Rodeo Queen

Rodeo Queen

Rodeo Queen

T. J. KLINE

AVONIMPULSE
An Imprint of HarperCollinsPublishers

Excerpt from *Rescued by a Stranger* copyright © 2013 by Lizbeth Selvig.

Excerpt from *Chasing Morgan* copyright © 2013 by Jennifer Ryan.

Excerpt from *Throwing Heat* copyright © 2013 by Candice Wakoff.

Excerpt from *Private Research* copyright ©2013 by Sabrina Darby.

EPub Edition DECEMBER 2013 ISBN: 9780062304742

Print Edition ISBN: 9780062304834

JV 10 9 8 7

For the man who first believed in me and fights
every day to help make my dreams a reality.
I love you with all my heart.
For my Baby Girl, don't ever give up on your dreams.

Chapter One

THE DRAWLING VOICE of the rodeo announcer boomed over the loudspeakers. "Ladies and gentleman, we'd like to welcome you to the Fifty-first Annual West Hills Roundup Rodeo! But first, let's have one last look at the ladies vying for the title of your rodeo queen!"

The array of glitter, sequins, and beads was dazzling in the April sunlight, nearly blinding her. She patted her dapple gray stallion to calm him as he shifted eagerly at the end of the line, kicking up dust in the newly tilled rodeo arena. Sydney looked down the line of young women on horseback, spotted her friend Alicia first in line, and gave her a reassuring smile.

"First, let's welcome Alicia Kanani!" Sydney watched as her best friend coaxed her gelding from the line, taking off into a slow lope along the fence. Alicia cocked a two-fingered salute to the crowd, her black tuxedo shirt glittering with silver and gold sequins, before filing back into the line of contestants. The next seven contestants duplicated Alicia's queen run. "And, last but not least, Sydney Thomas!"

Pressing her heels into Valentino's sides, Sydney made a kissing sound to the stallion as he took off from the line like a bullet from a gun. Leaning over his neck, Sydney snapped a sharp military salute while facing the audience. The sequins of her vest were a blinding flash of red light as Valentino stretched his body into a full run, his ears pinned against his head. Sydney reveled in the moment of flight as she and the horse became one, his hooves seeming to float over the tilled earth. As they rounded the last corner, Valentino slowed to a lope and Sydney sat up in the saddle. Reaching the end of the line, Sydney sat deep into her saddle, cueing the horse to bury his hocks in the soft dirt and slide to a dramatic stop. As the blood pounding in her ears subsided to a mild roar, she could still hear the audience cheering.

"There you have it, ladies and gentlemen, your con-testants for West Hills Roundup Queen," the announcer repeated. "May I have the envelope, please?"

Glancing at the fence line, Sydney caught her brother's gaze as he winked and gave her a thumbs-up. She smiled, appreciating that he had come to cheer her on when he had his own event to prepare for. The "crowd" was sparse in the morning hours before the rodeo actually began. It was mostly family and friends of the queen contestants and a few rodeo competitors who performed before the rodeo due to too many entrants in their events.

"Without any further fanfare," the announcer paused

for effect as the meager crowd immediately quieted to a hush. "Your princess this year is ... Alicia Kanani!" Cheers erupted from the grassy hillside where Alicia's family was seated with Sydney's. She cheered from the line, excited for her friend. "And now, the moment we've all been waiting for ..."

Sydney's heart raced. She felt it in her throat and in her toes at the same time as she waited for the name of the new queen to be called. Only her brother, Chris, knew how many hours of training and preparation had gone into this competition, all in hopes of having her name come to be associated with the best horse trainers in rodeo. As queen, she would be attending rodeos all over California, meeting and networking with stock contractors and other rodeo participants. She hoped that it would all lead to more exposure for her mounts, which meant more horses to train.

"The new West Hills Roundup Queen is ... drum roll please ... Sydney Thomas!" The applause rose to a roar on the hillside again as Sydney's family rose, laughing, cheering, and hugging one another. Sydney edged Valentino forward as the previous year's rodeo queen placed the silver-and-rhinestone crown on her red cowboy hat. She was soon encircled by the other contestants, who offered congratulations as they exited the arena and headed for the horse trailers.

They'd barely dismounted at Sydney's trailer when Alicia tackled her with an enthusiastic hug. "I can't believe we did it! You won!"

Sydney opened her mouth to respond but was cut off

by the massive arms that lifted her from behind and spun her around. "Congratulations, Queenie."

"Chris, put me down," she squealed. As her boots touched the ground she slapped him on the shoulder. Her brother might be a year younger than she was, but he'd inherited their father's tall, lanky frame.

"Ow!" He rubbed his arm. "You'll never find a king acting like that," he teased.

"Please. That is the last thing I'm looking for." Sydney rolled her eyes and turned to tie Valentino to the trailer.

"What about you, Alicia? Want to be my princess?" Chris asked as he snuck his arm around her shoulders.

Chris was a hopeless flirt. At nineteen, he was striking with his jet-black hair, aqua eyes, and broad shoulders— everything a girl would imagine from a cowboy, including the drawling charm. The fact that he and his roping partner were consistently ranked in the top of the national standings for team roping made him a pretty hot ticket around the rodeo circuit. But he'd never shown any indication that he would ever settle down with one girl.

"Why don't you go find yourself one of those 'buckle bunnies' that hangs out behind the chutes?" Alicia asked, shaking his arm off.

One of the drawbacks of rodeo were the women fans, young and old alike, who wanted to snag a cowboy. Too often Sydney found the cowboys around the circuit expected all of the other women to do the same.

"No thanks." Chris laughed. "When I find the right girl, she's going to outride and out-rope me."

"Good luck with that." Sydney laughed.

Alicia pulled her cowboy hat off, exposing her long, dark hair, and set the hat on the back of the truck. Sydney didn't miss the look of appreciation Chris shot her best friend. "You never can tell, sis." He tapped the red line her hat had left on her forehead before stepping back. "I'll never understand why you girls wear hats that tight"

Sydney slipped her sequined vest over her arms and unbuttoned the tuxedo shirt, grateful for the tank-top underneath, and hung her shirt in the tack compartment of her horse trailer so she could wear it again once the pre-rodeo events finished. "You guys should try doing a queen run sometime. If that hat hits the ground with a crown on it, my head better be in it. Rule number one."

She flipped the front of her brother's cowboy hat, knocking it to the ground. "Unlike you ropers, no one picks up our hats when they come off in the arena," she teased as she pulled a light cotton Western shirt from the trailer, wishing again that short sleeves were allowed. "Okay, I'm going to head back to find the stock contractor and see what they'll allow us to do during the rodeo."

It was typical for the stock contractor to allow the rodeo queen and her court to carry the sponsor flags for the events, but Sydney was hoping to network a bit and charm her way into being allowed to clear the cattle from the arena in the roping events. It was good exposure to show off Valentino and her accomplishments as a trainer. She exchanged her red cowboy hat for a baseball cap, pulling her russet curls through the opening in the back.

"Can you keep an eye on Valentino for me?" Sydney spotted their families heading toward the trailer. "Here comes the crew," she said, jerking her chin in their direction. "Let them know I'll be right back."

"Talk with Mike Findley," Chris instructed. "He's in charge. He should be pretty receptive to you."

"Thanks. I'll be right back."

Chris glanced toward Alicia, who was being hugged by both of her parents. "No hurry." Sydney smiled, wondering if the dance tonight wouldn't be the perfect opportunity to give Chris and Alicia a little nudge to take their friendship to the next level.

SYDNEY ROLLED UP the sleeves of her shirt to her elbows and pulled the shirt from her chest in an attempt to cool herself. It was only April, but her shirt was already sticking to her skin at nine in the morning. She couldn't help but smile and take in the smell of alfalfa, dust, and leather as she made her way through the jumbled maze of trucks and trailers, most with horses tied in the shade, dozing before their events. She knew how lucky she was; most people couldn't honestly say that they loved their life, but she loved every minute she'd spent growing up in rodeo.

Sydney heard the unmistakable pounding of horse hooves on the packed ground behind her and moved closer to the vehicle on her right. Usually there was more than enough room for riders and their rigs in the walkway, but with the unexpected turnout at the rodeo today, there was barely room to maneuver. The horse was jogging pretty quickly and she didn't have anywhere else to go, especially since another truck and trailer had chosen that moment to pull out of the gate ahead of her. The driver of the truck spotted her and waved her on. She tried to hurry through the opening he'd left her at the gate, but the rider behind her chose to slip between them, his mount's shoulder knocking her into the gatepost on her right.

Sydney reached up to massage her shoulder before registering the surprise on the face of the driver of the truck.

"Are you okay, Sydney?" It was Bobby Blake, a friend of her father's who must have been delivering some panels in the back of the arena.

"Yeah, I'm fine," she assured him before raising her voice. "I guess chivalry really is dead," she yelled at the cowboy's back.

She saw him jerk his mount to a stop before glancing back over his shoulder at her. "Look, honey, I don't have time for you girls who don't belong back here. This area is for contestants, not their groupies."

"Want me to set him straight?" Bobby asked.

Sydney smiled her appreciation. "No, but thanks Bobby. I've got this."

"Go get him, honey," he teased. "He doesn't know who he's dealing with. By the way, congratulations."

"Thanks, Bobby." Sydney made her way toward the obnoxious cowboy seated on the sorrel. "Look, I don't know who you think you are, but around here we tend to have a sort of unspoken code. When that walkway is packed with cars and horses like that, you slow down and you certainly do not push your way between a truck and someone walking. I don't really appreciate hoofmarks across my back."

She looked up at him as she came closer, refusing to let him intimidate her from his seat on the horse. "And as for being a groupie, I could probably outride you any day of the week," she challenged.

The cowboy arched his right brow and a slow smile spread across his face. "Maybe we'll have to see about that later." With a tap of his heels, the horse jogged forward a few steps toward one of the stock pens.

Sydney narrowed her eyes as he left. What a jerk, she thought. Shaking her head, she rubbed her shoulder again and searched the back of the arena for the stock contractor's trailers, noticing a lanky cowboy setting up folding chairs beside a Findley Brothers stock trailer.

"Excuse me," Sydney began, making her way across the short grass. "Can you tell me where I might find Mike Findley?"

A weathered face returned her smile and Sydney realized he was much older than she had first assumed. "What's that?"

Sydney realized that he probably couldn't hear her over the clattering of stock panels as the cattle moved into the pens. "Mike Findley? Do you know where I can find him?"

"Oh, no, I'm not Mike. I'm Jake," the man hollered.

"Hi Jake, I'm Sydney Thomas." She raised her voice as well. "I was just crowned rodeo queen and I'm looking for Mike to see if we might carry the sponsor flags or run cattle for him today."

Jake turned and faced her, crossing his arms. The cattle had quieted so he toned down his voice as well. "Well, Mike's up with the announcer right now working out of a few details. But he's not who you'd want to talk to about that." He leaned back against the trailer, crossing his ankles as if getting relaxed for a long conversation.

Sydney raised her brows in expectation. When Jake didn't say anything, she pressed. "So, who should I talk to instead?"

"That'd be Scott Chandler."

Sydney sighed, finding it difficult to restrain herself from punching something. First she'd been shoved into a fence post and now a cryptic cowboy was obviously enjoying a joke at her expense.

"And where would I find Mr. Chandler?"

The Cheshire-cat grin on Jake's face made her heart sink. No, life couldn't possibly be that cruel. Her gaze followed the direction of his finger as he pointed to the cowboy atop the sorrel at the stock pen, obviously eavesdropping on their conversation. Swallowing the dry lump that had suddenly materialized in her throat, Sydney squared her shoulders and raised her golden eyes to meet the black eyes of her foe.

"Well, I think you just finished telling him off." Jake grinned, anticipating the showdown to come.

Sydney had a few choice words that might have suited this moment if her mother hadn't ingrained in her how unladylike it was to curse. A blush crept up her cheeks as Scott Chandler dismounted his horse and bowed deeply before her.

"Your Majesty," he mocked. "I am at your disposal."

She realized that the noise from the stock pen hadn't kept him from overhearing her conversation with Jake. "I'm sorry. I didn't know who you were."

Sarcasm colored his chuckle. "Somehow I don't think it would have mattered if you had. Now, I am busy, so what did you need, Miss Thomas?"

Sydney took a deep breath and ignored the warmth flooding her cheeks. "I came to see about carrying the sponsor flags and returning the cattle during the rodeo."

"Experience?"

"Well, I've worked for Marks' Rodeo Company for the last four years doing both, as well as training for the last eight years, five of those professionally." Sydney's chin rose indignantly as she felt his gaze weighing heavily on her. She felt suddenly self-conscious in her red jeans and red-and-white plaid Western shirt. Did she look like an immature girl?

Scott gave her a rakish, lopsided grin. "Oh, that's right. You can outride me." His brow arched as he articulated her words back to her. "Any day of the week."

It took everything in her to try to ignore how good-looking this infuriating man was. He towered over her, well over six feet tall, and the black cowboy hat that topped a mop of dark brown hair, barely curling at his collar, gave him a devilish appearance. With sensuous lips and a square jaw, his deeply tanned skin reflected raw male sexuality. She wasn't sure if he was actually as muscular as his broad shoulders seemed to indicate due to his unruly Western shirt, but his jeans left no imagining necessary to notice the muscular thighs. However, his jet-black eyes almost unnerved her. Those eyes were so dark that Sydney felt she would drown if she continued to meet his gaze.

So much for ignoring his good looks, she chided herself. "Give me a chance out there today to prove it."

"I don't see why she can't run them, Scott." Jake must have decided that it was time to break up the showdown with his two cents. "She is certainly experienced enough, more than most of the girls you let run flags."

Scott glared at Jake before turning back to Sydney. She caught Jake's conspiratorial wink and decided that she liked this old cowboy. Scott would be hard-pressed to find a reason to deny her request now that Jake had sold him out.

"Fine, you can do both. But if anything goes wrong, if a steer so much as takes too long in the arena, you're finished. Got it, Miss Thomas?" The warning note in his voice was unmistakable.

Sydney flashed a dazzling smile. "Call me Sydney, and it's no problem." She clutched her shoulder. "Unless I'm unable to hold the flags since someone ran me into the fence post."

His look told her he didn't appreciate her sense of humor. "I mean it. Rodeo starts at ten sharp. Be down here at nine thirty, ready to go."

As the sassy cowgirl walked away, Scott shook his head. "What in the world possessed you to open your mouth, Jake?"

"Aw, Scott, she'll do fine. Besides, you did run her down with Wiley at the gate. You kinda owed her one."

Scott watched Sydney head for the gate, taking in her small waist and the spread of her hips in her red pants and down her lean, denim-encased legs. That woman was all curves, moving with the grace of a jungle cat. With her full, pouting lips and those golden eyes, it certainly wouldn't be painful to look at her all day. "I guess."

Scott mounted Wiley and headed to change into his clean shirt and show chaps, but he couldn't seem to shake the image of Sydney Thomas from his mind. He knew that she'd been attracted to him—he'd seen it in her blush—but he'd had enough run-ins with ostentatious rodeo queens over the years, including his ex-fiancée, to know that they simply wanted to tame a cowboy. It was doubtful that this one was any different, although she did have a much shorter temper. He chuckled as he recalled how the gold in her eyes seemed to flame when she was irritated. He wondered if her eyes flamed up whenever she was passionate. Scott shook his head to clear it of visions of the sexy spitfire. No time for that, he had a rodeo to get started.

Chapter Two

SYDNEY WAS STILL fuming as she sat on a prancing Valentino during the grand entry. As rodeo queen, now back in costume, she preceded the other riders into the arena, and Valentino quickly picked up on her turbulent emotions, which made him act more nervous than usual. At least they'd both gotten out some of their pent-up aggravation during her queen run. The procession finally filed out of the arena and waited along the arena fence line for the opening ceremonies to begin.

Sydney caught a glimpse of Scott riding by on a magnificent black-and-white paint gelding. He stopped at the arena gate, holding the American flag, waiting for the national anthem to cue his entrance. She noticed he'd changed into a long-sleeved white shirt and added a pair of red-and-blue chaps with silver fringe, accenting his slim hips and hugging his thighs. The shirt clung to his frame like a second skin, confirming his muscular upper body and emphasizing the broad shoulders she'd noticed earlier. He held himself as proud and erect in the saddle, but what captivated her most was his genuine smile and infectious laughter as he chatted with a child through the chain-link fence.

At the sound of the music, the paint's ears twitched. Scott tapped the gelding's ribs lightly with his heels and walked into the arena. As the anthem progressed, he cued the horse for gradual speed until he was charging around the arena. The horse's long black mane flowed backwards like silk as the flag snapped. Scott looked as majestic and regal as a knight going into battle. Suddenly he turned sharply into the center of the arena and slid to a stop as the music played its last strains. Once the music had faded and the announcer had welcomed everyone to the rodeo, he took the gelding for a final lap. The paint's body and neck stretched out and his ears lay back as he flew around the arena with Scott, who rode as if he and the horse were one.

Sydney watched in awe, not only of his riding abilities, which made her question her earlier challenge to him, but of the picture he presented in the opening ceremony. The crowd's hearts had been stirred with pride and he'd raised their excitement for the coming events to a roar in mere minutes.

"It's a beautiful opening, don't you think?"

Sydney turned, startled, to see a man in his mid-fifties beside her. She immediately noticed the Findley Brothers' rodeo tack as he flashed her the kindest, most grandfatherly smile she could have imagined.

"Great run, Scott," he hollered as Scott left the arena amid billowing clouds of dust. Turning his attention back to Sydney, he glanced at the rhinestone crown on her hat. "I hope I'm right in assuming that you're the new queen? The name's Mike Findley."

Smiling, Sydney shook his proffered hand, "I'm Sydney Thomas. I've heard great things about you. Chris Greenly and my brother chatted with you earlier this morning while I was competing."

"I remember. Your brother's a calf roper, right? Young guy?" Sydney nodded. Her brother had definitely been bitten by the rodeo bug early. At only nineteen, he was already in the top twenty standings nationally in his event.

"And who doesn't know the Greenly boys-?" Mike laughed. He jerked his chin in Scott's direction. "Have you met Scott Chandler yet? He's my arena director."

"I guess you could say that."

She was surprised when Mike laughed out loud. "Yeah, I guess Scott does kinda have an attitude problem when it comes to rodeo queens. Don't understand it myself. I never pass up a chance to be in the company of a pretty lady, especially if she can ride well."

"Attitude might be a bit of an understatement." Sydney smiled at the older man. "So, you've known him for a while, then?"

"He's worked with me since he could pick up a rope and been on the road with me since he was fourteen. His parents were my partners. I love him like he was one of my own."

Sydney made a mental note to keep her criticisms

about Scott Chandler to herself when Mike Findley was around. Her smile faltered when she saw the subject of their conversation approaching.

"Hey Mike, everything ready at this end for the first event?"

"It's all under control."

Scott flashed Sydney a mischievous smile. Before she could find out what he had planned, she cued Valentino to back up. "I'd better get the first sponsor flag. It was great to—"

"The princess—Alicia, I think?—She's already down there with it," Scott interrupted.

Sydney flashed him a knowing smile. "I wouldn't want to be responsible for anything going wrong." Her voice dripped with sarcasm as she turned Valentino to leave only to be stopped by his deep-timbre laughter. She glanced back at him over her shoulder. "Something funny?"

"Definitely," Scott replied, still laughing.

Sydney could see that Mike barely contained his smile while he pretended to be intently inspecting his rope. Her attempt at charming condescension wasn't having the effect she hoped for, and she felt her shoulders tense in irritation, wondering if there were any possibility of besting him in this instance.

"Besides," he added. "Someone needs to be down here to return cattle for the next event."

He was right, but Sydney knew that she couldn't stay around him without her nerves becoming strung tight, which in turn would aggravate Valentino. She scanned the arena, looking for any excuse, and saw Chris with her parents near the gate.

Turning toward Mike, she smiled genuinely. "It was so good to meet you. I hope we can talk more later."

"You can count on it."

Mike's chuckle followed her as she pivoted Valentino and broke the colt into a jog to meet her parents at the fence. She could feel herself relaxing with every step that took her further from Scott Chandler.

SYDNEY HAD NO more left earshot when Mike turned on him, his disappointment apparent. "The way you're treating that girl isn't right, Scott."

"What?" Even Scott didn't believe the innocence he tried to portray.

"She hasn't done anything but exactly what you've asked. Jake told me what happened earlier." Scott shrugged. "Have you seen that stallion she's riding? Her brother told me she broke and trained him. She's obviously talented." Mike eyed Scott.

"That girl happens to have a very sharp tongue. Just because she has you fooled doesn't mean I have to play her games."

Mike slapped his rope against his thigh absently. "You know, Scott, not every rodeo queen is like Liz."

"Right," Scott scoffed. "I haven't met one yet who *isn't* like Liz."

Mike looked to his right, where Sydney sat astride Valentino at the fence with her parents as they handed her a bottle of water. "Yes, you have. You're just too stubborn to see it."

As Scott watched the rodeo clown beckon Sydney into the arena, he couldn't stop the grin that spread on his mouth. He'd seen the prank hundreds of times before and wondered how this smart-mouth queen was going to react. The clown explained to the crowd that he would jump from the mini trampoline he was dragging into the arena and do a flip over his beautiful assistant while she swung a broom over her head. He would then pluck it from her hands and land on the other side of her. Scott watched him pull a well-worn bandana from his back pocket and shake it out.

"You don't mind if we blindfold you, do you?"

Scott could see the apprehension in her eyes, but the smile never slipped. "Of course not."

She held the blindfold to her eyes as the clown tied it just below the back of her cowboy hat. "You can't see anything?"

"Not a thing," she assured him.

Scott watched as the clown led her into the center of the arena, appreciating the sway of her rear as she made her way. The clown handed her the broom and helped her raise it overhead, adjusting her position several times to make sure her hands were well above her head. Scott tried to ignore the pleasure centering below his belt buckle as her back arched and her breasts pressed against the front of her vest. *Get a hold of yourself. She's a buckle bunny, just like the rest of them.*

The clown bounced on the trampoline a few times,

calling out instructions for Sydney to make sure that she continued to swing the broom in circles over her head. As he motioned the crowd to stay quiet, he pulled the trampoline from the arena, leaving Sydney alone in the center, twirling the broom. Minutes passed and a few chuckles from the crowd began to sound. The clown called out for her to continue, assuring her it would only be a moment longer. Scott saw her tilt her head, and he wondered if she wasn't growing suspicious.

"What do you think, ladies and gentlemen? Should we turn a bull loose in the arena so that our queen might leave sometime tonight?" The clown stood at the far end of the arena, rousing the crowd into full uproarious laughter. Sydney dropped arms to her sides and pulled the bandana from her eyes. As she looked around the arena, she could see she'd been duped.

Scott waited to see the fury rise in her eyes, wondering if she would be able to hide it as few had. With the bandana hanging around her neck, her full lips spread into a broad smile and she laughed out loud, surprising him. Brandishing the broom, she chased the clown, to the delight of the crowd. When he finally allowed her to catch him, he gave her a hug and whispered in her ear. Sydney turned back toward the crowd and waved to them, exiting the arena to the applause of the crowd.

Scott brushed away the incomprehension of her initial response, impressed by her composure. "Playing to the crowd," he muttered under his breath, certain that her reaction when she was out of the arena would be a tirade like every other queen.

Usually the clown used spectators because they loved being selected to take part in the rodeo, but in the few instances he chose to use rodeo queens, they always reacted the same way: embarrassment-fueled outrage accompanied by tears and screeching complaints. He wasn't sure why he'd suggested they play the prank on Sydney. Sure, he'd wanted to take her down a peg or two, but even now he could feel excitement churning in his gut, anticipating her anger, and wondered if he wasn't enjoying their verbal sparring too much for his own good.

He watched her, waiting for the good-natured smile to fade once the crowd could no longer see her. Instead, she nudged the clown playfully and suggested they repeat the prank on a friend. Scott narrowed his eyes, feeling the tension in his shoulders as he waited for her to unleash some sort of annoyance. The clown headed back into the arena to finish his act as Sydney mounted her horse. *Wait for it . . .*

She simply shook her head, her cheeks tingeing pink, as a cowboy at the gate teased her about the prank and she laughed with him. There was no anger or resentment, only a tantalizing playfulness, even at her own expense. He clenched his jaw, irritated that she hadn't reacted the way he'd expected. She was shallow; they all were. For some reason, the fact that she didn't act like the other one-dimensional girls that abounded behind the chutes bothered him. She might have fooled everyone else, but not him.

SYDNEY WATCHED AS the rodeo clown finished his act, the announcer teasing him from the loudspeaker. Usually she loved everything about the rodeos: the dust; the noise of the cattle loading into the chutes; the smell of leather, hay, and horses. But she couldn't wait for this one to be over. Scott had already been on her case twice about the way she worked the cattle, and the rodeo wasn't even half over yet. When he told her she was too slow on the flag runs, her temper had gotten the best of her, and she had allowed Valentino to slide to a stop, spraying him with dirt clods from the arena. She only wished she'd done it after they'd soaked the arena to keep the dust at bay. A mud bath might have done him some good.

She almost giggled at the thought and made her way into the arena as the clown gathered the last of his props and the announcer called for the steer wrestling. She looked behind her to make sure Alicia was ready, only to see Scott unceremoniously follow her inside and position himself in the far corner. She glanced over at Alicia, still by the gate, who just shrugged in confusion. Great, Sydney thought, trying to ignore Scott's glare, I'm running cattle with the tyrant.

Sydney watched as the first steer wrestler settled his horse into the box. As the steer burst from the chute, the rider reined his horse to the steer's left side. With a partner keeping the animal straight, the cowboy dove, head first. Sliding his arms around the horns and cradling the steer's head between his arm and ribcage, the cowboy angled the animal's head just enough for the momentum to carry both of them to the ground together. Sydney eased Valentino closer. When the cowboy let the steer up at the buzzer, she would be there to guide it back to the pen. The animal jumped up as the steer wrestler let loose and Sydney followed closely behind, moving to the right or left to direct the steer. Within seconds he was in his pen calmly munching on grass. Scott rode up beside her before she could make her way back toward her corner.

"Out," he ordered, and he rode through the arena gate ahead of her, expecting her to follow. "Mark, Alicia, go take care of those cattle," Scott barked.

Sydney saw confusion and a bit of worry for her friend in Alicia's eyes as she went through the gate. Whatever Scott was mad about now, they both knew Alicia still had a job to do in the arena. Sydney followed Scott outside the arena gates toward the trucks.

"What now?" she asked from behind his horse.

He shook his head, not even giving her the courtesy of a backward glance. "Not here. Where's your trailer?"

"Over here." Scott followed as Sydney led him toward her pickup. In the few minutes it took to reach her trailer, Sydney allowed her temper to grow into a burning rage. Scott had been critical of every move she made and she'd done a great job for him today. She wasn't his whipping post, and she refused to take any more, even if it meant losing the exposure for her training abilities that she hoped for.

Scott remained silent as Sydney dismounted and clipped the lead rope on her horse. He followed suit and tied his paint gelding with the lead rope already attached to the trailer beside hers. He stepped back as she spun, her golden eyes blazing, and forgot what he'd been about to say. It only took a glance to realize that she was ready for a fight. If that's what she wants, Scott reasoned, he was up for it.

"So, what was it this time?" Sydney stepped right up to him and stood toe-to-toe, even though he had a good six inches on her. "Wait, let me guess. I followed too closely behind that steer?"

"Actually, you were too far behind." Scott was careful to keep his voice even and calm. Her anger actually diffused his own irritation at having to be in such close proximity to her all day.

"Oh, really?" She sounded doubtful. "Is there anything else?" He could tell she was fuming.

"No, that's not all. Now look—" he began.

"No, you look," Sydney raged, and he briefly wondered if he hadn't been unfair to her. He squashed the thought. "I've been working my butt off for you today and you know it."

Realizing he'd pushed her too far, Scott knew he needed to diffuse the situation before everyone witnessed their argument. Fighting with her wasn't going to expose her for the fraud he knew she was. But if he could get her to let her guard down, he could prove he was right.

Scott leaned over her shoulder, looking behind her, and gave her his most charming smile. "Nope," he drawled, "It's still there. Matter of fact, it's kinda nice. Would be a shame to lose it."

Sydney continued, glaring at him. "Nothing has gone wrong, nothing has stalled the performance. So what, exactly, is your problem with me?"

"You really want to know?" He knew he wasn't being fair to lump her in the same category as Liz. Even Mike had said so, but he just couldn't bring himself to assume that she might be different.

"Yes," she emphatically replied. "I've had people who didn't like me or get along, but never this kind of open hostility for no apparent reason."

"I know your type."

"Excuse me?"

"I have to admit that you can ride better than most and you might not mind getting a little dirty," he continued. "But you're just like all of the rest of them."

"You mean rodeo queens." She wasn't asking so he didn't feel the need to answer. "And just what are the rest of us like?"

Scott leaned back against the side of her truck and cross his arms. "Spoiled little prom queens with buckles and cowboy hats. You think you can just gather your toys, break them, and then toss them aside for new ones." She stared at him, speechless. He could see the frustration in her flushed cheeks and the rapid rise and fall of her chest. He crossed his arms and leaned a shoulder against the truck. "Truth hurt?"

"I don't have to take this from you or anyone else." She turned back toward her colt. "Alicia can stay and help out, but I'll just get out of your sight since I disgust you so much."

Scott couldn't remember ever seeing anyone look this beautiful angry, and he hated that even knowing what she was like—what they were all like—he could still be so attracted to her. He couldn't tear his gaze from her blazing golden eyes as sparks flew between them and she faced him again. He wanted to kiss her smart mouth. His palms itched to be buried in her hair, and he clenched them into fists to keep from taking her by the shoulders. It was a primal desire, and he wondered what she would do if he gave in to it.

"Look, I apologized for my part this morning. Maybe I should have held my temper a little better," she admitted. "But you don't even know me."

Scott thought about what she said for a moment before pushing off the back of her truck. An idea began to take shape in his mind. "You're right."

Sydney gave him a wary look. It was obvious that his sudden concession confused her.

"I'll make you a deal." Scott wondered if he wasn't making the biggest mistake of his life with what he was about to propose.

"I don't think I'd like your deals."

"I'll lay off your case for the rest of the rodeo, but . . ."

"Of course there's a 'but.'" She sighed.

"But, you have to go to the barbeque and dance with me," he finished.

She stared at him in disbelief, and he hoped she wouldn't question his proposal. He wasn't even entirely sure why he'd suggested it other than to prove to himself that all rodeo queens really were the same. It's not like his heart was involved this time around; Liz had cured him of any delusions there. This was simply attraction. A few kisses to work her out of his system and prove his point. What could that hurt?

She grasped her horse's reins, her hand absently patting his neck and shoulder. "Why?"

"Let's test my theory. I think all rodeo queens are from the same selfish, conniving mold. You say you're different. Prove me wrong."

She eyed him cautiously. He could almost see the thoughts running through her mind. Did he have an ulterior motive? Would he be a jerk all evening? "And you'll stay off my case for the rest of the weekend?"

"Both days of the rodeo. Scout's honor."

He could see that she still wasn't sure she could trust him. "All right. I'll meet you here at—"

"I'll pick you up at five at your house."

"Why?"

"To meet your family, of course. To know you, I have to meet them, right?" He briefly wondered if he really wanted to go through this just to prove his "theory."

"Fine." She reclipped the colt to the trailer and reached into the truck for a scrap of paper and a pen. "Here." She handed him the paper. "Here's a map to my house and my cell number. Call me if you get lost."

Without another word, she unclipped the stallion, mounted him, and rode back into the arena. As he watched her ride away, Scott had the sinking feeling he'd just condemned himself to a very long, trying evening.

WHAT IN THE world did I get myself into? Sydney wondered. Whatever possessed me to agree to this ridiculous deal?

"Sydney?" Turning, she saw Mike Findley approach. "You're going to the barbeque tonight, right?"

"Yeah, I have to be here by six. Why?"

"Good. I have an idea to run past you, to see what you think about it." She wasn't sure what to say and wondered if he could see her confusion. "Don't worry." He chuckled. "I'll clear everything up tonight. See you then."

More confused than ever, Sydney watched him leave and made her way into the arena.

I CAN'T BELIEVE I'm actually going through with this, Scott thought as he pulled up to the address Sydney gave him. Five dogs, ranging from an enormous German shepherd to a wiggling cocker spaniel, ran from behind the house to greet him at the front gate, barking incessantly. Putting the truck into park, he reached for the long, rectangular package in the passenger seat.

"What in the hell am I doing?" he muttered to the dogs as he arrived at the front porch. He reached down and patted the shepherd on the head. "Like I don't already know that they are all alike, right? I must be a glutton for punishment." Just as he raised a hand to ring the bell, he heard the voices inside.

"Sydney, he's here!"

As the door swung open, Scott realized he hadn't made such a bad deal after all. Sydney stood before him wearing a form-fitted white leather dress, white hat, and white dress boots. The dress had obviously been tailor-made for her, hugging every curve she'd been blessed with.

"You look amazing," he said. He hadn't meant to speak his thoughts aloud but couldn't seem to help himself.

She gave him a brilliant smile. "Thanks. You don't look so bad, yourself." She moved away from the door. "Come on in."

Scott followed her in and stepped into the family room. He wanted to seem aloof, but he had a hard time ignoring the electricity that passed between them. He hadn't felt this nervous since he was a kid. *You'd better get it together or she's gonna eat you alive, just like Liz did.* The thought of his ex-fiancée brought his nerves back under control. He might give Sydney the benefit of the doubt, but he wasn't a fool. Not twice.

"Why don't we call a truce for tonight?" Scott handed her the package in his hand.

"I think we can manage that." She lifted the top from the box and gasped. Nestled atop green ferns were dark pink miniature carnations accenting a dozen white roses.

"They're gorgeous!"

"I'm glad you like them." Scott watched her face light up with delight as she pressed the flowers to her nose and congratulated himself on placing the rush order for the flowers earlier. He realized that there was a small part of him that almost hoped she would prove him wrong and wanted the night to go well.

"I love them, thank you. I better get them in some water."

"You must be Scott Chandler," the voice came from the hall. Scott saw a man making his way to where they stood and assumed it was her father.

He offered his hand. "Yes, sir."

"Bill Thomas. That was one hell of a rodeo this afternoon."

"Thank you, sir. You've got a nice ranch here." Bill Thomas had the look of a man who was no stranger to hard work but who definitely knew how to have fun when the opportunity presented.

"Hi, can I get you something to drink?" A petite woman with emerald eyes and elf-like features made her way into the kitchen. "I'm Sydney's mother, Julia."

SYDNEY BARELY LISTENED as her parents discussed the day's rodeo events with Scott. It was odd how at ease he seemed tonight in comparison to his demeanor earlier in the afternoon. He certainly wasn't an easy man to figure out. One minute he was arrogant and condescending. The next, he was charming and thoughtful. Her pulse quickened as she took in his dark blue jeans and the long-sleeved maroon shirt hugging his torso beneath his leather jacket. He stood confidently, laughing with her parents, his tanned, calloused hand tucked into his pocket. None of his moods changed the fact that he was rakishly appealing.

"Sydney?" Her mother's voice cut into her thoughts and she blushed, realizing that all three of them were staring at her. "Honey, are you listening?"

"Um . . ." she struggled to find any answer. Her father frowned, but Scott seemed to know exactly where her wayward thoughts had turned and arched a brow.

"I said I think you two should head out, don't you?" She silently thanked her mother for realizing she hadn't had a clue. She'd figure out what her mother's knowing smile meant later. For now, Julia Thomas was her savior.

Sydney glanced at the clock on the microwave. "You're right, I'm supposed to be there by six. Let me just get my sash."

"It was great to meet you both," Scott told her parents as he headed for the front door.

Sydney hurried out of the room, cursing her girlish fantasies with every step. *Pull yourself together, stupid. This night means nothing, other than proving to a chauvinistic cowboy that rodeo queens aren't groupies on horseback.* Pinning her sash at her waist, she made her way back to the front door where Scott waited.

"Sorry," she said. "I'm having a little trouble."

"Here, I'll help." He took the rhinestone pin from her trembling hands. Gently he slipped the pin through the shoulder of her dress and closed the clasp.

"Not your first rodeo, huh?" Sydney attempted to shake her nerves.

Scott's jovial mood instantly became dark and brooding. "Let's go." He reached for her arm.

Realizing she had just reminded him of his experiences with other rodeo queens, she cursed her big mouth and followed him to his truck. As he opened the passenger door, she wondered just how quickly this disastrous evening might end.

"SYDNEY!"

Whirling around, she looked for the owner of the voice. The band had just unloaded their equipment and it was becoming more difficult to hear by the minute. Dinner wasn't scheduled to begin for another thirty minutes, but the smell of tri-tips on the barbeque was already thick in the air. Just enough smoke wafted from the grills on the light spring breeze to tease her taste buds and make Sydney realize her hunger.

"Sydney, Scott! Over here." Spotting Mike Findley waving at them, they navigated the tables to reach him. "Join me for dinner."

"Sure," Scott said. He pulled Sydney's chair out for her. "Why don't you wait here and keep Mike company, and I'll get our food?"

"Scott, be sure that my steak is pretty rare. My teeth are too old for that tough shi- . . . stuff," Mike corrected.

"Okay. Sydney, what about you?"

"Medium is fine." She tried to hide her amusement at Mike's correction.

"I'll be right back," Scott promised as he walked toward the end of a quickly lengthening line.

As Scott left, Mike looked at Sydney curiously, cocking his head at an odd angle and smiling. "Did you two come together?"

Sydney nodded.

"Well, I'll be dam- . . . darned," he exclaimed.

"Mike, let's clear this up right away. My dad's a cattle-man. I've heard plenty of cursing." She laughed. "And what's the big deal about us coming together?" Mike shook his head, grinning like the cat that had just swallowed the proverbial canary. "What is so funny?" she asked again.

"It's nothing, although my idea may go over more smoothly now."

"Since you brought it up," she inquired, "what is this idea you have?"

"I know I was pretty cryptic this afternoon, so let me start from the beginning. I hear you have some horses for sale."

"Yeah, but . . ."

"How old?" Mike asked.

"Between four and six. But Mike . . ."

"I'd like to take a look at them on Monday if you don't mind."

"Sure, but will you tell me what's going on?" she asked, exasperated by trying to keep up with the conversation.

"I'm always looking for good stock. Besides," Mike added. "I like your work."

"What?"

"I've seen that stallion you ride, and I was told you trained him. I'd love to buy him too."

Sydney immediately shook her head. "Valentino isn't for sale at any price."

"Are you?"

Sydney furrowed her brow, not understanding what

Mike was trying to ask. Her confusion must have been obvious.

"I want you to come work for me," he clarified.

"What?" She breathed.

"I want you to travel with the rodeo as our trainer. You'd help set up the opening ceremonies, acts, keep the horses conditioned, train new ones, that sort of thing."

Sydney barely held in her excitement, wanting to leap across the table and hug Mike. This was more than she could have hoped for: the opportunity to train horses for rodeo with a world-class stock contractor. "Are you kidding?"

"I sure as hell hope he's kidding."

Mike and Sydney jumped at Scott's voice. She looked up at him as he placed the plates on the table and could see the anger smoldering behind those dark eyes.

"No way, Mike. Jennifer is bad enough. We don't need two women on the payroll."

"Scott," Mike warned.

"Forget it! For one thing, you'd have to pull another trailer for her to stay in. Her answer is no."

"Scott," Mike interrupted, his tone quietly authoritative. "Just because you own a quarter of the company doesn't mean you have final say on all decisions. Remember," he added, "I'm still the directing manager, which means I get to hire who I please." He shrugged and didn't bother to hide his smile. "Besides, you know Jen and Derek will side with me on this one. So you're outnumbered."

Sydney was tired of them ignoring her presence en-

tirely and rose from the table. "Have either of you considered the possibility that I might just say no? Now, it
looks like my family has arrived." She motioned to the
front gate. "If you'll excuse me for a moment, I'd like to
discuss this proposition with them." Without waiting for
an answer from either of them, she walked away.

"I DON'T KNOW what to do," Sydney complained to her
parents, throwing her hands into the air. "I mean, this is
a dream job, but I'd never see you guys."

"Sydney." Her mother's reasoning tone scolded. "Findley Brothers is only two hours from the house. That's not
that far."

"I know, but . . ."

"What is it you're really afraid of?" her father asked.

Sydney chewed on her lower lip. She hadn't really
thought that her hesitation was from fear. She had to
admit that it was scary to think of leaving the protection of her parents' ranch. She'd been training horses for
years, but she was barely earning enough to cover her
rodeo and business expenses.

"I'd have to relinquish the queen title," Sydney
pointed out.

Her father chuckled. "Wasn't the competition simply
a way to get the same opportunity you're being offered?
The committee will understand, and Alicia will take over
and do a wonderful job."

He was right. The queen competition was just a stepping stone, and Alicia would make a great rodeo queen.

"What about Scott Chandler?" Her father asked with a wink.

"Bill, stop it!" Julia slapped her husband's shoulder.

"What about him?" Sydney shrugged.

"Wouldn't you be working with him?"

"Well, that's actually part of the problem."

"Oh, I don't know about that," Julia teased. "If I was a young, single, not to mention beautiful young woman, I wouldn't consider him a problem."

Sydney laughed and shook her head at her mother. She knew her parents wanted to see her find someone, but she doubted that Scott was that someone. "Maybe if we'd met under different circumstances and he didn't hate the sight of me. He doesn't want me to have the job."

"Well, it doesn't really sound like it's his decision."

"Maybe not, but he could still make things miserable. How do I work with someone who doesn't want me around and doesn't care who knows it?"

"Sydney, do you want your mother and me to tell you not to take this job?"

Leave it to her dad to cut right to the point, she thought. "No, but . . ."

"Then you have to take responsibility for this decision on your own. You're a grown woman, and your mother and I will support you no matter what you decide is the best move."

Great, she thought. She was going to need more information to decide what the best move would be.

Chapter Three

"WHAT WERE YOU thinking? Why would you possibly do that?" Scott was furious, and he didn't care if Mike knew it.

"Do what?" Mike asked innocently.

"Offer her a job?"

"Because I think she'd be an asset." Scott could see the wheels turning in Mike's mind.

"Really? Because that doesn't sound like total bull at all. What's your real reason?"

"I happen to like her," Mike stated simply. "I think Jennifer could use the female companionship and I like her work. She's a good trainer, and we both know Derek isn't cutting it."

"Mike," Scott began, only to stop as he saw Sydney making her way toward them, the crowd separating for her to pass. If he'd realized how much trouble this woman was going to be, he would have said no to her request to carry flags.

"Well?" Mike sounded eager to hear her answer. He sounded far too confident that she would take the position while Scott prayed she'd turn him down and walk away for good.

"Actually, Mike, I'd like to speak with Scott privately for a minute if that's okay."

Scott was about to refuse when Mike answered for him. "Of course! I'll go and get a drink and meet you two in a couple of minutes." The warning glance Mike sent him clearly told him to behave. Scott hadn't seen that look since he was fifteen.

"Well?" Scott asked as Sydney lowered herself into the chair Mike vacated.

"I'd like to know why you don't want me to take this job."

He hadn't expected her to be so blunt, but since she'd asked he'd be honest, even if it angered Mike. "I don't think you have enough experience for the job."

"And?"

"And I don't think that the ranch is the best place for you."

"Why?"

Her rapid-fire questions were making him sound defensive, irritating him that he should be in this position at all. "Because I don't think the other hands will concentrate on their own jobs with you sauntering around the corrals," he answered harshly.

She arched a brow at him. "I don't *saunter*."

"This isn't a joke."

"Okay."

"Okay, meaning you're not taking the job?" He tried not to sound hopeful, but he had a feeling that her taking this job would only lead to disaster.

"Oh, I'm taking the job. I just wanted to know exactly where we stand."

"Sydney," he growled.

She sighed. "Scott, you said you wanted a truce for this evening, right? Mike's offer has nothing to do with tonight, so can we at least appear to get along?"

Scott hated the electric jolt that skittered through his veins at the sound of his name on her lips. It was the first time he'd heard it from her, and it rolled over him like a whisper on the wind. He couldn't help but wonder what it would sound like after a kiss.

"You can pretend for one night, right?" He hated that her innocent appeal made him sound like the bad guy.

Scott knew this was her best attempt to keep peace between them. "You'd better go tell Mike," he said through gritted teeth. "He'll be thrilled."

"Tell me what?"

Scott motioned toward a chair. "Have a seat. You've probably been listening to the whole conversation anyway."

"Why didn't I think of that?" Mike chuckled as he sat down. "Well, Sydney? What do you say?"

"What exactly would I be doing?"

Mike leaned forward in the chair as the band started to tune their instruments, making it more difficult to hear. "It really depends on where we are. At the rodeos, you'd be in charge of taking care of all the pick-up and special-event horses. You know—warming up, cooling down, watering, feeding, exercising, that sort of thing."

"Is that all?"

"Hell, no! You'd have to work with Scott and fill in wherever he needs you—flags, acts, opening ceremonies. And that's no small task, trust me."

Scott shifted in his seat. He hoped the evening shadows were hiding the frustration he was feeling. He leaned back in the chair and crossed his arms.

"What about during the off season, or when we aren't at a rodeo?"

"You'll be managing all of the riding horses at the ranch. Everything from exercising, breaking, grooming, training, breeding . . . the works."

"How many head?"

Scott was impressed that she seemed to ask all of the right questions, but he refused to let it show. He pretended to stifle a yawn. Mike shot him a warning look.

"About thirty. Of course, you'll have a few of the hands to help you whenever you need it."

Scott noticed that Sydney ignored him completely, focusing completely on Mike. It made sense, since he'd already stated his feelings about the situation, but it annoyed him anyway.

"Mike, I think you have yourself a new employee." Her smile lit up the room.

"Terrific!" Mike boomed over the band that had just started to warm up. The bass drum began to pound out a steady beat.

"Yeah, great," Scott grumbled. "Where is she going to stay?"

"In the ranch house. Where else?"

"What?"

"Oh, I don't want to impose," Sydney protested.

Why stop now? Scott thought.

"Nonsense," Mike decided. "You'll stay in the house with us."

"Us?" she asked.

"Us," Mike answered. "There's me, of course, Silvie, Jen, Clay, Derek, and Scott."

"Are you sure?" she asked, finally glancing over at Scott.

"It's decided," Mike insisted.

"She's gonna need a mount. You might want to figure that out now too," Scott reminded Mike.

"What about Valentino?" she asked, sounding hopeful.

Mike chewed on his thumb for a moment. "I'll make you a deal."

Sydney glanced at Scott. "What is it with you two and deals?"

"You could change your mind," Scott offered.

"I'll trade you food, shelter, and expenses for your stud in exchange for ten breedings during the season."

"You've got yourself a deal," she said as they shook hands.

He knew it was out of his hands now so he might as well get adjusted to her being part of their crew, which meant learning to get along with her. Scott watched Sydney; her eyes lit up with excitement at the thought of her new job. A few stray auburn curls fell over her shoulders, softly framing her face, accentuating the curve of her breasts, and Scott felt that electric warmth shoot through him again.

"Are we done talking business?" Scott asked. His voice sounded strained even to his own ears.

"I believe so." Mike speared the last of his tri-tip with the plastic fork. "Why?"

Scott rose and held a hand out to Sydney. "Dance with me?"

She seemed surprised by his sudden change in temperament, but her smile looked genuine as she wordlessly took his hand and followed him onto the dance floor. He twirled her before curling an arm around her waist and pulling her closer. As she lifted her face to meet his gaze, he noticed that her eyes had melted to liquid amber. She fit his body better than her dress fit her own. *This has to be the sweetest torture*, he thought.

As THEY BEGAN to sway to the gentle rhythm of a slow country ballad, the intensity of the desire she could read in his dark gaze made her knees weak and her breathing shallow. Yet, she couldn't tear her eyes from his and break the spell he'd woven around her. She could feel his every muscle taut against her body as they slowly moved with the music. He smelled of musk, horses, and leather, intoxicating her.

Scott pulled her closer and she gasped as his hand slid from her waist across her back. Silvery heat raced through her body, causing her to shiver and curl her fingers into his shoulders. A quiet growl escaped his throat.

"What?" she whispered, barely breathing. Scott shook his head in answer.

The final strains of the song came to an end, but he seemed unwilling to let her go. Sydney realized it was probably better if he didn't, because she wasn't sure she could stand. The band began to play a fast-paced song.

"Do you know how to swing?" His eyes glinted mischievously.

"Sort of." She'd only done it once with Chris, and not well.

"You're about to learn." Scott laughed as Sydney eyed him with distrust.

He proceeded to lead her through a pattern of twirls, turns, spins, dips, and even a flip. A crowd circled them while they danced, and when the song ended, people around them began clapping. Both of them were laughing breathlessly from the physical exertion.

"You want something to drink?" he asked.

"I would love a glass of water," Sydney replied gratefully. She watched him walk away, appreciating his physique, until a large cowboy stepped in front of her.

"You're the rodeo queen, right?"

Sydney politely smiled. "What gave it away, the crown or the sash?" she asked sweetly. The guy smelled so strongly of whiskey that Sydney wondered if she wouldn't get drunk off of his breath.

"Good, let's dance."

"I don't think . . ." She never got the chance to decline

his offer as he pulled her by her waist onto the dance floor.

SCOTT RETURNED WITH their drinks to witness Sydney trying to extract herself from the grip of a large, not to mention very drunk cowboy on the dance floor. He watched her push against the guy's chest, hoping to throw him off balance, but instead he leaned on her for support, staggering to the music. Scott's jaw clenched as he saw the man slide his hands from her waist to her firm bottom. Sydney grasped at the cowboy's hands, trying to pull them from her.

Normally, Scott would never allow a woman to be manhandled, but he stood his ground, hoping that this would make Sydney realize that she couldn't handle every cowboy she came across. Maybe this would be the event that would change her mind about taking the job. His intentions went out the window when he saw the foolish cowboy move his hand from her waist to the underside of her breast. An emotion he refused to acknowledge as jealousy enveloped him, and it took every ounce of self-control to keep from knocking the man to the floor.

"Mind if I cut in?" He could see the relief in Sydney's eyes.

"Yeah," the cowboy said. "Get lost."

Scott saw Sydney's plea for help and knew exactly how to handle this guy. "Tell you what, why don't you take this and go buy us a couple of beers, on me. You can have her when you get back, okay?" He handed the cowboy a twenty. "Keep the change, too."

"Now, that's a deal," he slurred, taking the money from Scott's outstretched hand.

As the cowboy let go of Sydney's waist, Scott pulled her behind him slightly, protecting her in case the cowboy changed his mind and punches were thrown. The cowboy left without further comment, heading directly to the long line at the makeshift bar booth, and Scott turned to face the woman behind him.

"You're welcome," he drawled.

"For what? You promised me to him when he brings you back a drink." She shook her head. "Yeah, you were a big help."

"If he comes back, then he's never seen your temper." Scott laughed as her eyes flashed angrily. "He'll forget about us and drink that twenty by himself." He wound his arm around her waist and pulled her close. "Come on."

Scott swayed with her on the dance floor as the male and female lead singers sang a duet about loving one another and their passion. Scott scoffed at the thought of love in the romantic sense, but in this moment, with Sydney's soft curves pressed against him, he could understand how desire could fuel passion.

"Scott," she whispered.

"Hmm?" He looked down at her, but she was staring at the base of his throat.

"Thank you."

Scott chucked and tipped her chin so she had to look him in the eye. "See, that wasn't so hard now, was it?"

She bristled and pulled away from him. "If you think this is all so funny, then why did you help me out at all? You could have stayed over there and laughed at me."

Scott pulled her back into his arms. "Because, princess, that guy had a few ideas for you in mind and they didn't include dancing." Hell, he was entertaining a few of them himself, he realized. He watched the blush creep into her cheeks as his words sank in, making her appear more vulnerable. He was almost disappointed when the band began to play an upbeat rock song and he had to release her from his arms.

AFTER THE INCIDENT with the drunk cowboy, he'd refused to let her leave his side, although he was sure that decision would lead to all kinds of speculation. He'd already seen Mike's knowing smile and a similar look on Sydney's mother's face while they'd danced. They could all think what they wanted; this was nothing more than an experiment, he reminded himself.

"Tired?" Scott asked as the night wore on.

They stood near the tables, sipping their drinks as the band took a final break before their last set. "A little," she admitted. "It's been a long day." She glanced at him demurely. "You see, the arena director is sort of a monster and he was on my case all day."

"And I'm sure you're an angel to deal with, right?"

"Of course," she answered innocently.

"Tell you what," Scott promised. "One last dance, and then I'll take you home."

"I think I'll take you up on that offer," she agreed as the band opened with the first notes of "I Will Always Love You."

Scott pulled her close to him and he felt the now-familiar desire for her spreading as his fingers slid along her spine. She curled her fingers along his shoulders and he wished she didn't have to wear the cowboy hat and crown so she could lay her head on his shoulder. He could feel her breath gently brushing his neck as he inhaled the musky scent of her perfume, trying to ignore the way her breasts brushed his chest. He could feel the heat radiating from her body and wondered if he wasn't on fire himself.

As their bodies moved in time with the music, the friction only served to fan the flame already threatening to blaze out of control. He sighed in pleasurable pain as her fingers tickled the curls at the base of his neck, brushing his already too-sensitive skin with her fingertips.

"Sydney," he whispered.

"Hey! I thought you said I could have her back!" Scott looked up at the cowboy who'd taken his money and disappeared, furious at the interruption. He edged Sydney behind him, knowing that the guy was even more inebriated than he'd been earlier.

"Where's my beer?"

"Wha . . .?" The cowboy looked confused in his stupor.

"It's okay, the lady and I were leaving anyway." Scott placed a hand at Sydney's back and started to walk with her toward the front gate.

He'd half-expected the shove that came from behind,

but it still made him stumble forward a few steps. "I think I'll take her home."

Instantly, a crowd began to surround them at the prospect of a fight. Scott spun around and dodged the first awkward swing from the cowboy, which caused him to stumble into the crowd. As he righted himself, Scott saw that Sydney had realized what was happening and stood frozen. The cowboy came at him again, this time tackling him like a football player, knocking him backward. Luckily, Scott had sobriety on his side and was able to twist quickly enough to throw the drunk man to the ground.

"Enough! Before security breaks this up, you idiot. I said, we're leaving."

"Whatever," the cowboy slurred from his seat in the dirt.

Scott turned back to Sydney as the crowd began to disperse and head back onto the dance floor. "Let's go before anything else . . ."

His words were cut off as a hand on his shoulder jerked him around and a solid fist connected with his jaw, knocking him backwards a few steps.

"That's for my buddy!"

Without hesitating, Scott rushed the assailant, grabbing him by the collar, and shoved the cowboy against the railing of the short fence of the exit gate. "We are leaving." Scott recognized one of the approaching security guards as part of the rodeo committee he'd worked with and motioned him over. "Can you escort us to the truck. These guys don't seem to want to let us leave."

The guard took one look at the situation and recognized the arena director and the newly crowned rodeo queen. "Sure thing. You"—he pointed at the cowboy Scott had just released—

"You might want to get lost and hope he forgets what you look like if you plan to ride one of his bulls tomorrow." The cowboy disappeared into the crowd as quickly as he had appeared.

Scott led Sydney to his truck silently and unlocked her door. Walking around to the driver's side, he lectured himself. It had been years since he'd gotten into a fight. As a matter of fact, the last fight had been over Liz, he recalled. So much for proving his theory wrong. If nothing else, this just proved how much Sydney Thomas was like Liz, including how easily and quickly he'd allowed her to get her hooks into him—enough that he would get into a fight over her.

Scott climbed into the truck and sat rigidly in his seat. Clipping the belt, he refused to look at her.

"Scott, are you okay?"

"Fine." He was determined not to let her affect him. He turned the key and the engine roared to life. Sydney took her hat off and scooted closer, laying it on the seat near the door.

"Then why won't you look at me?"

He turned to face her, just to prove her wrong. He realized it had been a mistake as soon as he saw the worry in her golden eyes.

"You're mad at me."

He saw the vulnerability in her eyes and wondered

momentarily how he could really think she was like his ex-fiancée. Scott cupped her cheek and ran his thumb across the velvety skin. "I'm not mad. I just didn't expect to get into a fight tonight." He gave her a lopsided grin.

She returned his smile. "I'm sorry. I really am." She touched the bruise already darkening the side of his jaw.

"Maybe you'll just have to kiss it."

She leaned back against the seat. "You seem fine," she teased as he pulled out of the parking lot.

SCOTT PULLED INTO her driveway and turned off the truck. Sydney had slipped off to sleep during the drive, her head against his shoulder, and he wasn't ready to wake her just yet. He stared down at her. Tonight had been an odd evening. No matter how he tried, he was having a hard time coming up with ways to even compare Sydney to Liz. He brushed the back of his hand against her cheek, amazed at how peaceful and innocent she looked. He brushed his thumb across her full bottom lip and wondered what it would be like to kiss her. She seemed so vulnerable, part of him wanted to completely forget what Liz had done and just trust that Sydney was exactly what she appeared to be. Then again, Liz had been a pro, acting vulnerable and sweet to get what she wanted, too. He felt like he was at war with himself, part of him wanting to trust Sydney and another part denying her authenticity.

He slipped his arm around her shoulders, shifting so that she lay against his chest, and traced her cheekbone before letting his hand slide down her neck to her collar where her dress began. She sighed softly and spread her fingers on his chest. Scott looked down, expecting to see her golden eyes burning into his own, dark with passion. Instead, he found her asleep.

He couldn't resist the temptation any longer. Cupping her face, he gently pressed his lips to hers. He slid his tongue along her lips before slipping past the barrier of her small, even teeth to encounter the sweetest honey he had ever experienced.

ONLY HALF-CONSCIOUS, SYDNEY marveled at the passionate dream she was having. She'd been wondering all night what it would be like to kiss Scott. At least in her dreams she didn't have to worry about the repercussions of following her desires. She gave herself completely to the kiss. Her pulse raced as she touched her tongue to his and felt herself tremble. Instinctively her hands found his neck, her fingers finding their way into the curls at his nape. She shivered as he blazed a path of burning kisses along her throat to her collar.

She let her head fall back to the headrest behind her. Headrest? Sydney blinked, realizing that this was not a dream. She instantly stiffened in Scott's arms. *Oh my God, what have I done?* Scott lifted his gaze to meet hers, and the blazing desire she saw there took her breath away. As if she had thrown a bucket of ice on him, his gaze hardened.

"So my theory was right, after all."

"What?" she asked, breathless.

Scott sat up, leaving the truck to open her door. "Save it, Sydney."

"Scott," she began, unsure of what she could even say about her behavior. How would she even begin to explain?

"You know," he said as he climbed back into the driver's seat and started the truck. "You're pretty good. I almost bought your act, but not quite." He dropped the truck into reverse and left her to stare at the taillights as he disappeared into the night.

Chapter Four

"Sydney," Alicia called. "That's your cue."

Sydney tapped Valentino's sides, giving him full rein to circle the arena with the sponsor flag snapping sharply in the April breeze. She exited the arena, cursing herself for not keeping her mind on the rodeo. She couldn't stop replaying what had happened in Scott's truck. Mike had even asked if she needed a break. As she made her way to drop off the flag at the trailer, she saw Scott leaning on his saddle horn, watching her intensely. His black eyes flared with raw desire for a moment before they clouded over. She was almost convinced that the bright sunlight was playing tricks on her.

"Good morning, Your Majesty." Scott raised a hand to his hat brim.

Sydney winced at his sarcasm, knowing she deserved it. "Scott," she began. "I need to explain about . . ."

"Don't want to hear it," he warned. He sat up in his

saddle and spurred his horse into a lope. Sydney sighed and wondered what chance she really had with this job if they couldn't even get along for one evening.

"Don't know what happened last night, but Scott's in one hell of a mood today." Jake handed Sydney the sponsor flag she would be taking for the next event.

"You guys were fine when you left last night," Mike pointed out. "A fight?"

"Yeah, there was a fight." Sydney took the flag and rode toward the arena before they pressed for answers.

"Finally." Sydney sighed as she rode back to the trailer.

She was mentally exhausted and was looking forward to getting home and relaxing before meeting with Mike the next morning. They would have a lot to discuss about whether or not they could actually make this job offer work. She loosened Valentino's cinch and carried the saddle to the tack room. She grabbed a pick and began to work out the dirt imbedded in his hoof.

"Sydney."

Her heart skipped at the sound of Scott's voice, but she refused to meet his gaze. It was the first time he'd initiated a conversation with her all day. In fact, he'd gone out of his way to avoid her. She dropped Valentino's front hoof and moved to clean the rear hoof. Balancing it against her thigh, she glanced up at him.

"What do you need, Scott?"

"I'll be by the ranch tomorrow around ten if that works for you."

She slid Valentino's foot to the ground and stood with her hand on his rump. "I thought that Mike was coming."

"Mike's taking the stock back to the ranch tonight. He wants me to check out the horses tomorrow and bring everyone back by Thursday."

She cleaned Valentino's other hooves before loading the horse into the trailer. Scott seemed to be waiting for an argument from her, but she was just too tired of fighting with him, trying to prove to him that she was genuine and not out to play games with him or any other cowboy. She closed the back of the trailer and locked it. She made her way to where he waited near the driver's side of her truck.

"Anything else?" She didn't mean to sound short, but she'd been trying to apologize all day, and he'd wanted no part of it.

He looked as frustrated as she felt. He removed his hat and ran his fingers through his hair before putting it back on. "Look, about last night. Let's just forget it and start over, okay?"

Sydney opened the door, not meeting his gaze. "Scott, from what I've seen, you don't really forget things that easily." She started the pickup and looked at him through the open window. "But, sure, we can start over if you think you can actually do that."

SYDNEY COULDN'T SLEEP. She tried to convince herself it was because someone would be passing judgment on her horses—and, therefore, her work—but that didn't explain the warmth that spread at the thought of Scott's dark eyes and his request that they "start over." She hoped he meant it, because if they couldn't resolve their differences, she could not accept Mike's offer, no matter how great it was. Today would be her only indicator as to whether they could have a working relationship.

Dressed in jeans and a t-shirt she headed outside to groom the horses. Hearing her enter the barn, Valentino nickered a quiet greeting. She headed for his stall as he hung his head over the gate, and she pressed her forehead against the cool bars before stroking his face.

"What is it about that guy?" she asked him. The stallion whickered a soft response and Sydney smiled at him. "You really think that's it, big guy?" Valentino was so different from most stallions; he was practically human most of the time. "I just don't get it." He sighed as she opened the door to the hay room, measuring out his grain ration. "He's so infuriating."

She put her nervous energy to use cleaning the stalls and adding fresh bedding. The radio in the tack room announced that it was fifteen minutes before Scott was due to arrive, then launched into a twangy country song. Sydney decided to saddle a couple of the geldings. She heard the back door slam at the house and her brother calling to their father as the dogs ran, barking wildly toward the front of the house, announcing what she could only assume was Scott's arrival.

The sounds of morning on the ranch were as familiar to her as breathing. She leaned her back against Valentino's gate. "Boy, am I going to miss this." The tug on her shirtsleeve brought her back to the present. "You have your food. Couldn't you give me a minute?" Valentino tossed his head, shaking his long silvery mane. She laughed at his antics, standing and patting the rump of the young gelding tied in the aisle of the barn. "Here we go."

She pulled the cinch tight and saw Scott leaning on the other side of the saddle as she stood. "Oh, I didn't see you come in."

He gave her a lopsided smile but didn't say anything as he stood aside for her to finish. Her heart skipped at his smile as she slipped the bridle over the gelding's head, trying to regain any shred of composure before facing Scott again.

"Ready?" She held the reins out toward him.

"You ride them. Let me see what they can do for you."

"You sure? They're bound to work better for me, I trained them."

"Show off for me, princess." His eyes glinted mischievously.

"Fine." She shrugged as she swung herself into the saddle.

SCOTT CLOSED THE arena gate behind her before leaning on it. He hoped he could pay attention to the horses rather than watching the rider. He'd tossed and turned all night, trying to forget how she'd felt in his arms and the heat that surged through him at the thought of kissing her again. He hated himself for it, knowing she'd probably get a good laugh at his expense, but he couldn't help the desire he felt for her. He watched as she warmed up the horse. She rode up to him with a smile gracing her lips.

"Can you rope off of him?"

Sydney rolled her eyes and cocked her head at him. "I live on a cattle ranch, what do you think?"

"Let's see how he handles the cattle." She made her way toward the chute at the end of the arena. "Don't worry about loading them."

Sydney walked the gelding to an adjoining pasture where a small herd her brother used to practice roping grazed. Pulling a weather-beaten rope from the fence post, she loped behind the young calf, expertly tossing the rope around the steer's neck. She dallied it to her saddle horn and stood in place.

"Good enough?" She loosened the rope from the calf's neck and shook it loose before letting the steer run off. "Or did you want to see a few other tricks?" At her cue, the gelding began prancing from one front leg to the other, appearing to dance in place.

"Okay, showoff, bring him back." Scott didn't want to admit it but he was impressed. She'd had a way of getting a horse to trust her and coaxing a performance each time he'd seen her ride. Not to mention that she made one hell of a nice picture astride a mount. She might have even been right about her ability to outride him. He patted the gelding's neck. "Are they all like this?" he asked. "Or did you start with your ringer?"

Sydney's smile grew wider. "Dakota is the most difficult of them all."

"What are you asking for them?"

"Three to five thousand. It depends on which ones you want."

"I'll give you twenty-eight for them all."

"Hundred?" she asked, confused.

Scott grinned. "Thousand," he said slowly. "Cash."

"Are you serious?" He nodded. "Don't you even want to see the rest?"

"It's not like you won't be at the ranch with them. I think I can trust you."

She climbed off the gelding. "Then I think we have a deal." She opened the gate and walked the gelding back to the barn. "Do you, Scott? Trust me, I mean?" She glanced back at him over her shoulder.

Scott wasn't sure how to answer her. He wanted to trust her, but he knew that wasn't what she wanted to hear. He was the one who had suggested they find a common ground, especially since they would be working together on a daily basis, practically living together. He just had to find a way to get past the desire he felt at the mere thought of her and forge a friendship.

"I'm trying." He followed her into the barn.

She hung the gelding's bridle on a hook and slipped the halter over his head. "I guess that's as good a place to start as any."

She loosened the cinch and slid the saddle off before disappearing into the tack room. Scott made his way to the gelding, grabbing the curry comb, and rubbed the horse down. She returned with two cold sodas and passed one to him. The radio still played quietly in the tack room and the gelding nosed the can in Scott's hand.

"So, you think you can be ready to leave by tomorrow? Mike wants us back at the ranch as soon as possible."

"I guess. I have a few things to tie up and to let the rodeo committee know. But none of it should take too long."

He was surprised she hadn't already relinquished her title, but imagined she'd been waiting to see if they were able to get along before completely committing to leaving.

"Jake will take the horses back into the stock trailer, Pablo can drive Valentino in the small trailer, and we'll take your things back with the fifth wheel. It's only a few hours up the road." Scott crushed his can and tossed it into a nearby garbage bin as one of the songs they'd danced to came on the radio. He wondered if she'd noticed. "I'll let you get started and take the horses down to the arena. That way they're covered by the company insurance."

Sydney helped him load the first pair of horses into the four-horse trailer he'd brought with him. When he'd closed the back ramp, he turned to face her and handed her a check. "I'll be in and out, so if you want to turn them loose in the arena, I'll pick them up."

"I'll leave the bill of sale and their registration papers with mom at the house."

"I'll pick you and Valentino up tomorrow at ten. We'll just put your things in the back of the truck, so pack light."

"Ten," she repeated. She stuck out her right hand, holding the check up to him. "It's been a pleasure doing business with you, Mr. Chandler."

He took her hand and felt the jolt of electricity that seemed to affect them both. "Let's hope it only gets better, Miss Thomas."

THEY SAT OUTSIDE, relaxing under the shade from the trailer as the sun began to sink, turning the sky blue with streaks of pink and orange. Sydney knew quiet moments on the rodeo circuit were hard to come by, and the men with her wanted to savor each one fully. She laughed at dinner as Jake spun a wild story about Scott as a young boy working his first rodeo, then she snuck away to Valentino's pen, pouring his grain into a bucket and reaching for a flake of hay. She put the horse between her and the men's laughter, laying her head on his neck for a moment before heading to check the other horses.

Entering the other pen, she ran her hand over the back of a large bay mare she'd nicknamed Pie. She knew the guys were trying to help her feel included, but they had known each other for years, so well that they could finish each other's sentences. She, on the other hand, was still an outsider and would be for a long time. It was difficult enough to be the "new kid" in any situation like that, but with the glances she'd seen from Scott today, it was nearly impossible for her to focus on anything other than his dark gaze.

Each time she'd caught his gaze, she'd read something in the smoky depths of his eyes that she didn't want to consider. It wasn't just desire, for she felt that herself. It was the feeling that everything she said and did was being weighed against a standard. Sydney felt like every comment he made was calculated for a reaction from her, which would then be measured on his scale of trust. She wasn't sure how they could form any sort of friendship while she was so conscious of his judgment.

"You okay?" Scott's voice startled her.

"I'm fine." She leaned on Pie's back and realized she felt more at ease with the horses between them. "Just checking on the animals before it gets too dark."

Scott slipped through the panels and made his way closer, patting the rump of Dakota, the horse she'd ridden for him the morning before. "Hmm, seemed more like you were hiding."

"Not hiding, just . . ." She searched for the word she wanted.

He leaned on Pie's rump, his arm pressing against hers, and patted the mare's neck. Scott looked into her eyes. "Hiding?"

Sydney's breath caught. He was close enough to kiss her, his breath fanning her cheek. He smelled of leather, horses, and grass. She wanted him to kiss her and bit her bottom lip. His gaze immediately fell to her mouth. She couldn't breathe; she had to inhale or she would pass out, but an inhale meant more of his scent filling her lungs. She stepped back from the mare, trying to put any space between them so that her brain would function.

"No, I just thought you'd like some guy time." It was a lame excuse, but it was all she could muster. Scott arched a brow, indicating his disbelief. "What time are we pulling out tomorrow?" she asked as she pretended to check the hoof of a gelding nearby.

"It will take a couple trips, so I'll start taking some of the animals over after breakfast." He made his way around the horse. "Why? Are you in a hurry to get there?" As she stood up, he had moved to stand in front of her and reached for her hand, his thumb caressing her palm. "Or just to have someone besides me to talk to?"

"I . . ." she stammered. Her breath caught in her throat as warmth spread through her veins. Just a touch from Scott and her entire body felt as if it were being consumed by liquid heat. She felt conflicted, her mind warring with her emotions. Her logic told her to jerk her hand away from his touch, but her heart wanted her to remain, which scared her even more.

"Scott," Jake yelled from the trailer. "Check the water while you're over there."

Sydney and Scott both looked toward Jake's voice. "No problem," he yelled back, breaking the spell he'd woven. Scott laughed, quietly. "Go ahead and hide, princess. I'll take care of this."

She knew it would look like she was running away, but she had to put some distance between them. *That man is far too sensual for his own good,* she thought as she hurried to where Pablo and Jake sat in folding chairs.

"I think I'm going to turn in, guys." She gave Jake and Pablo a wave. "Did you want me to leave this light on?" She pointed at the light above the camper door.

"Whatever, Sydney," Pablo answered. "The arena lights will kick on in just a few minutes."

"Night, Sydney. Don't worry, I'll feed the horses in the morning," Jake said.

Sydney stepped into the trailer and saw that Scott had put her overnight bag on the couch. She managed to find a long t-shirt and some track shorts she'd thrown inside and headed for the closet-sized compartment that housed a toilet and small area to change her clothes. She had just stripped off her jeans when she heard the trailer door open and close. She quickly changed shirts and gathered her dirty clothes. As she stepped from the bathroom, she saw Scott standing by the couch, bare-chested, removing his belt.

Sydney's jaw dropped. A blush flooded her face as heat spread throughout her entire body. Her legs felt like liquid, and she was shocked that they could still hold her upright. "What are you doing?" she asked, when she was finally able to speak.

"Changing," he answered, as if it should be obvious. "Why? Is there a problem?"

"Yes," she answered, trying to keep her eyes focused on his face and not on the bronzed skin of his chest and abdomen, which rippled as he turned toward her.

Realization of her discomfort suddenly dawned in his eyes, but rather than salvage her humility, he pressed her boundaries of decency. "You don't get any special treatment, princess," he began, taking a step closer. "We are sharing this trailer tonight."

Sydney stepped backward, her heel hitting the stairs going toward the only bed. She glanced over her shoulder: a queen size bed. *Of course*, she thought. "Then I hope you have someplace else to sleep."

Scott took another step toward her until she had nowhere to go but into the doorway of the bedroom. He placed a hand on the door frame on either side of her shoulders and leaned close so that her eyes had no choice but to meet his. She willed herself to ignore the apprehension creeping upon her and tried to appear bored, a sharp contrast to the dark desire she could read in his intense gaze.

"What's wrong, Sydney?" His voice was husky, seductive. "Didn't you want to start over?" His mouth was barely a breath from hers and she fought to not give in to his kiss. "Don't you want a repeat of the last evening we spent together?"

Sydney's cheeks blazed as she saw past his seduction. Why did everything have to be a test with him? Was everything a game? Scott pushed himself away and she mentally grasped the rejection with both hands, using it to fuel her anger and push the yearning he'd stirred up aside.

"I'm sleeping on the couch." He sounded as if the thought of being any closer disgusted him. "I've never had to force my way into a woman's bed." He glanced back at her over his shoulder. "But I'm not sure force would be necessary now, would it?"

"You horse's—" she mumbled, walking into the bedroom.

"So I've been told," he interrupted.

Sydney slammed the screen that separated the bedroom from the rest of the trailer. Trying to control her racing pulse, she took several deep breaths before she walked over to the bed and grabbed the comforter and pillow. She slid the screen back and stormed to the couch.

"Here!" She threw the pillow at him, only somewhat mollified when it hit his face with a soft thump. "I wouldn't want you to complain you're cold and try to make your way to the bed after all."

She almost laughed at him trying to dig his way out of the blanket tangled around him. "How very kind of you, Your Highness," he mocked.

"Go to hell."

"I'll meet you there," he said, rolling onto his side and turned his back toward her.

"You are the most arrogant, conceited ass I have ever had the misfortune to meet," she raged, assuring herself that if her mother had ever had to deal with Scott Chandler on a regular basis, she wouldn't think cursing was unladylike.

Scott's laughter reverberated in the small trailer. "Sweetheart, you need to get out more."

If I were a man, she thought, I'd punch him. She wanted to scream in frustration. Blinking back her angry tears, she reached down and grabbed a handful of the blanket. "On second thought, I hope you freeze!" She pulled as hard as she could, storming back into the bedroom, dragging the blanket as Scott fell off couch and hit the floor with a thud.

Chapter Five

"Damn!" Sydney heard a voice just before something clattered to the floor. "Crap!"

Sydney opened her eyes and raised herself onto her elbow to see what the commotion was about. She could only see Scott at the sink, but it sounded like he'd dropped every pot and pan at least twice. She slipped from the blankets and made her way to the doorway between the kitchen area and bedroom. In no way was she prepared for the sight that met her eyes.

Scott stood in the middle of the small trailer covered in milk and eggs. The small sink was filled with dirty dishes. The entire counter and some of the floor were covered with egg shells, raw egg, and milk. On the stove, smoke was pouring from a lump that looked as if it could have once been bacon. Scott was waving a towel, trying to push the smoke to an open window, so he didn't seem to have heard her approach.

Sydney stifled a laugh, but Scott heard it and turned her way, giving her a murderous glare. It might have been enough to end the humor of the moment if he hadn't already used the towel to wipe up some of his mess. He flipped the towel and raw egg yolk flung backward, landing on his forehead and slipping down, dropping from the end of his nose to land at his feet. At his look of utter distaste, Sydney's giggles exploded into outright gales of laughter.

"Are you going to keep laughing all day?" he asked as he turned off the stove and wiped the mess from his face. "Or do I need to drag you down here to help me?" His irritation only made her laugh harder. Scott glared at her, his black eyes flashing.

"Okay," she finally managed between spurts of laughter. "I'll help."

She had barely cleared the stairs when Scott pulled her into his arms, his body pressing fully against her own. "So," he growled. "You think this is pretty funny?" Sydney was sure her smile belied the negative shake of her head. "What am I going to do with you?" Scott asked as he maneuvered her toward the counter.

Her pulse raced wildly as he held her wrists behind her back. She was completely at his mercy but she knew his playful mood was only dangerous to her heart. "You could let me go," she suggested, trying to appear nonchalant.

Scott released her wrists and circled her waist with one arm, molding her body to his. He leaned closer, brushing his lips across her cheek to her earlobe. She closed her eyes in anticipation of his kiss, surrendering to the desire coursing through her. She'd dreamt about his kiss when sleep had finally claimed her in the early morning hours.

"I have something much more enjoyable in mind," he whispered, his lips brushing her earlobe, sending shivers down her spine.

Scott pulled back and looked her in the eye, his eyes as dark as she'd ever seen them but almost sparkling with wicked charm. Sydney was confused when he gave her the same smile she'd seen so often from her brother when he'd just pulled off a prank. She quickly realized she'd been had. She followed his gaze to his hand, raised in the air just above her head, just in time to see him crack an egg against the cabinet above. She squealed and tried to squirm away from him as the wet, slimy mess landed on her forehead.

"Bull's-eye." Scott's deep laughter rumbled through the trailer. "Now we're even."

"Ugh!" Sydney groaned as the egg yolk slid down her face and into her t-shirt.

"Need some help cleaning that up?" he teased, raising an eyebrow impishly, his eyes gleaming dangerously.

Sydney looked down to see her shirt clinging to her breasts and felt the egg yolk slide down her stomach. She spun away from him, reaching for the towel on the sink, and began to wipe the mess from under her shirt.

"You sure you don't want an extra hand?" Scott chuckled.

Sydney spotted the soapy water, complete with bits of cooked eggs floating on top. With her back still to him, she silently scooped up water in a dirty glass. "Actually, maybe you can help." She spun to face him, her hands around the glass of water.

"Don't," he warned.

"I think you need to cool off a bit," she threatened. He surprised her, moving quickly to disarm her of the glass, but she had quicker reflexes than he'd assumed. Sydney pitched the water at him, feeling satisfied as it connected squarely on his chest and splashed water in his face, momentarily blinding him.

Scott yelled in surprise, giving her a moment to scoot away from his grasp in the confined space.

"There!" she said, triumphant. "Now, we are even."

"Oh, sweetheart, we aren't even close." Scott's voice was too calm as he made his way toward her, and she realized exactly how a kitten must feel when it teases a snake, awakening danger it didn't expect.

She quickly searched the area for any sort of weapon. Grabbing a handful of cold scrambled eggs, she whirled to confront her attacker. "One more step and you'll be wearing these, too." Scott regarded her with an amused smile and took another step toward her. "I mean it, pal."

Scott dodged the eggs flung toward him. He wasn't as lucky, however, when a well-aimed handful of what had once been hash browns immediately followed and hit the side of his head. Sydney realized her folly too late and ran for the door, hoping to seek refuge outside. She flew out the door, leaping off the top stair just in time to see Jake walking toward the trailer, a worried frown creasing his brow.

"Jake," Sydney screamed, laughing again, trying to run toward the confused man.

"Oh, no you don't." Scott grabbed her by the waist and swung her over his shoulder like a sack of grain.

"Jake, help!" she screamed, pounding helplessly on Scott's solid back.

"Oh no, honey," Jake chuckled. "He's my boss. I'm staying out of this."

She cast him an evil glare but didn't think it had any effect with her hanging upside down. Jake was quickly forgotten when she realized that Scott was heading toward the water trough.

"Scott, don't you dare!"

"Well, Sydney, you seem to like water. Maybe you need to cool off." He stopped directly in front of the trough. She could see the leaves of alfalfa floating on top. "You did say you might need help cleaning up your shirt. I'm just being helpful, the way you were."

Begging for forgiveness wasn't usually her style, but then again neither was sitting in an icy water trough at seven AM in a deserted rodeo arena. She had to try. "Scott, I'm really sorry that I threw that water at you."

"And . . .?" he encouraged.

"And, um, I'm sorry I laughed at your attempt to make breakfast." He didn't move, and she wondered how long a person could hang upside down with all of the blood rushing to her head. "Well?" She was getting anxious to have her feet on solid ground again.

"You apologize real pretty-like, honey." Scott mimicked Jake's drawl.

"So, can you put me down now?"

"'Course," he agreed amiably.

Before she knew it she was flipped upright, waiting for her feet to hit ground that never arrived. Suddenly, water splashed overhead and she found herself seated in the livestock trough.

"Now, that would make a fun picture." Scott stood with his fists firmly planted on his hips, not even trying to contain his laughter as she swiped wet curls from her eyes. He reached down to pluck a piece of alfalfa from her hair and she swatted at his hand.

"Ass," she muttered under her breath.

"Is that any way for a lady to talk?" Scott leaned close and grasped her hands, helping her out of the water. "Besides, you're repeating your insults."

She glared at him as she stepped out before shoving him out the way, ignoring his laughter as he walked behind her back to the trailer. Jake led the way and stepped through the doorway, but stopped so suddenly that Sydney ran into his immobile form. He let out a low whistle as he looked inside the trailer.

He turned and faced them both. "Does this mean I'm heading out to pick up breakfast?"

Sydney's eyes met Scott's, and neither bothered to contain the laughter that burst from within.

"JAKE, GET THOSE horses in the trailer." Scott's shout echoed across the empty rodeo arena.

Sydney rode up on Dakota. "Are you sure you don't want me to come along?"

"No, we need those other horses exercised before we head out."

"Fine," she answered tersely as she turned the horse and rode toward the arena.

Scott shook his head as he watched her departure from his side mirror. He'd thought that after this morning they'd be able to call a truce, but she hadn't spoken to him while they cleaned up the mess in the trailer. He knew he was partially to blame. He'd allowed himself to get carried away this morning. But she looked so tempting in nothing but a t-shirt, her long legs bare to her shorts. He knew she was nervous about meeting everyone on the ranch later, and he probably should've allowed her on this first trip and gotten the instructions over with, but it was taking every ounce of control to be around her without kissing her senseless. And he was doubtful that being locked in a truck with her for the five-hour round trip was going to help any.

This morning after a sleepless night on the couch, he'd tried to do something nice and make her breakfast, but that only ended up with him needing a cold shower. Not that he'd entertained any ulterior motives like crawling into bed with her. He barely contained a groan at the thought. It was worth it for just a moment when he held her body pressed against his. He hadn't realized how a punishment could be so doubled-edged until he decided to give her the dunking she deserved. She'd looked so tantalizing as she stood from the water, her shirt clinging to her, he could just imagine how it would feel to hold her without the barriers of clothing. He shook his head to rid him of his reckless thoughts. *The last thing I need*, he thought adamantly, *is to get involved with someone like her, like Liz.*

Just the thought of the tall, waifish blond brought back the pain of her betrayal. He found out sooner than most cowboys that a rodeo queen's beauty, especially Liz's, was only skin deep. Looking back, he could see where she'd manipulated him. It had been easy, since he'd been so taken in by her looks that he'd forgotten how spoiled Mike's daughter had become when she returned to the ranch after college.

All he'd seen was her emerald eyes and long silken blonde hair; she was like an angel on Earth. Before she'd headed off to school, she'd always been the annoying girl that constantly pestered him and his best friend, Kurt. Once she'd returned fully developed after her first year, both men had vied for her attention. She had mastered the art of flirtation, but Scott was attracted to her vulnerability, as if only he could shelter her from the rest of the world. He liked being her knight. And the first time they'd made love had been initiated by her desire for him to hold and protect her. With professions of love, they were soon engaged. Everyone on the ranch was happy; it finally looked as if the two families would join in more than just business. Even Kurt was happy for them—or so he thought.

Arriving home from a trip to purchase cattle a day earlier than planned, he'd hoped to surprise Liz. He searched the house for her, and when he didn't find her he'd assumed that she must have gone shopping with his sister, maybe making more wedding plans. Scott made his way out to the barn to get some work done until she came back home. Entering, he could see that someone had left a light on in the office. The horses whinnied at his arrival, and he could hear voices over the sounds but couldn't make out words until he reached the doorway.

As if someone else were controlling his body, and with a calm his heart wasn't feeling, Scott cleared his throat. Kurt and Liz, caught in the middle of their lovemaking, looked up to see Scott in the doorway.

"Scott," she cried. Tears instantly welled in her eyes as she pushed away from Kurt. She tried to gather her clothing around her and ran toward Scott. "He tried to . . . I mean . . . he . . ."

Scott wondered what possible excuse she was going to try to make. "What, Liz? Spit it out." His voice was tight, and he felt like he could barely get the words out. His mind was beginning to cloud over with rage, and he wanted to beat someone senseless.

"Scott, he raped me," she whispered.

Scott's eyes met those of the man who had been his friend, or so he'd thought. Kurt was pulling his pants up and buckling them. Had Kurt feigned disbelief, anger, or even denied the charge, Scott would have believed her. Instead, Kurt leaned back on the desk, almost bored, and Scott knew this was another performance designed to reel him back into her web of deceit. For her to even claim something so audacious, she must not have realized how long Scott had been standing at the door. Long enough to hear her passionate words for Kurt and insults toward Scott, who was "too stupid to see what went on in his own office."

Scott wanted to hurt her, hurt them both, as he'd been hurt. He looked down at her and removed her hand from his chest, where she was trying to cuddle up against him. "I hate to be blunt, but you were riding that pony willingly."

The slap sounded like a gunshot in the small room. Liz shook her hand, but Scott refused to react. Instead, he looked at Kurt. "If I ever see you around this ranch again, if I ever see you on the circuit again, under any circumstances . . ."

"Don't threaten me, Scott." Kurt's gaze was dangerous yet slightly glazed. "You can't do anything. We both know I'm bigger, faster, and stronger."

"If I ever see you again, you will lose your card." Scott saw Kurt's eyes narrow. "I will report your drug use without a second thought." Kurt reached for his shirt.

"You bastard!" Liz spat at him. "If you'd really loved me, this wouldn't have happened."

Scott was struck by the absurdity of her words. His fault? Between him and her father, this woman had never wanted for anything. He looked down at her tearful emerald eyes, now glimmering with fury at not getting her way. He would never give her the satisfaction of knowing that she had ripped his heart out.

Scott turned on his heel, chuckling, and left the barn. He immediately loaded his truck, intent on heading out to the first rodeo he could find. Throwing himself into his work had proved to be his only distraction until the pain of her betrayal had been buried deep enough that it didn't rise up. And any woman who decided to flirt with him usually ignored the bitterness that tinged his intimacies. He'd been able to avoid any sort of emotional tie, until Sydney.

Liz had disappeared after that final confrontation. Scott never told Mike what had happened, but he hadn't needed to. When he returned home, Mike informed him that she had taken off that same day with Kurt, saying she had decided to "ride the circuit." Scott wasn't sure if Mike was more hurt because of the way Liz had treated him or because she had once again abandoned Mike and the ranch to run away.

"She acted like it was an adventure," Mike withdrew an envelope from his pocket. "She left this for you."

Scott reluctantly tore it open, its contents spilling into his hand. Mike picked up the engagement ring and held it up. "It just didn't work out, Mike."

Scott could see that Mike wanted to ask more questions but that he also wouldn't want to hear the truth. "So, how'd the rodeo go?" Scott's respect for Mike grew as he allowed Scott his privacy.

Scott had tried to focus on the endless stretch of road, watching for exits, leaving behind the highway for a road banked by lush, green pastures. They'd been lucky that Liz had stayed away the past two years. She'd only kept in contact with her father in short letters and emails with an occasional phone conversation, usually begging for more money, which Mike always sent her. The further away Liz stayed, the better off everyone was, Scott decided.

As Scott made his way down the driveway to the main corral, he saw bodies pour from the house. Mike led the way, followed by Clay, Scott's huge brother-in-law. He questioned whether the man had been lifting weights in his absence again. He saw his sister following behind and wondered again how the two of them could have such similar personalities and ethics, yet Derek, who hadn't even shown up, could be so different. Silvie, short and heavyset, with her apron still tied around her waist, brought up the rear.

"Scott," Mike yelled as he turned off the truck engine. "I didn't expect you here so soon."

Scott headed to the back of the trailer. "I wanted to get started since we're making two trips today." He opened the back gate and, unclipping the first two horses, backed them out together.

"How many horses did you end up getting?"

"Seven, plus the stud is coming back, too." He passed the lead ropes to Clay, who took the horses to the corral. Before he could say anything else, he heard Jennifer squeal as she threw her arms around his neck.

"Oh, I've missed you, little brother!"

Returning her enthusiastic hug, Scott laughed. "I've missed you too. But you're choking me," he teased.

Silvie looked around. "So, where's Sydney?"

"She's working the rest of the horses. I'll bring her later today when we bring the rest of the horses back." He hugged Silvie as he caught the I-told-you-so look she shot Jennifer.

"So what did we get?" Scott was thankful for Clay's interruption. He didn't want to answer the women's questions about his leaving Sydney behind.

"Four geldings and three mares. Plus, Sydney's got her stallion."

Clay raised a brow. "A stallion she uses in the rodeo?"

Mike laughed. Using stallions in rodeos was unusual due to their unpredictable nature. It was the same reason riders tended to use geldings instead of mares most of the time. "This isn't an ordinary stud, Clay. Trust me." Mike turned to Scott. "The mares are for breeding?"

Scott nodded as he handed Clay the lead ropes of the horses he had unloaded. "You should see the bloodlines, Mike. They'll throw some nice foals, especially with that stud." He closed and locked the back of the trailer.

"Okay," Silvie interrupted. "Let Clay finish with those horses. You get into the house. I just finished making lunch, so let's all hurry up and eat while it's still hot." She shooed them toward the house.

Scott leaned toward Jennifer as they headed toward the house. "Where's Derek?"

"Um." She stalled. "He was here just before you pulled in."

"He headed to the lake again," Clay answered as he came up behind them.

"What?" Scott couldn't believe how worthless his brother was on the ranch.

"Well," Clay said, matter-of-factly. "He was no help with the cattle, so he left."

Scott clapped him on the back. "How did we ever get along around here without you?" He was genuinely fond of his brother-in-law and had respected him as one of the best pick-up men in rodeo even before he and Jennifer had become a couple. He'd been thrilled when they had worked out their differences so that he was able to stand at Clay's side when they were married.

"Scott, Derek will come around. He's still young," Jennifer scolded.

"Derek is twenty-two years old. If he wants to be treated like a man, he needs to learn to act like one. Besides," he continued, "he's far older than we were before we started working rodeos with Mike, and he can't even handle the work around here."

Scott blamed himself for his brother's lack of responsibility. He and Jennifer had babied him after they'd lost their parents, and Jennifer had always been his valiant defender in every situation. Derek had always run to her for protection from their brother and had never hidden his dislike of Scott. Scott knew that Derek had always felt as if he came in second place, but that was usually because he wasn't willing to put in the hard work Scott had. Derek, like Liz, wanted everything handed to him.

"Scott," Jennifer pleaded. "Just don't say anything. I'll talk with him tonight."

"Jen, he's got to . . ."

"Please," she interrupted. "I promise. When you get home tonight, he'll be ready to work hard, okay?"

"Somehow, I doubt that." Scott didn't want to argue with his sister about their brother.

As they circled the kitchen table and sat for lunch, Mike didn't waste any time asking about Sydney. "Was she okay with the sleeping arrangements?"

Scott shrugged. "We worked it out. I took the couch." He didn't miss the knowing look his sister shot Clay, nor the smile that Mike tried to hide behind his glass. "Give me a break. There is nothing going on and there isn't going to be." He felt a slight twinge of guilt at the lie.

"Scott, if half of what Mike said about her is true, you should think twice. It might be good for you to date someone again." Jen tried to appear nonchalant without much success.

"And you think dating someone who works with us would be a good option?"

She shrugged. "All I'm saying—"

"Scott," Mike interrupted. "All Jen is suggesting is that you don't rule out the idea of dating anyone. Sydney's the type of girl we hope to see you settle down with someday—honest, strong, determined. And the fact that she's pretty doesn't hurt either." He chuckled.

Scott took a deep breath, letting it out slowly, clenching his jaw, and effectively ending the conversation. Clay changed the subject, discussing plans for an upcoming rodeo. Scott tried to keep his mind focused on his work instead of letting it stray to Sydney, who was waiting at the rodeo grounds. He glanced at his watched and realized that it was already past two o'clock. He hadn't planned on being gone so long and stood to leave.

"I'll walk you out," Clay offered.

Scott knew that Clay had something he needed to get off his chest as they walked to the truck. "What's the problem?"

"That obvious, huh?" Clay rubbed a hand over his stubbled jaw.

"Not really, I just know you. You don't usually walk me to the truck unless something's up." Clay looked like he was trying to figure out how to best approach bad news. "Just get it out. Don't worry about sugarcoating it." Scott wondered what Derek had done that had Clay this worried.

"Liz is coming home."

"What?" Scott felt as if someone had stuck a knife in his gut. Mike hadn't even heard from her in the last three months. "Are you sure she just doesn't want Mike to send her more money?"

"I wish, man." Clay looked uncomfortable. "But she called Mike today and I knew that with everything that happened, you deserved a heads up. Besides, I'm a little worried that with this new girl staying in the house, there might be some trouble."

"You mean Liz won't like Sydney stealing her spotlight?" Scott guessed.

"Exactly."

Scott laid his hand on Clay's shoulder. "Thanks for letting me know." He climbed into the truck. "As if this wasn't going to be difficult enough."

Scott started the engine, unsure if he meant dealing with Liz or having Sydney in such close proximity all of the time.

Chapter Six

SCOTT CURSED HIS luck. He'd already been late leaving the house to get back to the arena, but then a flat tire on the trailer had made any chance of getting back to the ranch tonight an impossibility. He hadn't even been able to call Jake or Sydney because his cell phone battery was dead and his car charger wouldn't work. Finally, just as he was about to turn off of the freeway, traffic slowed to a stop due to a big rig that had dumped its entire load on the freeway, shutting down all but one lane of traffic. What should have been a two-hour drive back had now taken him almost five hours. If nothing else, the long drive had given him plenty of time to think about what Mike said at lunch.

Sydney was strong and honest and determined, but she was so much more than Mike even realized. She was passionate, with a temper that rivaled his own, but she also had a soft vulnerability that he couldn't ignore. He was beginning to see that Sydney was nothing like Liz. She'd had plenty of opportunities to use him, Jake, or Mike to get what she wanted. Mike's job offer had come as much of a shock to her as it had him, and she'd been undervaluing her horses and her training. He had to admit that he'd been wrong about her, and he had never been so relieved to be wrong.

When Scott finally pulled into the rodeo arena, he just wanted to get something hot to eat and to fall into a deep sleep. He parked the truck and went to check in with Jake to see how the day had gone for them, then he glanced in on the horses to see them relaxed and fully cared for by Sydney and Jake. Finding everything in order, he headed for the small trailer where he hoped to find Sydney waiting.

Walking into the trailer, he was surprised to find her asleep on the couch that served as his bed. He made his way to her sleeping form and squatted on the balls of his feet. She lay curled up, facing the door with her hand tucked under her chin. He saw that the small table was set and a chicken dinner had grown cold. A pang of guilt for abandoning her all afternoon crept up. Scott brushed her cheek with his fingertips. Soft and pink, with her curls falling around her face and down the side of the couch, she appeared so innocent.

"Sydney," he whispered, trying to rouse her.

She leaned into his warmth, and her hand covered his on her cheek. Scott was unable to help himself when faced with her sweetness. He leaned down and lightly kissed her pouting lips. At the touch, a soft sigh escaped her throat, relaying her pleasure at his caress.

"Sydney," he whispered again, this time along her jaw. "Wake up, princess." He traced his thumb along her cheek and ear before allowing his lips to explore both.

"Scott?" She blinked, her eyes still clouded with sleep, and smiled up at him as she cupped his cheek. "I was worried about you."

Her eyes widened as she came fully awake, realizing what she had just revealed. The blush that colored her cheeks made her look even more appealing. Scott arched a brow before placing a quick kiss on her protesting lips. "Long drive and my cell died. I see I missed dinner?"

"Wait, before you say anything I have something I have to tell you." She sat up on the couch, but Scott stayed squatting in front of her, remaining eye to eye.

Scott took her hand and placed a kiss on her palm, feeling the pulse in her wrist speed up. "Go on."

She drew her hand back as if it were on fire. "I ... um ... I just wanted to say," she stammered. He knew their kisses were affecting her the same way they affected him. "Just that I know we didn't meet under the best of circumstances and I hope you don't think I'd normally treat someone the way I've treated you."

"Thanks." He smiled. "I think."

"No, I mean ... I don't mean it like that." He could see she was getting frustrated, so he rocked back onto his heels, giving her a little room to breathe and think. "What I mean is that I've been rude to you, and I'm sure you haven't deserved all of it." She gave him a coy smile. "But I hope you'll accept my apology and we can be friends."

Scott stood and made his way to the cold meal on the

table, preparing to warm it up. "Friends?" he asked, letting the word slide off his tongue.

"Sure. I mean since we'll be seeing each other almost daily, it would make it easier on us both." Her curls bobbed around her face as she nodded.

"Just friends?" He arched his brow again and gave her his most rakish grin.

"Well," she stammered. He chucked as she struggled to find the answer she thought would work before giving him a scolding glare. "You're doing this on purpose," she accused.

"What am I doing, princess?"

"You're trying to make me feel . . ." He could see she was searching for a safe word.

"Uncomfortable."

"Touché," Scott chuckled as he grabbed one of the chairs and set it down in front of her. "Okay, since you want to lay everyone out on the line, I'll take a turn. I did a lot of thinking today and I agree, we didn't get off to the best start. I also apologize for the shabby way I've treated you. I've let past experience cloud my judgment without giving you a chance. You didn't deserve that and I think a clean slate is in order."

Scott reached for her hand and she allowed him to take it. "I know that it took a lot for you to be that honest with me, so I'm going to be honest with you. I'm all for us being 'friends', sweetheart, but that's not all I want from you."

"What do you mean?" Her breath caught as he cupped her cheek with his hand and stroked the silken skin.

"I mean that I want you. I have from the first moment I laid eyes on you, more than anyone I can remember." He watched as her blush returned, but her eyes flamed with smoldering desire before she tore her gaze from his. "I'm not a romantic guy, I don't believe in love at first sight, but I do want you. I want you going into this 'friendship' with your beautiful golden eyes open."

Sydney chewed at her bottom lips as if unsure how to respond. "Don't worry; I don't expect you to say anything to that little revelation." Scott chuckled, lightening the anxiety of the moment, and rose from the chair, pushing it back under the table. "How about if we warm up this chicken? Now that I've satisfied my appetite for you." Scott wiggled his eyebrows. "For the moment at least," he clarified. "I'm starving."

Scott laughed as Sydney's cheeks grew even more pink as she stepped over to the stove, placing the chicken in the oven to reheat it. Reaching into the refrigerator, she pulled out a pitcher of iced tea and poured him a glass. As she placed the glass in front of him, Scott reached out and captured her wrist, pulling her to his lap.

"Come here."

She smiled. "I thought you said you were hungry."

"Oh, I am," he agreed, his eyes ran over her face, hungry to taste her lips again. "Besides, I missed you today."

"I missed you too," she admitted. He was lowering his head to take possession of her mouth when the timer went off.

Scott growled as he let her up. "Saved by the bell."

Sydney retrieved the chicken and dished up two plates, putting a green salad on the table. "So, ready to meet everyone tomorrow?"

"A little nervous," she admitted. "But other than that, I think I'm ready to get going."

"What can I do to help you feel more comfortable?"

She laughed slightly and tipped her head to the side. "Are you serious?" Scott nodded. "Because that was not your concern a few days ago. You didn't want me to even take the job."

Scott sighed, realizing how difficult his stubborn ego had made this challenge for her. "That was a mistake on my part. You're going to do a great job; you're an amazing trainer. I'm more worried that you might get hurt."

"Scott," she said, shaking her head at him. "I've been breaking horses since I learned how to ride. I grew up in the saddle. I'm more comfortable there than on my own feet." She took a bite of her salad.

Scott took a bite of his own food. He wasn't worried about her getting hurt on horseback. He was worried about the damage he might cause to her heart, or what Liz could do.

SCOTT WASN'T SURE what woke him but he was upright on the couch. Something had broken through the haze of his subconscious and grabbed his attention. Then he heard it: Sydney's voice, so full of pain that he ran to the bed. She was caught in a nightmare, tossing her head on the pillow as tears rolled down her cheeks. He grasped her shoulders.

"No, please," she begged. "Don't."

"Sydney," Scott reached for her wrists as she fought against him, scratching his cheek in the process. "Sydney, wake up. You're dreaming." She opened her eyes and stared at him, dazed. "You were dreaming," he explained, letting her wrists loose.

"Scott!" He could hear panic in Jake's voice from outside the door.

"It's okay, Jake. We're fine," he assured him.

"You're not killing her, are you?"

Scott raised his eyebrows at Sydney expectantly. "He's expecting your voice."

"I'm fine, Jake. Just a bad dream."

They heard Jake leave the steps, muttering as he made his way back toward his bed. Scott lay beside her, pulling her onto his chest protectively. He looked down at her and smoothed a curl from her cheek. "You want to talk about it?"

She shook her head as a tear slid down her cheek and landed on his chest. She refused to meet his gaze. "I don't remember."

He knew she was lying, but wasn't sure why. He stroked her head, not wanting to force her but concerned. "You were telling someone to stop and you fought me like a wildcat." He brushed his thumb across the tear streak. "You can talk to me," he coaxed.

"I ... I can't," she whispered, her fingers curling against his chest.

"Okay." He wrapped his arms around her, tucking her head below his chin. "When you're ready, you can tell me. But you'll be safe for tonight, I promise."

"Thank you," she whispered, her breath warm against his bare chest.

Scott felt his pulse rage as desire shot through him. He willed himself to think of anything other than the soft, warm temptation lying in his arm. She needed his comfort right now, and that was what he would give her. He pressed a kiss to the top of her head and heard her breathing grow deep and even. Her fingers twitched on his chest. She was falling back to sleep. Now if only he could do the same, he thought.

SCOTT AWOKE THE next morning as the sun peeked through the curtain across from him, but it wasn't the rays that woke him. It was Sydney's rear, pressed firmly against him as he found himself curled around her back with his hand cupping her breast. He stifled a groan, settling instead for a sigh, and forced himself to scoot away from her on the bed. He didn't want to think what would have happened if she'd wakened to his fondling, and he hated himself for his weakness.

He rose onto his elbow and looked down at her profile. She looked like a child, with her hand curled into a fist under her chin as she slept. Scott leaned forward and lightly placed a kiss on her temple. "Sydney," he whispered as he kissed her jaw. "It's time to get up."

"Hmm." She sighed, stretching her torso and raising her arms above her head. She rolled over and landed on his bare chest.

A soft groan escaped his throat. She was putting him

through hell without even knowing it. "Come on, sleepy-head. You have a long drive ahead and a busy day."

Sydney opened her eyes and, realizing they were in bed together, tried to pull away from him. He wrapped his arms around her back and held her close. "Good morning."

Her smile was shy as she looked at him. "Morning," she mumbled. "Want some breakfast?" She appeared ready to flee at the first opportunity.

"Sure, in a minute," he said, enjoying this moment of holding her against him. He tipped her chin up and touched her lips with his. Her mouth tasted so sweet he wanted to deepen the kiss, but he didn't want to imagine where that might lead him this morning. "I wanted to say good morning properly." Her smile was relaxed and her eyes liquid, which had been his intention.

"Now, would you like me to fix breakfast?" she asked.

Scott loosened his arms and began to stroke her back. "Unless you want me to fix it."

"No, I think I'd better do it. I remember cleaning up your mess last time."

Scott reluctantly moved away from her and left the bed to find his shirt near the couch. "Why don't you get started and I'll go feed the horses? We'll be loading up and pulling out after we eat."

Scott returned to the trailer to find Sydney showered, changed, and placing the food on the table. She looked as fresh as a spring flower and smelled nearly as sweet. Had Jake not been right behind him, he would have forgotten breakfast entirely and kissed her senseless until they had to leave.

As they sat down at the small table, Scott stared at the woman across from him. He wasn't sure what had changed on his drive back from the ranch yesterday, but he knew that Sydney was different. In fact, she was the polar opposite of Liz, and he couldn't believe he'd ever thought they were alike. Sydney was tough as nails when she wanted her way, refusing to back down, even running headlong into a fight to stand up for a cause where Liz wouldn't have lifted a finger for anyone but herself. Where Sydney sought out hard work, Liz ran from it. She had a passion for life and had stirred a passion in him unlike anyone else. But he'd also glimpsed her vulnerability and a pain in her eyes that he knew few had seen. He wasn't sure what had caused it, but he wanted to protect her from any of her fears. Scott's eyes followed her as she rose to clear the breakfast dishes.

"Sydney, honey," Jake drawled, sitting back in his chair. "That was fantastic."

"Thanks, Jake."

Jake jumped from his chair and took the plate from her. "Why don't you go load the rest of the horses and Scott and I will take care of these?" He gestured at the dishes. "You cooked, we'll clean."

"You sure?" she asked.

She pulled a hair tie from her wrist and used her fingers to comb her long curls back into a ponytail. Scott felt his breath leave in an instant, as if he'd been kicked in the gut by one of the horses. Her every curve was accented as she raised her arms, her shirt clinging to her breasts and raising enough to give him a peek at the bare, silken skin of her stomach. He couldn't tear his gaze from that small expanse of skin, and he wondered when he'd become a fifteen-year-old boy again, so given over to his hormones. He was almost grateful when she headed out the door so that he could breathe again.

"Ahem." Jake cleared his throat and a broad grin filled his face.

"What are you laughing at?"

"How the mighty fall."

"What?"

"You've finally met your match." Jake chuckled. "And I've gotta say, she's a perfect match."

"What are you talking about?" Scott rose and attacked the plates in the sink. "Since when do you play matchmaker? Isn't that still Jen and Silvie's job?"

"Boy, you've got it bad. A blind person could see it." Jake clapped him on the shoulder as he reached for a towel to dry the dishes. "And there is nothing wrong with that. It's been far too long."

"For what?" Scott passed another dish to him, jamming it into his hands. He knew that Jake was just trying to watch out for him. Most of the older hands thought of him as their nephew since they'd known him most of his life, but he didn't like the turn this conversation had taken.

"Scott, it's been a long time since you were in love."

"Love?" Scott scoffed at the thought. "You know I don't believe in that crap. It's right up there with Santa Claus and the Easter Bunny." Scott pressed the last dish into Jake's hand and headed for the shower. "Maybe you should mind your own business."

As Jake headed out the door, Scott barely heard him mumble, "Maybe you should cowboy up and just admit the truth."

SYDNEY HAD JUST finished loading the horses when Scott stepped out of the trailer. She could just make out his damp curls at the collar of his t-shirt.

As she made her way toward him, her pulse quickened. Even clean shaven, he had a rugged air about him, and her heart skipped at the mere sight of him. She wasn't sure what had happened yesterday before he'd arrived, but his change had, at the very least, pleasantly surprised her. And his kisses, well, those had turned her every bone to Jell-O and her limbs liquid. Waking in his arms this morning had caused buried yearnings to rise up, demanding fulfillment.

Scott had admitted that he wanted her and she couldn't help but desire him, but they couldn't base a relationship on mere need. She wasn't sure how she felt about him. To call them friends seemed too mild, but she couldn't say that this was love either—not after only knowing him a few days, even if those days felt like a lifetime. There was definitely something other than desire between them, and it was growing stronger, but she wasn't convinced they should explore it further. She wasn't naïve enough to think she was more than a fling for him; he'd practically admitted that love had nothing to do with it. And he was her employer, or might as well have been. If this fell apart, she'd be back to training at her parents' house.

"Ready?"

"Yep, let's head out." Scott waved Jake over as he opened the passenger door for her. "Hop in."

During the two-hour drive to the ranch, Sydney tried desperately to control her nerves. Questions swirled in her head. What if the family didn't like her? What if she didn't like them? What if there was too much work to keep up with by herself? Scott tried his best to keep her talking about rodeos she'd attended and the horses she'd trained. He asked questions about her training methods and her father's ranch. But her nerves practically vibrated as they turned off of the highway onto the gravel road before stopping in front of the barn and corral. She was jumpy, unsure of what kind of welcome to expect from the family Scott had told her about.

Scott jerked his chin at the people pouring from the house as if the first one to the truck won a prize. "Looks like the gang's all here."

Mike was the first one to her door, and he swung it open for her. "Come on out, Sydney. We're so glad to see you made it in one piece."

As Scott climbed out of the truck, he was bowled over by a brunette with the same mischievous dark eyes. "I'm so glad you're back!" She hugged him tightly as Mike walked Sydney to the driver's side.

"Hey," Scott choked out. "Loosen up before you strangle me."

"Sydney, this is Jennifer, Scott's older sister," Mike introduced.

The woman pushed Sydney's outstretched hand aside

and drew her into a warm hug. "Call me Jen. We've heard so much about you! And you're far prettier than even Mike's description." As she drew back, she elbowed Scott in the ribs. "I hope this one behaved himself."

Sydney smiled as Scott cringed at Jen's teasing. She was so bubbly and warm, and willing to push Scott's buttons, that Sydney felt an immediate bond. "Yeah, I can hold my own against the likes of him." Jen's eyes were full of laughter while Scott's held the glint of desire, and she realized her unintentional double meaning.

Sydney felt the blush immediately stain her cheeks, and Scott's lips spread into a knowing smile as he winked at her. "And this is Clay, Jen's husband and our best pick-up man." He clapped the towering, blond beast of a man on the shoulder. Scott looked around. "Where's Derek?"

"I'm right here." At the mention of his name, a tall young man stepped forward. He looked so much like Scott it was eerie, but he was obviously younger and his body lacked Scott's muscularity. He was less tanned as well, as if he'd been indoors more than out. He walked forward and scooped up Sydney's hand, kissing her knuckles. "It's so good to meet you. If I can do anything for you, be sure to let me know."

"Um, okay." Sydney was a little embarrassed at his display, so she wasn't sure how to react and took a step back. The rest of the group burst out in boisterous laughter. Derek frowned at Scott and hurried to the back of the trailer.

"Now, all of you leave this poor girl alone," ordered a

plump woman in a motherly tone as she shooed everyone away. The short, gray-haired woman wound a chubby arm around Sydney's waist.

Scott leaned in and whispered in her ear, loud enough for everyone to hear. "This is Silvie. Mike calls her the housekeeper, but she really runs everything around here."

"Oh, you . . ." Silvie waved her hand at Scott modestly. "You just go and get those horses settled."

"Oh, I should go do it," Sydney protested.

"Nonsense," Silvie said as she guided Sydney away from the men. "You just follow me."

SCOTT ENTERED THE kitchen after getting the horses settled in their new pasture. As the screen door slammed behind him, all three women at the kitchen table immediately stopped talking and turned to look at him. They all watched silently as he reached into the refrigerator and grabbed a cold soda. He'd heard them talking as he reached the door, but all conversation had stopped upon his entrance.

"Everything okay?" He popped the flip tab on the soda, barely letting the fizz settle before gulping back almost half of the can.

"Sure," Jen answered. "Why wouldn't it be?" She looked at Sydney and Silvie and suddenly all three women burst into hysterical laughter, sounding just like Jen and her friends had during their teenage sleepovers.

Scott rolled his eyes and shook his head as he opened the screen. "I'm not even going to ask," he said in mock disgust. In truth, he was thrilled that Jen and Silvie were already making Sydney feel at home. He knew they'd welcome her in; they both shared that mothering instinct, as he knew too well, but they also seemed to be bonding in a mutual friendship.

"How's it going out there?" Sydney tried to hide her grin between her thumb and first finger.

"It's fine." He shot her a sideways glance. "Why? How are things in here?"

"Silvie and Jen were just warning me to stay away from the giant snakes near the water troughs."

Scott cringed. So that's what they'd been in the kitchen laughing about? The one time when he mistook an old, knotted rope in front of a horse trough for a rattlesnake? He arched his brow and put his hands on Sydney's shoulders, lowering his voice but still whispering loud enough that everyone could hear.

"You should tell them about your last encounter with a water trough." He gave her shoulders a squeeze, watching a flush rise from her neck as he brushed a kiss on her cheek and hurried outside.

"What happened with the water trough?" Scott heard Jen's voice carry through the screen, wondering how much of the truth Sydney would actually admit.

Chapter Seven

DESPITE THE OLDER woman's protests, Sydney helped Silvie clean up the dinner dishes. Afterward she found herself sitting on the end of a very comfortable bed, staring at the boxes stacked beside the closet on her right. She felt so odd to be unpacking her clothes and mementos in someone else's home. Well, they weren't going to unpack themselves. She had just picked up the first box and moved it when she heard a knock at the door.

"Come in," she called, assuming Scott had come to check on her again. He'd been staying close all day, as if he was making sure nothing went wrong on her first day at the ranch. She glanced over her shoulder and caught a glimpse of dark eyes and dark hair, but it took a second for her brain to process the leaner, taller frame. "Oh, Derek. Come on in, sit down." She motioned to the easy chair in the corner.

"Thought I'd come and see if you needed anything."

He slid down into the chair, staring at her intensely with those black eyes, which were so much like his brother's.

"Not that I can think of. I'm just getting started unpacking so . . ." she left the suggestion hanging.

Derek rose and grabbed the box labeled "Stuff" from the stack, laughing. "Hope there's nothing I shouldn't see in here."

"That's just pictures and knickknacks I couldn't do without." She smiled as he held up a picture of her with her parents, taken of her at four on her first "big-girl horse." "Those are my parents and Jedi."

"That horse is enormous. And you're what? About five?"

"Four, and yes, he was big, but he was such a teddy bear. We actually just lost him a few summers ago." Sydney took the picture and placed it on the dresser. "So, Derek, I know what Clay does, and Jen helps Silvie. Are you going to the college?" She guessed he was about twenty, so she'd assumed that with his lack of muscle from outdoor work he must not be at the ranch full-time.

"I graduated a couple semesters early, last fall."

Sydney realized that she must have misjudged his age. "I see," she teased. "You're a genius."

Derek laughed and placed another picture of her parents on the dresser. "That's me, genius extraordinaire." He grabbed a picture of her brother, his arm looped over her shoulder, taken at a rodeo last year. She saw him frown before holding it up for her to see. "Boyfriend?"

"Ew, no! Younger brother," she corrected. She saw the flash of anger on his face, but it was gone almost as quickly as it appeared. She almost wondered if she hadn't imagined it. "So, you're the youngest?"

"Yeah, I'm the baby of the family." His tone told her he wasn't happy about it either. "Ask anyone and they'll tell you."

Sydney wasn't sure what sort of family dynamic was at work, but there was some sort of tension. "So Jen said she's the oldest. You guys must be pretty close in age."

"Jen and I are five years apart. Scott and I are three years apart, although sometimes it feels like a lot more." He didn't hide the bitterness in his voice at the mention of his brother.

"You two don't get along, I take it."

"That would be an understatement." He turned back to the box.

So that was the reason for the odd tone when Derek talked about his brother. "What about your sister?"

"Jen's great. She just . . . she gets me, you know what I mean?" He shrugged and put the picture next to the others. "Scott wants me to be him. Just because we look alike doesn't me we are alike."

Sydney didn't really want to delve any further into the dark waters of a family disagreement. "So what do you do now that you've graduated, smart guy?"

"I actually work for you."

Sydney's hands froze. "What? You mean you work for Mike."

Derek shrugged and shook his head. "No, for you," he repeated. "Well, technically, with you, I guess, since I'm a part owner. But you're my boss and I'm supposed to report to you, so I work for you."

"Doing what?"

Derek reached inside the box for the last few pictures and laid the photo albums on the bed before flattening the box. "I never liked working with the bulls or cattle. No," he corrected, "I think *hate* would be a better word. But I love working with the horses. I've been trying to do the exercising and training, but when it comes to training, I'm just okay. So when Mike hired you, he said I'd be your right hand."

Sydney realized that while she was filling a need Mike had for a trainer, she'd actually taken Derek's only position on the ranch. She wondered if he was bitter about the situation. She'd have to be very careful not to step on his toes.

"You know," Derek drawled as he grabbed another box, "I think for the first time in a very long time, I might enjoy my job." He winked at her and gave her a lopsided smile.

Sydney wasn't oblivious to his flirting but wasn't sure how to deflect it. She certainly couldn't say she didn't date people she worked with. On the other hand, she couldn't really say if she and Scott were actually dating. She chose instead to pretend she hadn't noticed his flirting. "So when do we get started?"

"Why don't we take a tour tomorrow morning? I'll take you out to the barns, then we can ride to the pastures and you can see the stock. Then I can get you up to speed on our paperwork after lunch."

"That sounds like a great way to start. Silvie said breakfast is at eight?"

"Yeah, I'll get up early and saddle a couple of horses. Mike will feed them about six so we can leave around nine, if that works for you."

Derek placed a box on the bed and Sydney noticed it said "Clothing" on the side. Unsure of what might be inside, she placed a hand on the lid. "It's okay, I'll finish this tomorrow. I'm pretty beat."

Derek looked down at her hand then met her gaze. He looked hurt, but she really didn't want him unpacking her underwear. "Uh, okay, I guess I'll see you in the morning then."

Derek shut the door behind him and Sydney plopped back onto the bed. She really liked Derek. He was fun and quick to laugh and tease, but she didn't want him to construe any sort of friendship as flirting. And she certainly didn't want to cause any more sibling rivalry between Derek and Scott by telling him about her relationship with Scott. Not that she was sure what she could even tell him. It wasn't like she or Scott had actually defined their relationship.

Sydney sighed and stretched. The unpacking could wait. Her back was as tight as her nerves. Her mind whirled with questions about how to handle Derek's flirting tomorrow. Maybe a walk would do her some good. She could head over to the barn and check on Valentino.

She tiptoed down the stairs, careful not to disturb anyone in the nearly silent house. The only noise she heard came from a television in a room down the hall, the faded light shining from under the closed door. Sydney took a deep breath of the brisk nighttime air as she stepped onto the porch. As she made her way down the stairs, she noticed a shooting star and smiled. She and her mother always made wishes on comets. She wondered what her mother would say if she told her that tonight's wish was to get through tomorrow with no confrontation.

She opened the main door of the barn and heard Valentino whinny. "Shh, you don't want to wake everyone else, do you?" She hurried to his stall and he met her at the door, hanging his head over the gate. "So what do you think of this place?" She rubbed a hand over his forehead.

"Couldn't sleep?" The familiar voice sent her heart racing. Scott stood beside her but didn't touch her. His rigid stance told her that he was upset, but she had no idea why.

"Not yet. Too much excitement, I guess." She looked over her right shoulder. "What are you still doing up? I thought everyone in the house was asleep."

"Seems like you are getting along fine with everyone already." She couldn't read anything in his face, but his tone and the fact that he refused to look at her sent up warning signals.

She matched his nonchalant tone. "I'd like to think so."

"Derek seemed quite taken with you."

"What's that supposed to mean?" Sydney bridled at the suggestion.

"It means I saw him when he first laid eyes on you and I heard the two of you in your room." He faced her and she could see the barely contained anger glinting in his eyes. "I know you guys are going to be working together with the horses—if Derek actually works."

Was Scott jealous of Derek? Sydney turned and faced him. "Scott, I am not interested in your brother." She laid her hand on his forearm, trying to reassure him.

Scott cocked an eyebrow, his eyes still dangerously clouded. "Really? So you told him about us?" His tone clearly assured her that he knew she hadn't.

Sydney drew back, hurt by his accusation. "I'm not sure what you think you heard. Derek was helping me unpack and, sure, he flirted a little. But I was trying to figure out what to tell him about us without causing any trouble between the two of you."

He shrugged. "So you thought leading him on was the best decision? What's next? A little seduction scene while you are out riding tomorrow?"

"I wasn't leading him on. What was I supposed to say, Scott? That we kissed? That you want me?" Sydney's voice was dripping in sarcasm as her frustration flared into anger. Hadn't he realized by now that she wasn't out to seduce anyone?

"I don't think that's really a concern any longer," Scott interrupted. His black eyes narrowed, his voice suddenly calm.

She wouldn't allow him to see how his words wounded her. His accusations hurt enough, but to know that she'd imagined the desire she'd thought he felt . . . She felt like a foolish, lovesick teenage girl. "Fine. Then I'll just do my job, and we'll have as little to do with one another as possible."

"Keep your distance from Derek, Sydney. He's trouble."

"At least he was nice and welcomed me. You've been

the one who was nothing but trouble. You don't have the right to warn me about anything, Scott." She spun to leave but felt his hand at her elbow. She jerked it free of his grasp and whirled on him, causing Valentino to jump backward. "Don't ever touch me again."

He arched a brow and his gaze swept from her head to her knees and back. "Next time, princess, you'll beg for me to touch you."

"Don't bet on it." She wished she could slam the door of the barn but had to suffice with storming toward the house.

Sydney hurried back to her room and flung herself onto the bed. How could she have believed that Scott Chandler cared about her? She felt the hot tears streaming down her cheeks, hating herself for crying for him but unable to find the strength to stop the flow. So much for their budding friendship, let alone any sort of truce for the sake of working together in peace.

SYDNEY WAS UP early the next morning after a long night of tossing and turning in the unfamiliar room. She glanced at the clock just before hearing Mike greet the giant black lab on the porch. The horses immediately started whinnying in anticipation of breakfast. Every sound seemed to reverberate in her aching head. She groaned, wishing for aspirin, before tossing back the covers and grabbing her robe. She might as well get an early start on what she was sure would prove to be a trying day. In fact, that would probably prove to be an understatement.

She grabbed a towel from the hall closet Jen had showed her the night before and headed for the shower. She stood under the warm water and closed her eyes, willing her headache to go away. Sydney let the spray of the water soothe her sore muscles and relax her mind. A knock on the door brought her crashing back to the present and her eyes flew open.

"Any day, Sydney. You're not the only one in the house."

Did Scott really have to intrude on her shower the way he'd intruded in her fitful dreams last night? Was a moment's peace too much to ask for?

"If you don't open this door in two minutes, I'll break it down."

"That I'd like to see," she muttered as she turned off the water and pulled her robe over her shoulders.

Apparently the acoustics in the bathroom were better than she'd thought. Just as she fastened the sash on her robe, the door swung in.

"What in the hell are you doing?" she yelled.

"I warned you."

With her wet hair plastered to her head and tendrils sticking to her cheeks and neck, Sydney pushed her way past him, proud of her ability to contain her anger and not slam the bedroom door.

Sydney heard the bathroom door close and the shower turn on before a deep baritone began singing a haunting country ballad. She frowned, pulling on her jeans, as she realized Scott was singing the same song they'd danced to at the barbecue. She wasn't sure what he hoped to accomplish by trying to aggravate her at every turn, but she wasn't about to give him the satisfaction of knowing he'd succeeded. She buttoned a faded Western shirt over her tank top and stepped into her boots before checking her reflection in the mirror. Maybe a little mascara? She dabbed it on quickly before running a comb through her wet hair, pulling it back into a ponytail, and hurrying down to help Silvie with breakfast.

"Need any help, Silvie?"

"Thanks, honey, but it's all under control." She motioned toward the set table. "Take a load off." She poked her head into the oven to check her breakfast casserole before glancing at Sydney over her shoulder. "Something wrong?"

"What?" She had to get her head on straight. "No, nothing I can't take care of."

Mike stomped his feet at the back door before entering. "Hey, Silvie, how much longer 'til breakfast? I'm starved!" He blinked as he noticed Sydney at the table. "Morning, Sydney." He made his way to the cupboard and grabbed a mug. "Want some coffee?"

"Sure, thanks." She smiled at her employer as he placed the steaming mug in front of her.

"Milk? Sugar?" he offered.

"This is fine, thank you." She raised the mug to her lips, inhaling the tantalizing aroma before sipping it.

"So, where are you starting today?" Mike took the seat across from her, leaning back in the chair as he sipped his coffee.

"We're heading out after breakfast so I can show her

the stock and what she's working with. After lunch, I figured we'd get started on the paperwork," Derek answered as he entered the room. "Morning." He reached out as he passed by and slid a finger down her arm.

Sydney didn't miss Silvie's raised brows or the questioning look she shot toward Mike. And why wouldn't they wonder? They had no idea what had happened between her and Scott the night before. She didn't even get a chance to answer Derek before he gave Silvie a squeeze around her shoulders. "Morning, Sil. Smells good this morning. What are we having?"

"Your favorite, as if you didn't know." Silvie reached for a mug and handed it to Derek. "I have some lunch already packed for you and Sydney to take too."

"Are we going to be out that long?" Sydney glanced at Derek and caught his wink.

"Who knows?" He laughed.

"Isn't it a bit early to be laying the charm on so thick, Derek?" Scott strode into the room. "Morning, Mike, Silvie."

Sydney glanced from Mike to Silvie before settling her gaze on Derek's storm-clouded eyes. It hadn't escaped anyone's notice that Scott hadn't greeted her, ignoring her presence entirely.

Derek glared at his brother. "I thought you'd have left early with Clay. Sleeping in?" Sydney was sure she wasn't imagining the sarcasm and resentment dripping from Derek's words.

"Nope, just taking a shower." Scott arched his brow at Sydney as if daring her to comment. He sipped his coffee and leaned against the kitchen counter. She simply frowned at him when Derek's eyes flickered over her still damp hair. "Oh, and Mike, I'll need to pick up a new lock for the bathroom door."

"Do I even want to know why?" Mike's brows shot up between the weathered creases of his forehead.

"Probably not." Scott chuckled and looked pointedly at Sydney. "Ask her." He jerked his chin at her. "I have to head out and get some work done. We can't all take picnics and joyrides around the ranch all day."

Derek blanched at Scott's open animosity before Sydney saw the color flood back into his cheeks. His pride wasn't allowing him to tolerate Scott's mocking. The chair scraped the wooden floor before toppling backwards. Derek was standing toe-to-toe with Scott before anyone realized what was happening. Derek had the height over his brother but his youth and lanky frame wouldn't match Scott's experience and powerful physique.

Scott calmly rose to his full height, the counter still behind him, and slid the cup to the counter. "I'd advise you to take a step back, little brother. I don't want to have to help Silvie clean the mess your blood will make."

Sydney held her breath. This was exactly what she'd been worried about. The dangerous gleam in Scott's eyes left no doubt that his wasn't an empty threat.

"Knock it off, you two," Mike warned. He hadn't even looked at the two men but his tone left no room for argument.

She watched anxiously as Derek's lips split into a wide grin as if he'd just pulled one over on Scott. He glanced back at Sydney before stepping away from Scott and, reaching over, righted the chair.

"It's fine, Mike." Derek sat down as Silvie reached for the casserole in the oven as if the fight between the brothers was typical morning chatter. "I guess Scott's just nervous to see Liz tomorrow for the first time since their breakup."

Sydney shot a quick glance at Scott. He wouldn't meet her gaze and she couldn't read his expression. Was that why he started the argument with her last night? Did he still have feelings for his ex-girlfriend and want her out of the way now that she was returning? Well, she'd make sure that she wasn't anywhere near either of them. Scott and his ex could get back together and she wouldn't even care. Sydney knew it was a lie, even as she thought it. She knew she was stupid for even getting involved with Scott. There'd been nothing about him that suggested any sort of relationship. For him, it was all about desire, and he'd made that clear from the start.

Silvie placed a plate of food in front of her, squeezing her shoulder in sympathy. She was grateful for even that little bit of offered comfort, as if Silvie understood her thoughts while the three men in the room seem oblivious to her inner turmoil. She had never felt so foolish, or so used. She moved the food around the plate, unable to eat. Scott put his cup in the dishwasher and left through the back door. He hadn't denied Derek's accusation.

Sydney sighed and rubbed her temple with her fingertips. Silvie rose from the table without a word, and grabbed Sydney's plate before returning to the chair, slipping two aspirin into her hand. She reached over and squeezed Silvie's hand in thanks. She wasn't sure if she should be grateful or worried about how much Silvie seemed to see.

"Sydney, honey," she suggested sweetly, "why don't you head out and get those horses ready and I'll send Derek on his way in a sec."

Sydney mouthed a "thank you" as she slipped out the back door, leaving Derek and Mike, and giving her time to gather her wits after the war zone that had been her first breakfast on the ranch.

Chapter Eight

SCOTT WAS HEADED back to the ranch after a trip into town for some medicinal supplies for the stock. Mike had insisted he needed them immediately, although Scott had his suspicions it was to get him off the ranch and away from Derek and Sydney for a while after this morning's scene at breakfast. He wasn't sure what had prompted him to break down the bathroom door—although seeing Sydney's shock was almost worth the trouble—and then to nearly come to blows with his brother. He hadn't been that mad at him since they were teenage boys.

Of course, he had to admit that Sydney had them both acting like teenage boys again. He knew that Derek had always been a flirt, even if he wasn't interested in a girl; it was just his personality. He was the charming one and Scott was the quiet one. To hear him flirting with Sydney, however, had brought something to the surface that he hadn't felt since Liz. It was more than just jealousy, although the thought of Sydney with Derek was certainly enough to make him want to punch a wall. The scene he'd caused in the barn last night wasn't like him. He couldn't explain why he'd been so angry that she hadn't told Derek that there might be something beginning to develop between them. But this was more than his ego being worried to lose a woman to someone else. It was about an underlying suspicion that every word between them, every shared touch, every kiss, had been some sort of act. It had all been a lie he hadn't seen through—again.

Just like with Liz, he feared that Sydney was playing him for a fool. He wanted to believe that the past week was real, that the passion he'd felt was more than just desire. But he couldn't risk what little pride he'd managed to salvage out of the situation with Liz on a fairy-tale notion of love that might or might not prove real. Even if he had convinced himself just a few days ago that Sydney was nothing like Liz. Even if it felt completely illogical, he wouldn't chance having that wall he'd built chipped away, and being betrayed again. It was all enough to give him a headache. He pressed a button on the truck's radio, blaring AC/DC through the speakers, hoping to drown out the part of his brain trying to convince him that pushing Sydney away was a mistake.

By the time he'd returned and passed the supplies off to Clay, it was nearing lunch. He was starving and knew he should settle for a quiet meal in the house with Silvie, Jen, and Clay, but before he could talk himself out of it, he headed to the barn to saddle Noble, his black-and-white paint. He headed toward the creek in the east pasture, knowing his brother would pick that secluded spot for a romantic tryst, as he had so many times before. It was where they both had taken dates all through high school, but while Scott had grown up quickly, Derek still seemed to be a boy in a man's body.

Scott reached the creek to find it deserted. He loosened Noble's reins, letting him graze on the surrounding grass, and leaned back on a tree to wait in case they showed. He cursed his own jealousy, especially when there were animals that needed vaccines, fences always in need of repair, and stock to check on, but he couldn't shake the need to be close to Sydney, even if it was only to prove she was a gold digger.

DEREK LED THE way and Valentino flipped his head, pulling at the reins, wanting to run. Sydney reined him in as they headed toward the creek Derek had told her about. She'd already checked out the stock she'd be working with and had to admit that Mike and Scott had a great eye for horses. The animals were well kept, healthy, and seemed intelligent. The two of them had enjoyed a fun afternoon of chatting about horses, rodeos, and their childhoods. She was grateful for the light conversation that didn't hold any indication of romance, and her earlier headache from breakfast had long since disappeared. Of course, the fact that Scott had disappeared immediately following the scene in the kitchen had helped immensely.

"Whoa." Derek drew his gelding to a quick halt.

Sydney followed suit, unsure of what had him pulling

up short. "What is it?" she asked as she followed his suddenly somber gaze toward a stand of trees. She spotted the unmistakable black-and-white paint grazing in the trees.

"Scott," Derek muttered.

Wonderful, she thought. There goes the rest of the afternoon. Didn't he have anything better to do than to torment her? Derek glanced over at her and she tried to hide her frustration, but she knew she'd never been good at hiding her feelings from anyone. Her mother had always said that her eyes gave her away.

"Okay, I'm not the biggest fan of my brother, but I've gotta ask. What's going on with the two of you?"

Sydney opened her mouth, ready to tell Derek a condensed version of what had happened at the rodeo grounds, but changed her mind as she saw the mix of hope tinged with reservation. If the argument with Scott last night had proven anything, it was that she'd been nothing more than a fun distraction until he'd become bored with her. She felt like a mouse being toyed with by a very irritating tomcat.

"I think it bothers him that I took this job. He didn't want me to," she confessed.

"I think it's more than that." Derek tapped his horse's sides and they began walking toward the creek. "He likes to be the boss, have things his way with no surprises. I think you challenge that control and he's not sure how to handle it. You push him out of his comfort zone."

An image of Scott trying to make breakfast popped into her mind. He'd definitely been out of his area of expertise there. A smile found its way to her lips. "I guess I do."

Her smile faded as quickly as it appeared when she saw Scott seated by the trees, one knee bent, head back against the tree, his straw hat settled on his knee. She was struck by the raw sexuality he possessed and her pulse quickened, butterflies suddenly appearing in her stomach. She could say he didn't affect her, but she'd be lying.

"Hey guys," he greeted as they rode up, not even glancing their way. "What are you guys doing all the way over here?" He stood up, placed his cowboy hat back on his head, and brushed the dirt and grass from his jeans.

Derek stopped his horse and dismounted, reaching for the lunch packed in a small saddle bag. "Just giving Sydney the tour."

Sydney noticed that Derek's jovial mood had disappeared as soon as he'd noticed Scott's horse. She dismounted and tied Valentino to a nearby shrub, away from the geldings. She reached out for the sandwich and water bottle Derek held out to her.

"Thanks," she said as she sat on the grass at the edge of the water. "Derek thought we'd have lunch here before heading back to start the paperwork."

"Makes sense," Scott agreed. "Make-out Creek has always been a pretty spot."

She caught the deliberate look he shot at Derek. What Scott didn't count on was that Derek had already told her the antics he and Scott had always pulled at the creek. He'd spun the tales, with embellishment she was certain, of dates, drinks, and parties that the creek had hosted. "From what Derek said, this spot has a pretty colorful past."

Scott raised a brow and nodded toward Derek. "For some of us more than others, right?"

"What do you want, Scott? I'm sure you didn't ride all the way out here in the middle of your busy day just to have a picnic by the creek." Derek narrowed his eyes, his gaze dark and brooding. Sydney only hoped they wouldn't come to blows out here with Mike nowhere in sight to diffuse the situation as he had earlier.

"Clay needs help rounding up some of the stock for vaccines."

"And you couldn't do that?" Derek shot Scott an ominous glare, answered only by Scott's raised brow and clenching jaw. Derek crumpled up the bag from his lunch and made his way back to his gelding. "Guess we'll have to cut our tour short."

Sydney was frustrated that Scott had intruded on the first relaxing moments she'd had since arriving. She wasn't about to let whatever objection he had about her presence destroy the friendship she'd created with Derek so far. "I'll head back with you." She put her garbage into her own saddle bag.

"We will all head back," Scott clarified. "Tell Clay we'll be right there. Sydney, I'd like to talk with you for a second so hang back."

Derek rolled his eyes before mounting his gelding. "Sounds like a direct order from the boss, Sydney. I'll meet you at the chutes in just a few minutes." He glared at

Scott. "And if you're not there, I'll be sure to come looking for you."

Sydney watched Derek ride away and tightened Valentino's cinch. "Well? What could possibly be so important that you want to be anywhere near me?"

Scott chuckled as he inched toward Valentino's side. "Trust me, I just saved you the bumbling advances of a boy."

"What makes you think I wouldn't have returned them?" Sydney instantly regretted the words as they fell from her lips. They only gave him more fuel to accuse her of being a tease, but she'd wanted to wipe the smug smile from his face.

Her plan worked too well as his grin disappeared and his eyes narrowed. "If you're just looking to pass the time, I'm sure I can satisfy far more than Derek."

The tender passion she'd heard in his voice as he'd comforted her after her nightmare seemed like it came from a different person entirely. She felt the shiver of desire trickle down her spine at the mere memory of that night. But there was no gentleness in his eyes now.

She slid her foot into the stirrup and mounted the stallion. "Don't you think you should be saving your energy for reuniting with your ex?"

Scott arched a brow and gave her a lopsided grin. "Don't worry, princess. I have energy to spare."

She hated that just the thought of him holding her could still cause the rush of heat through her veins. Sydney glared at him before turning her horse back toward the house. "You're an arrogant ass."

He swung himself into his saddle. "So I've been told," he answered as he spurred his paint, leaving her to catch up to him.

SYDNEY AWOKE FRIDAY morning to a knock on her bedroom door. She stretched her arms above her head and curled her toes as she heard Derek's voice call again.

"Sydney! Come on, sleepyhead. You've got horses to break today."

She opened her eyes to the shaft of light through the curtains and was shocked that she'd slept so long. She glanced over at the clock. Eight-thirty? She could just imagine the snide comments Scott would make if she wasn't down to the corral soon.

"I'll be down in just a second," she called.

"I'll meet you at the corral," Derek informed her.

Sydney threw back the covers and pulled on her terrycloth robe. She could hear voices in the kitchen below and realized that everyone else had already started their day. She hurried to the bathroom and splashed cold water on her face before brushing her teeth quickly. She glanced in the mirror and decided she didn't have time for makeup today, then rushed back to her bedroom. She pulled on an old t-shirt and jeans and ran a brush through her chestnut curls. She glanced at the unmade bed and prayed Silvie would forgive her for not making it today, then closed the bedroom door behind her.

She didn't see anyone in the kitchen as she passed through on her way out the door, and she made it to the corral just in time to see Derek leading a young bay filly into the round pen.

He smiled as she approached and held the long training reins out for her. "She's all ready for you."

"What's she like?" she asked, running her hands over the filly's rump, cooing to her in soothing tones.

"This one's pretty rank," Derek warned. "There's been some talk of putting her into the bucking string if we can't get her broke." Sydney arched a brow at him. "I'll hold her for you to get on." Derek smiled. "And catch you when you come off."

"Thanks for the vote of confidence." She tugged the cinch, watching the filly's reaction. Her ears twitched back and forth at the sound of their voices.

"Nothing personal, but she's thrown our best hands."

"We'll see." Sydney walked around the filly while Derek continued to hold the reins. She wasn't ready to mount the filly for the first time yet. Sydney wanted the horse to be used to her voice and touch, to relax and realize that she wasn't a threat. She patted the horse's neck, talking to her in soft, nonsensical phrases while rubbing her shoulders and tugging on the saddle.

"Sydney?" Derek's tone told her he wanted her attention. She met his gaze. "This filly threw Scott last week before they left for the rodeo."

Sydney rubbed her hand on the filly's forehead, causing her to drop her head, obviously enjoying the attention. A smile lifted the corners of Sydney's lips as she whispered to the filly. "Aren't you the smartest girl ever?"

Derek tried to stifle his laughter as Sydney took the reins and crossed them over the filly's thick black mane. "I'll ride her," she said confidently. "Go ahead and wait outside the corral."

"Are you sure you know what you're doing?" Derek asked.

Sydney tuned out everything around her but the bay filly. She stroked her neck calmly then waited as the filly raised her nose to Sydney's face, curious about her. The filly's ears twitched as Sydney gently blew on the horse's muzzle. The filly nickered softly before flipping up her top lip and nudging Sydney's shoulder. Sydney turned her back to the filly, walking away a few steps but keeping her eyes always looking over her shoulder for any signs of aggression from the young horse.

The filly slowly walked behind Sydney, pressing her head against Sydney's back for attention. Sydney was always quick to reward her curiosity. Sydney ignored the cowboys that had begun to wander toward the corral, eager to see the filly toss yet another body to the ground. She refused to let her ego crowd out her common sense and gave the filly plenty of time to grow accustomed to her touch, both on her body and on the saddle, all the while holding a one-sided conversation with the animal.

SCOTT ROUNDED THE corner and noticed the crowd at the corral. His foul mood after seeing Sydney and Derek together had only grown worse after listening to the two of them joking while rounding up animals yesterday.

He'd managed to avoid them both this morning, but he knew his luck would run out eventually. Seeing the hands standing around with so much work to be done lit his already too-short fuse.

"What in the hell is going on here?" he demanded as he walked up to Clay. "And why is everyone just standing around?"

Clay pointed into the corral. Scott's eyes followed, and for the first time he noticed Sydney walking around the pen with the filly following behind like an obedient dog. He could hear Sydney's voice, calm and soothing.

He hushed his voice, his tone still betraying his apprehension. "What is she doing with Cougar?"

"She's going to ride her," Clay stated. "Or, at least that's what she says."

Scott clenched his teeth. "No one can ride her. She's going to break her damn fool neck." He looked around him at the various men, frustrated that they were all allowing this nonsense, especially knowing what the filly had done to most of them. "And why is she in there alone? Dammit!" Scott cursed as he headed toward the gate on the other side of the corral, prepared to order Sydney out.

"Scott." Mike's tone stopped Scott in his tracks. "Give her a chance to do her job." Mike walked over to where Clay stood, the other men moving to allow him a front row seat for the coming excitement.

"You can't be serious?" Scott pulled his hat off and ran a hand through his hair, frustrated that no one else seemed to be thinking clearly when it came to this woman.

Mike grunted and both men stood at the fence to watch. Sydney stepped up to the left of the saddle and snapped the stirrup against Cougar's side. The filly turned and looked back at her but turned her head forward when Sydney began talking to her again. Scott held his breath as she reached for the reins and put her left foot into the stirrup. With excruciating slowness, she stood with all of her weight in the left stirrup, still talking to the filly calmly. Scott could hear the collective intake of air from the men watching as she bounced lightly in the stirrup. The filly's ears twitched as she listened to Sydney's voice but appeared completely at ease otherwise.

Cautiously, Sydney swung her leg over the filly's back and sat lightly into the saddle. Sydney sat still on her back, allowing her to walk wherever she wanted in the corral, all the while rewarding Cougar with nothing more than her voice and strokes along her neck. Scott watched as she was able to get the filly to begin following the guidance of the snaffle bit in her mouth and finally to stop and back up. He looked around at the seasoned hands surrounding the pen. They were as transfixed as he was at watching her break the filly. With this one ride she'd managed to earn their respect simply by proving she was worthy of the chance Mike had taken in hiring her.

Scott watched as Derek stepped into the arena, taking the reins as Sydney dismounted Cougar.

"Sydney," Mike said, beaming. "You are one amazing horsewoman."

She looked around the arena as if noticing the crowd of cowboys for the first time. A modest smile graced her lips. "Thanks Mike. She's a nice filly."

"You ready for the next one?" Derek asked, leading Cougar back to the barn.

Scott tipped his head toward her as their eyes met, hers practically sparkling yellow. "Bring it on."

DEREK WATCHED AS Mike and the other hands wandered off to what they'd been doing, most of them talking about how Sydney had been able to do what none of them had. In spite of his embarrassment at Sydney riding a horse he hadn't, it was even more fun to watch Scott being taken down a peg in front of the other hands. He brought a sorrel two-year-old gelding in to Sydney. He watched as she began to repeat the process.

"So, this is the new bimbo daddy hired?" The feminine voice purred behind him.

Derek glanced behind him and saw Liz approaching. He had been at college when she and Scott had been dating, but he'd been around the ranch enough to know that Liz had slept with most of the ranch hands right under his brother's nose, not to mention several of the cowboys on the rodeo circuit.

"You might want to watch who you're calling a bimbo, Liz." Derek jerked his chin at Scott, who stood near the corner of the barn, still watching Sydney and oblivious to Liz's arrival. "Especially since Scott seems to have a thing for her."

"Really?" She turned her emerald eyes toward the barn. "But will she give him what I can?"

Derek laughed. "What? Leftovers?"

She raised her slim, manicured hand to slap him, but he easily deflected the blow. "Want a word of advice, Liz? I don't know why you came home, but Scott isn't the guy you left anymore."

She tilted her head to the side, her blonde curls falling forward. "I came home for Daddy, of course."

Derek narrowed his eyes. "Why, now, after all this time?"

Liz flipped her blonde curls over her shoulder. "I don't owe you an explanation. I'm not even sure why I bothered to say hello to you."

"Whatever," Derek mumbled as he turned his back on her. "But I'd leave Sydney alone if I were you. She could probably tear you apart." A broad smile spread across his face as he chuckled at the thought.

"Now I remember why I never liked you much Derek," Liz hissed. "Because you're nothing more than a little boy trying to imitate his big brother."

SCOTT WATCHED AS everyone left and headed back to work. He couldn't take his eyes off of Sydney. She had a way with the horses like he'd never witnessed before. He'd never seen anyone so patient breaking them. Not only was she rewarded with their trust, but they craved her attention. He could understand how they felt; he fought the desire for her attention himself. He wanted to feel her hands on him, to hear her voice go soft and languid again.

He barely caught a glimpse of blonde hair before the voice erupted from the other side of the corral. "Scott!" The smile that formed on Liz's lips never reached her eyes as she ran around the corral and threw herself into Scott's arms, squealing as she pressed her lips to his. Scott cringed at the thought of her touching him, but who knew what kind of scene she would create if he pushed her away?

Scott heard Sydney's voice and tore himself away from Liz. He hurried to reach the corral, leaving Liz standing by the barn.

"Whoa! Easy boy!" Sydney pulled the colt's head to the right until it touched her knee as he continued to buck seconds before rocking backward on his hind legs. He dropped back to his front, throwing his hind legs into the air, dropping his head, and twisting the rest of his body. He spun wildly in circles as Liz began to whoop from the shade of the barn.

"Whoo, ride him!"

The other hands, hearing the commotion, hurried back to the corral. Scott watched with terror as the colt stopped suddenly, snorting loudly before rearing again and stumbling backward. As the colt lost his balance and began to fall onto the saddle, he saw Sydney jump off. She hit the ground roughly, managing to roll a safe distance from the horse's feet just before the colt twisted his body and fell onto his side. He rose unharmed and shook himself then stood in the center of the arena. Scott and Derek jumped the fence from either side of the corral.

"Sydney?" Scott asked, dropping to his knees next to her. "Are you okay?"

"Don't," she hissed through clenched teeth. "Don't even touch me." Scott could see where her tears had streaked her cheeks through the dust.

"Sydney, you need to lay still."

"Just go away, Scott." She shoved him with her palm.

Derek put a hand on Scott's shoulder. "Scott, go grab the horse. I'll take care of her."

Scott shot his brother a burning glare before turning back to Sydney. A stab of jealousy shot through him as she reached past him for Derek's hand, allowing him to pull her to her feet.

"Both of you, out!" Sydney ordered. She turned her back on them and made her way back to the colt. As she mounted him again, amidst several objections from Derek and Mike, Scott could see the determination in her eyes. Surprisingly, the colt acted as if nothing had happened and walked calmly around the corral. Sydney took him around a few more circles before dismounting.

Liz giggled as she made her way to the fence where Scott stood watching Sydney. "Looks like someone needs a riding lesson."

"If your coyote howl hadn't spooked him, he would have done fine," Sydney answered.

Scott saw Liz's jaw drop in shock before her eyes glittered like dark jewels. "If you were any good, you'd have been able to ride him down."

Sydney handed the reins to Derek, who led the gelding toward the barn, and turned to face Liz. "I saved that horse's life by getting off when I did, and if you had even half a brain in that bleach-blonde head of yours, you'd know not to run around horses screeching like a hyena."

"Why, you little . . ." Liz rushed the fence, ready to leap over, but Scott grabbed her by the arms. He wondered if Sydney even noticed that Liz had four inches on her.

Derek held the gelding, so he would have been no help separating the two women. But, even if she was shorter, his money was on Sydney.

"I think maybe now is a good time for a break," Scott suggested to Derek.

"Sure," Derek agreed, chuckling. "Come on, Sydney, let's leave the lovebirds alone."

Scott shot his brother a glare before grabbing Liz by the arm and dragging her toward the barn. He pulled her inside and slid the door shut behind him.

"So eager to be alone with me again?" She slid up to him, pressing herself against the front of his body.

"Don't kid yourself. I hoped to never lay eyes on you, again."

"Oh, Scott." She pouted, winding her arms around his neck. "You haven't forgotten everything we shared, have you?"

Scott reached behind his neck and grasped her hands, pulling them away from him. "And everything you shared with everyone else?"

"A misunderstanding," she clarified, her hand snaking out from his hold and grasping the front of his shirt. "You loved me once." Liz stood on her toes, her lips a mere fraction from his. "Don't try to tell me that, deep down, you don't still love me." She snuck her tongue out to lick his lower lip.

He leaned back against the barn wall. "Just let me know when you're finished." Liz pulled away from him and looked up at his face, feigning innocent seduction. "What we had was nothing but a lie. I'm not playing your games anymore. Whatever you're here for, get it and leave." Scott brushed her off and headed for the door.

"Don't turn your back on me, Scott," she threatened, her innocent act forgotten. He turned back to look at her. "I can make your life a living hell."

Scott laughed. "Liz, you don't matter to me one way or another. You're no different than any other buckle bunny on the circuit." He slid open the barn door as she let out a frustrated scream. The hay hook crashed into the door and dug into the wood, bouncing in the air as it lodged mere inches from his head.

"You missed," he observed as he left the barn laughing.

DEREK HAD HEARD most of the argument between Liz and Scott. He heard Liz curse and kick one of the stall doors. He chuckled when she spun at the sound of hooves on the concrete floor. "Didn't go the way you planned?" Derek laughed.

"Go away, Derek."

"Well, I guess you can't get your way all of the time." He just couldn't rouse any sympathy for her. "So now you want Scott back?" He opened the stall and led the gelding inside.

"What I want is to get rid of that little . . ."

"Watch it," he warned. "And she has nothing to do with Scott rejecting you. Again," he added suggestively.

Derek knew his little jibes would find their mark. Liz had never taken any sort of rejection well, even as a child. It actually drove her to pursue something with even more determination. And she certainly didn't seem to be enjoying Scott's rejection of her advances now. But he also realized that something was brewing between Sydney and Scott. There was a tension there he wanted to see disappear. If Liz could distract his brother long enough, then it would give him that much more opportunity to try to win Sydney over. Not only would he not be bested by his brother again, but Sydney was a mighty fine woman, and he was certain that they could have something special together. A plan began to take shape, but he'd need Liz's cooperation.

"How long are you planning on staying, Liz?"

"That depends. Why?"

"Maybe we can work out some sort of arrangement."

She arched a brow at him, cocking her hip to the side. "I'm listening."

"I'm not sure what has you rushing home to Scott after all this time." Derek paused, waiting for her to fill in the blanks. When Liz simply crossed her arms, refusing to fill him in on her motives, he continued. "But it's pretty obvious that you want him and I want her."

"Wow, genius! Did you come up with that one all on your own or did you get some help?"

Derek wrapped a hand around the bars on the stall

door and squeezed, briefly imagining it was her neck. "You know what, you're right. You seem to be doing just fine with Scott on your own. Forget needing my help." He turned and started down the horse barn's aisleway.

"No, wait." Liz reached for his shoulder. "What do you want me to do?"

"I'll do my part in keeping Sydney away from Scott. They can't be in the same room right now anyway without a war breaking out." He pushed her hand from his shoulder. "But you need to keep Scott distracted. Keep him away from her as much as possible. Keep the rift between them growing." Derek gave her his most charming smile. "You just do what you do best: destroy relationships."

Derek left her standing in the aisleway, staring after him as he stepped back into the sunlight. Sure, he felt a little guilty about misleading Sydney, but he wasn't really lying. He was just stacking the deck in his favor where she was concerned. The less she was around Scott, the more one-on-one time he could have with her. And the more time they were together, the more likely their attraction could become more substantial.

Chapter Nine

As everyone gathered around the table for dinner, Sydney wasn't surprised to see the blonde bombshell from earlier enter. She saw her frown when she realized the seat beside Scott was taken and the only available chair was beside Sydney, directly across from Scott.

"Sydney." Mike motioned at the young woman. "This is my daughter, Liz."

Liz flashed her father a winning smile. "We met at the corral today, Daddy." She turned to Sydney, her green eyes glinting maliciously. "I believe you'd just taken a nasty spill." Her tone dared Sydney to join her game of innuendos.

"Are you okay, Sydney? What happened?" Mike's concern was evident.

"I'm fine, Mike." Never one to pass up a challenge, Sydney smiled at Liz. "He only spooked because a snake slithered past the corral."

"Snake?" Jen asked, her face wrinkling in disgust.

Sydney shook her head. "Yeah, ugly but harmless."

Derek choked on his tea, nearly spitting it onto his plate, and had to cover his mouth with a napkin.

Clay reached over and slapped his back. "You okay?" he asked.

"Yeah," Derek answered between coughs. "Just went down the wrong pipe." He cleared his throat again. "So Liz, how long are you planning on staying?"

Everyone but Sydney turned to look at Liz for an answer. Sydney couldn't care less; she just hoped the woman would stay far from her. She wanted no part in watching Liz and Scott rekindle their relationship.

"I'm not sure. Probably for a while." She curved her lips into a pout. "I missed you guys and the horses."

"Liz was a rodeo queen," Mike explained to Sydney. "She's a pretty good barrel racer too." Mike smiled brightly. "Since you're going to be staying a while, you should help Sydney with the horses."

Liz grimaced, and Sydney tried to not look horrified at Mike's suggestion. It was the worst idea she'd ever heard. Before Liz could even protest, Scott interrupted. "I don't think that would be a good idea."

Sydney glared at Scott. Was he afraid that they might compare notes on him? Did he worry that she'd ruin his chances at reuniting with her? He needn't be concerned. As much as she hated herself for still being attracted to Scott, she could see it was one-sided. And she wasn't about to throw herself at someone who didn't feel the same in return.

"Why not?" Mike asked. "I think it would be good for Liz to help out while she's here."

"Daddy," Liz protested.

"Don't 'Daddy' me, girl." Mike shook a finger at her. "It'll keep you out of Silvie's hair."

Yeah, Sydney thought, *and make my life hell.* She watched as Liz looked around the table for an ally to her argument. She pinned Scott with a stare, giving him a look that spoke volumes, and nodded at her father.

"I can't tomorrow, Daddy. Scott promised to take me riding with him. Didn't you, honey?" she purred.

This time, everyone's eyes swung to Scott, who looked furious. He pushed his plate away and rose from the table. "Sure," he agreed, pushing the chair in and storming out the kitchen door, mumbling something about checking the horses.

So, that's why Scott hadn't liked the idea of Liz helping with the horses? Because it would ruin his big plans for an intimate rendezvous? A sharp stab of jealousy shot through Sydney as she imagined the two of them at the creek, his lips on hers, his hands . . . Sydney sighed, forcefully pushing the image from her mind.

"No," Mike insisted. "You and Scott can go ride another time. My mind's made up. You can help Derek and Sydney tomorrow. Maybe she can even show you a thing or two about breaking."

Sydney hid a smile behind her napkin as Derek winked at her conspiratorially. She glanced at Liz just in time to see her eyes blaze with emerald fire. Mike may have done it unintentionally, Sydney realized, but he'd just lit the fuse on a powder keg. There was no way this was going to end well.

"Um, can you excuse me?" Sydney rose and loaded her dishes into the dishwasher.

"Don't worry, honey," Silvie scolded. "I'll take care of that."

"Where are you headed?" Derek asked.

"Just to finish the paperwork from today and check on Valentino." Sydney laid a hand on his shoulder as she passed. She didn't really want company and was hoping he would understand. "Go ahead and finish. I'll only be a minute."

As she stepped onto the porch, she looked up at the indigo sky. She was tired from the day's work but pleasantly so. She and Derek had worked the two-year-olds, one right after another, until sundown, but she knew they had accomplished a lot for one afternoon. A full moon lit her way to the office inside the barn, and the horses nickered a soft greeting as they heard her approach. She switched on the office light and pulled out the files of the horses she'd ridden, writing notes about what had been accomplished. After only a few minutes, and several scribbled-out notes due to her wandering thoughts, she gave up.

She couldn't seem to keep her mind from returning to Scott. She found herself wandering down the dirt path that led to Valentino's pen just behind the barn. Sydney peered through the pipe fencing to see the familiar gray stallion prancing across the large pen towards her. Valentino swung his head over the fence and nudged her arm for attention. She absentmindedly raised a hand to his forehead.

"How could I be so blind? He's just using me. It was just a cat-and-mouse game at the rodeo, and I fell for it without even suspecting anything. I'm an idiot," she whispered. "When am I going to learn?"

Valentino pressed his soft muzzle to her cheek, blowing softly, filling her nose with the scent of sweet alfalfa and horse. She kissed the side of it, grateful for the comfort he offered. "How could I be so stupid after Kurt played that same game?" she asked the stallion, swiping at the tears she'd just realized were creeping down her cheek.

"Kurt . . . Willits?"

Sydney saw Scott's muscular frame emerge from the shadows behind the barn. Embarrassed he'd heard her most intimate thoughts, she turned her back on him and laid her forehead against Valentino's. She didn't want to face him while her feelings were so close to the surface.

SCOTT HAD BEEN heading back from a walk to try to clear his thoughts when he'd seen Sydney leave the barn and head for Valentino's enclosure. The pain and regret he'd heard in her voice tore at his heart. He knew he'd been the cause of it and wanted to kick himself for not telling her about Liz sooner. Even if he was able to get her to listen to the truth now, it would seem like he was covering a lie. How could he prove to her that he'd only been trying to protect her from Liz and from himself? And what did Kurt have to do with this?

"How do you know Kurt?" Scott stepped closer, reaching out a hand to pat Valentino's neck. "I had a feeling you'd end up over here." He tipped his head to see her face.

She sighed and turned her back to him, ready to walk away.

"Sydney." She stopped. His voice was low and husky, even to his own ears, as he placed his hands on her shoulders and turned her to look at him. "Please don't walk away now."

She remained silent, with only the moonlight glowing on the stallion's coat. Scott slipped his knuckle under her chin and tipped her face up. He wanted to look into her eyes, to make sure she understood he'd never meant to deliberately hurt her. What he saw instead made him feel like Valentino had just kicked him in the gut. Her tears glimmered in the moonlight as they left silvery trails down her cheeks.

"Oh, Sydney," he whispered, wiping away a tear with his thumb.

She brushed his hand away and he could see the flash of yellow in her eyes. "Don't."

Her anger had returned; the stallion flipped his head as if her anger spurred his own. He could deal with her anger better than he could her pain. He clenched his hands in fists at his side to keep them from pulling her to him. He wanted desperately to bury his fingers into her hair and kiss her into submission so that she would believe him about Liz.

"Don't what, Sydney?"

"Don't you dare pretend to care about me." Her fury spurred her on. "I won't be the next notch on your belt. Go find someone else." They both knew she was talking about Liz.

"Is that what you think you are?" This had to be a sick joke. She was now charging him with the same motive he'd accused her of having.

"You told me once that rodeo queens gather their toys, break them, and then toss them away. How is what you're doing any different?" Her eyes blazed with golden fire and he tensed at her allegation. From her point of view, he realized, he'd simply been using her until Liz's arrival.

"You don't understand my relationship with Liz. I should have told you—" he began.

"You're right," she interrupted. "I don't understand. Nor do I want to hear about it." Sydney brushed past him, turning back toward the house. The stallion spun and raced into the center of the pen, kicking his feet high into the air.

Scott grasped her arm above the elbow and pulled her back into his arms. "Will you listen to me?"

"No, you listen to me." She pushed against his chest. "I won't play your games. Just let me do my job and stay the hell away from me."

Scott let her go. He knew he couldn't force her to believe him. He watched as she ran back to the house. Somehow, he had to convince her that there was nothing between him and Liz. He could tell her what had happened in the past, but there was no way he was allowing anyone to know what a fool he'd been. He didn't even want to think about it, let alone admit it to anyone else. And he'd be damned if he ever allowed himself to feel that vulnerable again.

DEREK WAITED UNTIL he heard Sydney return to her room. He'd heard the kitchen door slam when she reentered and caught a glimpse of her tear-stained cheeks as she headed down the hall. Damn Scott. She must have run into him while she was in the barn. Derek snuck down the hall to Liz's room and gave a light tap on the door.

"Come in," Liz purred.

Derek entered to find her stretched out on the bed in a translucent nylon robe with very little lingerie underneath. Her eyes glimmered like a cat, waiting to pounce on its prey.

"What are you doing?" Derek rolled his eyes. Did she really think she was irresistible?

"I expected you a while ago."

"Yeah, well, I was busy keeping an eye out for Sydney. Who, by the way, ran into Scott while she was at the barn." Liz sat up and he knew he had her attention. "You're not doing a very good job at keeping his attention diverted."

"Shut up. It's a lot harder to do when Daddy is thwarting my every attempt to spend time with him." She slid back against the pillows suggestively. "I'm lonely."

"Too bad. Get a dog," he suggested. "What do you want me to do?" He was already tired of her games.

She shrugged. "You're so smart, figure it out." When Derek glared at her, she went on. "Just be her friend. There is already tension between her and Scott. She obviously wants nothing to do with him, so just be there to offer an ear and a shoulder to cry on. Hopefully you'll be man enough to keep hold of her interest."

"And I hope you've got some trick to pique Scott's at this point." Derek laughed, knowing exactly how to hit her weak point. "He didn't seem too thrilled at your suggestion for a ride tomorrow."

"Ass." Liz glared at him. "Get out of here and stay away from me. We don't want anyone to suspect we are trying to massage the situation between them."

"Oh, I will try to control myself," he assured her sarcastically. "But it will be so hard to stay away."

"Get out," she hissed.

SYDNEY ROSE THE next morning and wondered what, if anything, she could do about her swollen eyes. She'd hurried to her room, not wanting to face anyone after her confrontation with Scott. She cursed herself for being a fool. She'd known better than to trust someone like Scott Chandler, but the tears had continued to flow even as she tried to will them away. While exhaustion had finally claimed her, her worthless tears had left their calling card on her eyes this morning. She splashed cold water on them and hoped it would do the job.

Sydney hurried through the kitchen, hoping to avoid running into anyone else—especially Scott. She had just stepped off the porch when she felt an arm slip around her shoulders.

"You look terrible. Are you feeling okay?"

"Thanks, Derek."

"Come on. You know I didn't mean it like that." He stopped and turned her to look at him, his hands on her upper arms. "Maybe you should go back inside and rest. You might be coming down with something."

Yeah, she thought, a stupid broken heart. She sighed. "I'm fine, Derek." He looked skeptical. "Really," she assured him. "I just want to get to work."

Derek shrugged. "If you say so."

"So, where's our little helper this morning?" Sydney looked at the empty corral.

"Who? Liz?" he asked, laughing. "She won't drag her butt out here before noon."

"You want to bet?" As much as she didn't want to work around Liz, she really wasn't going to be the one to break the news to Mike that his daughter was a spoiled witch.

"Where are you going?" Derek asked, following her back to the house.

"To wake up Her Majesty and get her perfect hide out here to help us." Derek chased her up the stairs, trying every tactic to convince her to leave Liz alone. Sydney wasn't about to defy Mike's orders, and she certainly wasn't going to give Liz any excuse to pin the blame on her when Mike found out she had ignored him.

She pounded loudly on Liz's bedroom door. "Go away." She heard the muffled whine from the room.

"Come on, Your Highness." Sydney's voice was sickeningly sweet. "Time to wake up and get to work."

"Oh, it's only six-thirty," Liz complained. Sydney could hear the rustle of blankets and bedding. Finally the door opened a crack, just enough for Sydney to see Liz's tousled hair and one eye glinting with hatred. "If you enjoy your life in the slightest, I suggest you leave before you lose it," Liz warned.

"Does that mean you're refusing to do the work Mike wanted you to do?"

"You could say that."

Sydney smiled. "I was hoping you'd say that. It's exactly what I'll say when your father asks." She spun on her boot heel and headed back to the barn. She looked over at Derek as they reached the porch. "You're my witness."

Derek laughed. "Now that was worth getting up early to watch." He shook his head. "I don't think she's ever had anyone call her bluff."

They went into the barn and began grooming the horses. Sydney put the entire ordeal out of her mind as Derek brought Cougar out for her second ride. She rode the young horses until lunchtime and sent Derek inside to eat.

"What about you?"

She didn't want to chance a meeting with Liz or Scott. She waved him off. "I just want to get some notes down first. I'll grab something in a bit," she said, leading a cute sorrel paint toward the barn. "I'll take care of this guy. You go on ahead."

Sydney unsaddled the colt and brushed him down

before putting him into a stall and tossing him a scoop of grain. As she made her way out of the barn, she spotted Scott riding in from the west pasture. She figured she could handle Liz and hurried out of the barn toward the house before Scott arrived, congratulating herself for good timing. Out of the corner of her eye, she noticed that he'd turned his paint in her direction and sped up. She didn't want to appear to be running away, but definitely wanted to avoid him.

She'd barely reached the halfway point when he cued Noble to stop in front of her, cutting off her route. She took a deep breath and looked up at him expectantly. He looked like he wanted to say something, but she had no idea what could be left to say. She stood rooted to the spot as he spun the horse and wordlessly left. Her heart began to slow its racing pace and she inhaled deeply, her shoulders slouching before she rolled her head from side to side to alleviate the stress she could feel building in her muscles. How was she ever going to work, seeing him day in and day out? *I'll just have to deal with that one day at a time*, she reasoned.

"Sydney," Mike's voice broke into her thoughts. "I've been looking for you."

"Sorry." Sydney rubbed her neck with her hand. "Just in the barn finishing up the paperwork for the two-year-olds. What did you need?"

"Just wanted to let you know that you'll officially be working your first rodeo this weekend."

"A rodeo? This weekend? But what about the two-year-olds we just started?" Butterflies seemed to flock to her stomach at the thought of a rodeo. She knew what to do with the animals, but the idea of spending a weekend at a rodeo with Scott had those butterflies doing cartwheels.

"Derek will stay here to keep working the horses. Just be sure to let him know if there's anything special to be done." He put a hand on her shoulder as if he could read her thoughts. "It's a Friday-Saturday-Sunday performance in Oregon, so you'll be leaving on Wednesday morning. Be ready for a long drive."

"Okay." She mentally ran down the list of things she'd have to tell Derek before she left. "Which horses do you want me to take?"

"We'll sort them tomorrow with Scott and see what he's thinking. It'll be you, Scott, Jake, and a couple of the other boys."

"You're not going?" She was hoping there would be someone who could be a buffer between her and Scott.

"No, I'm going to stay here and visit with Liz since she's home. You can stay in the trailer with Jen. I know she and Clay are going too."

Sydney practically breathed an audible sigh of relief. At least she'd be able to stick close to Jen, and with his sister near there was little chance of confrontation with Scott.

"No, Mike, I'll take someone else. Let Derek come." Scott's voice carried to the balcony just outside of her second-story room as if she were standing beside him.

"Look, I don't care what is going on with you. Fix things with her."

"Fat chance!"

"Stop it, Scott. You can't blame her. Derek may have dropped hints about Liz, but have you told her the truth? Taking her this weekend will give you guys some time to talk this out where neither of you can run off and hide."

"My past with Liz isn't anyone's business," Scott insisted. "I don't need to explain anything. She can believe what she wants."

"The same way you are?" Mike's voice sounded frustrated as he finally lost his temper. "Scott, I can't believe you! Here is someone I know you care about, and you're going to throw it away because of your stubborn pride?"

"I love you like my father, Mike, but leave this alone. I'll handle it my own way."

"Right. Well, 'your way' better not include driving my new trainer off this ranch. Dammit, open your eyes, boy! I never thought that you were stupid, but I'm beginning to wonder."

Sydney chanced a peek over the railing of the balcony to see Scott's back as he stormed off toward the barn. Mike followed him down the steps and, shaking his head, glanced toward her window. She jumped backward to avoid being seen and stumbled, crashing into the chair beside the window. The chair shifted sideways and jarred the lamp and pictures on the small table so that the frames clattered loudly to the ground. *Way to stay inconspicuous*, she scolded herself. Maybe Mike hadn't noticed.

She heard Mike's chuckle from downstairs as he entered the house through the back door. *So much for him not noticing.* She picked up the frames that had fallen. He'd obviously realized that she'd heard the entire conversation but didn't seem too upset about it. She paused as she placed another on the table. *Unless his intention had been for her to hear what was said.* She thought back, recalling the men's conversation.

Everything had seemed so cryptic. Scott had never confessed having a current relationship with Liz, just that they'd had one in the past. Was it something ongoing or was it over? He never said he had feelings for her, although Mike insisted on it. *But he never denied it either,* her heart whispered to her mind. *No,* she rationalized. *I can't start hoping. Especially when we aren't even on speaking terms.*

SCOTT LEFT MIKE and headed toward the barn to find Clay. He needed to get everyone in place and settled with their duties for the rodeo. Clay could let Sydney know which horses they wanted to take for riding stock. The less he had to be around her, the better. He could still see her face, tear stains on her cheeks, and it tore at his heart to know that he was the one causing her pain. He didn't want to be that guy and wasn't sure how to fix the situation. Every time he tried, he only seemed to make things worse. Especially since he wanted nothing more than to take her in his arms and kiss her until nothing else mattered. There was no way he was even going to start thinking about collaborating on a grand entry for this weekend's rodeo. He'd just stick with the same one he'd been doing on Noble.

"Clay," Scott called, meeting up with him at the barn door.

"What's up?" Clay stopped to wait for him. "You're in a hurry. Where's the fire?"

"Pack up. We have a rodeo this weekend. We're leaving tomorrow morning."

"Are you kidding?" Clay threw his hands in the air. "My anniversary is on Thursday."

"Not a paid vacation day." Scott laughed.

"Very funny, Scott. Your sister is going to kill me for this one." He pulled open the barn door and started to walk inside.

"Hey, don't get mad at me. Wait and see what she says when she finds out she's going."

"She's going?" Clay stopped suddenly. "Why is she going? She never goes. Not that I mind," he clarified.

Scott shrugged. "I think she's going to make it easier on Sydney."

"Things are going that good, huh?"

"Could be worse," Scott said, reaching for his saddle. "Liz could be going."

"What's going on with her? She's been awfully possessive of you since coming home. Something going on that we don't know about?"

Scott frowned at him. "Are you kidding? I learned my lesson where she's concerned a long time ago. The only thing I want from Liz is for her to leave town." Scott tossed the saddle blankets they'd need onto the floor of the tack room. "I thought you knew me better than that by now."

"I'm glad to hear it." He shot Scott a look of warning. "Why don't I finish this and let the guys know? You go get everything else situated."

Scott dropped his head back on his shoulders and sighed. "You mean I should go talk to Sydney and straighten things out before we leave?"

Clay smiled. "Something like that." He threw his hands up in defense. "Hey, I'm married. I know what it looks like when a man is in the doghouse."

Scott shook his head and walked back to the house. Why couldn't everyone just let him take care of his personal life? *Because you're making one hell of a mistake*, his inner voice warned. Smothering the urge to go and find Sydney, Scott headed toward the tack compartment of the trailer and took inventory of the gear for the bucking stock. As much as he wanted to tell Sydney about Liz, he wouldn't risk looking weak and stupid. He wasn't the same naive kid who lost his head for love. *Love*, he scoffed. He knew better than anyone that there was no such thing as a fairy-tale romance.

Chapter Ten

"SYDNEY?" JEN'S VOICE at her door wasn't unusual. They'd become good friends over the last week, and Sydney assumed she wanted to talk about the coming rodeo plans. "Are you in there?"

She rose to answer the door, pasting a smile to her face, hoping the conversation wouldn't steer toward Scott. "Come on in."

Sydney silently envied the grace Jennifer had as she made her way across the room and settled onto the end of the blue checkered comforter on the bed. She could read the uncertainty in Jennifer's eyes as her friend took a deep breath before glancing at her.

"What?" Sydney cocked her head to the side. She could see that Jennifer was struggling to decide how to approach the conversation.

"Scott."

"I don't want talk about Scott." Sydney shook her head and shut the door.

"I know, but Sydney," Jennifer paused and shook her head and frowned, looking unsure. She shrugged. "Okay, we'll talk about something else then."

Sydney knew that Jennifer was not one to give up easily, and she raised a questioning brow at her friend. "Like . . .?"

"Let's talk about Liz."

"Couldn't you have at least picked something nice to talk about? We could talk about the weather, horses, even the rodeo this weekend," Sydney offered as she crossed the room to sit in the chair by the window.

"That's Liz, all right." Jennifer laughed. "She always brings out the benevolence in others."

"I don't know what I did to her, but she's really got it out for me."

Jennifer furrowed her brow and bit her bottom lip. "You know why, right?"

Sydney shook her head. "I didn't realize she needed a reason."

Jennifer sucked in a breath and her mouth formed a circle of disbelief. "Scott didn't tell you?"

"I thought that subject was off limits." Sydney held her hand up defensively. She certainly didn't want to discuss any topic that included Scott and Liz.

Jennifer shook her head emphatically. "Oh, Sydney! I can't believe Scott didn't tell you himself. There's a lot you don't understand, especially where Liz is concerned."

Sydney thought of Scott's earlier comments to Mike.

"I guess he just feels like his relationship with her is none of my business." Sydney couldn't meet Jennifer's eyes. She was afraid that all of her feelings for Scott would be reflected in her eyes.

"Maybe. And he may kill me for telling you this, but I'm going to tell you anyway." Jennifer reached over and took Sydney's hand in her own. "I know you care about him."

Sydney looked up, her eyes filled with tears, in spite of her attempts to will them away. She didn't want everyone to see her humiliation, and she certainly didn't want the truth to get back to Scott. It would only make the situation between them harder to face.

"Let me finish the whole story before you say anything." Jennifer released Sydney's hand and settled herself at the foot of the bed. "You know a little about what happened to our parents, right?"

Sydney nodded. Derek had told her a bit about how his parents had been partners with Mike. When they were killed in a car accident coming home from a rodeo, Mike had accepted guardianship of all three of them.

"Before our parents died, Liz was just a little nuisance to Scott and his friends. Her mother had died when she was two, so Liz didn't remember her. My mother had been the only woman she'd really known as a mother figure. When she died, Liz looked to me and I was only a girl as well. Somewhere along the line, she decided she wanted to go to a fancy boarding school. Mike always gave her anything she asked for." Jennifer lowered her voice. "It's his only real flaw."

"There could be worse flaws than a father loving his daughter too much," Sydney commented, smiling as she thought of her own father.

"I know. And in most cases it wouldn't be too big of a deal. But Liz was beautiful."

"Is this supposed to make me feel better? If so, it's not working," Sydney interrupted.

"Just listen," Jennifer instructed. "Most of the time, she just stayed at school for vacations or competed in high school rodeos. But late in her junior year of high school, she visited. She was a rodeo queen by then and used to plenty of male attention. She flirted with every guy on this ranch and every single one of them was head over heels for her. Especially Scott. Mike and I tried to talk him out of dating her, but he wouldn't listen to us and he refused to see her flirting with other men. Once they got engaged the next summer, it was even worse. It seemed like the more he committed to her, the more openly she'd flirt with anyone else. Even Mike recognized it and tried to talk Scott out of it, pointing out that Liz was too much of a 'free spirit,' which I think was his way of admitting how spoiled she was."

Jennifer shook her head as she recalled the memories. "Scott was working every day with Mike by then. He came back early one afternoon and found her in the barn with his best friend." Sydney met her gaze and could see the compassion Jennifer had felt for her brother's broken heart. "She tried to lie to him and say it was rape, but he'd seen their lovemaking and knew better. He broke off the engagement and she took off again. She'd barely been back since and he hasn't seen her at all since that day . . . until now."

Sydney leaned forward in the chair and covered her face with her hands. She couldn't help but feel sympathy for the young man he'd been. He'd once been the romantic in love until he'd had his dream crushed by a heartless vixen. She held her hands against her cheeks and sighed. Scott's first impression of her made so much sense now.

"He said he knew my type," Sydney whispered.

Jennifer raised her brows as if Sydney's statement only confirmed the facts. "Liz was a rodeo queen, and you know a lot of them are spoiled like she is. And it's not hard to see that Scott has a hard time opening up to people. He didn't even tell Mike or me the truth about what happened until Liz came home for a visit a few years ago and he insisted on being gone."

"But why didn't he just tell me this instead of being so obnoxious about it?"

Jennifer cocked her head, pursed her lips, and raised a brow. "Are you kidding? I love my brother, but do you really think that macho Scott is going to confess any frailty or vulnerability?" She rolled her eyes. "Nope. Dust off those britches and cowboy up," she drawled in a humorously elaborated accent. "It's stupid, but I know he thinks he's protecting you. I don't know why Liz is so interested in him again, but the fact that he's interested in you has put a target on your back as far as Liz is concerned."

Sydney realized that in an odd, slightly warped way

Scott was trying to deflect Liz's attention from her. He'd tried to keep them away from one another at every turn. She'd assumed it was because he was interested in rekindling his romance with her, when in fact he'd simply been using himself as bait. Was he interested in her? It had seemed so. But, she wondered, was he too wounded by his past with Liz to ever trust again? She knew that her past had left scars as well. Were they both too damaged to ever feel vulnerable enough to fall in love?

"So," Jennifer encouraged, "now that you know what happened, what are you going to do about Scott?"

Sydney threw up her palms, shrugging, and sat back in the chair. "Nothing."

"What?" Jennifer stared at her in disbelief.

"He doesn't want me, Jennifer." She held up her hand as Jennifer began to protest. "I overheard him say as much this morning. And sometimes the scars from our past just don't ever heal."

Jennifer gave Sydney an odd look and she hoped that her friend wouldn't ask her to elaborate. She wasn't ready to confess her past with anyone yet. She knew she could trust Jennifer, but she was afraid that the truth would make her look weak and she couldn't stand pity. She and Scott had more in common than he'd realized.

"Sydney, if you ever want to talk, I'm here." Jennifer reached out and squeezed her hand.

"I know Jen." Sydney rose from the chair, squeezing her friend's hand before releasing her. "And I appreciate that more than you know. But right now, there's nothing to talk about." Sydney hardened the protective shell around herself, pulling it close like a trusted talisman. If they knew the truth, would they blame her?

CLAY PICKED UP the suitcases and piled them into the trailer. "Come on, ladies," he complained good-naturedly. "Let's get this show on the road before the sun rises."

"My cases are right there," Jennifer said as she pointed at the two very large suitcases and overnight bag on the porch.

Winding his arm around his wife's waist, he pulled her close. "And this is why I never take you, woman. You bring everything but the kitchen sink."

"Fine." Jennifer shrugged, standing on tiptoes to kiss his beard-roughened jaw. "I guess I'll just stay home then."

He growled and placed a quick kiss on her lips. "Like hell you will."

They both laughed as Clay loaded Jennifer's bags into the truck. Sydney watched their exchange with hidden jealousy. Jennifer had explained that they'd shared a rocky start to their relationship as well, but had quickly overcome it because of their mutual love. But Sydney and Scott didn't have a mutual love. Their relationship was nothing more than lust, at least on his part, and she just couldn't allow herself to be swept away by that tidal wave.

"Everyone here?" Scott stepped from the back of the horse trailer. Sydney hated that her pulse raced every time she saw him.

"Hold on," a voice called from the porch. All heads turned to see Liz come running down the steps, curls bouncing, an overnight bag in her hands. "I'm coming too!"

Mike reached for her arm. "But, honey, I stayed home so that we could have time to visit."

"But, Daddy," she whined. "I want to go too."

Sydney could see the flicker of disappointment in Mike's eyes. How could Liz not see or seem to care that she was hurting her father? And what sort of grown woman actually thought that whining would help her get her way? Sydney rolled her eyes.

"Not this time, Liz," Clay insisted. "We barely have enough room as it is. Stay and visit with your dad for a while." He turned and opened the truck door for Jennifer, helping her inside.

Sydney met Liz's glare with a smile tugging at the sides of her mouth. She was only able to keep her composure because she could see what Liz's request had done to Mike. She could deal with Liz's hatred, but she was worried at how Mike almost seemed to age from the disappointment of knowing his daughter preferred anything other than his company.

"Let's move out," Scott ordered.

Sydney slid into the back seat of the truck Clay was driving, but not before she saw Scott walk over to where Liz still stood. She couldn't make out his words, but if the unmistakable look of fury in the woman's face was any indication, Liz didn't like what he had to say.

THE CREW PULLED their caravan of trailers into the rodeo arena just as the sun began descending behind the hills. Scott, Jake, and Clay hurried to unload the stock and make sure they were fed and had a plentiful supply of fresh water. Sydney and Jennifer unloaded the riding horses and led them to a pen separate from the bucking stock. Sydney threw flakes of alfalfa over the fence and stooped to dust the loose flakes from her pants as she saw Jennifer going into one of the fifth-wheel trailers brought to house them over the long weekend.

"Wonder how they plan on working out these sleeping arrangements?" Sydney mumbled as she stomped her feet to shake off the leaves and stood.

"You'll be sharing a trailer with Jen." Sydney's heart leaped into her throat as Scott's familiar voice intruded.

"Oh, okay." She was so surprised by his nearness that she practically forgot what she'd even said.

"At least, for now," he added.

Sydney saw the flame of desire in his eyes and her pulse quickened at the sight of it. *Stop it*, she scolded herself.

"What?"

Scott wiped his hands on the sides of his pants. Was he actually nervous? She tried to look busy watering the horses.

"There are so many entrants that we'll be running slack well into Sunday evening. We'll have to stay an extra night or two to close up the deal. Jen and Clay will head home with most of the guys, and we will stay and finish up with Jake."

Sydney bit her lip, trying to control the nervous flutter in her stomach at the thought of spending one night, let alone two, nearly alone with Scott. This was the longest conversation they'd had in days without it ending in an argument.

"Sydney." Her name was barely spoken as he turned her to face him, but she could hear the longing in his voice.

She turned to him, hoping that her eyes wouldn't lay her heart bare for his perusal. Scott tipped up her chin and she trembled at the contact. His thumb caressed her jaw and it took every bit of willpower she had to not lean into his touch.

"Hey, Sydney." Jennifer's voice carried through the fading light of the arena grounds, breaking the trance. "I need your help with this."

"I have to . . ." Sydney stammered.

Scott let his hand fall. "Saved again."

SYDNEY HURRIED TO the trailer, grateful for Jennifer's interruption. That man could tempt the devil, she thought. One look from him was all it took to get her heart racing. And with only a touch, she'd practically melted in her boots. She considered herself lucky to have been able to escape with any shred of her pride still intact. The last thing she wanted Scott to know what that being around him was like the first time she'd been on a roller coaster: scary, yet oddly thrilling. He made her constantly feel like she was on unstable ground, trying to maintain balance where there was none. If she wanted to have any sort of sanity left, she'd have to stay as far away from him as possible. *Now, if only I can figure out how to do that when everyone leaves*, she mused.

She saw Jennifer putting the sodas and beer in the small trailer's refrigerator as she walked inside. "What did you need?"

Her friend looked over her shoulder and smiled at Sydney. "Nothing. I just happened to see you with Scott, and you looked pretty uncomfortable." She looked back into the refrigerator. "I thought I'd rescue you."

"Thank you." Sydney sighed as she flopped onto the small sofa. "It'll be worse when you guys leave."

"I thought you said he wasn't interested in you." Jennifer glanced at her again, raising a brow. "He didn't look *disinterested*, that's for sure."

Sydney looked around the trailer and changed the subject. "So, why is this trailer away from the other two?"

Jennifer shrugged and stood up, arching her back to stretch it. "Because we're women and I told them we wanted some privacy."

"But what about your anniversary?"

"How'd you know about it?" Jennifer looked pleased that she'd remembered.

"Silvie mentioned it a couple days ago before we knew about the rodeo."

"Yep, number seven." Jennifer sighed. "Doesn't seem like it's been that long."

"We should celebrate tomorrow."

Jennifer scoffed at the thought. "Scott would never let us have a party the night before a rodeo."

"Jennifer," Sydney scolded, "Aren't you the oldest?" She continued when Jennifer nodded and looked at her as if she'd grown a third head. "Then that makes you a senior partner, doesn't it?"

Sydney watched the myriad of expressions that passed over Jennifer's features. She laughed out loud as Jennifer smiled broadly. "A party it is," she agreed.

THE MEN GATHERED outside, eager for dinner, as Sydney and Scott's sister finished preparing the meal in the trailer. The easiest way to feed a crew of this size was buffet-style, and Jen had promised the crew her famous fried chicken. Both women appeared, carrying platters of crispy, golden chicken, biscuits, gravy, and an enormous tossed green salad to a folding table. When everyone had eaten their fill and several of the guys were groaning from eating their share plus quite a bit more, Sydney and Jennifer jumped up to clear the table.

"Do you want some help?" Clay moved to rise from his chair.

Jen stopped him with a hand on his shoulder. "You know you never do dishes," she teased. "Don't pretend to be chivalrous just because Sydney is here."

The women retreated as the men continued to tease Clay. They returned within moments with four home-made pies, courtesy of Silvie's kitchen.

Scott laughed as Jake groaned beside him. "I can't eat another bite, but how can I pass up Silvie's boysen-berry pie?"

"I'm sure you'll find a way to fit it in," Scott teased.

He hadn't taken his eyes off of Sydney all night. It was amazing to see her relax and enjoy herself with his sister. She seemed to let her guard down, and he could almost see the woman he'd spent time with at the last rodeo. He knew that much of the tension between them had been inflicted by his desire to protect his ego. When she had smiled at Paco's teasing early in the evening, he'd clenched his fists, wondering what it would take for her to smile at him that way.

He watched as she moved to clear away the dessert. He couldn't help but notice the way her jeans clung to her every curve, or the way the v-neck of her t-shirt dipped just low enough when she bent over that he could see the shadowy curve of her breast in the light of the lanterns and the fire pit Jake had set up. He shifted in his folding chair, hoping to calm the warmth that was spreading through him. He was disappointed when she didn't emerge from the trailer and he realized that Jen had also turned in for the evening.

Scott looked around to see that several of the men had headed off to bed, either in the fifth wheels or in the tack rooms. He'd been so focused on Sydney that he hadn't realized anything else going on around him. *That is not a good sign, cowboy*, he thought to himself.

"Sydney's a nice girl," Clay observed aloud. "Jen sure seems to have taken to her."

"What brought that up?" Scott sounded defensive, even to his own ears.

"Nothing." Clay pulled a can of Skoal from his pocket,

flipped it a twice, and then pressed a pinch between his lower lip and teeth.

"If Jen sees you with that, you're a dead man," Scott reminded him, nodding at the chew. "And if you have something to say about Sydney, just get it over with."

"She's a good match for you."

Scott shook his head. "Why is everyone so fired up about my love life all of the sudden?" Clay's only response was to spit off to the side of the chair. "She's not my type anyway."

Clay laughed. "Not your type? I've never seen two people more suited for each other than the two of you." Clay rose and spit the chew into the fire. He swished a mouthful of soda to rinse his mouth and spit it out before walking into the trailer and leaving Scott with his thoughts. But Scott didn't miss Clay's laughter as he headed for the trailer, or his comment as he entered.

"Not your type, my ass."

Scott sighed in frustration and bent over to put the fire out. Hell, he thought. Okay, he was big enough to admit that Sydney was exactly his type of woman. She was feisty and strong, hard working and beautiful. She shared the same interests he did, and she was kind. Beneath the wall he'd given her reason to build, she had a tender heart that was made for loving. He'd seen glimpses of the passion she kept hidden, and he was dying to be the one to release it.

Who was he kidding? She didn't want anything to do with him. If he even tried to make a move for her, she'd probably die laughing. Although she didn't seem inclined to laugh today, he realized. She'd seemed like she was longing for his touch as much as he craved hers. He crumpled up his empty soda can and tossed it into the garbage bag tied to the end of the trailer. There had to be some way that they could co-exist. He'd just have to figure it out, and soon.

SCOTT STEPPED OUT into the cool morning. The sun had just crested the hills surrounding the rodeo grounds, casting a pink and orange hue to the sky. He knew that the coolness now would burn off quickly, but the weather here was always cooler, even in mid-spring, than at home. He made his way toward the horses and saw alfalfa leaves and stalks scattered. Several of them were already finished eating and were saddled and tied outside the arena gate. He headed toward the standing horses and saw Sydney in the arena on his horse, Noble. He leaned against the fence, watching her ride, loping in gradually arcing circles before sliding to a halt. She didn't appear to move a muscle or cue the gelding as he began to prance sideways before taking off in a smooth lope in the opposite direction. Scott marveled at her knack for getting the animal to do things he hadn't even thought of trying. She practically had his horse dancing.

She patted Noble's neck and spotted him at the fence. Reining the gelding toward him, she came to a stop behind the fence.

"Morning," she said brightly.

"Morning. You're up early." Scott pointed at the paint. "How's he doing?"

"Noble?" She leaned forward and rubbed the gelding's neck. "He's a good boy. Aren't you?" The gelding's ears twitched at her voice and he turned to look at her. "But he loves to run."

Scott pointed at the horses tied to the fence. "You ready for the next one?"

"I was up early so those have already been ridden and cooled off. I just need to unsaddle them."

Scott did the mental calculation. It was barely seven in the morning, and allowing for the horses to eat, she must have been up around three o'clock. He wondered what had kept her awake and remembered the nightmare he'd witnessed. He'd have to remember to ask Jennifer if she'd heard anything.

"So, you're already finished for the day?"

Sydney shrugged. "Unless you have anything else for me to do today."

"Good, you can come to breakfast with me." He hadn't planned on asking her to join him, but it seemed like a good idea in the spur of the moment. Maybe, away from everyone, they could just talk. Sydney arched a brow and he could only imagine the questions running through her mind. He hadn't exactly given her reason to trust him.

"Is that an order from my boss or an invitation from you?"

Scott rubbed his hand across the overnight growth of stubble. Why was she making this more difficult? "Does it have to be an order?"

Sydney tipped her chin up in defiance. "No."

Scott couldn't help but smile at her courageous façade.

"Then I'll unsaddle the horses and you finish cooling off Noble and clean up. I'll meet you at the trailer in fifteen minutes."

AFTER WALKING NOBLE until he was cooled off, unsaddling him, and hurrying to the trailer to clean up, Sydney stepped out to see Scott waiting at the truck. She tried to think of any reason Scott would want to have breakfast with her and nothing had surfaced. While a small, hopeful part of her was looking forward to their time together, her logical, pessimistic side dreaded the battle that was sure to come from the two of them talking. She'd come to wonder if they weren't more like oil and water: completely incompatible, even as friends.

She started walking to the truck and was surprised to see him get out of the driver's side and open her door. She sat down and eyed him speculatively. Scott frowned as he got back into the truck but said nothing and she wondered what she'd done wrong already. They rode in uncomfortable silence for several miles until he pulled into an empty parking lot. It was surrounded by ponderosa pines and sagebrush with a few daisies peeking through. Just past a worn trail, a small creek flowed.

"I thought we were going to breakfast."

Scott smiled mischievously. "We are." He exited the truck and reached into the back for a backpack in the bed of the truck. He hurried to her door and opened it before she could. "Come on."

Sydney didn't know what to say. It was not what she'd

expected, and she was a little surprised to say the least. Scott ushered her down a wide slope, not stopping until they reached an open, flattened area along the bank of the creek. He pulled a light throw blanket from the backpack and spread it on the ground, motioning for her to sit. She followed his lead and leaned back on her palms, crossing her feet in front of her.

She still wasn't sure where he intended for this breakfast to lead, but she decided to take a chance. "Pretty spot." She stared out across the water gurgling slowly past them.

"Yeah, I found it a few years ago by accident when I was looking for a mechanic to fix a flat tire. I didn't have GPS and got turned around on the map. Luckily, the mechanic wasn't too far from here and I eventually got the tire repaired."

Sydney laughed quietly. "And now you have the GPS in the truck, I see."

"Not gonna make the same mistake twice." Scott smiled. "I try to come by if I have time when we are up this way. It's a relaxing spot. At least now," he clarified when she looked at him skeptically.

She liked seeing him relax and let his guard down. She watched him stare at the water. His entire being seemed to lighten. He shoulders didn't seem so straight, his face relaxed, and his eyes almost gleamed with delight. Away from the worries of the stock, schedules, and responsibilities of the rodeo, Scott seemed almost serene. He turned toward her, his lopsided smile curving his lips.

"What?" He chuckled.

Sydney returned his smile, not worrying about anything that had passed between them previously. This almost seemed like a different man—except his smile still sent her heart pounding like a racehorse. With the shadow of scruff still on his jaw, he looked dashing. "I'm just wondering why you act like such a tough guy?"

His face clouded over instantly, and she felt guilty for dampening his lighthearted mood. "What do you mean?"

"You only let people see the rough cowboy side." She lowered her gaze. "You obviously enjoy this." She waved toward the water. "There's more to you than this cowboy persona."

"You think so?" His lopsided smile returned and she could tell he was teasing her. "Like what?"

Sydney decided to play along. "Are you fishing for a compliment, Mr. Chandler?"

"Maybe."

"Okay, well, we know you like to cook." She laughed out loud when he raised his brows and gave her a dubious look. "Sort of."

"Anything else?" He reached into the backpack and pulled out a loaf of fresh French bread, some spreadable cheese, and a plastic container of fresh fruit. He reached in again for a thermos and two Styrofoam cups and filled them with steaming coffee. "Can't think of anything else?" he asked as he handed her the cup.

"Give me more time. I'm sure I'll think of at least one more," Sydney suggested as she took the cup from him and reached for a green apple in the container.

Scott's eyes shone wickedly. "I think you're going to have to pay for that one, princess," he promised.

Sydney could feel a blush spread to her cheeks, anticipating the payment his eyes said he had in mind. She feigned sudden interest in the food before her. "Okay," he conceded. "Enough about me. Why don't we change the subject?" he offered.

"These strawberries are delicious." Sydney caught the juice as it started to run down her chin and reached for another. She closed her eyes and savored the sweet berry.

"Now Sydney," Scott scolded. "I'm sure you can think of something better than the berries to talk about."

She lifted the cup in her hand and blew on the coffee to cool it. "We could talk about your girlfriend," she suggested, refusing to meet his eyes.

Scott bent his knee and settled back into one arm, lifting the coffee to his lips and sipping it. The muscles of his triceps flexed as he leaned back, his t-shirt tightening across his chest, revealing a solid wall of muscle beneath the thin cotton. Sydney shifted her gaze to his face, waiting for his anger, surprised when it never materialized.

"What did you want to know?" he asked agreeably.

Sydney shrugged, suddenly unsure of how to react to this candid version of Scott. "Nothing. Never mind, it's none of my business."

Scott looked over at her. His face held none of his usual imperviousness. "You brought her up, Sydney, so there must be something you want to know about her."

Sydney rose and walked to the edge of the water, sorry she'd even said anything. She'd opened up a can of worms she wasn't sure she was ready to deal with. She certainly couldn't confess that Jennifer had told her about his past with Liz without betraying her friend. But she hadn't expected Scott to be open about their relationship.

"Maybe you'd like to know who Liz is? Or why she showed up without warning? Or what my relationship is with her?" She heard Scott stand and start walking across the short distance that separated them. "What is it that you want to know, princess?"

"Yes . . . no . . . I don't know!" Sydney threw her hands up in frustration and turned to find that he stood mere feet away, watching her.

"Sydney, come here." No matter how softly spoken, it was another command. She was tired of feeling confused and ordered around by him, so she remained where she was, quietly defiant. "Please? Don't make this any harder than it already is for me."

She met his gaze and recognized the courage it was taking him to open up to her. He was offering her something she had yet to see him give anyone other than Mike. His eyes promised her complete vulnerability. Sydney prayed she could give him the same. She wanted to touch him, her fingers itched to reach out to him, to make it easier to release his pride.

She stepped closer and Scott reached for her hand, pulling her back toward the blanket. He sat down but remained holding on to her fingers, playing absently with her nails as if to distract himself from the memories.

"Tell me."

Scott sighed and recounted a brief version of his past

relationship with Liz. He didn't omit anything about how much he'd cared for Liz or how foolish he'd felt when he realized she'd betrayed him with his best friend. "Now can you see why there is nothing between Liz and me anymore? At least, not for me."

"But it's not over for her, Scott."

"Sydney, any feelings I had for her died the day I found her with Kurt." She felt her heart stop. It couldn't possibly be the same person.

"Sydney, what's wrong? You look like you just saw a ghost."

"Kurt . . . Willits?" Her voice was barely a hoarse whisper. She hated that after all this time, even his name still held the power to make her feel weak.

Scott nodded. "He's lucky I didn't kill him then. I haven't seen him since, but I heard he was traveling the circuit." He slipped his finger under her chin. "Are you okay?"

Sydney nodded. "I'm fine, it's nothing. Just feeling a little light-headed, I guess."

"Sydney, you mentioned Kurt once before. We can talk about it."

His voice was so kind and her heart pleaded with her to tell him, to open up and be as vulnerable as he was being. She wanted to share with him, but her mind refused to take part. If she told him now, he'd see her differently. He'd always view her as the weak Sydney who needed rescuing. *As opposed to the lying Sydney*, her heart argued. She found a compromise between the two.

"Not yet, Scott." She prayed he could understand that she needed more time. "Someday. But not today."

Sydney could see that he wanted to push her for more, to ask questions she wasn't ready to understand. Instead of pressing her, he nodded, but there was a lingering feeling of distrust. Scott placed the lid back on the fruit.

"We should be heading back soon." He put the rest of the food back into the pack.

Sydney wanted to stop him, hating that he had just begun to start opening up when she slammed on the brakes. "Okay." She rose and picked up the blanket, shaking the dust off of it before folding it and giving it to him.

As they headed back to the truck, Scott placed a hand at her lower back. She hoped his touch was an indication that he wasn't giving up on her just yet. Dropping the pack into the bed of the truck, he reached around her and opened the passenger door.

"Sydney?" His voice was quiet as she slid into the truck. He stood in the open doorway looking down at her. "Is this going to change anything between us?"

Did he mean breakfast, his vulnerability, or her refusal to open up? "I don't know, Scott. Will it?"

Chapter Eleven

SYDNEY HAD BARELY entered the trailer doors when Jen began to grill her about her breakfast with Scott. "Whoa!" She held up her hands to her friend in retreat. "I give up. He told me about his past with Liz."

"Finally!" Jennifer breathed a sigh of relief.

"I'm not sure it changes anything." She shook her head and sat on the couch. "There's just so much water under the bridge already."

"And some words still left unspoken?"

Jennifer was far too observant, Sydney realized. "That too."

"Look," Jennifer said as she sat on the couch and put her arm around Sydney. "I don't know what it is that you are keeping bottled up, and you don't have to tell me, but maybe the reason Scott didn't tell you was because he wanted to keep those memories in the past where he thought no one would have to deal with them, just like you're doing."

Sydney could understand those reasons. They were the same ones she had tried to convince herself were true. The problem with Jennifer's logic was that it wasn't true. The past always came back and haunted the present.

"Okay, so here are the plans for the party." Jen deftly changed the subject. "We have a radio and some MP3 players, so there will be plenty of music. The boys are going to keep Clay and Scott out working later than usual tonight to give us more time."

Sydney couldn't help but be caught up in Jennifer's enthusiasm as she finished telling her what she needed her to do before the evening arrived.

"WILL YOU GUYS come on?" Clay yelled. "I need to get back to the trailers." Scott wasn't sure what was holding the other guys up today, but they were moving like turtles.

"The little woman got you on a leash?" one of the senior hands teased.

"Shut up," Clay growled. Scott could see that this might turn ugly quickly, and knew he had to stop it.

"All right, that's enough for tonight. We can finish up tomorrow." Scott was ready to collapse, but he'd promised Sydney that they could talk more tonight. She was hiding something, but the pleading in her eyes had convinced him not to push her to talk about it before she felt ready. He wanted her to trust him, and that meant giving her time and space if that was what she needed. But he wasn't about to let her pull too far away from him.

"You just want to get back to your own *señorita*, eh?"

"Enough," Jake warned. Scott was grateful for Jake's interference this time.

"Grab the gear and let's head back to the trailers," Scott ordered.

Two of the hands glanced at one another before shooting Jake a sideways look. Scott narrowed his eyes. If he didn't know better, he'd think they looked nervous. He slipped several horn wraps across the front of his saddle to use in the morning for the slack. They'd managed to get the arena ready, which had taken most of their energy and time. In the morning, they would be wrapping the horns on the steers before they started allowing the overflow of contestants to compete early.

As he rode behind the rest of the crew, Scott heard Clay mumbling about how Jen would kill him for being so late for dinner on their anniversary. The rest of the guys had hurried ahead of them, leaving Scott and Clay to close the gates. Scott couldn't blame them for rushing off. He and Clay had both been in foul moods due to the delays all day, but it didn't seem to bother the men now as they chatted in a group.

Scott rode through the gate to find the trailers silent and deserted. The barbeque they used for meals sat in the center, between the semi-circle of trucks and trailers, but it was cold. Sydney and Jen were nowhere to be found.

"Now, where could those ladies be?" Jake asked, raising his voice.

"Surprise!" The men turned and yelled. Sydney and Jen appeared from behind the nearest trailer.

Scott wondered what sort of surprise included a cold barbeque, seven hungry cowboys, two cheerful women, and too many saddled horses. Clay dismounted and walked over to his wife, a rare boyish grin stretched across his face.

"Happy anniversary," Jen whispered as she pressed her lips against his.

Jake patted Clay's back before reaching into the horse trailer, pulling out a radio, and turning on music. He tied his horse before taking Clay's animal and tying him to the trailer.

"Come on," Jennifer grabbed Clay's hand and pulled him toward her trailer. "Help me get all of the food and bring it out."

Scott shook his head and smiled. Leave it to his sister to plan a party at a rodeo. He tied his horse to the stock trailer and began to unsaddle the animal.

"Are you mad?" Sydney appeared on the other side of Noble, looking slightly hesitant.

"Who, me?"

She shrugged and glanced back towards Jen and Clay trying to find an empty spot on a table full of food for yet another dish. "Jen wanted to do something special for Clay. All of the guys were in on it, even Jake."

Scott followed her gaze and smiled, shaking his head. "Why doesn't that surprise me?" He lifted the saddle and set it inside the trailer. "No, I'm not mad."

Sydney came around and began to unsaddle Clay's mount. The other boys were already taking care of their own horses, knowing that the animals came before their own stomachs.

"Really?" She pulled the saddle from the animal's back and placed it on the ground while she groomed the gelding.

Scott picked up the heavy saddle and placed it beside his in the trailer. "Really. Come on." He took the brush from her hand and led her back to the barbeque as Jake came back to move the horses to the pen and feed them.

Clay and Jen were already seated in the center of the others amidst a wealth of congratulations, well wishes, and food by the time he and Sydney joined them in the folding chairs.

"So, Clay, how does it feel to be tied to this ball and chain for seven long years?" Scott teased.

"It hasn't been easy," Clay commiserated, rolling his eyes.

"Watch it," Jennifer said as she slapped her husband's arm. "And don't worry, little brother, your time will come too." She glanced pointedly at Sydney.

After eating a hearty meal of tangy barbecued steak, baked beans, a fresh green salad, and an orange pudding dessert Jennifer had whipped up earlier in the day, Clay reached for Jennifer's hand and pulled her into his arms as Mark turned up the radio. The small speakers were surprisingly loud as the country ballad played across the open pasture that served as their dance floor. Scott watched as his sister's eyes gleamed with love for her husband. Clay tightened his embrace and placed a light kiss on the tip of her nose.

Scott looked at Sydney seated beside him. Why was it so easy for him to believe that Jen and Clay were in love and so hard to believe that he could ever fall in love again?

He wondered if it was just a matter of having the courage to allow it to happen. For so long he'd convinced himself that love was nothing more than unresolved desire, but he felt so much more for Sydney than desire. He wanted to erase the pain he'd seen in her eyes when she thought about her past, and he wanted to see her smile with pleasure the way he'd seen when she worked Noble.

He saw the wistful shimmer in her golden eyes as she watched Jennifer and Clay dance. She deserved that, and while he was unsure he could give it to her, it pained him to think of her having it with anyone else. Scott reached over and twined his fingers between hers, feeling a jolt of electricity at her touch.

"You think that there's something like that for everyone?" Her voice was tinged with doubt. He wondered if she'd been reading his thoughts.

"Like what, princess?"

"That kind of love," she clarified. "They are so happy and perfect for each other." She turned her eyes to him and the flames from the fire reflected in them. Her cheeks were highlighted by the light from the flame and she seemed to glow from within. It almost took his breath away.

"They've gone through a lot to get to where they are. I'm not sure if everyone is capable of the kind of sacrifice it took."

"Looks like it was worth it."

"I think what they have only comes around once in a lifetime and you just have to pray you don't miss it."

"Why, Mr. Chandler," Sydney teased. "Are you getting romantic in your old age?"

Jen and Clay stood before them, saving him from having to answer. Sydney started to slip her hand from his, but he held on. Scott realized the music had been turned off and the others were heading to bed.

"We'd better head into the trailer, Sydney. Morning will come before we realize." Jen's voice sounded disappointed, and he understood exactly how she felt. He wished now that he'd asked Sydney to dance with him and had the chance to hold her in his arms, even for just a moment. He stood and pulled Sydney to her feet.

"Clay, why don't you stay in the trailer with Jennifer tonight?" Sydney suggested.

"What?" Jen's voice was breathless. She smiled up at Clay.

"Um," Clay cleared his throat. "That's really nice and all, but where will you stay, Sydney?"

Scott raised his brows. Leave it to Clay to let the voice of reason cheat him out of a night with his wife. "You and Jen can stay in our trailer and I'll sleep on Sydney's couch," Scott offered. Three pair of eyes spun to watch his face. "What? It's not like we haven't shared a trailer."

Sydney shrugged. "He's right. And you two need some time alone for your anniversary."

"Just let me get a few things." Jen was practically leaping out of her skin with eagerness. She reached for Sydney's hand and pulled her with her to the trailer. "Scott, just come over in a few minutes."

"Are you sure about this, Sydney?" Jennifer asked her, yet again.

Sydney sighed. "I told you, it's perfectly fine. We won't kill each other, I promise."

Jennifer shot her a cynical look over her shoulder as she threw her toothbrush into a small bag with her jeans and shirt for the morning. "Just because you guys are getting along right now doesn't mean it will stay that way."

"Thanks for the vote of confidence," Sydney joked. Watching Jennifer jump around the trailer giggling like a girl on her first date was enough to convince Sydney that she was doing the right thing, no matter how nervous she was at the thought of staying in the trailer with Scott.

The knock at the door made her stomach drop to her toes. Jen stuffed the last items of clothing into the bag and hurried out the door, scooting past her brother with a quick kiss on his cheek and a murmur of thanks. Scott entered the trailer cautiously, closing the door behind him, but he kept his fingers around the handle.

"Are you sure you don't care about me staying in here? I mean, I can sleep outside, or in my truck for that matter."

Just the fact that he seemed more concerned about her comfort than his own touched her. He was making a conscious effort to put their past arguments behind them.

"It's fine, Scott, really," she assured him. "I'm just going to change."

Sydney walked into the bathroom and changed into a long flannel shirt and some running shorts. She looked at her reflection, tipping her face to the left and the right before stepping back. Not exactly sexy lingerie, but that wasn't the look she was going for, was it? She pulled back the screen and stepped into the living area to find Scott scanning a piece of paper.

"What's that?"

"Jen pressed this into my hand as she walked out. It's about you." Scott glanced her way and his eyes turned to molten obsidian. She may not be wearing lingerie, but it seemed to have the same effect on him. She felt her stomach tighten with a longing that matched what his eyes revealed.

"What does it say?" she whispered, barely able to string more than a couple of words together.

"She thought that now would be a good time for us to apologize for the things we've said to one another."

Sydney eyed him speculatively and reached for the note. "What?" His fingers caressed the back of her hand and he handed her the paper, sending liquid heat coursing through her veins. "You weren't kidding."

She lay the note on the table, unwilling to chance his touch again. She already felt as if the trailer was closing in on her, her breath coming in short gasps as he continued to gaze at her with a fiery hunger that both scared and excited her. She noticed that his own breath was uneven as he finally looked away, severing the trance he'd cast over her.

"We should probably get some sleep." He removed the cushions from the couch and pulled out the sofa bed. She retrieved the pillows from the closet near the bed and took them back to him. "I'll set an alarm in here."

Sydney walked back to the bedroom, glancing at Scott on the couch, and fought off a sense of déjà vu. She only hoped the next morning didn't end the same way. Sydney slipped between the cool sheets and willed sleep to come. After counting sheep, mentally balancing her checkbook, and staring at the ceiling for what seemed like hours, she heard Scott on the couch, still tossing and turning.

"Scott," she called out.

"Yeah, what's wrong?" He sounded irritated.

"I really am sorry for the things I said."

"So am I," he admitted. "I accused you of a lot of things that I know you didn't deserve."

They were silent for a moment and Sydney heard him shifting on the sofa bed again. She felt guilty that he had to sleep on the uncomfortable bed while she had a full mattress to herself, knowing that he had a much harder day ahead of him than she did. But did she dare offer to share the bed with him? A blush crept up her cheeks and burned her face.

Before she could offer, she heard Scott's muffled voice. "Goodnight, Sydney."

"Goodnight," she whispered.

ALTHOUGH HE WAS exhausted, Scott couldn't sleep. He lay on the couch with a metal bar pressing into his lower back listening as Sydney's breathing evened out. He'd already conjured up at least a hundred indecent proposals he wanted to make. His entire body felt like it was on fire, wanting to crawl into the bed with her, if only to hold her close. He couldn't remember ever wanting a woman as badly as he wanted her at that moment. Scott noticed when her breath went rapid and shallow and he held his own, listening. She began to murmur in her sleep incoherently and toss on the bed.

He rose, assuming that she was, once again, having a nightmare, and made his way to the bed. She had become twisted in the sheet; the blanket had been tossed to the floor at some point. She whimpered and cried out softly.

"Sydney." Scott said her name, trying to gently rouse her from the nightmare. When he heard her sob in her sleep, he slipped into the bed beside her, wrapping his arms around her. "Shh, Sydney, it's okay," he whispered, stroking her hair.

"No," she cried. "Get off me! You said you loved me."

"Sydney, wake up. You're dreaming." Scott shook her slightly.

"Please, don't." She awoke with a start, confusion clouding her eyes. Scott could just see the tears streaming down her cheeks, glistening in the dim light he'd left on over the stove.

"Scott?"

He could tell that she wasn't sure whether or not she was still dreaming in her barely conscious state. "Yeah, it's just me."

Scott gathered her into his arm and held her gently, kissing her forehead, temples and eyes. He didn't understand her tears, but he wanted to make sure she felt safe enough with him that she would talk about her dream. As her tears passed, she clung to his bare chest as if she wouldn't let him go. In truth, he didn't want her to let go, but he also realized that his body was responding to her soft curves in a way that certainly didn't instill feel-ings of safety. He grasped for every ounce of self-control within him.

"Sydney, I can't help if I don't know the problem."

"I can't talk about it." Scott could hear the pain in her voice, even with her face buried against his chest.

"You obviously need to talk about it," he whispered as he tipped her chin up with a finger, forcing her to meet his eyes. "Princess, trust me."

"I want to, but I just . . ."

Scott ran his thumb across her cheek and smoothed away a stray curl at her temple. "Who hurt you?" She im-mediately stiffened against him, and he knew he'd hit the mark. Sydney tried to pull away, but he held her close.

SYDNEY HAD JUST begun to feel safe and content in Scott's arms as the last of her tears fell against is chest. She'd had several nightmares about what had happened, but this was the first time anyone had been there to hold her as the fear and pain were purged. And then he asked her to talk about it. To talk about it would be to relive everything, including her failure. She couldn't do that, not yet.

She tried to pull away from him, to withdraw from his too perceptive gaze, but he held her to him firmly. Instead of feeling imprisoned and trapped by his embrace, she found compassion in the muscular wall of his chest. His shoulders offered her a foundation of strength she could cling to. And when she saw his eyes she knew they weren't just reflecting her torture; his own was there as well. He wanted her to trust him, and she desperately wanted to finally exorcise the anguish that had pursued her for the last eighteen months.

"Kurt," she barely whispered, as if speaking his name would cause his appearance.

She could see the moment that understanding dawned. They had both been betrayed by the same person. "What happened?" he asked, cupping her face with his calloused hand.

"We were friends," she began. "At least I thought we were."

"When?"

"Almost two years ago. He came home from a rodeo and he'd had a bad ride. He wanted me to come over and watch a movie, have dinner with him. I thought . . ." Sydney searched for the right word. "I guess I thought he might be interested in more than just friendship. I was barely eighteen, and I had this girlish crush on him. But the last time was different. He left the room for a while."

Scott's eyes never left her face. She could read the fury in them and wondered if it was directed at her or Kurt. Did he think she was a stupid, naïve girl for being at his apartment at all? She forced herself to continue.

"When he came back, he was a completely different person. He started pressuring me, grabbing me, and when I pushed him away he shouted at me, called me everything he could to insult me. He claimed I led him on, that I was sleeping around, and those were the nicer comments. I assumed he'd been drinking, so I got up to leave, and he threw me back against the couch and said that if other guys were already having me"—Sydney's voice caught as she remembered her fear—"he would get his turn too."

Scott's thumb gently traced the line of her cheekbone and down to her jaw. "Oh, Sydney," he whispered.

She pressed on, wanting to have it all out now that she'd started talking about it. Like an open sore, this wound had festered for too long. She had to open it wide in order to find healing.

"He tore my clothes apart. I begged him to stop and fought as much as I could, but he was just too strong. I remember trying to claw his eyes out." Her words caught on a sob as she tried to choke back her tears. "I don't remember anything else. I don't know if I passed out, or got knocked out. I don't know if he . . ." She met Scott's eyes. "I just don't know."

"Did you ever report it? Go to the hospital?"

She shook her head. "I woke up on the floor and he was gone. I felt so . . . dirty and used and stupid. I've never told anyone about it." Scott tucked her head under his chin and held her to his chest, stroking his hands along her spine.

"Sydney, I'm so sorry that you ever had to go through anything like that." She felt his shoulders stiffen and his arms around her grow protective in their embrace. "If I ever see him again, I'll kill him with my bare hands."

"It was my fault," she confessed against the wall of his chest. "I shouldn't have been so stupid."

He pulled away from her and looked down at her. "Don't ever say that again. It was not your fault. That bastard doesn't deserve to live." His eyes hardened with hate. "But you," he began, smoothing her hair back from her forehead, "didn't do anything except trust someone you thought cared about you."

Scott smiled at her, his eyes softening to liquid onyx. She was surprised at how the fear diminished after confessing to him, although it didn't disappear entirely. His reaction had eased her worries that he would blame or reject her. It was as if sharing her ordeal had finally shed light of day on a nightmare, removing some of its power to hurt her. She might never know exactly what happened that night but she didn't want to let it haunt her future.

She laid her head on his chest and listened to the strong, steady beat of Scott's heart. He offered her strength and compassion. It touched her that he was willing to protect her without viewing the need as weakness on her part. He had reacted completely opposite to what she had expected from him. Sydney began to relax. Her breathing slowed to match his as she curled her hand under her chin. Scott had given her an unexpected gift of freedom and she didn't know how she could thank him, but she knew that their relationship had completely changed in the last two days.

SCOTT STROKED SYDNEY'S chestnut curls, letting the soft waves flow through his fingers. Her breathing had slowed, become deep and even, and he knew she had fallen asleep hours ago. His mind swirled at what she had told him.

Had Kurt actually raped her? Would she know subconsciously, or could she have simply blocked the memory? And what could he do about it? Just the thought of anyone hurting her made him want to hit something, but knowing that it was Kurt . . . fury boiled within him.

He glanced down at the woman asleep on his chest, her fingers curled, her breath fanned against his skin. It was killing him to lay with her. Even after what she had told him, he couldn't help but desire her. No amount of self-control could stop his body from responding to her nearness, and he cursed himself, praying that the evidence of his arousal would remain his secret. His fingers grazed the silken skin of her lower back where her shirt had slipped up, and electricity shot through him. His abdomen tightened almost painfully. He longed not only to protect her but to possess her as well, and he hated himself for even thinking about his needs. He had to move away from her before she realized how little control he really had over his hunger for her.

Scott slipped his arm from under her and tried to slip out of the bed unnoticed. He had barely sat upright on the edge of the bed when he heard her voice, still groggy with sleep.

"Scott?" He froze in place and didn't answer. "Don't go," she whispered. "Please?"

He clenched his hands. "Sydney, I don't think I can stay in this bed any longer without touching you," Scott confessed, looking at her over his shoulder. Sydney's eyes were like liquid amber, soft and so inviting.

She bit down on the corner of her lip. "Please stay."

Scott groaned inwardly. "I can't do that to you, not after what you shared with me."

Her eyes glowed with the sheen of unshed tears of rejection. "And you don't want me now?"

"Dear God, I can barely keep myself from you. That's why I had to get up." He shook his head, wanting to hold her close, to press his lips to hers, but knowing it would be his undoing. He ran his fingers through his dark hair. "I don't want you to see me like him."

"Scott, you are nothing like him." He felt the warmth of her hand touch his forearm, and he knew he couldn't deny the pleasure any longer. He lay back down, facing her on the bed, and cupped her face in his fingers, his thumb tracing the outline of her lips.

"But are you sure, Sydney?"

She touched his face, brushing back a stray curl that had fallen forward. "I'm sure, Scott."

He groaned and pulled her tighter to him, wrapping her in his arms, his hands finding the skin of her lower back warm and inviting. Scott hesitated, his lips just a fraction of an inch from hers, in order to gain some modicum of control over his raging desire. He wanted her to remember this night as something beautiful, and to do that would require restraint on his part.

Scott touched the corner of her mouth with his lips and heard her sharp intake of breath. Her lips parted as he licked her lower lip. He groaned in defeat as she cupped his face in her palms and her small tongue slyly captured his own in a deep kiss filled with all of the longing and passion she felt. He reached down and unbuttoned the flannel shirt she wore, pulling away from her to view her flesh as he revealed it, inch by delectable inch. Sliding his hands over her shoulders, he slid the shirt down her arms and stared at her.

"My God," he whispered, his voice raw with desire, "You're beautiful."

Her breath came in short gasps and he could tell that she was just as lost to the sensations as he was. With his hands at her waist, he lowered his lips to her throat, kissing the hollow below her ear, and was rewarded with a sigh of pleasure. He felt her tremble while he blazed a trail along her throat and collarbone with his teeth and tongue. Scott's hand slid up the delicate skin of her back, caressing her ribs before finding a breast. His thumb coaxed the nipple to a tight bud as his fingers caressed. Sydney gasped and pressed against him, intertwining her legs with his. White-hot lightning shot through him as her skin touched his own scorched flesh.

Growling, he lowered his head and kissed the top of her breast before stroking it with his tongue. Sydney cried out and arched her back, her nails digging into his bared shoulders as a blazing fire consumed them. Scott nipped at the sensitive flesh with his lips, encircling her waist with his arm and exploring her body with his other hand. He slid her shorts down her long legs before allowing his fingers to trail up her inner thigh. The wisp of lace that she wore for underwear was gone in an instant.

Scott groaned against her skin, the feel of her sending spasms of need through him. He slid from the bed, giving himself a much-needed respite to control his raging passion and rid himself of his pants. He stood before her, completely naked as her eyes darkened with longing. She unconsciously licked her lower lip.

Scott fluidly lowered himself over her, every inch of his body on fire where it touched hers. "Princess, if you keep looking at me like that, tonight will be over before it begins."

His hands framed her face as he branded her with a searing kiss that reached the depths of his soul, leaving him wanting more of her. His hands explored her body as he kissed her neck and breasts, following his hands with his lips. He caressed her flat abdomen as he slid his fingers up her inner thigh. Scott paused at the juncture of her thighs before he allowed his fingers to dance magically over her waiting heat. She cried out, arching against him, holding on to him as she drowned in the sensations she was riding.

"Scott, please," she begged.

Unable to bear the exquisite torture any longer, Scott nudged her legs to open for him. He rose above her and placed a slow, sensuous kiss on her swollen lips as he pressed himself against her. Slowly, he entered her. Sydney's eyes flew open and Scott groaned as he froze, waiting for her to adjust to him. A sweat broke out on his back as her heat clutched and held him tightly.

"Dear God." He sighed as he pressed into her further.

Sydney's fingers clutched at the corded muscles of his back and he rocked with her to a rhythm as old and instinctual as time. She met his every penetrating thrust as she rose with him high into the heavens on the crested waves of rapture.

"Sydney," he whispered, her name a prayer on his lips.

He felt her tremble as she cried out in release. He thrust into her as the heavens exploded and filled her with his passion.

They floated back to earth in one another's arms.

Chapter Twelve

SYDNEY LAY WITH her head on Scott's chest, his body cradling her own. He brushed a stray curl from her cheek.

"You're mine now, princess." The intensity of his voice left no doubt for either of them. "You realize that, don't you?"

She smiled up at him and curled tighter into his embrace. Within minutes, she had dozed off, leaving him to wonder what had happened that night with Kurt. After all this time, they may never know if Kurt had raped her. *Unless he found Kurt and beat the truth out of him*, Scott thought ruthlessly.

Scott looked down at Sydney's sleeping face and smiled. No woman had ever felt as good in his arms as she did. It just felt right. He almost laughed at himself and wondered where this sentimentality had come from. Somehow in the last two weeks, this beautiful, outspoken vixen had snuck past the walls he'd built in his past to his carefully hidden heart. She'd been able to see beyond his pain, bitterness, and regret to emotions he thought he was no longer capable of. He didn't believe in fairy tales and love, but he knew he cared for her deeply. He finally fell asleep thinking about the princess he held and how maybe fate had finally dealt him a decent hand.

THE POUNDING ON the door woke them both. "Are you guys going to sleep all day?"

Scott squinted as he raised his watch to his face. "Crap!" He looked down at her, stretching against the pillow. He jumped from the bed and reached for his pants on the floor. "Get up. It's almost eight!"

She clutched the sheet to her chest and yawned. "You're such a slave driver." She tried to hide her smile when he shot her an evil glare. "Okay, okay, I'm getting up. But I get the bathroom first."

Scott reached over and pulled her against him, his dark eyes gleaming mischievously. "No time for separate showers. Guess we'll have to share."

She eyed the shower, which was barely big enough for one, and raised a brow. "Really?"

Scott lifted her, dragging the sheet with them as he carried her to the shower. Moments later, he was exploring her body, covering her with a soapy lather. Soon, they were both gasping for breath. Being late was no longer a concern as Sydney cried out her release, the water streaming down her face and mingling with her tears. Scott held her, kissing her eyes and cheeks until their breathing returned to normal. She faced the spray, attempting to rinse off.

"We've really got to get going," he said as he nibbled on her earlobe, his hands sliding around her waist. "But you are just too tempting." Scott spun her around and took possession of her mouth once again.

The warm water sluiced between them and she broke the kiss. "You aren't giving me a chance to tempt you." She turned off the water and reached for a towel, making her way toward the bedroom.

Scoot stepped out of the shower and reached for the bottom of her towel, pulling her back into his arms. "You are absolutely beautiful."

Sydney squealed, gripping the front of the towel to her, and blushed at the desire she could see still smoldering in his eyes. "If we don't get out there and help get this rodeo ready, we will be absolutely dead."

She slipped from his arms and hurried to get dressed in jeans and a t-shirt as Scott brushed his teeth and shaved. As she walked past the bathroom area, she wrapped her arms around his waist and laid her cheek against the muscles of his back, listening to his steady heartbeat. She sighed and looked at his reflection over his shoulder.

Scott paused mid-shave. "What?"

"Nothing." Sydney shrugged. "I'm just content."

He smiled as he washed off the last of the shaving cream, wiping his face with a towel, before turning and kissing her nose lightly. "Good. Let's keep things that way."

Scott moved aside to give her access to the sink as she

watched him head to get dressed, appreciating the view. He was an incredibly built specimen of manhood. She washed her face and applied her minimal makeup as she heard him open the trailer door and yell to Clay.

"You ready?"

"Coming," she said as she grabbed her boots from the side of the bed and hurried to the door. "Okay, let's go."

Scott placed a hand over the door, not allowing her to open it. "One more, since I won't be able to do this all day." Scott dipped his head and melded his lips to hers. Time stood still and he pulled her into his arms, fitting her against his frame. She could feel his arousal. Sparks of electricity shot through her and she wound her hands around his neck. She held on tightly as he kissed her. She'd never known this sense of dizzying longing. Every nerve ending seemed to vibrate at his touch.

Scott cupped her face in his palms and broke the kiss. He leaned his forehead against hers. "If I don't stop now, I'll never get out of this trailer." He opened the door and hurried out without looking back.

Sydney held onto the door frame, still trying to catch her breath. She could hear the crew outside as they shouted at the cattle, but nothing seemed to penetrate the storm of desire Scott had stirred. Her fingers touched her tender lips, still swollen from his kiss, and her eyes sought out his frame as he mounted his gelding.

"Earth to Sydney," Jennifer called.

"What?" She felt the heat rise over her neck and cheeks as she turned to face her friend. Jennifer was grinning like a Cheshire cat. "What are you so happy about?"

"You'll find out soon enough." Jen jerked her chin at Valentino and her gelding, Sable, which were tied nearby at the back arena gate. "Scott's meeting with the group putting on the rodeo, but he wants us to use the usual opening since you guys haven't worked out the kinks in the new one yet."

Sydney nodded her understanding. She was on pins and needles. As much as she wanted to lure Scott back into the trailer and make love all day, she was terrified that the rest of the crew would discover the extent of her relationship with him, ruining her professional reputation. She had worked too hard to get to this point to ruin it with a fling. Although Jen assured her that none of the guys knew, or would care if they did find out, Sydney knew better. She was certain her feelings for Scott were as obvious as the nose on her face, but she had no clue as to where she stood with him.

She began to question his motives throughout the rodeo when he barely glanced her way. He hadn't done more than bark a few instructions at her, and a bystander would have thought he was simply talking to any of the cowboys working for him. As grateful as she felt, her heart took a beating from his indifference. As the rodeo came to a close and the last of the trailers pulled out of the arena, Sydney could hear the band tuning their instruments and the cooks warming up the barbeques on the hill overlooking the arena. It wouldn't be long before the crowd of party-goers returned, freshly showered and clothed, for the dance.

"Are you heading up?" Jen asked. Sydney knew that

Jen and Clay were planning on going up, which would free her from putting in a supportive appearance as a representative for the stock contractor, but the tantalizing scent of the mesquite barbeque was tempting.

Clay approached the two women and placed a kiss on his wife's forehead. Winding an arm around her waist and pulling her close, he glanced at Sydney. "All packed and ready to head home?"

"Packed?" Sydney glanced over at Jen. "Already?" Jen snuggled into Clay's embrace and smiled as if she had a secret. "Okay, what's going on?"

Clay shrugged. "Scott wants to see you over at his trailer, ASAP." Clay smiled down at Jen.

Sydney raised a brow at the couple. "Okay, I don't trust either of you." She pointed a finger at one, then the other, before narrowing her eyes.

Jen rolled her eyes. "Just go already." She planted a palm firmly against Sydney's spine and pushed her toward Scott's trailer.

Sydney tapped on the door gently before stepping inside the doorway. "Scott, Clay said you wanted to see me?"

The trailer was silent and dark. There was no sign of Scott in the kitchenette and the bathroom door was open. She tried to see into the darkened bedroom, climbing the three stairs toward the bed. "Scott?"

Strong arms appeared from the dark to encircle her waist, pulling her close against his chest. "I always want to see you." Scott's lips nuzzled against the sensitive flesh of her neck. "I have some good news."

His words barely registered; her body's response superseded her brain's ability to think. "News?"

Scott chuckled seductively. "Everyone is heading home tonight."

Her shoulders slumped as she realized what he'd said. "We are?" She wished she were able to hide her disappointment better.

"Well, not quite everyone." Sydney wrinkled her brow. "You're staying with me to make sure we tie up any loose ends."

Sydney smiled. "What loose ends?"

Scott's thumb traced the fullness of her lower lip. "I'm sure I can find a few. I've been waiting all day for this." He captured her lips in a soft caress that left her limbs weak and her heart willing.

SCOTT AND SYDNEY headed toward the others to bid everyone goodbye. As Scott slipped an arm around her shoulders and leaned to whisper into her ear, he saw Jake approaching from the back of the trailer.

"Looks like the two of you finally made peace."

Glancing down at Sydney, Scott could barely hide a smile at her embarrassment as her cheeks flamed in the last light of the dying sunset. Jake chuckled and shook his head as he slipped behind the wheel of the cattle rig.

"Sometimes it don't matter how big a wall is if someone can just find a chink to break through." Jake arched a brow at Scott.

"Have a safe trip home, and tell Mike we'll be back by tomorrow afternoon."

"Will do."

Jen hung out of the passenger side of the truck Clay was driving. "I'll see you both tomorrow! Love ya, baby brother!"

Sydney waved furiously while Scott simply raised a hand toward the trucks pulling away from the arena. Scott looked down at the woman nestled against his side.

"Hungry for some dinner?" He jerked his chin toward the barbeque already in full swing at the top of the hill. "Since Clay and Jen left, we should probably put in an appearance for the company."

"Just give me a few minutes to get ready." Sydney slipped from his arms, and he instantly missed the warmth from her body. He wanted to pull her back into his embrace and brand her as his, once and for all.

SYDNEY HURRIED BACK to the trailer and reached into the closet where she had hung the dress that Jen had insisted she bring along. She suspected that Jen had planned this all along, but she didn't have time to ponder the implication of it. She slipped the coral dress over her head, grateful that the rayon was just clingy enough to be provocative without being hot and that the spaghetti straps would be cool in the summer evening breeze. She tightened the mesh leather belt and slipped on her brown leather dress boots.

She knew she only had a few more minutes before

Scott came looking for her, so she rushed to the bathroom mirror to touch up her makeup and add a touch of eye shadow before piling her curls onto her head, pinning them in place, and allowing a few stray curls to trail down her back. As the trailer door opened, she heard a low whistle.

"Does that mean you like it?" she asked.

Scott took a step closer and reached for her hand, twirling her toward him and pulled her close. Sydney's hands instinctively curled against his chest. Scott pressed his lips to her palm before moving to the pulse racing at her wrist. Her knees turned to liquid and she felt as if his touch had set her skin ablaze.

"I thought that you said we had to make an appearance." Sydney wondered if that husky voice was really her own.

"Are you sure you want to?" His eyes grew dark with the passion she knew could consume her completely at any given moment.

"I think Mike would probably appreciate it."

"Then, by all means, let's get this evening started so we can get back." He arched a brow at her and she felt the heat in her stomach spread outward toward her limbs.

SCOTT LED THE way to the truck and opened the door for her. They could have walked up the path to the barbeque, but he wasn't about to ask Sydney to do that dressed the way she was. She seated herself near the passenger door and buckled her seatbelt out of habit. He climbed into the driver's seat and looked over at her as he slipped the key into the ignition. She took his breath away. The dress clung to her in all of the right places and left the rest to his hungry imagination. After making love to her last night, he couldn't wait to explore every inch of her body again.

"What are you doing all the way over there?"

Sydney smiled, unbuckled her seatbelt, and scooted closer to him before planting an innocent kiss on his scruffy cheek. "How can it even be possible?"

"What?" Scott asked.

"Are you sure you're the same man that tried to run me over at the rodeo three weeks ago?"

Scott laughed at her recollection of their first meeting. "That's me."

As they reached the top of the hill, Scott followed the directions given by the parking attendant and pulled the truck off to the side, into the area set aside for reserved guests. Scott reached for her hand as they made their way through the crowd buying tickets at the front gate. The band was already tuning up, reminding him of the first barbeque and dance he'd attended with Sydney.

"Here you go, Scott." Jeff Garretty, the president of the group who had contracted Scott and Mike, handed him two passes for dinner, free drinks, and wristbands for the dance.

"Thanks, Jeff." Scott held up the passes. "We appreciate it, really."

"No problem." Jeff glanced at Sydney appreciatively and nodded. "After the performance you guys put on for us this weekend, it's the least we can do."

Scott slipped his hand to Sydney's lower back, preparing to lead her to an empty table set up for diners under the ancient oak trees. The trees sparkled with millions of tiny lights strung through the branches; the little lights looked like fireflies.

"Actually, Scott"—Jeff interrupted their retreat—"we thought that you might want a more private area so you aren't totally bombarded by people recognizing you from the rodeo."

Scott was surprised that anyone would have been considerate enough to think of their privacy. He followed Jeff to a table behind a large oak, set away from the rest of the tables yet still in view of the festivities. At this table, he and Sydney would be almost completely hidden unless someone knew to find them. Jeff pulled Sydney's chair out for her.

"I'm assuming you are both ready for some of our famous T-bones with all of the fixings?"

Scott looked to Sydney for her agreement before answering. "That would be fantastic."

"I'll bring you a beer." He assured Scott before turning to Sydney. "Would you like wine or beer?"

"I'll have a glass of white wine, if it's not too much trouble."

"None at all." Jeff hurried away from them toward the barbeque.

SYDNEY LOOKED AROUND her in awe. As they were seated at their table overlooking the empty rodeo arena, tiny lights sparkled in the trees above while the band launched into a quiet ballad. The entire evening had an enchanting ambiance as the sun melted into the hills, giving way to the moonlight overhead.

"I'm not sure how they did it." Sydney shook her head in admiration at what a few lights had been able to achieve. "They turned this into a mini-fairyland."

Scott's eyes darkened with desire as his gaze swept over her. He leaned forward to respond when he caught a glimpse of Jeff returning with their food and jerked his chin at him. "Ready to eat?"

Sydney's mouth watered with anticipation as the wonderful aroma of the steak wafted to her nose. She watched as Scott cut into his with relish. As soon as she tasted her own she could understand why. The food was delicious and cooked to perfection. The sourdough country rolls had just enough tang to bring out the richness of the baked beans. She took her time, savoring every bite of the meal and sipping the wine Scott kept refilling from the bar. As a result, she was starting to feel a bit lightheaded.

"Would you like to dance?" Scott asked as he dropped his fork onto the table.

Unable to take another bite and feeling like she should loosen her belt a notch, Sydney smiled across the table at him. His midnight eyes revealed his desire. "I'm not sure that I can stand, let alone dance."

Scott rose from his seat and took her hand into his calloused palm. "I promise not to let you fall."

"Too late." She smiled up at him, the room beginning to tilt slightly. "I fell for you a while ago." Sydney's eyes widened as she realized how loose the wine had made her tongue and what she had just revealed.

Scott's chuckle rumbled in the back of his throat. "I seem to recall our meeting somewhat differently."

Sydney shot him a sly grin. "I'm a good actress."

His laughter erupted as he led her in front of the tree and the other diners turned toward them. Embarrassed, Sydney pressed a finger against her lips. "Be quiet," she whispered loudly. "Everybody is staring at us."

He leaned close to her ear, sending chills down her spine as his warm breath caressed her neck. "They're staring at my beautiful date. I think it's jealousy."

"Nope." Sydney shook her head. In her inebriated state, she lost her balance and felt her legs give way beneath her as the floor rushed toward her. Sydney giggled as Scott caught her in his warm embrace and lifted her onto his toes. "This is how my dad taught me to dance when I was little."

Scott's eyes twinkled. "I think it's a bit easier than trying to hold you up all night."

Sydney felt like they had been dancing for hours. When she needed something to quench her thirst, Scott was right there with a glass of something refreshing, but whether it was wine or water, she could no longer tell. When she found herself still leaning against Scott's shoulder with no music playing, Scott decided it was time for them to head back, and she wasn't about to argue. While the dance floor spun around her, Scott led her to his truck and helped her into the passenger side. When he slipped behind the wheel, she scooted close to his side, curling up against his arm with her head against his bicep.

Scott put the truck into gear and looked over at Sydney, fully prepared to kiss her senseless, when he found her already asleep against him. "So much for a night she'll never forget. I'll be lucky if she even remembers anything tomorrow," Scott mumbled and turned the key in the ignition awkwardly with his left hand in order to leave Sydney undisturbed.

As he pulled into the arena below and parked beside the trailer they would share, he realized that Sydney was quietly snoring and had passed out. He left her in the truck to unlock the door of the trailer before returning to her, gathering her gently into his arms and carrying her inside. Scott laid her on the bed and stared down at her. Her soft sigh of contentment pounded in his brain, sending a pulsating need throughout his body, making him ache for her. But he knew he couldn't live with himself if he were to take advantage of her in her less than conscious state. He reached down and brushed a curl from her cheek.

Sydney's eyes opened. "Scott?" Her eyes remained glassy but trained on him as he dropped to a knee at the side of the bed.

"What's the matter, princess?" Scott cupped her jaw in his hand, brushing her cheek with his thumb.

"Gimme a kiss."

Although she slurred the words slightly, he could understand the need that drove them. He prayed he could retain control of his senses as he gently placed a chaste kiss on her pliant lips.

"No, no, no . . . not like that," she scolded as she cupped his face with her hands and pulled him toward her.

As she pressed her lips to his he stiffened, knowing he should break the kiss now before he lost all sense of control, yet unable to tear himself away from her. When Sydney darted her tongue past his lips to meet with his own, sighing deeply in her throat, he knew he was lost. Her tongue began to duel with his and he could taste the sweet honey of her mouth, nearly driving him insane. She pulled at him, urging him to join her on the bed. He tightened his fingers on her shoulders, wanting nothing more than to lose himself in her. Scott growled, a sound that to his ears was a mixture of pleasure and pain, forcing himself to end the erotic kiss.

Sydney sighed. "That was a kiss."

Scott smiled down at her, although he despised himself for his lack of control where she was concerned. He started to rise. He had to put some distance between them or she was going to be his undoing.

"Jus' where do you think you're goin'?" Surprisingly quick in her inebriated state, Sydney reached out and grasped his wrist.

Scott's chest was tight as he faced her. God, she was beautiful. "Princess, you've had a lot to drink tonight. I'm just going to let you sleep it off."

"What if sleep wasn't what I was thinking about?" She smiled up at him wickedly.

Scott felt his loins burn at the thought. "I don't think that's a good idea tonight."

"You don't want me?" Scott saw the disappointment in Sydney's eyes as embarrassment colored her face.

Hell, this is what he'd been trying to avoid. Scott dropped to a knee beside the bed again and cupped her face in his hands. His desire for this woman flooded his senses, the sweet scent of her driving him insane. He tipped his finger under her chin, forcing her to meet his gaze.

"Do you really believe that?"

Sydney tried to turn away from him. "I'm not sure what to believe."

"Princess, do you really think you mean so little to me?" His voice was husky with desire. She wouldn't meet his gaze. "Sydney, answer me."

"I don't know what to think," she shot back, defensively.

Scott realized that she had taken his concern for rejection. He kissed her cheek. "Don't you see how much I care about you? I have never felt this way about anyone."

Sydney's eyes brimmed with unshed tears, but he wasn't sure if they were due to pain or joy. "Liz . . ." she began.

"No," he assured her. "I never felt this way about her. I wasn't leaving the room because I don't want you. I was sleeping on the couch because I don't want you to hate me in the morning for taking advantage of you." Scott stared at her perfect lips.

"Really?"

Scott sighed and closed his eyes before meeting her questioning gaze. He couldn't resist the desire to taste her lips again. He lowered his head, intent on tasting her mouth again, when he saw her face contort. Knowing what was about to happen, he jumped from the bed, clearing a path for her to the bathroom door.

"I'm going to be sick," she explained as she hurried toward the toilet.

Scott followed her, reaching for a washcloth and wetting it at the sink with cool water. He reached the bathroom door in time to see her sit back on her heels, trying to pull the loose tendrils of hair back away from her face. He handed her the washcloth and helped her hold back her hair.

"Are you okay?"

"I think so." Wiping her face with the cloth, Sydney rose and walked to the sink. As she reached for the sink's handles, she lifted a white rose from behind them. He hadn't even noticed it in his hurry to get to her. He watched her fingers pluck a note from the wall behind the flower. As she read it silently, he saw her eyes brighten before misting over. She turned and smiled brightly at him, holding the note out for him to take.

"What does it say?"

"Read it." She continued to hold the paper out until he took it.

Scott glanced at the handwriting and instantly recognized Clay's scrawling script. He'd expected it to have been from Jen.

Sydney,
   I realize that I haven't known you long and I don't know you as well as Jen does, but it's obvious to

everyone that you are a wonderful, talented, and loving woman. It's no wonder that Scott fell for you from the start. Don't let his evil looks and foul moods fool you. He is happier than I have seen him in years because of you. Thank you for giving us back the "old" Scott.

Clay

Scott wasn't sure what to say. Clay had always been pretty quiet about the situation with Liz, and he certainly hadn't mentioned that he thought Scott was unhappy since, but he was right. Scott had allowed his feelings about one failed relationship to color every chance at finding what Jen and Clay shared.

"So, are you happy now?" Sydney rinsed her mouth at the sink before sitting on the couch.

Scott tried to judge Sydney's motive for asking. He didn't like reminiscing about the past, seeing no point in bringing up buried things, but he'd almost lost Sydney once when Liz returned. He didn't want it to happen a second time. But Sydney didn't pry; she simply waited for his answer expectantly.

Scott sat on the couch next to her, urging her to curl into his arms. "I didn't exactly have a picture-perfect childhood, but at first it was pretty great. My parents were partners with Mike and his wife. Jen was about twelve when my parents left to do a no-name rodeo on the coast."

Scott paused and took a deep breath. It had been so long since he'd allowed himself to think about his parents and what he had lost, what each of them had lost.

"How old were you?" Sydney asked, looking up at him.

Scott dropped his cheek to the top of her head, her soft curls tickling his lips as he inhaled the sweet scent of her, reminding him of raspberries and leather, femininity and strength.

"I had just turned eight. Derek was only about two." Scott kissed the top of her head. "Anyway, they were gone a lot back then and we stayed with Mike, his wife, Ellie, and Liz. But this time, they didn't return home. They were killed instantly by the semi that hit them head on in the fog."

Scott tried to swallow the lump that had formed in his throat, making any further comment impossible. He willed back the moisture in his eyes that threatened to spill over. He would not cry—not now, not ever, especially for something that couldn't be changed. He had become the man in their family at eight, and a father figure to Derek as a child. There was no time for regret or sorrow. *Cowboy up*, Scott instructed himself.

Sydney's hand twined in his, cooling his temper and dissipating his anger. "Derek never knew your parents then?" Her lips moved against his shirt, but he could feel the heat of them through the material.

Scott shook his head. "Everything they had was left to the three of us. Their share of the company has supported us since, and Mike took us in like we were his own children."

SYDNEY SAT ENVELOPED in Scott's embrace on the couch, her legs curled beneath her, until she wondered if he hadn't fallen asleep. Scott's head lay against the top of her own and his chest rose and fell rhythmically. She wanted to be there for him as he relived his past, sharing a part of him that she could tell he still hadn't made peace with. She had heard the haunted note in his voice as he told her about his parents, and she desperately wanted to share his pain. Her heart broke for the boy who had tried to step into shoes only a man could fill, leaving his own childhood behind.

Sydney could feel the heat of his skin through his shirt and her fingers itched to touch him, to offer him any comfort. But she couldn't bear to take her hand from his, which was curled against his chest. She heard his breath hitch and he lifted her hand to his lips, kissing the palm and sending liquid fire racing from her hand to her shoulder and into the pit of her stomach. She felt the heat of his touch spread to her loins.

Scott looked down at her. "I want you, princess."

Sydney cupped his face with both of her hands, his rough jaw scraping her palms. She lifted herself onto her knees and straddled his lap, allowing her full access to his mouth. Slowly, she kissed him. With her lips she tried to take away the sorrow she could see he had never fully allowed himself to feel. Her tongue danced with his, urging him to release the pent-up grief. When she finally pulled away, she knew that her heart was in her eyes, the love that she felt for this man shone like a beacon.

Scott's eyes fell to the spaghetti straps at her shoulders and he slipped a finger under the thin material, letting it fall to her upper arm. Scott's fingers followed his eyes as he slipped them from the column of her throat to her collarbone and over the crest her breasts. He reached up and pulled the pins from her hair, allowing the curls to fall around her shoulders, and buried his fingers inside the waves, urging her head back and allowing him access to her throat. His lips rained burning kisses on her face and neck. Sydney arched her back at the sweet torture, and he rewarded her with his lips at her collarbone. Scott pulled the dress down and it slid easily to the indentation of her waist. He wasted no time removing the thin barrier of her strapless bra, the only thing between his hands and her flesh.

Sydney felt as if her body were aflame. Scott caressed the hardened rosy buds as he nibbled at her ear, gently probing the pink shell with his tongue. Sydney gasped and pulled him closer, trying to become one with him. She arched her back as his mouth neared her breast. Scott pressed kisses in the valley between them before tasting the underside. His tongue was wreaking havoc on her senses, and she cried out as white-hot lightning shot through her when he took her fully into his mouth.

After turning his attention to the other tight, rosy nipple, Scott lifted his smoky gaze to hers, forcing her to look into his passion-darkened eyes. "Undress me, Sydney."

With trembling fingers, she fumbled with the buttons of his shirt, pulling it down his arms. She moved off of his lap and fumbled with the waistband of his pants, slowly unbuckling his belt and then the button of his pants. She reached for the zipper, her fingers grazing the swollen flesh beneath, and Scott growled.

"I can't take this." He stood with her, cupping her bottom, and she wrapped her legs around him as he carried her to the bed.

Scott laid her back with her knees hanging over the end of the bed and pulled her dress from her body, dropping it at his feet. He quickly shed his boots and pants, creating a puddle of clothing on the floor. Then he allowed his eyes to travel the length of her form, starting at the jumbled mass of auburn curls and pausing at the rise and fall of her breasts before continuing to her flat abdomen and the gentle swell of her hips.

Scott leaned over her, wrapping his arms around her waist and pressing his unshaven jaw against her stomach. He held her as she curled her fingers into his hair; he breathed ragged puffs against her skin, and she wondered if he felt as out of control as she did. He trailed his fingers down her ribcage and pressed a kiss to her navel—a kiss that was both tender and incredibly erotic. His fingers continued their explorations across her hips, as if memorizing every detail of her skin. As he fell to his knees on the floor, he tugged the thin wisp of fabric with him, leaving her bared to the sweet torment of his hands. Pressing a kiss to her inner thigh, his rough jaw heightened her soaring ecstasy while his fingers found the nest of curls and taught her new pleasures. Scott's lips inched up her thighs and Sydney arched, unable to control the physical response she had to his touch.

"Scott, wait," she cried, her voice husky.

Scott's tongue touched the center of her being. She

had never known that a feeling like this existed. He worshiped her with this tongue and she felt her body cresting before exploding into dazzling points of light. Scott slid onto the bed, curling himself against her side, cupping her breast in his hand and pressing kisses to her shoulder. Sydney's body hummed with pleasure.

"Scott?" she whispered. Sydney rolled over so that her body was pressed against his.

Scott smiled as he pressed a kiss to her lips. "Hmm?"

Sydney slid her knee to Scott's hip, pressing against his chest so that he fell onto his back. "I think it's my turn," she whispered against his lips.

Sydney straddled Scott's hips and met his eyes, blackened with desire. She leaned down and pressed a kiss to his lips, slipping her tongue inside tentatively. She had no idea how to please him, but she wanted desperately to give him even a fraction of the pleasure he had given her. She took his sigh as a sign that she was doing something he enjoyed. She pressed her lips to his neck, moving down to his chest and licking his hardened nipples. Scott growled in his throat and reached for her, intent to pull her against him, but she batted his hands away.

Her fingers trailed lightly against the hard muscles of his abs, every ridge of them standing out in the pale light. Sydney allowed her fingers to venture further, roaming across the muscles of his hips and thighs before remembering how he had touched her. When her gentle fingers touched him, he twitched and gasped for breath. She pressed a kiss to his hip, wondering if she could give him the same sense of pleasure she'd just experienced.

"Sydney, don't," he began, but stopped short as her tongue slid along the length of him.

A moan sounded deep in his chest as she pressed a kiss to the tip of him softly before taking him into her warmth. He shook as she teased him with her lips and mouth.

"No more," he growled and pulled her up against his chest. He lifted her hips and slid her down the shaft of him, burying himself within her. Sydney arched as they both groaned in mutual pleasure. Scott slowly lifted her hips, teaching her the rhythm when she tried to speed up to keep time with her racing pulse.

"Slow, princess," Scott purred. "Feel what I'm doing. Feel me inside you."

She moaned at his erotic words, feeling the pleasure coursing through her body. Sydney felt the waves of rapture pulling her under as Scott reached for her, joining their mouths and tongues as their bodies were joined. Scott thrust into her deeply, quickly, and she cried, surrendering to the crescendo of their passion.

SYDNEY WOKE TO the sun shining through the window at the foot of the bed and found black eyes staring down at her. Scott brushed a stray curl from her forehead.

"You're breathtaking," he whispered as be bent his head to steal a kiss.

Sydney smiled and stretched, wondering when they had found their way under the covers last night, as she raised her arms from under the sheets and over her head.

Scott cupped her breast and she squealed in protest, reaching for his hands.

"Don't we have to get going?"

Scott pressed a kiss at the pulse beating rapidly at the base of her throat, brushing her hands away. "No one is expecting us until this evening. I just have to collect a final payment this morning at the rodeo office," he murmured, his lips teasing the flesh of her neck and ear. He rolled onto his back, carrying her with him onto his chest as she pretended to consider the implications of his words.

"What shall we do until then?"

He growled low in his throat. "I know what I'm going to do." His fingers tickled her ribs as he ran them down her side to her hip and then lower. She sighed and threw her head back, giving herself up to the exquisite sensations surrounding her every fiber.

Chapter Thirteen

LIZ FINDLEY WAS fuming. The entire rodeo crew—minus
Scott and that tramp her father had hired—had returned
yesterday, and there was still no sign of the other two yet
today. She wasn't stupid; she knew that Scott had a *thing*
for her and that they had probably resolved any issues
they'd had, including her roll in Scott's past.

So much for Plan A, on to Plan B.

Scott still had feelings for her, she was sure of that.
Not that she really cared one way or the other, but she
knew that she could exploit any tenderness he still had
to get what she wanted. And what Liz wanted was to get
her hands on the ranch and sell it. She knew there was
no way that Daddy would ever sell the ranch as long as
the Chandlers were still working rodeos. She knew that
he still thought of them as his own kids, and it infuri-
ated her.

She'd had to share her father with them as kids, and

while she admired her father for taking on his friend's kids, she hated the connection that all three of them had with her Daddy. When he'd called her last winter to tell her about his stroke, he'd sworn her to secrecy. It was the first time since her mother had died that he'd ever shared something that was just between the two of them. She realized then how frail he'd become, and she was determined to make sure that he was able to take it easy. And none of the Chandlers were going to get in the way of her selling off the ranch and helping Daddy live a life he deserved—one without the Chandlers, where she could take care of him.

If she could just get him away from this miserable ranch and rodeos like the doctor had recommended, she would know that her efforts to impress him to prove that she was more worthy of his love than Scott were worth the sacrifices she would have to make. It had ripped her heart out when her father had taken Scott's side after their breakup. He hadn't even given her a chance to explain—not that she would have told him the truth—before encouraging her to leave the ranch. It was Scott's fault that she'd never had all of her father's love, and she was intent on making him pay dearly.

She was going to destroy the one thing he loved most: the ranch. She was going to sell it off piece by piece to investors. She'd already had some incredible offers, and once the ranch was sold, she and Daddy could take the money and get as far away from here as possible—away from this place and the Chandlers—and maybe head to the coast. Let those three fend for themselves and stop relying on her father for everything. But her first goal was getting Scott to fall for her again.

Liz stepped in front of her mirror and surveyed her image. She had realized quickly that Scott's flavor-of-the-month was going to be an irritation, but she hadn't expected it to be this difficult. She was proving to be a sneakier adversary than Liz had expected. She wasn't even sure what Scott saw in her.

Liz ran her hand through the highlighted blonde tresses at her forehead. He had always preferred blondes. In fact, he'd only dated one brunette that she'd heard of, and she'd kept close tabs on Scott over the years. She knew exactly which rodeos he was attending and who he was with at all times. She had enough girlfriends who rode barrels to be able to hear the latest gossip about Scott. From what she'd heard over the years, he was always a hot topic with a new girl every weekend.

She leaned closer toward the mirror, squinting at her reflection. She might have a couple of small wrinkles around the corners of her eyes from being in the sun. She would have to get those taken care of the next time she was near Los Angeles for the circuit finals. She smoothed out the Western shirt she had tucked into her fitted jeans. She was slim and long-legged, but well endowed, which intimidated most girls, but Scott had always preferred her body shape to that of the shorter, curvier girls. What was it that he saw in this girl Daddy had hired?

A pounding at the door interrupted her thoughts. "Who is it?" Liz sighed. She wasn't in the mood for visiting with anyone, unless it was Scott.

"Liz, let me in."

Great, she thought irritably. Scott's little weaselly brother. "What do you want, Derek?"

"I want you to let me in."

"Fine," she said. "I'm coming." She swung the door open, blocking the entrance. "What?" Liz arched a dark brow, hoping to intimidate the younger man.

At his full height, Derek was taller than Scott but not yet as broadly built. Given time and hard work on the ranch, he would fill out as Scott had. But there was a broodiness that surrounded Derek, especially when Scott was around. Liz didn't know him as well as Scott or Jen did, but she could recognize sibling rivalry; she could see that Derek wanted to move out of Scott's shadow.

"I want to know what's going on. Why didn't Sydney and Scott come back with everyone else?"

Liz rolled her eyes. "It doesn't take a brain surgeon to figure out that they're together, does it, Boy Wonder?"

Derek put a hand on either side of the doorway, his biceps flexing against his t-shirt, and leaned toward her, narrowing his eyes. There was nothing overly threatening about his pose, yet Liz held her breath as his coffee-colored eyes slid from her face to her waist before meeting her gaze again.

"Guess your plan wasn't as fool-proof as you thought," he goaded. "I'll just handle this on my own."

Liz ignored his taunts and left him standing at the door. "Nothing is ever fool-proof." She flashed a vicious smile his way. "Especially where you are concerned."

Derek narrowed his eyes and walked through the

door, shutting it behind him and advancing on her. Liz refused to cower. It wouldn't be the first time a man had hit her, but if Derek tried he'd be sorry.

"We had a deal. You take care of breaking them up and I make sure to keep them apart."

"Just how do you propose that I do that when they are at a rodeo? It would be different if he were here."

Derek shrugged his massive shoulders. "I highly doubt that you're above using that body of yours to get what you want. Use that, make him jealous. Do something or I will."

"Jealous," Liz murmured as she looked at her reflection again. "I can do that." She spun to face Derek. "Any idea where I might find Kurt Willits? He might be just what we need around here to drive a wedge between those lovebirds."

Liz knew that while Derek had never interfered with her relationship with Scott while they were dating, he was young enough to still idolize his older brother and old enough to know what had transpired between her and Kurt.

"Let me see if I can find his number."

SYDNEY COULD FEEL Scott's eyes on her as she stared out the window, pretending to be engrossed in the scenery whizzing past her. She'd been silent for most of the ride home, and Scott didn't seem inclined to make conversation. She wasn't sure what to say now that they were headed back to the ranch. The past weekend had woven a magical spell around them, and the thought of returning to the ranch with the trials she suspected were waiting for them there would only serve to sever the ties they had created.

Sydney knew that things would change as soon as they arrived at the ranch. There would be no privacy and too many eyes to witness any exchange between them. And she still wasn't certain where she stood with Scott. He'd admitted to having feelings for her, but he'd never said where he thought those feelings were leading, if anywhere at all.

She jumped as Scott's hand found hers on the seat. She felt the now-familiar rush of desire flood her chest and inhaled the scent of musk and leather that was his alone. She pasted a smile on her face before looking over at him, hoping that he wouldn't look too closely and see the worry in her eyes.

"You okay, Sydney?" His voice was husky, and it reminded her of how it had sounded last night when they made love.

"Fine," she answered quickly.

"Then why do you look worried?"

She couldn't help the sadness that crept into her voice or the half smile that she mustered. "What would I have to be worried about?"

"Us," Scott answered matter-of-factly.

Sydney met his dark gaze and read nothing but honesty in his eyes. She knew that her own eyes were giving him the only answer he needed and there was nothing she could do to hide the truth from him. Scott eased the truck to the shoulder of the deserted highway and turned it off. He turned and faced her on the seat.

"Nothing is going to change what we shared this weekend." Sydney sighed and looked at their clasped hands. Scott tipped her chin up with his free hand. "Nothing."

She gave him a faint smile and nodded. "Nothing," she repeated, trying to convince herself but falling short.

"Okay," Scott said as he reached for his cell phone, which was plugged into the dash of the truck. "You'll see."

"Who are you calling?"

"Mike. I'm going to have him saddle the horses and have them ready for us when we get there."

"Why?"

"You'll see."

LIZ RUSHED OUT of the ranch house and into the waiting arms of the blond Adonis on her porch. Passionately pressing their lips together, he held her tightly. When she finally separated from him, out of breath, she stroked his cheek with her thumb, her fingers running over the long scar that marred his cheek from his eye to his jaw. Liz loved the dangerous appeal it gave him.

"I knew I could count on you, Kurt."

"Yeah, that's me," he drawled. "Reliable Kurt."

Liz gave him a husky laugh meant to draw him in. "Let's not push it."

"Okay, sweetheart. This reunion is great, but you didn't call me here to rekindle old flames."

Liz thought about trying to string him along. He

would be a fun distraction while he was in town, but he couldn't give her what she wanted: the ranch and Scott's demise in her father's heart. "Same old Kurt, right to the point."

Kurt jerked her roughly to his chest, towering over her and grasping a handful of hair, forcing her to look up at him. "I'm happy to *rekindle* things with you, but I don't think you would have chanced a meeting between me and your lover boy for that."

Liz knew it was hazardous to rile Kurt. His temper had always been unpredictable. "You always could see right through me, couldn't you?"

Kurt released her instantly and she almost lost her balance. "We're two of a kind, you and me. We always have been."

Liz caught herself and glared at him. "Come on." She held open the front door. "Daddy is in the barn working, the others are in the north pasture, and Silvie took off to go to town. Let's go talk in the kitchen before anyone gets back. You want something to drink?"

Kurt arched a brow. "What do you think?"

Liz rolled her eyes as she led him towards the kitchen. If she didn't need his help—if he weren't the most immoral person she'd ever met—she never would have called him. But he was such an ass to deal with. She pointed at the kitchen table as he pulled out a chair, stretching his long legs out in front of him and leaning back. She reached into the refrigerator and pulled out one of the cold beers she kept in the back, holding it out to him.

"So what's the deal, Liz?"

"I need you to help me get Scott's share of the company so I can sell it off."

Kurt laughed as he took a swig of the beer. "Sure, no problem. I'll just ask Scott and I'm sure he'll hand it over." He tipped the bottle in her direction. "Just how do you suggest I do that?"

Liz narrowed her eyes at him and arched a brow. "Don't be a smartass." She didn't have time for him to play around. One of the hands could come back to the house at any moment.

"Okay, let's say you *can* get Scott to give up his shares to you. What about Jen and Derek? They aren't going to give you anything."

"Derek is weak. He practically hates Scott and will do just about anything to see him fail. And if both of the boys give up their shares, Jen will cave too. She'll be outnumbered."

Kurt shrugged. "Why do you want to sell this place all the sudden anyway? You think your dad's gonna let you do that?"

Liz shook her head. "I'm doing this for him. The doctor told him to stay away from stress, and for him that would be this company and the Chandlers. He won't say anything."

"Why not just sell Scott your dad's share?"

"Since when do you care about seeing Scott succeed?" Liz shot back. Kurt just rocked the chair onto the back legs and shrugged. "I want to see him beaten off that pedestal he puts himself on. The perfect Scott Chandler needs to see he's not so perfect after all."

Kurt chuckled viciously. "So is this because he dumped you, or is it some kind of 'Daddy' thing?" Liz glared at him. "Okay, both. So what do I get out of this proposition?"

"My undying gratitude?"

Kurt slid the empty bottle onto the kitchen table. "Your undying gratitude almost got me killed the last time I saw Scott. Not interested."

"You always said you wanted to get your own revenge. Steal his girl."

"Hmm . . . Who is this girl?" A faint smile played at his lips. Liz knew he loved a challenge, and no girl really stood a chance against him when he turned on the charm.

"Some rodeo queen Daddy hired to train horses." She shrugged. "I'm not sure how she convinced him . . ."

"A name, dear. Give me a name."

"Sydney something, I think. I only met her for a second, and she's pretty forgettable." Liz was bored with the turn of conversation. She didn't want to talk about Scott's little bimbo.

Kurt bolted upright in the chair, upsetting the bottle on the table. "Thomas?"

"Geez, Kurt," she reprimanded. "Be more careful." Liz reached for the towel on the sink to wipe up his mess.

Kurt jumped up and grabbed her shoulders roughly. "Thomas, Liz?" He shook her when she didn't answer right away. "Is her last name Thomas?" he yelled.

Liz slapped at his hands, trying to push him away. "That hurts!"

"Answer me, dammit!"

She'd seen Kurt get angry at other people, but he'd never launched his attack her direction. For the first time, she was truly afraid of him. She liked to be in control of every situation, and he suddenly seemed uncontrollable.

"I think so," she finally managed, still trying to unlock his grip on her shoulders.

"I'll do it."

Liz was curious what sort of person could elicit a reaction like this out of Kurt. "What the hell?" She rubbed the spots she knew would be bruised by tomorrow morning. "I take it you know her?"

"I guess you could say that." Kurt nodded, fingering the scar on his face.

SCOTT PULLED INTO the driveway and headed straight to the barn with Sydney following close behind. He knew that her curiosity was probably killing her, but she would be happy for the distraction when she saw what he had planned.

"Come on, slowpoke," he teased.

Sydney stopped in her tracks. "I'm not taking another step until you tell me where we are going."

Scott walked back to her and slid his hands down her arms, leaning down to whisper in her ear. "Come on, princess. Don't ruin my surprise."

Scott felt the pulse in her wrist speed up and pressed a kiss to her cheek. She looked up at him, her eyes glowing with unspoken doubt. "Trust me." Scott pulled her into the barn where Noble and Valentino stood, saddled and waiting patiently. Valentino whickered a greeting before she even came into view. "I guess that's two of us eating out of the palm of your hand, huh?"

"Right." She laughed at his teasing and he was thrilled that they could spend a little more time together, even if they did have to work during the day.

Scott checked the gear in the pack strapped to the back of his saddle. Since Mike had gone ahead and set everything up for him earlier, he simply needed some provisions for their ride. "Okay, we have everything we need."

Sydney mounted Valentino, and, to her credit, didn't ask where they were headed. He wondered if she recognized the path out to the lake, where she and Derek had shared lunch right after her arrival. Scott looked over at her and marveled at how relaxed she became when she was on the back of a horse. It was as if nothing else in the world mattered any longer. She and the animal were part of the same body, sharing every breath and enjoying each experience with the other. Her joy was almost childlike.

"Want to stop and let the horses get a drink at the lake?"

"We aren't staying here?" Her eyes shone brightly as she dismounted and led the stallion to the water's edge.

Scott shrugged his shoulders, refusing to give her any hints. Dropping Valentino's reins and letting him step into the cool water at the edge, Sydney twirled in place, laughing.

"I love this place."

Scott chuckled at her antics. "Just wait until we get to where we are headed."

"And that would be?" she said, trying to trick him into giving their destination away.

"Someplace where we'll ..." Scott stopped mid-sentence, looking out beyond the lake.

"What is it?" Sydney asked, moving closer to him.

Scott stared at the approaching figure until his mind registered the rider. He sighed and turned back to the horses. "It's only Derek."

"Derek? I've missed him the past few days."

Sydney's voice registered a little too much enthusiasm for his liking. A sharp stab of jealousy shot through him and he tried to shove it away. He realized that he usually didn't feel jealous of any man, not because there was no reason to, but because he never let himself feel enough for any particular woman to warrant any possessive emotion. Scott hated the feeling, but couldn't stop himself from slipping his arms around her waist and branding her as his as Derek approached.

"When did you guys get back? I never even saw the truck."

"We haven't." Scott's curt answer was meant to send Derek back to work. Sydney's tight laugh was obviously an attempt to lighten the tension between the brothers.

"We just got back and Scott said he had a surprise for me, so we came for a ride."

"Oh." Scott didn't miss the disappointment he heard in Derek's voice, nor did he miss Derek's glance at his arm draped around Sydney's shoulders. "Maybe we can catch up over dinner then. You can let me know how the rodeo went."

Scott arched a brow. Since when did Derek care how any rodeo went? "We'll be gone for dinner too."

Nice try, bro, but Sydney is mine.

Sydney and Derek both turned, looking at Scott incredulously, and he wondered if he'd actually spoken his thoughts aloud.

"Fine." Derek mounted his horse and glanced back at Sydney over his shoulder, adjusting his baseball cap. "I can see I'm interrupting here, so I guess I'll just be going."

"Don't worry," Scott said as he slid his arm around Sydney's waist and pulled her closer to his side. "She's safe with me."

Derek glared at his brother. "She'd better be."

"You have something you want to get off your chest, Derek?" Scott challenged. Scott could tell his brother was fishing for Sydney to ask him to stay, but he wasn't about to let it happen, not today. "Why don't you just get back to work. I'll make sure that Sydney's in good hands."

Derek shot a sad, pleading look toward Sydney before kicking his horse and taking off at a lope across the pasture. Scott pulled Sydney into his arms.

"Don't you think you were a little bossy with him?" She shook her head. "What's with you two?"

Now that Derek was gone, he could relish the feel of her in his arms, her body pressed up against his, causing a slow burn through his clothing. He felt his body tighten in response to her breasts pressed against his chest. Scott smiled down at her and gave a husky laugh. "It's you."

"What's me?" She tried to pull back, but he refused to release her.

"Derek's jealous because he wants you but he knows you're mine." Scott pulled her against him, one hand caressing her back while the other found its way into her hair and tipped her head back.

"Somehow, I don't think that's it. Derek and I are just friends."

"Wanna bet? Derek the lady-killer wants the one person he knows I won't let him have."

"What's that supposed to mean?" Scott felt her tense up. He didn't want to talk about his brother; he wanted to kiss her silly. To do that, he'd have to get where they were headed.

"Nothing." He released her and headed to gather the horses from the edge of the water. He handed her Valentino's reins and saw that she wasn't happy with his answer. "Don't get defensive, I just meant that you're mine and I'm not letting you go anywhere." He leaned down and placed a quick kiss on her pouting lips. "Come on, it's not much farther."

Sydney swung into her saddle. "Where are we going now?"

"To your surprise." Scott checked his cinch and swung into his saddle. "You coming?"

"I'm right behind you, cowboy. Lead the way."

SCOTT LED HER around the small lake and over a high hill to find a hidden valley. In the distance was a log home, towering over the terrain like a rustic castle. He directed her to a corral behind the massive house. Scott unsaddled

Noble as Sydney followed his lead, removing Valentino's tack and following him into the barn. Scott turned Valentino loose in the corral and put Noble into a stall.

"Come on." Scott's eyes shone with childlike excitement as he reached for her hand.

Sydney was too awed to speak. The house was amazing. Scott walked her past the comfortable-looking Adirondack chairs up the stairs that led to a deck that surrounded the entire back of the house. He opened the double doors to an open living room filled with overstuffed leather couches and a stone fireplace reaching to the second-story ceiling. The room was filled with light from the many windows that gave views of the gorgeous vistas beyond the house.

Scott leaned down and brushed her temple with a kiss. "Wait here."

She watched as he left the room before wandering around the living room. The leather furniture lent a rustic, masculine air to the house. It still smelled of pine and leather but had a hint of lemon cleaner and didn't seem lived in. She made her way past the dining table on her left to the kitchen. The dark granite countertops were obviously a modern addition, but the dark cabinetry still reflected the homey atmosphere family gatherings are built upon. Sydney immediately recalled memories of Thanksgiving dinners in her parents' home.

"Ready?" Scott came down the stairs with two oversized towels.

"Just what are you planning?" She arched a brow, suspicious at what he might have in store for her.

"I told you. It's a surprise." He reached for her hand, handing her one of the towels, and made his way out the front door.

"What is this place?"

"You like it? It was my parents' home before they died. A few years ago I was able to hire a friend of mine to restore it and make some additions."

"You grew up here?" She spun around, taking in the full impact of her surroundings. "It's beautiful."

"It wasn't quite this big and elaborate when we lived here, but Davis did a nice job." He guided her toward a grassy path that led to the right of the house into a wooded area. He had obviously landscaped the surrounding property to blend with the natural terrain. As he ushered her over the path blanketed with velvety grass, she heard the unmistakable gurgle of water. Scott stopped suddenly, turning her to face him. He cupped her face with his palms and placed feather-light kisses on her forehead, eyes, cheeks, and nose before finally reaching her lips.

Sydney's heart pounded in anticipation and her knees turned to liquid. She leaned against him for support as he tasted her, her tongue mating with his. She was breathless when he finally broke the kiss.

"This place is special to me, princess," Scott began. "This was where I came as a child, either to hide or to think. When I restored the house, I had Davis turn this into my own private retreat. Jen and Derek have never even been here. I wanted to share it with you."

Chapter Fourteen

THE SIGHT THAT greeted her stole her breath. They were surrounded by a thick wood with the trees blocking out any entrance other than the one they had used. Directly in front of her was a pool of bubbling water, steam rising from the top, but what caught her eye was the waterfall to her right. She could hear the birds twittering and squirrels chattering in the trees above. She could almost imagine a deer stepping from beyond the trees to drink from the water. While it wasn't dark, the only light that filtered into the hidden sanctuary came from above the trees, lending a magical, ethereal aura to the haven.

Scott's arms circled her waist. "Want to take a dip with me?"

"I don't think I can in jeans and this shirt."

Scott reached up and slipped the straps of her tank top over her shoulders. "You won't be," he hinted.

"Anyone can see us!"

Scott laughed. "Who? Like I said, only a couple of people even know this place exists. I doubt that Davis or Mike are going to show up. Besides, that is the only entrance." Scott pointed at the grassy path. He reached for her shirt again and this time she let him remove the garment. He slid her jeans down her legs, removed her boots, and left her standing in only her underwear. She stood rooted in place, watching as he rid himself of his clothing. He stepped into the water and turned to watch her join him. Hesitantly, she lowered herself into the pool.

"It's a heated pool?" she cried out, surprised.

"I told you this was my private oasis." Scott laughed. "All of the controls are over there." He pointed toward a moss-covered rock that perfectly blended in with the surroundings.

"This is amazing!" She swam toward the waterfall and the deeper water, finding a step designed to look like a rock at the edge. She watched as Scott moved fluidly through the water to where she waited.

"You look like a mermaid."

"Right." She laughed. "I probably look more like a wet poodle."

"No," he disagreed. "More like a water nymph, put here to tempt me."

Sydney smiled mischievously as she wound her arms around his neck. "It's too bad," she said, forcing a note of remorse into her voice.

"What's that?"

Sydney could barely think of what she'd been about to say. When her body had pressed up against his heated torso, fire exploded inside her. Wanting nothing more than to touch him, her playful side overtook her desire. She slid her fingers into his wet hair. "It's too bad you're a sucker for temptation." She pressed her hands on top of his head, pushing him under the water.

Scott rose to the surface, sputtering water and threats as she swam back toward the shallow end. But she wasn't fast enough as he reached for her ankle.

"Woman," he growled as he pulled her back toward him in the water. "You could have drowned me."

Sydney's reply lodged in her throat when she twisted around to fight back and realized that Scott had released her and was nowhere to be seen. "Scott?" she called when he still hadn't surfaced after several seconds.

Her scream pierced the air when she was pulled under the water by two unmistakable hands. When she surfaced, she was not surprised to see him just out of her reach.

"Are we even?" he asked as she gasped for breath. She sent him a wilting look. "Would you rather I leave?" Scott laughed as she considered the offer. "If I go, princess, I'm taking your clothes with me," Scott warned.

"You wouldn't dare." Sydney's chin rose with a confidence she didn't really believe. Scott swam toward the bank where her clothing lay. "Okay, okay, we're even," she conceded quickly.

Sydney and Scott played in the water like children until Scott mentioned how dark it had become. Sydney followed his glance toward the sky, seeing the first stars beginning to twinkle in the darkness. Scott pulled her into his arms, brushing his thumb across her nipple, causing it to tighten in reaction. He bent and kissed the hollow behind her ear.

"We should probably head back." She trembled in his arms, arching her back and pressing her into closer contact with him. "You're cold."

She didn't have the heart to tell him she was as far from cold as possible. In fact, she was on fire with need for him to touch her. She climbed from the water, modesty overtaking her as she wrapped herself in one of the warm towels before dressing behind a bush to hide the way her bra and underwear had become transparent.

By the time they walked back to the cabin, the stars were twinkling brightly overhead and the moon had completely risen. It cast an otherworldly glow over the path; the sounds from the night animals beginning to rise from their slumber made her feel as if they were the only humans on earth.

Scott led her back into the cabin, built a small fire, and ushered her to the couch in front of it. He kneeled before her. His eyes darkened with desire as his thumb caressed her collarbone. Sydney just sat before him, silent, waiting for him to say something, anything. Sucking in a deep breath, Scott rose and left the room. She heard him moving around in one of the rooms behind the kitchen. She heard what sounded like drawers opening and closing before what sounded like a door closing. Moments later he entered wearing nothing but a baggy pair of sweatpants. He handed her a thick robe and a dry towel.

"If you want to shower, the bathroom is straight down the hall. I'll fix us something to eat."

Sydney rose, wondering at the change in him. She felt as if she'd almost been dismissed. Her body was aching for his touch, yet he didn't seem to desire her at all.

SCOTT WATCHED AS Sydney made her way to the bathroom and almost breathed a sigh of relief when she left the room. He had to use this limited amount of time to gain some semblance of control over his need for her. Every second he was around her seemed to wear down the defenses he had placed around his emotions. She had a way of turning his body into a raging storm of desire that he had no control over. He pulled in a ragged breath as he visualized Sydney as she had looked stepping from the water, her bra revealing more of her bronzed flesh than it hid. Scott felt himself harden. He'd never met a woman that could push him to the brink of ecstasy at the mere thought of her.

He pulled a bottle of wine from the cooler on the counter and removed the meal that Silvie had sent with Mike for them, reading her instructions and placing the tin foil-covered dish into the oven. He was trying to focus on anything that might take his thoughts from the last night he'd spent with Sydney. His hand shook as he poured the white wine into two glasses.

When he turned around, Sydney was standing behind him, her hair lying in wet strands on her shoulders. She looked warm and desirable with his robe tied around her waist. It was far too big for her, falling at her shins. He handed her the glass of wine.

"Dinner is heating up, thanks to Silvie."

Sydney took the glass and sat on the couch, burying her feet under her.

"Sleepy?" he asked, sitting down on the opposite side of the couch.

"Um," she said, "a little." She curled her arm on the back of the couch and pillowed her head with it. "So, why'd you rebuild the house?"

"I told you how we lost our parents and moved in with Mike when I was eight? I still wanted to have some sort of connection to my parents. I missed them, but I knew I had to grow up and be a man for Jen and Derek. There was no one to take care of them but me."

"There was Mike," she pointed out. Sydney's voice was soft with pity. She was the last person he wanted to pity him.

"Yeah, but Mike had a daughter to take care of. He didn't need three more kids. I was determined to make sure that we weren't a burden on him. Jen took care of Derek when she wasn't in school and I worked on the ranch. I started heading to rodeos with him when I was fourteen."

"When I first met him, he said you'd been working with him since you could pick up a rope." She yawned. "He said you were like his own kid."

"We've been pretty close. Especially since I took over most of the rodeo operations. I got my diploma early and took night classes until I got my degree in business." He smiled as Sydney's brows arched in surprise. "I was always good with numbers. It's the reason why our operation has grown while so many others failed. I've been able to keep us in the black by running several businesses in conjunction with the ranch. Like breeding Valentino."

She blinked slowly and took a deep breath. She relaxed as the warm pool, shower, and wine were started to take effect. Her hair was starting to dry, bouncing into ringlets that shone red in the firelight. He longed to touch them, to see that they were indeed as silky as they appeared.

"Anyway"—he returned to his original topic—"after my parents died, I was so busy trying to hold the world together on my own shoulders that I didn't want to complain to Mike, or to anyone else for that matter. When I felt like I couldn't take it anymore, I'd saddled up my horse and headed over here. Mike knew where I went, encouraged it actually. Once the operation really started to earn I decided to repair the wear and tear on the house from age. By then, Jen and Clay were already dating and she knew what the house meant to me. Derek never remembered living here, so he didn't really feel the connection to it. They both let me have it to do what I wanted."

Scott ran his hands through his hair and arched his back, stretching his muscles, which were tight from lack of actual work.

"I think your parents would be thrilled to know their home is still in your hands. It's obviously well loved." She looked around the room. "But you don't stay here most of the time?"

"Most of the time I'm in the trailer at a rodeo, but when I'm home for more than a few days I come back here." Scott leaned back into the soft leather, watching Sydney intently, wondering what she was thinking.

"That explains where you were some mornings."

"Were you looking for me?" Scott gave her a rakish grin.

"Maybe." Sydney couldn't stop the smile from spreading across her face.

Scott took her empty wine glass into the kitchen to refill it and check on the food. "I was about nine when I found the stream," he called from the stove. "Well, back then it was a stream. I remember making a campfire and sleeping by the water. A couple of raccoons woke me that first night, stealing my food." Scott chuckled at the memory. "That was the one place I could just be me. So when I renovated the house, since the stream had long dried up, I decided to give it a renovation as well."

He made his way back to her, holding out her wine. Sydney lay with her head on her arm against the back of the couch, sound asleep. Scott set the wine onto the table and lifted the sleeping woman into his arms. He inhaled the scent of her, like honey and leather, and her curls tickled his jaw. He fought the urge to bury his face in them as he carried her into the master bedroom. He laid her down on the thick comforter and reached for the quilt lying over the back of a nearby chair. He spread the blanket over her and stared down at the vision.

Her hair had spread across the pillow and she had curled a hand below her chin. With her eyes closed, her face had softened, losing any pretense at controlling her emotions. She looked angelic. Her lips parted slightly as if waiting for a kiss. His gaze dropped to the robe that had slipped from her shoulder and revealed the satiny bronze skin beneath, giving him just a glimpse of her breast. Oh, how he wanted to reach out and touch her. Just the thought sent lightning coursing through his veins. There was no way he would be able to sleep next to her and not touch her tonight.

He forced himself to turn from her and walk into the kitchen, taking out the meal and turning the stove off. He considered dishing himself up a plate of the pasta but rejected the thought. His hunger had nothing to do with food. He put the food into the refrigerator and headed for the bathroom. He was going to need a cold shower if he was going to get any sleep. Although he'd had all three of the guest bedrooms decorated with comfort in mind, none of them held any appeal to him. He wanted to be curled around the soft form in his bed, feeling her hips pressing against him. He headed to the shower downstairs.

He stifled a groan as he stepped into the spray, letting the cool needles beat against his skin; they cooled his flesh but did little for his desire. He tried to keep his thoughts from drifting to the woman asleep in his bed. Working the soap into a lather, he recalled the shower they had taken together. He sighed and turned the knob, forcing even colder water out. He turned his back to the stinging cold.

Had Sydney really said that she loved him? Maybe he'd simply heard what he'd wanted to hear; he wasn't even sure that was what he wanted. He'd sworn off loving anyone after Liz. The way he was feeling right now, this could certainly be nothing more than lust.

Would you really be standing in this ice cold water, letting her sleep, if it was just lust?

Scott knew that somehow Sydney had breached the wall he thought he'd built too thick for any woman to penetrate. She may not have torn it down completely, but she'd slowly been able to chip away at it, enough to remind him that his heart still beat and that he could love someone. He hung his head, water dripping from his forehead and nose. There was no doubt that he was in love with Sydney Thomas, and the thought scared him to death.

He stepped out of the shower, taking the towel from the sink and wrapping it around his slim hips. He stood in front of the mirror, drying off his head with the hand towel. He braced his arm and stared at his reflection. What would happen if he allowed Sydney to know how much he cared for her? He couldn't allow another woman to have that power over him again. "This has to stop right here."

"Scott?"

Sydney stood by the bed. The light from the bathroom spilled through the doorway and illuminated the hesitation in her eyes. She was a vision, her curls haloing her face, her lips full and pouting. Scott couldn't hold back his passion for this woman any longer. He covered the few steps to her side and slipped the robe off of one shoulder, causing it to gape open. He pulled her with him toward the bed until the mattress hit the back of his calves.

Scott sat on the bed, pulling her between his thighs as he untied the knot at her waist, and the robe fell, catching on her arms. Sydney cradled his head against her stomach as his fingers held her waist. His fingers drifted over her ribs to the sides of her bared breasts. She looked down at him as he placed a gentle kiss along the swell before meeting her gaze.

"What do you want from me, princess?" His question delved into his very soul. How much was loving her going to cost him?

Sydney twined her fingers through his hair, her eyes glowing as she stared down at him. "I want you to love me, Scott."

He heard the unspoken plea in her voice and knew that her answer held as much double meaning as his question had. He obliged her the only way he could. Sydney trembled at the touch of his lips on her skin. He lay back onto the bed, taking her with him so that she lay atop him. He lifted her until she straddled his hips. Reaching up, he cupped her face in his fingers.

"Sydney." He breathed, winding his fingers into her hair, pulling her down to kiss her fully. His lips and tongue ravished her mouth, stealing her breath, wanting to allow her to feel every bit of his love but unsure of how to express it without becoming vulnerable.

He guided her movements with his hands at her hips. He felt his heart stop as he found ecstasy in her arms, torn between his desire to protect himself and his need to open his soul to her. His heart was still pounding as he rolled her onto the bed, bracing himself above her on his arms, and stared down into her glowing golden eyes.

She reached up and touched his face, the ghost of a smile gracing her kiss-swollen lips.

He slid the back of his hand down her cheek, and he could see the tears well in her eyes. "What?"

Sydney bit down on the corner of her lower lip and shook her head. Scott hated knowing that he was the cause of her tears. He couldn't give her what he knew she wanted, so he pressed a kiss to her lips. Nothing was going to stop him from falling asleep tonight with her curves pressed against him.

LIZ WATCHED SCOTT and Sydney ride into the yard from her bedroom window. Derek had informed her that he'd run into both of them at the lake but didn't know where they were going afterward. She assumed that Scott was just taking her out to dinner, but neither of them had returned to the house; she'd been watching for them all night.

"That's her." Kurt's voice held a deadly note of malice. "What do we do now?"

Kurt turned and faced her, his blue eyes filled with icy hate. Liz took a step backward, putting as much distance between them as the small window would allow.

"The less you know, the better off you'll be." He grasped her chin with his finger and thumb, kissing her roughly. "My gift to you is deniability."

SYDNEY TURNED VALENTINO into one of the stalls near the breeding shed. As she shut the door, Scott reached for her waist, pulling her up against him and kissing her soundly.

"What was that for?" she asked breathlessly.

"I'm going to miss you while I'm working today."

"Me too," she admitted, certain that he could hear the heavy thudding of her heart when he looked at her like he wanted to have her for lunch.

"Be careful breeding him today." Scott jerked his chin toward Valentino, who stood at the door waiting for his oats.

Sydney tilted her head to the side. "Really? Because I haven't done this before, right?"

Scott arched his brow at her, giving her his look that meant he was serious. "Just tell me you will be careful."

"Yes, boss." She laughed. "Go. We'll be fine. Derek will be here, too."

"That's not instilling any confidence." Scott rolled his eyes before pressing another quick kiss on her mouth before she could argue. "Okay, I'm leaving."

Sydney watched as he sauntered out of the barn, admiring the way his jeans and t-shirt hugged his frame. That man was far too desirable for his own good. He'd discovered a wanton side of her personality that she'd never known existed. She scooped grain from the bag in front of the tack room into a bucket and opened Valentino's stall, pouring the sweet molasses mixture into his feeder.

"Well, boy," she murmured to the horse, patting his neck as she stood in the open doorway. "What do you think of this whole situation?"

"I can tell you what I think."

The deep voice she'd heard for the last two years in her nightmares couldn't possibly be real. Sydney turned to see him near the doorway of the tack room. The air was momentarily knocked from her lungs as her chest constricted painfully. "Kurt." She breathed.

"Aw, I'm touched that you still remember me." His blue eyes glittered with hatred, belying the friendliness of his words. "Did you miss me?"

"Get out of here," Sydney ordered with a courage she didn't feel.

"That's no way to talk to a guest of your employer." He must have seen the surprise register in her eyes. "That's right, there's no way you could have known that Scott and I were old friends. Small world, isn't it?"

Sydney couldn't believe that Scott would have asked Kurt to come to the ranch, not after she'd told him what he'd done to her. "Scott didn't invite you."

"Your other employer, Liz." He laughed and shook his head as she narrowed her eyes. "I see you're still as naïve as ever."

"Liz is not my boss." Sydney's eyes blazed with fiery hatred. "Get out."

"I've missed that passion." He sighed as if the thought made him remorseful, and she knew he was toying with her like a cat with a mouse. "Why did I ever let you go?"

"Because I saw you for the sadistic monster that you are."

"Speaking of which ..." Kurt's smile spread evilly across his face as he stepped closer, the way she imagined a lion would stalk an antelope. "Now that you brought it up, I believe we have some unfinished business."

Sydney felt physically ill at the suggestion that Kurt might touch her again. She shot a glance to the heavy wooden door of the barn. It was closed tightly. Even if she could get past the hulking man who blocked her way, she couldn't get it open in time to escape him. Kurt noticed the direction of her gaze and advanced on her. She took a step backward, her spine hitting the metal frame of Valentino's stall door. She was trapped unless she went into the stall with the stallion, who had begun to paw at the floor mats. She abandoned the thought, knowing that an agitated stallion could kill either of them. Valentino stood with his ears pinned against his head, his front hoof pounding the stall door.

"Stay away from me, Kurt. Derek will be here any second."

"And you think that's a threat?" As quickly as a striking cobra, Kurt grasped her shoulders and shoved her away from Valentino's stall, slamming her back against the wall, stealing the breath from her lungs and the fight from her pained limbs. He held her throat between his thumb and fingers, restricting her ability to breathe.

"Do you see this?" Kurt traced the pulsing pink scar marring his cheek. "You did this. Now I'm going to take what you denied me that night."

Sydney gasped for air. "Denied you? You took what you wanted. You raped me, you bastard."

Kurt's eyes narrowed. "You don't remember what happened, do you?" Kurt pressed his body against her, his breath fanned against her cheek as his eyes blazed with fury. "After you ripped open my face, I had to go to the hospital." Spit hit her face as the wall jolted from the stallion's escalating assault. "You'd passed out so I left you there and you were gone when I got back. I never got to have my . . . fun." He looked at her chest, heaving to take in any oxygen.

"Passed out?" she choked out. "Or knocked out?"

Kurt ignored her. "See, we still have unfinished business. And taking what Scott regards so highly will make the pleasure that much sweeter." He trailed his hands across the front of her shirt, squeezing her breast roughly.

Sydney arched her back in an attempt to dislodge his hand from her jaw. Kurt laughed evilly and lowered his face to hers, grinding his lips against her mouth. She could taste blood in her mouth when he pulled away. She spit in his face with all of the venom and strength that she could muster. The blow came before she could block it and she fell to the concrete flooring in the barn walkway. She heard the pounding of Valentino's hooves on the stall door, now a constant staccato.

Kurt gripped her upper arms, shoving her once again against the wall before slapping her in disgust. She tried to stop the yelp of pain before it escaped her swollen lips, knowing it would only excite him further. He continued to deliver blows on her abused body as she slid to the ground, then he picked her up and shoved her toward the tack room.

She hit the floor again, the concrete tearing at her jeans. She could feel the blood trickling down her chin from her split lip. Her limbs hung useless, unable even to help her stand. Sydney could see her bloody handprint on the concrete as she threw her hands out to break her fall. She could feel herself losing consciousness and knew it would be the death of her if she did. Through her clouded gaze, Sydney saw Kurt coming toward her again. She curled into a tight ball on the floor, fully expecting his scuffed boot to connect with her lower back.

The shatter of metal pierced the air and she saw Kurt's eyes widen in shock. She saw the blur of white and heard the dull thud of Valentino's hoof connecting with flesh. Kurt yelled as he hit the ground. She saw him glance up in time to see Valentino coming after him, teeth bared, ears pinned against his head. He ran for the barn door, dragging his left leg limply behind him.

"You and that horse are going to pay for this," he threatened as he disappeared from sight.

Sydney knew she needed to get up or Valentino could turn on her as well, but her body wouldn't cooperate. She heard the stallion kick at the wooden wall of a stall before pawing at the concrete walkway. She tried to force her knees to push her toward the tack room. She felt the soft nudge at her cheek before her nose registered the smell of alfalfa and molasses. Valentino puffed air against her neck and she knew that he had spent his agitation against her attacker. She tried to open her eyes but realized they were swollen shut.

She would just close them for a second . . .

Chapter Fifteen

SYDNEY WOKE IN a dark room. She could hear someone nearby, then the soft rush of water from a faucet. She tried to look around, but the pain shooting up the left side of her neck convinced her to stop any movement. As her vision started to clear, she could barely make out the large window off to one side and a television on the wall in front of her. A hospital?

"Hello?"

Was that croak her voice?

She had no idea why her body wouldn't cooperate. She pushed her hands against the soft mattress, attempting to sit up, but there seemed to be no connecting her brain with her muscles. She curled her hands into fists. This was no dream. Sydney shifted on the mattress, trying to arch her back as pain shot across her ribcage and she groaned.

"SYDNEY, ARE YOU awake?" Scott poked his head out of the bathroom.

He thought he'd heard something and went rushing to the side of the bed. Scott knew that her condition was serious, even without the doctor confirming it. Sydney had been in and out of consciousness for the last two days. Her face and body still bore the bruising from the beating she'd taken. Sydney lay motionless in the hospital bed, fighting through the pain of a cracked rib and an infection that had set in.

No one had seen anything until Clay had found Sydney lying on the floor of the barn, Valentino standing beside her with his head to the floor. The trip to the hospital had been agonizing. Scott had watched helplessly as the hospital staff searched for internal injuries, warning him of the danger she might be in. He hadn't left her side and had even given the sheriff the limited information he had from her hospital room. So far, no one had any clues as to who might have done this or why. He heard the groan from the woman on the bed.

"Sydney?" He brushed her cheek with his thumb.

Her lashes batted on her cheek as she tried to pry her eyes open. "Scott?" Her voice sounded more like a pained moan.

"Princess, it's okay. Don't worry about talking yet. Let me get the nurse." Scott pressed the call button on her bed, surprised when the nurse came into the room only moments later.

"Did you need something?" she asked. "Oh! You're

awake." She reached over the bed and brought the blood pressure cuff to Sydney's arm.

"What happened?"

Scott reached for her right hand as the nurse took the cuff off of her arm. "We were hoping you could tell us."

"You're pressure is good. I'll just go page the doctor on call." The nurse nodded at Scott before leaving the room.

"I don't . . ." Sydney blinked and lifted a hand to her face, touching her swollen lip. "Ow!" Scott could see when the memories returned as panic flooded her eyes. "Valentino!"

"Shh, he's fine." Scott tried to calm her. "He was standing guard over you when we found you in the barn."

"You have to go check on him, Scott." She began to tremble.

Scott could see her distress. If he didn't ease her worry, she was never going to get any rest. "Okay, I'll call Derek and have him check on him. Try to relax and get some rest, okay?"

"Scott." Sydney stopped him with a hand over his wrist. "It was Kurt."

Scott felt the lump of hate forming in his throat. What in the hell had Kurt been doing on the ranch? How had he even known Sydney was there, or had he come looking for Scott and found Sydney instead? He cleared his throat, trying to hide his fury from the woman recuperating. His jaw clenched tightly and he took a deep breath, letting it out slowly, not trusting his voice. He gave Sydney a nod and brushed past the curtain separating the beds before heading into the hallway to call Derek.

He punched Derek's cell number into his phone. It had barely rung once when Derek picked up. "How's Sydney?"

"She's awake." Scott didn't want to let jealousy cloud his better judgment. Right now, he needed his brother's help. "I need you to check on Valentino."

"What?" Scott could hear the confusion in his brother's voice.

"Sydney is having a fit about Valentino and I told her I'd have you check on him."

"He's out the in corral. He was pretty agitated when Clay found them, and the siren from the ambulance just made it worse, so I put him into the corral where he could stretch his legs a bit."

Scott sighed. Why couldn't Derek just do what he asked him to? "Can you just go out and look at him?"

"Fine." Scott could hear the sound of a door slamming from the other end of the line and his brother's boots crunching over the gravel that separated the house from the corral. "There. I see him. He's fine. You can actually tell Sydney that he seems a bit interested in Betty."

"We need to get the broodmares bred or we're going to miss our window," Scott said.

"You want me to do it? I could get Clay to help out," Derek offered.

"No. Sydney will want to be there." Scott saw the doctor approaching from across the hall. "I have to go, the doctor is here. I'm hoping that we can head home by tomorrow."

SCOTT HAD BEEN avoiding his own work all week to keep an eye on Sydney. Kurt had completely disappeared off the grid. The sheriff had been watching for him, even checking with a few of the towns nearby, but he'd warned Scott that he didn't hold out much hope of finding him. Scott knew that the best bet was to find him on the circuit, but the sheriff wasn't interested in sending his limited manpower on a wild goose chase and Scott wasn't about to leave Sydney's side to go looking. If he ever saw Kurt again, he would cold-bloodedly kill the man with his bare hands.

It had been hard enough to persuade her to slow down and take it easy for a while. She'd been trying to convince him that she could still work the animals with cracked ribs and had pointed out that bull riders did it all the time. Scott had only been able to sway her by allowing her to be present while Scott and Derek bred the stallion to the mares. She'd stood valiantly by, ever watchful of the stallion, insisting the barn door was locked with him inside each night. If he hadn't watched her come into the house each night, he'd have wondered if she weren't sleeping in the tack room. He didn't understand the fear for the stallion and she refused to discuss it.

Scott stared out of barn office at Sydney, lost in her own thoughts, as she leaned over the corral fence. She watched as Valentino pranced around the corral, showing off. He'd been a bit on edge since the attack, pinning his ears back more often than was typical for him, and he hated being locked in the barn for extended periods. But he seemed otherwise unharmed, and Scott thought he'd be back to normal before Sydney was. The bruises had faded to a dull yellow-brown over the past week, but her fear hadn't seemed to fade. Scott knew she had every reason to be afraid. He'd let her down and hated himself for it. He wasn't sure how to make it up to her, or to not let it happen again.

"It's over, Liz." Scott heard his brother's voice from behind the barn and had to strain to hear her reply.

"Don't you *dare* back out on me now." There was a warning note to her voice, but Scott could barely hear her from his office. He slipped out the doorway and made his way toward the back of the barn where it sounded like they were conversing. They'd obviously assumed that the barn was empty. Scott stood with only a thin wall separating him from their conversation.

". . . and given you everything I promised." Damn, he'd missed the rest of Liz's comment.

"You said that Kurt was going to make Scott jealous, not kill Sydney."

"Shut up!" Scott heard the dull thud of flesh being pounded and assumed that Liz had hit Derek, which was less than he wanted to do to either of them right now. "Someone is going to hear you." Scott could hear the impatience in her voice. "Yeah, Kurt got out of hand, but I had no idea that's what he had planned. I don't even know where he is now. He caused this mess and took off."

"Poor Liz." Derek's sarcasm was unmistakable. "That was not a little out of hand. He broke her ribs and she was unconscious for the better part of two days." The wall shook near Scott's face with the force of Derek's anger. "This stops now."

"No, I'm too close."

"Now, Liz, or I tell Scott everything."

There was nothing but the sound of ragged breathing for a moment. Scott could tell that they had reached a standoff. Liz was the first to cave. "Fine, it stops." He heard footsteps walking away, Derek's from the sound of them.

"It stops when I say it stops, you coward." The voice was deceptively soft and lilting, almost sweet, and Scott knew he had to get Sydney as far from Liz as possible.

SCOTT WALKED UP behind Sydney and circled her waist with his arms, placing a kiss behind her ear. Sydney jumped.

"You okay?" She shrugged her shoulders. "I've been thinking." Scott turned her in his arms so that she faced him. "I want to take you away for a little while."

"But the horses," she argued.

"Not that far. What if we just stay at my house? You could keep Valentino there, we can put the mares in the barn, or take the horses you need to break."

"Scott," she began.

"I want you safe and I'm not sure you are here." He thought about the discussion he'd just overheard and the threat that had been unmistakable in Liz's voice.

"I've already caused enough trouble for you and Mike." She rested her hands on his arms, and he was alarmed at how cold they felt. It was almost as if the attack had taken the fire out of her. "I mean, you haven't even been able to get your own job done. And I know you sent Clay and Jen to the rodeo last weekend instead of going yourself." She shrugged and looked back at the stallion in the corral. "Maybe I should leave the ranch completely."

"No." Scott wasn't about to leave any room for argument. "Do you really think I'd let you out of my sight after what happened?" He tipped her chin up so that she met his gaze. "I want you where I have more control over our surroundings, at least for now."

Scott could read the relief in her eyes, and he pressed his lips to her temple. "Don't you realize what your leaving would do to me?" he whispered into her hair.

THE KNOCK AT her bedroom door halted Sydney's packing. Before she could even open the door, Derek barged in uninvited.

"Just what the hell is going on?" he yelled.

Sydney had never seen him like this and wasn't sure how to respond. When she didn't answer, Derek reached for her shirts, stacked neatly on the bed, and tossed them into her suitcase.

"Where do you think you're going?"

"Scott wants me to stay somewhere else for a little while. At least until he feels like it's safe to return." She wasn't sure why she felt obligated to give him an answer.

"Why didn't you just ask me? I'd stay with you during the day. You'd be just as safe with me."

A smile played at the corner of Sydney's lips. "I know, Derek." She knew it wasn't true but didn't want to hurt his sensitive ego. "But this will keep everyone safer. If I'm not here, there's no reason for Kurt to return. And if he does, he'll leave if he doesn't find me."

"And this isn't just because of Scott?"

"What?" How had he even heard that she was leaving with Scott?

"I'm sure Scott's staying with you." Derek didn't even try to hide the bitterness from his tone. Maybe Scott was right about Derek's jealousy. She shook her head, refusing to answer him, and turned back to her clothes, stuffing them into the bag.

Derek grasped her by the shoulders and turned her to face him. "Sydney, can't you see that he's trouble? He's caused you nothing but heartache. I've seen him do it to other women hundreds of times. Just look at Liz."

She jerked away from him and held a hand up to ward off any further conversation. "I don't want to talk about this now." She tried to shut out Derek's voice, but seeing he'd hit a tender wound, he pressed on. "She wasn't always like this. This is what happens when Scott gets tired of you. I would never treat you the way he has—or the way I know he will."

Sydney pressed her hands against her forehead. "Please, Derek, just leave."

"Sydney." He reached for her arm.

"Go!" The slamming door echoed with the foreboding of finality.

"So maybe that was a little mistake." His voice held a rasp. He tipped the shot glass back and downed the liquid.

"That wasn't a *mistake*, Kurt. That was an out-and-out failure. You just drove them closer, and you may have ruined any chance I have at getting this ranch away from Scott."

Kurt chuckled at her rage. "So where are they now?"

"I have no clue." She pushed at his shoulders. "Thanks to your stunt, he took off with her and a bunch of the horses last night." She reached for the icy mug in front of her and took a sip, wrinkling her nose at the beer foam. "They don't have a rodeo, but if anyone knows where to find them, they aren't talking to me."

Kurt twirled a toothpick between his fingers, slipping it into his mouth. "Are they gonna be working tomorrow?"

Liz rolled her eyes. "How would I know what they have planned?"

Kurt rolled the piece of wood to the other side of his mouth. "Then I'll watch tomorrow and follow them back to where they are staying."

Liz pursed her lips and arched her brow at him. It might work; it was better than anything she could come up with right now. Kurt leaned forward and pressed a quick kiss to her mouth, making her jump backward.

"Trust me."

Liz turned and stared at the people making their way to the dance floor of the loud country bar. She tossed back the rest of the beer and stood to leave, leaning to whisper into Kurt's ear. "Not in a million years."

SYDNEY WOKE THE next morning curled against Scott's chest, her fist tucked under her chin. His arms held her in a tight embrace, as if he'd been afraid to let her go, even in sleep. She placed a light kiss against his stubbled jaw, savoring the salty roughness. Scott mumbled unintelligibly and rolled onto his back, pulling her with him.

"Scott," she whispered, running her fingers up his hardened thigh, feeling his arousal against her hip. She felt his muscles bunch and tense under her fingers.

She kissed her way down his chest, smiling as his abs contracted as she ran her fingertips across them. In a flash of movement Scott rolled over, pinning her beneath him on the bed. His eyes opened, dark with desire, sparkling with mirth.

"I certainly hope you plan on waking me like this every morning."

Sydney pushed against his shoulders. "You were awake the entire time, weren't you?"

Scott shrugged his broad shoulders, a sly grin gracing his lips. "Guilty as charged, I'm afraid." She tilted her head and tried to appear disappointed in him. "Well, can you blame me?" he laughed. Scott rolled onto the bed beside her. "You seemed to be enjoying yourself, so who was I to interrupt?"

She fought to hide the smile trying to break through. "And you weren't, I suppose?"

Scott's eyes grew darker than she thought was possible, becoming inky. "What do you think?" He pressed himself against her leg, silently encouraging her to continue her explorations.

Sydney smiled, reveling in her feminine power. "I think . . ." she began. A wave of nausea flooded her and she pushed herself away from him, running to the bathroom. Slamming the door, she raced to the toilet in time to be sick, holding a hand to her still painful ribs. She laid her forehead on the cool porcelain, wondering whether she had caught a bug or this was her infection returning.

"Sydney," Scott called from behind the door. "Are you okay?"

The nausea passed as quickly as it had hit and Sydney emerged from the bathroom, pale and trembling slightly. She didn't want him to worry that she was getting sick. "Yeah, probably just that flu going around."

Scott didn't look convinced. "You want me to call Clay and tell him you're not breeding Valentino today and won't need his help?"

"No, I'm fine. Really," she assured him. "Those mares aren't going to wait forever."

FOR THE NEXT two weeks, Sydney spent her days breaking a few of Mike's newest colts, breeding the mares, and working with Scott on a new opening for an upcoming rodeo. Scott had informed her that it was one of the biggest rodeos they would do during the year and that they always expected something new and spectacular. With what he and Mike were planning, she wasn't sure that they could pull it together in time. The rodeo was only two months away and they were going to need some elaborate props.

She poured herself a glass of iced tea and sank into one of the Adirondack chairs behind Scott's house that overlooked the corral. Valentino circled the arena, sprinting from one side to the other. She could sympathize with his need to run. She was tired of being under Scott's ever-watchful eye. Kurt still hadn't turned up, but instead of relaxing him it had only seemed to make Scott even more tense. He'd been neglecting the cattle, pushing the work off to the other ranch hands in order to keep an eye on her. It had taken Mike to convince him to go with him to check on one of the bulls who had seemed sick.

Sydney made her way to the corral. Valentino pranced to the fence, eager for her attention. His fuzzy lips tugged at the sleeves of her shirt. He'd almost returned to his usual spirited self after the attack, and she was excited to think of the mares that would be heavy in foal to him over the coming months.

"Have you missed me, boy?" The young stallion flipped his upper lip back as if smiling at her in response. Sydney rubbed the flat spot between his eyes, her hand slipping under his long forelock. They both felt cooped up and needed to run. Scott had made her promise to stay at the house, but he wouldn't be back for a few hours—enough time for her to take a quick ride and be back before he returned. She left the fence and stepped into the barn, intent of checking on her favorite mare first. Cougar nickered as she peeked into the stall.

"Hey there, little lady. Are you ready to be a mama?"

The sorrel mare snorted and shook her coppery mane. She had come along nicely once Sydney had been able to get her to accept a rider willingly. She had perfect conformation and she and Valentino were going to have a beautiful foal next spring. Cougar took a step toward the door in anticipation of the treat Sydney always had for her. Pulling the latch on the door, Sydney stepped inside, greeted by Cougar thumping her stomach with her nose.

"All right, here you go . . ." A wave of nausea overwhelmed Sydney and she pressed the back of her hand to her mouth, fighting the urge to retch as her stomach clenched and roiled. She took a deep breath, inhaling the scent of sweet alfalfa and molasses, and was amazed that the queasiness passed as quickly as it had hit.

This is the strangest stomach flu ever.

She closed the stall door and dropped the bridle over the horn before carrying the saddle from the tack room. She quickly groomed the anxious stallion before slipping the saddle onto his back. She had every intention of getting rid of this pent-up energy they both had with a run to the lake. Valentino continued to prance in place as she swung her leg over his back and settled herself. She understood his anxiety; she, too, had the desire to break loose and run forever, feeling the wind whip her hair behind her, dragging at her shirt.

She leaned close to his neck and loosened the reins. She wound her fingers in his silvery mane before making a kissing sound. Valentino, sensing her exhilaration, broke into a fast gallop.

"Come on, boy. I know you can do better than this." She tapped him with her heels.

Valentino flattened his ears and stretched out his majestic body as he raced across the emerald pasture. Sydney's laughter was carried on the wind, circling her and reminding her of less challenging times. She sat up, slowing the horse as they approached the lake, allowing him to choose his own path to the waiting refreshment.

She slid from his back, loosened his cinch and, let him roam, knowing that he wouldn't stray far. She sat on a rock on the bank, kicked off her boots, and rocked her foot back and forth, dipping her toes into the cold water. It had been too long since she'd come back here. The last time was the first time Scott had taken her to his home, after the confrontation with Derek. She'd been able to avoid Derek since he'd stormed into her room. Maybe Scott was right and he did have feelings for her, but she had never encouraged him. Not even when Scott had accused her of it.

A nudge to her shoulder shook her out of her reverie. Sydney turned to see Valentino waiting patiently for the attention he felt he deserved. She reached up and petted the velvet softness of his muzzle.

"I've missed riding you the last couple weeks." Valentino's deep nicker made her laugh. "I take it you missed me too, huh?"

The horse shook his shining mane and brushed her cheek with his nose. Sydney glanced at the sun, which was gradually creeping toward the horizon. She had to get back or Scott would be at the house before she returned. With a sigh of regret, she tightened the cinch.

"Guess it's time to head back." She climbed onto his back and headed the way she had come.

As the barn came into view, she saw Scott's unmistakable profile against the corral. He met up with her before she even reached the barn.

"Where in the hell were you?"

Sydney shrugged. "I just went out for a ride."

"I got here and you and that stallion were gone. Why didn't you leave a note? Something?"

"Scott, I . . ."

"What was I supposed to think? I'll tell you, I thought that Kurt . . ."

"Scott, stop!" She climbed from the saddle and slipped the bridle from Valentino's head, replacing it with the halter. "We just went to the lake. I'm sorry I didn't leave a note, but I expected to be back before you were. I'm sick of being cooped up like an animal. He needed the exercise and I needed some freedom."

Scott pulled her away from the horse and into his arms, exhaling a breath she hadn't realized he'd been holding. "Next time, leave a note. Or call my cell." He stroked her tangled curls.

"I'm sorry I worried you." Her voice was muffled against his chest.

"I know." He kissed the top of her head, breathing in the scent of the grass, the wind and honey. "I know."

KURT HAD KNOWN his patience would pay off eventually. He'd watched Scott arrive at Mike's ranch without Sydney several days in a row only to see him leave, heading toward town. He knew that Scott wasn't staying in town. The wagging tongues there would have been in full swing. Then he remembered the old road Scott's parents had used to take to town instead of cutting through Mike's part of the ranch. The chain locking the old gate was brand new and the rusted gate had been oiled. It didn't take much effort to cut the link enough to allow access for his truck. The road was overgrown with weeds that now lay pressed down in tracks from Scott's truck. Kurt's four-wheel drive climbed the hills easily, crossing ruts and rocks as if they were speed bumps.

He'd worried momentarily that the sound of the loud diesel engine would carry, alerting Scott and Sydney to his presence on the hills overlooking the monstrosity Scott called home. Luck had been on his side as the wind carried any sound away from them. He followed Scott's tire tracks until he reached the crest and parked behind trees to keep his truck hidden as a precaution. Kurt limped to the top of the hill and lay in the weeds, watching them through the high-power binoculars. Scott didn't look happy; his shoulders were practically tensed to his ears as Sydney rode up. There was obviously something causing tension between the lovers, and

Kurt smiled, wondering if he wasn't the reason for the stress.

He watched Sydney unsaddle the stallion and turn him loose into the corral. If they thought they had stress now, tomorrow was going to bring an entirely new definition of the word. A smile spread across his lips as he limped back to his truck, climbing into the driver's seat and pulling his baseball cap down to shade his eyes. Once the sun went down, he was going to be busy.

Chapter Sixteen

SYDNEY LAY WITH Scott's body curved around her back and listened to his even breathing, trying to sort out her feelings for him. He could rile her temper faster than any man she'd ever known, and more often than not she wanted to smack that smug, arrogant smile from his face. But sometimes, there was something so kind and gentle about him, a sensitiveness he tried to hide. It wasn't as if he were difficult to look at either. She ran her fingertips over the arm at her waist, the solid muscles of his forearm protectively surrounding her with his warmth. He was the most virile man she'd ever met, and his rakish charm never let her catch a breath. There was no doubt in her mind that she loved him.

But even after the past few weeks, she still had no idea what permanent place, if any, he saw for her in his life. She'd told him how she felt, albeit accidentally, and he'd never let her in on his thoughts. She didn't want to believe Derek that Scott was merely using her, but she couldn't help the doubts from creeping in when he refused to open up. How long was she going to be willing to offer up her heart and soul to him only to be shut out, simply a body to keep him warm at night? How much longer would he make her pay the price for the unfaithfulness of another?

"I love you, Scott," she whispered as she caressed his powerful arm and surrendered herself to sleep.

SCOTT OPENED HIS eyes slowly. He had heard her confession. This was the second time the words had left her mouth, and he couldn't deny that this time it had been deliberate. Sydney had offered him the greatest gift he could have ever asked for. If she was so afraid of his rejection that she couldn't voice her feelings in the light of day, had he really earned it? And how would he respond if she did? Could he really profess a love he wasn't sure he even believed existed?

The questions swirled unanswered as he held Sydney in his arms. He knew that the thought of her with anyone else drove him mad, but jealousy didn't equate with love. He had learned that lesson from his experience with Liz, and he never wanted to make the same mistake again. Love was for suckers, he convinced himself. He cared about Sydney a lot, and he could admit that to her, but love? That term was better left for fantasies and fairy tales.

The unmistakable thud of a hoof hitting the rail of

the corral and the resulting crack of the board cut off all thoughts of the soft woman in his arms. She bolted upright, awake immediately.

"Scott?"

He placed a finger to his lips and slid from the bed, pulling on the sweats he'd thrown at the foot of it. "Stay here. I'll check it out."

Sydney reached for his arm. "No."

"It's probably just the horses spooked by a coyote."

She rose and reached for the robe that he had thrown on the floor. "I'm coming with you."

He wanted to argue with her, but the determined set of her jaw advised him of the futility. It would only waste time and energy. "Fine, but stay behind me."

He unlocked the back door and stepped onto the deck, scanning the horizon for anything that looked out of place: shadows that didn't fit the landscape or anything that instinctively struck him as odd. When nothing stood out, he headed down the stairs to check on Valentino. Sydney brushed past him, slipping into the corral and cooing to the agitated stallion. One of the corral boards hung awkwardly from the break. The horse was anxious but seemed unharmed, even as he snorted loudly one last time.

Valentino pranced away from Sydney to circle the corral before returning to her, nudging her shoulder. "I don't see anything," she whispered.

Scott held a finger up, listening. He'd heard a rustling near the barn, but that could have been one of the mares inside. He circled the corral before waving Sydney to follow him to the barn. After checking each of the mares and the tack room, Scott peered into the dark feed room. Nothing seemed amiss, but he couldn't shake the feeling that he was being watched. He reached for Sydney's hand and led her from the barn. As she reached back to turn the light off, he stopped her.

"No, let's leave it on tonight." Scott hoped the presence of the light would deter anything unwelcome from entering the barn or coming anywhere near the corral illuminated by the fluorescent glow.

"I didn't see anything, did you?" Sydney asked, her voice wavering.

Scott pulled her into his arms once they had entered the back door. She didn't seem any more at ease than when they had first heard the noise. "Like I said, a coyote probably went past the corral and Valentino kicked at it. I'll have to fix that board in the morning." He brushed a stray hair from her forehead. "Let's go back to bed."

Scott followed Sydney back to the bedroom. He knew that his reasoning was only meant to reassure her. There had been no other sounds since the crack of the horse kicking the fence. Had it been due to wildlife, they would have heard its retreat into the pasture as it made its escape. He stopped just before reaching his room and unlocked the gun cabinet under the stairs.

"Scott, are you coming?" Sydney called from the bedroom.

"Just checking the doors again." His first priority was to protect Sydney with any force necessary. If anyone tried to touch her again, they would pay with their life.

SCOTT WOKE AS the sun turned the clouds along the horizon pink and orange. He'd only had small fits of sleep last night after checking on the horses, mostly lying awake to listen to any sound outside. He'd known that if he rose and stayed on the porch it would only rouse suspicions with Sydney, and he didn't want to be far from her in case there was any trouble. Maybe he was just being overly cautious, especially considering they hadn't had any trouble for several weeks, but he couldn't shake the feeling of unease that seemed to settle in his spine, as if he had overlooked something in his inspection.

He poured a cup of coffee and stepped out the front door, heading toward the feed barn. He couldn't see if the barn light was still on from his angle, but he would know soon enough. He prepared the mixture of mash, grain, and alfalfa pellets for the mares, grabbing a large flake of alfalfa for Valentino and pushing the wheelbarrow of food toward the barn door. Approaching, he could see the light, faint in the morning sunrise, through the doorway as he heard the mares nicker a breakfast greeting. He poured the mixture into each bucket, relaxing a bit more as he fed each one. The animals seemed fine. Maybe they were all just letting the trouble with Kurt unnerve them.

Scott left the wheelbarrow in the barn and turned off the light. He carried the flake of hay to the corral but dropped it the moment Valentino came into view. The stallion lay flat on the ground, facing away from him. He rushed toward the fence, stopping when he saw the blood pooling beneath the animal. Scott's hands shook as he reached for the cell phone in his pocket and immediately hit the speed dial for the veterinarian's emergency number. The machine instructed him to leave a message. Scott made his way into the corral to see Valentino's empty eyes staring skyward. Feeling for a pulse at his neck, he touched only cold fur.

Valentino was gone, and there was nothing the vet could do now. Scott dialed the sheriff instead, giving them directions to Mike's house. After hanging up, he stood and dialed Clay's cell phone. He reached him on the second try.

"I need you to show the police how to get here, Clay." Scott was devastated. He'd failed Sydney again. This was going to destroy her. Valentino had been the culmination of her life's work. "Valentino's been killed."

"What? How?" Clay stuttered. "Are you guys okay?"

"We're fine." Scott sighed as he stared down at the lifeless horse. "I've got to go tell her. The police should be there shortly. Just bring them here. I don't want her alone right now."

"Kurt?"

Scott rubbed a hand over his eyes. "I don't know. I think so." He scanned the horizon. There was no trace that anyone had been on the ranch recently other than the two of them. "He could still be here for all I know."

"I'll be there as soon as the police get here."

"Thanks."

"And Scott," Clay began. "Hang in there, brother."

Scott wondered how he could break the news to Sydney. Whatever monster had done this had been right under their noses.

SCOTT HUNG UP the phone as he entered the house through the back door. He turned and dropped the blinds that hung over the doors.

"Scott?" Sydney called from the kitchen. "Do you want some more coffee before we head over to Mike's?"

Sydney came around the corner, sipping her own coffee. "I can make you a cup if you'd . . ." Her words died in her throat and he could see the worry slip onto her brow. "What is it?"

She must have read it in his face. "I want you to stay inside."

"Why? What's wrong?" A slight tremor coursed through her voice as she tried to control her panic. "Scott, you're scaring me. What happened?"

Scott wasn't even sure how to break the news gently. He reached for her shoulders. "It's Valentino."

"I need to get out there." She tried to brush his hands away from her, spilling hot coffee on both of them, sucking in air as the liquid scalded her arm. "Ow!"

Scott rushed her to the kitchen sink and turned on the water, letting it cool the angry red coloring her arm. He held her arm under the water while pinning her against the sink, his chest against her back. Sydney hung her head.

"Scott, please. Tell me what's going on."

He leaned to her ear. "He's gone, Sydney."

"Stolen?" He could hear the hint of hopefulness in her voice. He pressed a kiss to her temple, hating that his next words were going to break her heart.

"No, princess."

Sydney's body slumped against him, allowing him to hold her upright. He turned off the water but felt her tears burning his forearms. She sobbed in his arms but said nothing. Scott heard the tires crunching on the gravel driveway, but he wasn't about to let Sydney see the horse in the corral. He turned her to face him and cupped her jaw in his fingers.

"Wrap your arm while I go meet with the vet and the sheriff. Do *not* come out there until I come get you." She nodded but wouldn't meet his gaze. "I mean it, Sydney."

She looked at him, the tears still streaming down her cheeks, and he could read the questions she left unasked. He couldn't give her the answers she sought right now. He couldn't even offer her a moment of shared grief. "I promise I'll come back in as soon as I have any answers for you," he whispered before pressing a kiss to her mouth.

SCOTT HURRIED TO the corral where Clay waited with Dr. Mitchell and one of the local sheriff deputies.

"Scott." Dr. Mitchell barely acknowledged him as he continued to inspect the lifeless stallion. He knelt by Valentino's head, running a hand down his neck before rubbing at a spot with his finger. "Right there." He rose and turned to the officer. "Scott, this is Deputy Barnes."

The officer held a hand out to Scott. "Sorry to meet you under these circumstances." Scott shook the man's hand.

"Any ideas who might have done this?"

"I have my suspicions, but I can't prove anything." Scott turned back to Dr. Mitchell. "What was it you were pointing out?"

"A puncture wound. This animal was drugged. Someone planned this out."

Clay rose from his position, squatting near the horse. "What?"

"See this?" The vet pointed toward the majority of blood pooled near Valentino's hindquarters. There was a mangled mass of flesh lying by the horse's leg. "He was given enough drugs to take him down, but then he was castrated."

Dr. Mitchell shook his head. "Whoever did this had the tools with him—or her," he clarified, "and then took them when they left." He pointed toward the spots of blood on the grass heading toward the barn.

"But there's no evidence left behind?" Clay asked.

The deputy shook his head. "So far, nothing. A few shoe impressions in blood, but nothing with prints, and some tire marks near the barn. I'll check the gate on the corral and in the barn for prints, but I'm not hopeful."

Scott turned to Clay. "You know this has Kurt written all over it. That sadistic bastard."

"He had no idea where Sydney was staying."

"Who?" The deputy asked.

"You guys have been searching for the past couple weeks for Kurt Willits. He assaulted Sydney at Mike's and the only reason he didn't kill her was because this stallion got out. According to Sydney, the stallion attacked him."

"Yeah, but it's not like this place is easy to get to."

"We grew up together as kids. He was out here almost as much as I was growing up. He even worked with Mike for a while." Scott explained. "He knows the property like the back of his hand."

"But he couldn't have gotten past Mike's house without someone seeing him."

Scott frowned. Clay was right. Someone would have seen the truck, at least. Dr. Mitchell reached into the back of his truck and pulled out a tarp.

"I'd like the doc to do an autopsy on the animal."

Scott nodded. "But not here. Sydney's in the house."

"I'll need to speak to her as well." Barnes jotted down a couple of notes on his pad while Dr. Mitchell went back and covered Valentino with the tarp. "Anything else you can think of that might help us?"

Scott sighed. "No, I . . . last night we heard the horses making a bit of noise, so I came out and checked on them." He remembered the broken corral board. He pointed toward the broken board, hanging askew. "We assumed that Valentino had just gotten worked up about an animal when he'd broken that board."

Barnes moved closer and inspected the broken wood. He reached into his pocket and pulled out a small manila envelope and some latex gloves. He slipped the envelope under the board and Scott saw him pluck at the wood before dropping something into the yellow package and seal it. He stood and made his way back to his beat-up Chevy.

Clay helped the vet cover the horse with the tarp so that only his head was exposed. "Did you want to get Sydney?" Clay jerked his chin toward the house and the shadow they could see behind the blinds. "At least let her come say goodbye."

Barnes made his way over to where Scott and Clay stood. "You didn't see or hear anything last night, did you?" he asked Clay.

"Jen and I were up watching a movie, so we wouldn't have heard a truck over it, but we would have seen lights and we didn't see anything at all."

"Is there any other way to get to this property other than the road?" Barnes asked Scott.

"I've been using the west gate. But no one else even remembers it's there."

"Are you sure? Have you driven that way since last night?" Scott shook his head. "If you show me where it is, I'll check for tire tracks. Maybe we can get lucky and get a set other than yours."

"Sure. The road cuts behind the bar and up over those small hills. It's pretty rocky but . . ."

"And the other horses?"

"I headed to the barn first this morning. Everything was fine in there. I left the light on last night when we went back into the house and it was still on this morning. Whoever did this was only looking for Valentino.

It was personal." Scott had no doubt that any evidence was going to point to Kurt, and he wasn't about to wait around for them to find him. They hadn't found him after Sydney's attack, and they certainly weren't going to waste too many man-hours searching for him for killing an animal, no matter how valuable Valentino might be.

"I'm going to get Sydney." He turned to Barnes. "Can you keep your questions for her until later?"

Barnes gave a curt nod. "But I'll need to talk with her about it after I check out that hillside."

"All right." Scott made his way back to the house and Sydney stepped from the doorway. He'd expected her to be watching, but peeking through the blinds couldn't prepare her for the sight that would meet her in the corral. He met her on the deck and escorted her down the stairs. She held his hand but didn't seem to want him for support as she pulled him toward the corral. He tried to hold her back as she hurried, wanting to prolong every moment before the grief he knew she was about to experience.

Sydney stopped at the corral gate, as if the sight of the tarp-covered animal on the ground had stolen the air from her lungs. She dropped Scott's hand and both of hers flew to cover her mouth, holding in a silent scream of horror. Seeing the reality for herself was far more painful than her imagination could have prepared her for. She slid between the wooden slats of the corral, ignoring the gate altogether, and kneeled down beside Valentino's head. Scott saw blood near the back of the horse and moved the tarp to cover it, but Sydney simply ignored him.

Tears fell, slipping down her face too quickly for her cheeks to contain them. She stroked his face, her hand slipping over his glassy eyes and closing them eternally. Her fingers caressed the velvety muzzle and Sydney leaned down, pressing a kiss on Valentino's cheek.

"Goodbye, my friend," she whispered, her tears flowing unchecked. She laid her cheek against the horse and closed her eyes.

Scott placed his hands on her shoulders. "Come on, princess. Let's go inside."

She let Scott lift her from the ground and surveyed the men in the corral as if seeing them for the first time. She spotted the sheriff's vehicle making its way toward the hillside.

"You know who did this." She pointed her finger at Scott. He nodded in agreement.

"He's not going to get away with this."

"He said he was going to do this, and he did. And they didn't do anything to stop it." She aimed her anger at the deputy, out of earshot.

"Sydney, they have a warrant out for him." Clay argued.

"Hell of a lot of good that did."

"Now that Kurt knows where she is, you might as well take her back to Mike's. The more eyes you have around, the safer she's going to be. This place is just too secluded now," Clay pointed out. "Sydney, go get your things together and I'll take you back to Mike's."

She looked to Scott and her eyes flashed with fire when he nodded his agreement. She was looking for a fight. Someone would go after Kurt, but it wouldn't accomplish anything just yet. Kurt was going to pay, but first Scott had to make sure that Sydney was out of his reach and safe, although he wasn't even sure what that might entail at this point. She stormed from the corral, shoving the gate open, and headed back to the house.

"I don't want her here when you load up the horse. That's not something she needs to see."

SYDNEY THREW HER case onto the bed, wadding up shirts and throwing them inside. She was sick and tired of being treated like a possession, of everyone making decisions for her. She had just walked into the bathroom and reached for her toothbrush when she heard the slight creak of the bedroom door. Scott entered quietly, almost as if he was waiting for an explosion.

"Sydney?"

She stepped through the doorway and threw the toothbrush in the bag, barely glancing his way. "What? Any more instructions, boss?"

"Stop," Scott said, reaching for her arm, attempting to pull her into his embrace.

"Why?" She jerked her arm from his grasp. "What difference does it make? Valentino is gone, Kurt is still out there somewhere plotting his next revenge, and you are still ordering me around like one of your ranch hands."

Scott ran his fingers through his hair. "I am trying to keep you safe."

"I don't want you to keep me safe." She threw her

jeans into the bag and zipped it up. "I'm not even sure it's possible." She hated the defeat she heard in her voice, but she was tired of running.

"Look, I'm sorry I failed you last night. I should have trusted my gut and moved Valentino." Scott threw up his hands and punched the door.

Sydney was taken aback by his admission. She didn't blame him for Kurt's actions. She simply wanted to be with Scott instead of playing this cat-and-mouse game with a lunatic. She placed a hand on the back of his shoulder. "Scott, there was no way you could have known what Kurt was going to do. I don't think anyone would have guessed that he was this far gone."

Scott turned and faced her, pulling her into his arms and burying his face in her hair. She felt her hair rustle as he breathed a sigh of relief. "He could have killed you last night," she whispered.

"He could have killed either of us." He pulled her close, as if the threat were still near. "Clay is taking you back to the ranch where there will be more people around. More eyes will keep you safer. I'm not going to let anything happen to you."

"And what about you?"

"I'll bring the mares back tonight. It's not me that Kurt is after."

"Fine." One of these days, she was going to have to push Scott for a commitment, but Sydney didn't have the strength to argue with him. Her fight had left her when she saw Valentino's body in the corral. She shrugged and reached for her bag. "Promise me you'll be careful."

Chapter Seventeen

SYDNEY BRUSHED THE mare, trying to ignore the fact that there were four new ranch hands making ridiculous excuses to enter the barn. Scott had brought the mares back after the vet had taken Valentino for an autopsy, promising to notify them of his findings. So far, they hadn't heard anything. The only thing that returning to the ranch had accomplished was that Clay had to hire more hands so that the work was completed while someone stood lookout over Sydney. She felt like a child.

Scott was hard to find. He was usually out in the pasture; he claimed to be checking the cattle. She wasn't sure if he was telling the truth or not, but in the week since Valentino's death, he'd been reserved. While he was staying at Mike's house, he kept his distance from her, almost as if no one knew about their relationship. Every time she tried to talk to him, he gave her simple, one-word answers and was off again. She wasn't sure what she had done to cause the rift between them or if she was imagining it, but when she wasn't grieving over Valentino she was doing her best to settle her sour stomach.

Liz had been smirking continuously, and she continued to flirt shamelessly. While he hadn't encouraged her, Scott hadn't put a stop to it either. Poor Mike was beside himself, pacing the floors, cursing a blue streak in between apologies about Valentino.

Sydney felt bad for Jen and Silvie. They were doing everything that they could to try to help her over her grief about Valentino—everything from spending as much time as possible with her to offering to do her job for her. They must have realized that her work was keeping her busy, even as it reminded her of the stallion at every turn. Derek had tried to come to her aid, but she'd refused to talk with him. After the last conversation, she wasn't sure if it was jealousy or genuine friendship that fueled his actions.

She pulled the comb through Cougar's silken mane, ignoring the mare's stomping back foot. She dropped the comb back into the grooming bucket and reached for the finishing cloth.

The only person who seemed pleased with her return was Liz. She was more than happy to offer her assistance at every turn, but to Sydney it seemed she was intent on aggravating her, pouting when Sydney refused her attempts at friendliness. She didn't trust her, and on top of everything else she couldn't stomach the way she continued to flirt with Scott, even though she knew about their relationship. Or what Sydney had thought was a relationship.

"Ow!" Sydney yelped as the mare twisted her head back and nipped at Sydney's leg. "What is your problem?"

The mare flipped her upper lip back and shook her head, tossing her mane and tangling what Sydney had just brushed. She sighed, the sweet scent of the alfalfa suddenly making her feel nauseous. She finished brushing the mare and put her back into a stall before dropping to sit behind her desk in the barn office. She was so tired, she realized. Not just mentally but physically as well.

"Taking a break?" Sydney jumped and saw Jen leaning against the doorjamb.

"Yeah, I just finished the mares and was going to take the geldings out for some exercise."

"You look tired."

"I was just thinking that." Sydney gave her a sad smile. She wanted to feel optimistic but just couldn't bring herself to force it.

"Have you eaten today?" Jen looked concerned, and Sydney hated that she was causing anyone else to worry needlessly.

"A little this morning, but I was feeling sick to my stomach again." She waved Jen off. "I'll have lunch in a little bit."

Jen entered the office and pulled two cold bottles of water from the refrigerator, passing one to Sydney. "Do you still think this is the flu?" She didn't sound like she was seeking an answer, but she was ready to offer one.

"Maybe. Maybe it's just because of Valentino."

"I think it's time that you face the fact that this could be something else." She sat in the chair facing Sydney. "I don't think this is just a viral infection."

"WE NEED TO talk," Mike called from the front porch as Scott headed toward the barn. He turned and jogged to where Mike waited. "We have an issue."

What now? This week had seemed plagued with problems. Everything had gone wrong, from trucks breaking down to one of the new hands getting kicked by a steer. Scott wondered if bad luck was the only kind he had.

"Another one?"

"Cheyenne is less than two weeks away. Are the travel arrangements set?"

"Crap," Scott muttered. How could he have possibly forgotten that their biggest rodeo was next week? It took them three days to get the stock across state lines and well rested. And what was he going to do about Sydney? Should he take her with him or leave her behind at the ranch? They hadn't found out anything about Kurt, and he wondered how the man could simply disappear from the face of the earth.

"I need you and Clay there."

Scott realized that Mike was worried about Sydney. "I'll take Sydney too."

Mike shook his head. "I don't think that's a good idea. She's still sick."

Scott frowned. He knew he had tried to keep his distance from her since they returned to the ranch, but he hadn't noticed that she'd been ill. Had he been so focused on finding out any bit of information about Kurt's where-abouts that he was ignoring her? Scott opened his mouth to protest, but Mike cut him off.

"Scott, she'll be fine here. Take as many of the guys as you'll need. You'll be there for a week, so don't skimp. The rest of us will take care of Sydney."

"She won't like the idea of being left behind."

"She won't argue with me." Mike chuckled. "I'm still the boss, right?"

"Good, then you break the news." Scott rolled his eyes. He tried to block out the nightmarish images of the stallion, castrated and lifeless. How could he possibly be in two places at once?

Mike placed a hand on his shoulder. "Scott, Kurt would expect Sydney to go with you anyway. She'll be safer here than there."

LIZ PACED THE length of her room. She had to figure out a way to end up in Cheyenne with Scott. Ever since she overheard her father and Scott talking, she knew this was going to be her chance. With Sydney out of the picture for a few weeks, she was sure that she could get Scott to rekindle what they once had, even if it was only to obtain his shares of the ranch. She cornered her father in his office after lunch, while everyone else cleaned the gear they would need before loading it into the stock trailers.

"Daddy, I want to go to Cheyenne." She forced sappy sweetness into her voice. It might be a bit too much, but she would play on her father's distraction.

"What?" He arched a fuzzy brow. "Since when do you want to work the rodeos?"

Liz sighed and made her way around the massive oak desk and hugged her father. "Since the doctor told you to take it easy, you stubborn man." She smiled up at him. "Besides, I heard you and Scott talking. With Sydney staying home, he's going to need some female assistance with the horses."

She didn't like the way her father frowned down at her. Maybe he knew more than she gave him credit for. "Nothing more than that, Daddy. And you know that I can handle those animals as well as anyone on this ranch. I know exactly what needs to be done." *With the rodeo and with Scott.*

Her father stared down at her for a moment and pursed his lips. It wasn't like him to refuse her anything, and she wondered if this was going to be the first time. He sighed and shrugged. "Scott needs the help and the opening will need a woman. Go tell Derek to set up the extra trailer for you. I'll let Scott know."

Liz squealed and threw her arms around her father, hurrying out before he could change his mind. "Thank you, Daddy." She wasn't going to rely on Derek or Kurt to do anything this time. They had both managed to complicate everything. This time, she was going to do this the old-fashioned way: outright manipulation.

SYDNEY AND JEN waved as the trailers pulled out. Scott was leaving for almost two weeks and Liz was going with him, taking her place. They had barely spoken in the days leading up to the crew's exodus. At first she'd been furious that Scott and Mike had made arrangements for Liz to take her place, but when Scott continued to ignore her, barely speaking to her at all unless absolutely necessary, she resigned herself to the fact that it would be easier to work with the horses on the ranch instead of working directly with Scott right now.

She wasn't sure what had changed between them after Valentino had been killed. He'd apologized several times and she'd assured him that she didn't blame him, but she wondered if he didn't blame himself. He'd been withdrawn, avoiding her at all costs. She'd known all along that he would have to come to a crossroads in deciding what sort of relationship they would have. It seemed as if he had decided, and it was breaking her heart.

"Sydney, Scott cares about you." Jen wrapped an arm around Sydney's shoulders and she wondered if her feelings were that transparent or if her friend was just that perceptive. "Things are just a little crazy right now. He needs some time to process everything and sort it out."

Sydney shrugged. She knew that there was nothing she could do about the situation even if she wanted to. Scott would be spending the next two weeks working closely with his ex-fiancée, the woman who had crushed his illusion of love and seemed to be intent on destroying his chances for happiness with anyone else.

"While he's gone, I think you need to go see a doctor."

Sydney waved Jen off. "I told you, it's just from stress."

"Then a quick trip into town to visit the drug store will be no biggie, right?"

"Other than a waste of time," Sydney answered.

"We can make a girls' day of it then and do some shopping. Not that our little town has anything other than a few feed stores." Jen laughed. "But we can have a nice lunch."

It certainly couldn't hurt, Sydney realized. She was late this month, most likely from stress, but there was definitely the possibility that she *could* be pregnant. Scott had never taken any precautions to avoid a pregnancy and she had been too consumed by their passion to even consider protection. The more she thought about a baby, the more she realized it was a probability.

Jen must have seen the change in her demeanor, because she pulled Sydney into an excited hug. "I knew it!"

"We don't know anything yet," she cautioned Jen. She would take the test to confirm what her body and her heart were already assuring her. Her heart thumped heavily in her stomach at the thought of a life growing inside of her.

Jen flipped open her cell phone and dialed a number. "I'd like to set up an appointment this afternoon with Dr. Webster, please."

"You have the doctor on speed dial?" Sydney whispered.

Jen covered the mouthpiece of her phone. "It's a small town, Sydney. Yes, I'm here." She turned back to her conversation. "Okay, two o'clock would be perfect. We'll see you then." Jen pressed a button, disconnecting the call.

"Guess I'll go grab my purse and freshen up a little bit."

LUNCH HAD BEEN forgotten as the two women stared at the stick in Sydney's hand.

"I'm going to be an aunt," Jen whispered, barely containing the excitement in her voice. She surrounded her friend with a bear hug. "I'm so happy for the both of you."

"I'm going to be a mom?" Sydney wished now that she had taken the test privately, or at least waited to return to the ranch. But at Jen's prodding she had taken the test just before her doctor's appointment. Sydney felt guilty that her first reaction wasn't the same pleasure. Her initial thought at seeing the plus symbol on the stick had been fear, followed closely by worry. How was Scott going to react? Would he even care? How was she going to continue working? Her future on the ranch was going to be entirely dependent on Scott's reaction to the news.

"The doctor will be calling us in any time. We should head back into the office," Jen suggested.

Sydney knew she was right and, willing her feet to move, followed Jen into the immaculate pastel blue office. Picking through the various magazines on a table nearby, Sydney wasn't even sure what sort of periodical she'd picked up as she flipped past ads, barely giving any a glance. A baby? What would her parents say? This was the last thing she expected when she agreed to work for Mike. Her relationship with Scott had been a wonderful surprise, but was either of them prepared to deal with a baby? Their baby?

Scott couldn't even admit his feelings for her, let alone commit himself to being a father.

"Sydney Thomas?" The nurse appeared at the door, looking at the chart in her hand. "Good afternoon," she greeted Sydney and Jen as they approached. "Just follow me."

Both women stepped into a narrow hallway, moving aside as another nurse brushed past, excusing herself. "We'll just head to the scale over there." The nurse pointed at the scale ahead.

After registering her weight and height, the nurse led Sydney into an examination room. "So what brings you in today?"

"Well," Sydney began, then chewed at her lower lip. "I'm not sure, but I think, that is, I might be . . ."

"She's pregnant!" Jen poked at Sydney's leg. "Show her the test. We just took it," she informed the nurse.

The nurse chuckled at Jen's enthusiasm. "Jennifer, let her talk."

Sydney rolled her eyes. She should have known that Jen would be friends with everyone in town. She didn't want Scott to find out through the rumor mill. She had to be the one to tell him.

"Oh, Hailey, I'm about to be an aunt. Don't rain on my parade." Jen waved her friend off. "Hailey and I went to high school together," Jen explained.

"The doctor will be in shortly," Hailey informed them as she slipped the chart into the rack on the door. "Congratulations!"

"Thanks," Sydney mumbled.

As soon as the nurse shut the door, Jen spun on Sydney. "What's wrong? You don't seem happy about this."

"Jen, I have to tell Scott. No one else can know about this until I tell him," she explained. "I should have gone further from town to see a doctor. I don't want the small-town gossip to get back to him."

"Hailey won't say anything, and neither will Dr. Webster," Jen assured her. "You don't think he'll be happy."

Sydney didn't miss that Jen had made a statement rather than asking a question. She shrugged. "I don't know. He doesn't seem inclined to commit to any sort of lasting relationship. I'm not sure how a baby would even fit into the picture."

"Then we'll need to make a trip to Cheyenne."

"We don't even know for sure yet," Sydney pointed out.

"Really?" Jen cocked her head and arched a brow at Sydney. "Are you going to try to tell me you don't think you're pregnant? Then why are you so worried about what Scott will say?"

"Okay." Sydney closed her eyes and rubbed her temples. She could feel a migraine coming on. "We will get the results from the doctor. If it turns out positive, then I'll drive to Cheyenne. I might be able to catch up to them."

"Wrong," Jen argued. "*We* will drive to Cheyenne."

TWO HOURS LATER, with a doctor's confirmation of her pregnancy and a suitcase in hand, Sydney was sitting in the driver's seat with her destination programmed into the GPS device in Jen's Jeep. She wasn't sure how Jen had convinced Mike to let the two of them leave without telling him about the pregnancy, but somehow Jen had persuaded him that it would be in everyone's best interest if they went. But that hadn't stopped Mike from grumbling that two women shouldn't be driving alone.

The drive was going to be intense for them, but Jen insisted that they only stop long enough eat and to sleep in a real bed. After the second day of taking shifts, Jen taking longer ones and insisting that Sydney nap, they stopped at a truck-stop diner near the Wyoming border. The waitress, a gum-smacking, coffee-drinking smoker named Florence, informed them that the stock trailers had just been through during her last shift twelve hours earlier. With the realization that they would meet up with the crew at the rodeo grounds by midday, both women decided to find a room for the night.

The trip was taking a toll on Sydney. She was sore, and sitting so long in the car was making her crabby. Her apprehension was causing her to have nightmares about the baby, which in turn fed her natural fears about being a mother. As she woke with the sunrise and poured herself a cup of the bitter decaf the motel provided gratis, she fretted about seeing Scott.

Today would decide their future. She slid a hand over her still-flat abdomen and wondered if the baby would look like Scott or if it would have her golden eyes. Would they have a little cowboy or a future rodeo queen? Sydney closed her eyes and tried to lose herself in fantasy, trying to visualize them as a happy family, but the image just wouldn't come. That worried her more than anything else.

She woke Jen and waited while she showered and had a cup of the brew. "Ugh, we need something better than this. Let's get breakfast, then we'll head out. We should be there by dark tonight."

Jen was driving when they finally arrived at the rodeo grounds. The GPS had given them the wrong directions, so they had pull over and search for the correct address. It was nearly midnight before they finally pulled up to the back gate. The stock was quietly milling in pens near the trailers as they pulled behind the arena. Only a few of the crew remained awake, sipping on their beers and comparing stories of rodeos past, trying to outdo one another.

"Hey Pablo," Jen greeted as they parked the jeep. "Where are Clay and Scott?"

Pablo pointed to the right. "Over there is Scott." He gave Sydney a meaningful smile. "And Clay's trailer is behind his."

"Thanks Pablo."

Jen climbed back into the Jeep and parked it beside Scott's trailer. Sydney reached for her overnight bag on the floor. Her heart thudded heavily in her chest, her stomach roiled, and she fought to keep down the last latte she'd had to stay awake after dinner.

Jen reached for her arm. "Surprise him tonight, but wait to tell him about . . ." She looked around them in case someone might overhear. "You know, tomorrow."

She slipped the keys to the Jeep into Sydney's hand and grabbed her own bag from the back of the vehicle. "I'm going to go see my husband." Jen smiled broadly and slipped into the darkness behind Scott's trailer.

Sydney forced herself to open the door to the trailer and climb the stairs. She laid her bag on the couch before heading to where Scott's quiet snores told her he slept soundly. As she reached the bed, a dread suddenly overwhelmed her. She stared in disbelief at the blonde head nestled on Scott's naked chest. His arms encircled the bare shoulders of Liz Findley, and he sighed deeply as she curled closer to the heat of his body under the sheet.

Sydney's heart stopped mid-beat and shattered. Had the time they shared been nothing but lies? Even after she'd told him about Kurt's betrayal, comforting her as her nightmare released its hold, it had all been nothing more than a ruse, a ploy to have his way. How stupid could she have been to believe his story about Liz breaking his heart? Had he been wishing she were Liz the entire time? Had they been just waiting for a chance to rendezvous?

She closed her eyes tightly, willing away the image of them in a passionate embrace. They hadn't wasted any time rekindling their romance once they left the ranch. Was this the reason he'd been so distant? Sydney ran from the trailer. She had to get as far away from Scott as she could. Without thinking, she hurried to the Jeep, fished the keys from her pocket, and revved the engine, spraying dirt as she raced through the back gate of the arena. She wasn't sure where she was headed, but she certainly couldn't stay in Cheyenne.

Chapter Eighteen

THE SLAMMING DOOR jolted Scott from a sound sleep. Still groggy, he wondered at the sound of a speeding vehicle but ignored it when he realized that he held a woman in his arms. He pulled her closer.

Ah, Sydney, you came after all.

Now it wouldn't matter that Liz had been trying every trick in the book to get him into bed with her. She'd been relentless in her pursuit the past two days, and he'd never felt so relieved to arrive at a destination and be busy meeting with clients so that he could ignore her advances. He looked down at the woman he'd grown to care so much about.

The shock of light hair, glinting in the moonlight through the open window, caused him to bolt upright. "What the hell?"

Liz stretched her thin frame against him seductively. "What's the matter, honey?"

Scott pushed her from his chest and jumped out of the bed, just missing creating a nasty bump on his head. She smiled at him. "You might want to put some clothes on."

Scott glanced down at his sweats and saw that his body was still in a state of full arousal at the thought of holding Sydney. Scott ran a hand through his disheveled hair as Liz sat up, wrapping the sheet around her bare breasts.

"Aren't you going to come back to bed?" She brushed her hair back from her face.

Scott struggled to remember how she had ended up in his bed. The last thing he remembered was having a few beers with the guys by the fire pit. He'd been tired, so he headed inside. He stared at the woman in his bed. "Get out," he ordered.

"But, honey, you told me . . ." Scott saw the tears welling in her eyes and wasn't sure if they were real or a product of her manipulation.

Scott shook his head. "What the hell is going on? How did you get in here?"

Liz climbed off of the bed, pulling the sheet with her and pouting. "Fine!" She reached for her shirt and pulled it over her arms, barely fastening a few well-placed buttons. "I see you just wanted to play games with me. Well, I guess this makes us even then, doesn't it?" She pulled her jeans over her long legs.

Scott strode over to where she stood, glaring at him. She flinched as he came closer. He had never struck a woman, but he'd never felt closer to losing control than he did right now. There was no way he would have ever allowed Liz Findley into his bed. Would he?

"I'm not sure what it is you're trying to accomplish, but I want you off the ranch for good. You'll leave this rodeo, say goodbye to your father, and you can disappear like you did before."

"I'm not going anywhere, Scott. Not until I get what I came for." She met his gaze, her eyes gleaming. There were no tears in her eyes now. She appeared calm, but her eyes flashed with hatred as she sauntered toward the kitchenette of the trailer. "Have a seat, and we can talk business."

Scott stood immobile and was sure his contempt was clear. She arched a brow at him. "Suit yourself." She curled her frame onto the couch and crossed her slender legs. "I'll leave when you sign over your shares of the company."

"What?" Scott stared at her in shock. *All of this was to get him to sign over his shares? Did she realize what she was asking?* It would be a betrayal to his brother and sister, not to mention the legacy their parents had left behind. "Why?"

"So I can sell the company." She flipped her hair back over her shoulder. "You want me gone, that's my price. I'll go and leave you and the little mouse alone." She played with the handles of an overnight bag beside her.

"Why sell it? Why not just sell me your father's shares? Then the company can still continue."

She shot him a baleful glare. "Because Daddy would never willingly let this company go. He'll never do it himself, so I will."

Scott crossed his arms over his chest and smiled astutely. "That's why you came back. You thought that if you could get me to hook up with you again, you could convince me to give up my share. But with Sydney . . ."

He wouldn't talk about what they shared with the woman before him. He couldn't believe that he'd once thought himself in love with her. She was a despicable excuse for a human, willing to use anyone to get her way.

His laughter reverberated in the trailer, and Liz glared at him. "You're too late," Scott informed her.

"What are you talking about?" She was trying to control her temper, but he could see the indecision in her eyes. She wasn't as certain as she had been moments ago.

"You should have discussed this plan of yours with Mike. He already sold me his shares."

"What?" Her breath caught as she gasped. "No, he . . . the stroke . . . he said . . ."

"I was in the hospital with him when he had the stroke. I was the next of kin they called." He leaned down and narrowed his eyes. "Where were you?"

The sound of her hand connecting with the flesh of his cheek only served to assure him that his barb had hit its mark. "You bastard," Liz hissed.

"I think it's time you go, Liz. There's nothing left here for you. And as the majority owner, I can order you from my property."

Liz rose and headed for the door. "This isn't over yet."

"Don't forget your bag." He held the overnight case out to her.

Liz's emerald eyes gleamed viciously. "Oh, that's not

mine. I believe that bag is Sydney's. You must have been sleeping when she rushed out of here after seeing you and I locked in a tender lover's embrace. Naked. In your bed." She smiled at him before trying to appear innocent. "Oh my, I wonder what she will think?"

Scott clenched his fists at his sides as she opened the door. "I want you packed and off the ranch when I get back."

Liz shrugged as she made her way down the stairs. "Maybe. Or maybe I will stick around and see what new excitement ensues . . . attempts on her life, horses slaughtered. Trouble seems to follow her."

SYDNEY DIDN'T CRY. She didn't have the luxury of time any more. Her naiveté might have cost her her pride and her heart, but time was no longer a commodity that she could waste. Her pregnancy was six weeks along and she only had another two months or so before she would start showing. She couldn't risk Scott finding out about the baby until she was ready to tell him.

"Sydney?" Silvie's voice sounded from the hall as she knocked softly on the bedroom door. "Do you want to come have some lunch? You need to eat."

Silvie was right, and she could only imagine what the housekeeper and Mike had been thinking when she returned alone, only days after leaving for Cheyenne. But she couldn't bring herself to face them yet. She was going to have to tell Mike something, since she was planning on quitting and going home. She wasn't sure how her parents were going to react, but it was a temporary solution, at least until she could figure out something else.

"Just give me a few minutes, okay, Silvie?"

"No problem, sweetie. Just let me know when you're hungry and I'll fix you something." Sydney heard her steps as she clumped down the hallway toward the kitchen.

She sat at the end of the bed and collapsed backward, the mattress cushioning her. How was she going to break the news to Mike? She didn't want to tell him what she'd seen in Cheyenne, or how wrong she'd been about Scott. She'd thought that Scott cared for her, that there might be some sort of future for them. Now the only future she saw was that of a brokenhearted single mother. The man who had seemed like her knight in shining armor had, in reality, been a tarnished and broken imitation. Her heart couldn't take seeing him again, especially when he returned with Liz. She had to tell Mike she was going home.

Sydney rose from the bed and searched the house for her boss. When she couldn't find him, Silvie suggested she try the barn. True to his cowboy roots, he was in the barn office, reviewing the records for the bulls and making notes. Butterflies swirled in the pit of her stomach at the thought of what she was about to do.

Scott will be home with Liz in less than a week. You can't stay and see them together.

"Mike, I need to talk with you."

"Sydney, come on in." Mike smiled warmly. "Have a seat." He gestured to one of the chairs beside the window that overlooked the corral. "What's on your mind?"

Sydney opened her mouth to speak but was cut off as Mike continued to chat. "It's good to see you up and around. I know you haven't been feeling well."

His small talk was doing little to calm her nerves. She spit out the words in a rush. "I need to give you my notice. I have to quit."

"Quit?" Mike stumbled over the word before catching his voice. "I know what happened to Valentino was hard on you, but you don't have to quit. It will get easier over time."

Sydney felt the tears prick her eyes at the mention of her horse. "That's not it." She shook her head, unsure of what excuse to actually give him. "I can't work here anymore."

Mike reached between them and took her hand. The calluses on his palm scratched her hand, but his touch was comforting all the same. "I don't understand. I thought you were happy working for me . . . and Scott." Realization dawned on him. "It's Scott."

Sydney bowed her head, not wanting him to see the tears that welled for the love that was now lost. "Did something happen? Is that why you came back so quickly?"

She couldn't tell him what she'd seen. Liz was his daughter and Scott was like a son to him. Of course he'd be elated at their reunion. She was nothing more than a new face caught in an old love. Sydney shrugged her shoulders. "I just can't stay," she whispered. She prayed that he wouldn't press her further for information.

"Sydney, is this about more than just you and Scott?"

Her eyes shot to his face. Could he have guessed her

condition? She could understand Jen guessing, but had it really been obvious to everyone else?

"Silvie has her suspicions. She thinks you're pregnant."

Of course. Silvie. Sydney dropped her gaze, unable to confirm or deny his hunch.

Mike leaped from his chair and pulled Sydney into a bear hug, squeezing her. "That's great news! What did Scott say?"

"Scott doesn't know . . . he can't know. Not yet."

Mike's arms fell from around her. "What do you mean he doesn't know? You haven't told him?"

"I just found out for certain. But he's not in love with me. There is someone else." Her voice broke and Mike sat her back in the chair, reaching for her hand again.

"You love him, don't you?" Mike asked, sympathetically.

"Yeah," she whispered before clearing her throat. "But that won't do me much good now."

"Come with me for a sec." He pulled her out toward the aisle of the barn. The horses whinnied their greeting. "Do you see these horses? These horses, these wonderful animals, are a product of you."

"What are you talking about?"

"If it hadn't been for what you brought to these animals, none of them would be what they are right now. You have a gift. Anyone can break a horse, but only a special trainer can tame one without breaking its spirit." Mike put his hands on her shoulders and forced her to meet his gaze. "You can gentle anything without breaking its spirit. Anything." He gave her a pointed look.

He meant Scott. But she didn't want to tame him, she simply wanted his love in return for her own. That wasn't something she could control.

"You can't really want to leave this behind?" Mike laughed. "If I have to, I'll sue you for breach of contract," he teased, his eyes glinting mischievously.

She gave him a weak laugh as she looked at the horses she had trained, a few in foal to Valentino. "No," she admitted. "I don't want to leave. I *have* to leave. I just can't stay."

"Sydney, you can't keep the baby a secret from Scott. He has a right to know."

"I'll tell him, eventually." Mike gave her a sardonic glare and pursed his lips. "I will, but I can't just yet. It's still too early."

"I'll keep quiet, but on one condition."

"Mike—" she began.

He held up a hand to halt any conversation. "Nope, it's this, or I tell him. You stay here." She opened her mouth to protest, but he pressed on. "I'll make sure that you are gone when he's around. We have enough rodeos in the next few months to keep you both gone. Just let me know when you're ready to tell him, and I'll schedule you guys some time to be together."

Sydney sighed. It would solve her predicament for the next few weeks at least. She wouldn't have to see Scott with Liz, and it would buy her time to figure out a way to tell Scott without running away. She didn't want to keep him from his child, but she didn't want him to feel trapped by her either.

"You'll keep this to yourself?" She hated asking Mike to deceive Scott, but she couldn't risk him finding out until she was ready to talk with him about what he wanted.

"I promise, Sydney."

"SCOTT, YOU HAVE to go after her." Jen was frantic. He'd never seen his sister act like this. She was always animated, but this was even beyond her usual animation. She pushed against his chest. "Get in that truck and go find her."

"Damn it, Jen, you know as well as I do that she wouldn't believe a word I say right now." He ran his fingers through his hair before settling the baseball cap again.

"Then *make* her believe you, you stubborn idiot!" Jen cried.

Scott was torn. He wanted to find Sydney and explain what she had seen. But he still wasn't even sure what the truth was. He *had* been in bed, nearly naked, with Liz. How she had gotten there, he still couldn't prove, but from the pounding headache the next day, he assumed she'd slipped something into one of his beers.

If I ever see Liz Findley again, I'll kill her.

"Even if I could explain why she found me in bed with another woman, do you really think she'd ever trust me?"

"Look, Scott," Clay began. "You know that Jen and I can handle things here. Go find Sydney, tell her that you love her. Fix this."

Scott eyed Clay. How could he admit to them that he wasn't sure that he loved her? That he didn't even believe in love?

"Scott, it's in your eyes every time that her name is mentioned. Go tell her already."

"Look, I'm a big boy. I don't need you to 'mother' me right now. I will handle this my way, in my time. Back off." Scott stormed off, leaving his sister and brother-in-law to wonder what would happen next.

SCOTT RETURNED HOME after meeting with the rodeo production company and settling the accounts to find Mike waiting for him on the porch. "How'd it go?"

"Where's Sydney?"

"That's a fine 'howdy-do.'"

It had been nearly ten days since she'd driven away from Cheyenne. That was far too much time to have let her speculate about what had really happened between him and Liz. He should have called her, but he didn't want their conversation to get out of hand over the phone. He needed to see her face, hold her in his arms, when he finally told her how he felt.

"I don't have time for this, Mike. I need to talk with her."

"I know you do." Mike shook his head. "Jen told me what happened between you and Liz." Mike sighed. "I'm sorry, Scott. I had no idea of what she had planned. Had I known . . ." Mike's words trailed off.

"I know, Mike." He didn't want to talk about Liz. "Tell

me where she is so that I can talk with her and try to clear this mess up."

"Can't do that." Mike pulled out a cigarette. "You know the doc says I'm not supposed to have these."

Scott was growing impatient. Mike was wasting precious time, time he needed to explain, time he could be holding her. "What do you mean?"

"Because of the stroke." Mike was deliberately avoiding Scott's question.

"What do you mean, you can't tell me where she is?" Scott clarified, quickly losing his patience with his friend.

"I made her a promise, Scott," Mike said matter-of-factly. "She was going to quit, leave and head for who-knows-where. I promised her that if she would keep working here, I'd make sure she wouldn't have to see you until she informed me she was ready. She's at a rodeo."

"With everything that has happened, and Kurt still running around looking for her, you let her go?" Scott threw his hands into the air. "Are you nuts?"

"Have you told her that you love her?"

"What? What is it with you and Jen butting into my love life?" Scott turned away guiltily.

"I didn't think so," Mike called after him. "Maybe if you had, if you would have put your stubborn pride aside for fifteen minutes, she would have seen through Liz's scam."

He spun on Mike and unleashed his fury, his hands slashing through the air. "Enough. When is she getting back?"

"Not until after you're on the road this week for Texas."

"I'll be gone for three weeks."

"Exactly." Mike turned on his heel and walked into the house, leaving Scott staring after him, feeling betrayed. Mike looked back at him as he reached the front door. "Scott, I'm sorry, but I made her a promise." He shook his head. "You should have told her."

Chapter Nineteen

SYDNEY TRIED TO put Scott out of her mind as she circled the arena with the sponsor flag. Jake held open the gate for her as she exited the arena, allowing the pick-up men to slip in before the next event. So far, everything for the small rodeo had gone off without a hitch. Derek had taken control, and she was surprised to see how well he ran the event. She appreciated his attention to detail, except when he turned that attention her way. So far she'd been able to deflect any questions, but Derek was persistent. No matter how often she tried to change the subject, he managed to turn the conversation back to Scott.

When he cornered her at the trailer as she loosened the gelding's cinch, she spun on him.

"Fine, Derek. It's over. Is that what you want to hear?"

"Yes." His honesty surprised her. After the last private conversation she'd had with him, she'd managed to avoid any personal discussions. She knew he didn't like the idea of a relationship between her and Scott, but his blunt reply stung.

"Thanks for your sympathy." She hoped he could hear the pained sarcasm. "I don't need an 'I told you so' right now."

"Are you all right?" His voice softened, reminiscent of their earlier friendship. She didn't trust her voice, so she nodded. "Do you want to talk about it?"

"Not right now."

"How about over dinner? We can finish the new opening for tomorrow, and if you want we'll talk then." He wiggled his brows at her. "I promise I won't seduce you."

She couldn't help but smile at his impish charm. He was so different from his brother. "Fine." She pointed a finger at his nose. "But no funny business. Got it?"

He snapped a salute to her. "Yep, nothing but boring business."

DEREK KNEW EXACTLY what had happened between Sydney and Scott. When she returned from Cheyenne, Liz had informed him that her plan had gone awry. She'd even informed him of her intentions to take over the ranch in hopes that he would give her his share. He felt like a fool for ever helping her. He certainly wanted Sydney for himself, but not at the expense of his brother and sister. And if Scott was the person who made Sydney happy, he cared for her enough to seek her happiness over his own desire. He had been a spoiled screwup long enough. It was time to grow up and take some responsibility, even if that meant giving up his jealousy of his brother.

He glanced over at Sydney, glad they had opted for a dinner at a local restaurant rather than the rodeo BBQ and dance. They would be able to get the opening ceremony details finalized, and then they could have a private conversation without the rest of the crew around to overhear. He opened her door when they arrived. He appreciated the long expanse of curved thigh as he helped her from the truck, reminding himself that she loved his brother.

It didn't help that she was incredibly beautiful with her curls framing her face. He pulled out her chair as the waiter led them to a table and ordered for both of them. He couldn't help but wonder what it would have been like if this had been a real date.

"Is everything okay?" Sydney had barely picked at the food on her plate.

She gave him a sad smile. "Besides Scott?" She shrugged. "Sure, why wouldn't it be?"

He shook his head and narrowed his eyes. "I don't know. You seem more distant lately . . . like you're off in your own world."

"Do I?" she muttered, laying the fork down and curling her hands in her lap.

"Are you sure you're not still sick?"

She shook her head. "I'm fine. You haven't asked about what happened with Scott yet tonight?"

Derek shrugged. "I figured you'd talk about it when you were ready."

"You were right."

"About Scott." He wasn't asking.

"You told me exactly what would happen and I didn't listen to you. I should have."

"Sydney, about what I said. There's a lot between me and Scott you don't understand. Jealousy, I guess." He folded his hands on the table, staring down at them. "Scott has always gotten whatever he wants. Things just always seem to go his way. When I first saw you, I knew he wasn't right for you. I think you realize by now that I want more than just a friendship with you." He glanced up at her nervously, then back to his hands before he hurried on. "I know you don't feel the same way, but I would take care of you. I would never hurt you."

Her eyes misted. Derek couldn't believe he was revealing his feelings to her, but he didn't want to lose the one opportunity that had presented itself. If he didn't take this chance to tell her, he never would.

"I know, Derek." She reached across the table and took his hand. "I care about you, I really do, but I'm in love with someone else."

His heart fell like a stone to his stomach. "Have you told him?"

She nodded. "I guess it wasn't enough."

Guilt assailed him. Should he tell her that Scott had ordered Liz from the ranch? If he did, she'd find out that they had been working together to destroy her relationship with Scott. She would hate him if she found out, but could he live with the lie?

"Sydney, Liz set out to ruin anything you and Scott had from the start."

"I know that." She sat back in her chair. "It looks like she succeeded."

Derek took a deep breath, pressing on before his bravado failed him. "What you don't know is that I was helping her." The look of horror on Sydney's face was almost his undoing. "At least, at first. Sydney, I'm sorry." He reached for her hand but she jerked it from his grasp, her eyes flashing fire across the table.

"You what? Why?"

"I told you, when I first saw you . . . I couldn't stand for Scott to have you. He doesn't deserve you, and I guess I thought I did. I knew she wanted to break you guys up, but I didn't know why, at least not then."

"And Kurt? What did you have to do with that?"

"Nothing, I swear!" Derek threw his hands in the air. "All I knew was that she wanted him to help her make Scott jealous, like before." Derek ran his fingers through his hair, hating himself for what he had done. "She wanted to play on Scott's feelings for her, so he would give up his shares of the ranch. You were in her way. When you went to Cheyenne, you played right into her plan."

A tear slid down Sydney's cheek, and Derek could barely keep himself from wiping it away. "Looks like Scott did too."

Derek sighed. He might as well get it all out in the open now. His part in Liz's schemes had cost him any chance with Sydney, but he couldn't stand to see her unhappy, even if that meant losing to his brother again. "No, he didn't. Nothing happened between them. Liz drugged him and was going to try to trap him the next morning. You just made it easier for her."

"None of it matters anymore." She sounded defeated, a tone he would never have imagined he would hear from her. "It's more complicated than Liz."

SCOTT WAS ALREADY gone when Sydney returned from the rodeo. She wanted to see him. After her dinner with Derek, it had been a sleepless night. She had to make some decisions, but she couldn't do that without knowing how Scott felt about her and their child. She'd had short, stilted conversations with her family, not wanting to give anything away, and the secrecy was wearing on her.

Not to mention the way Jen and Mike seemed to hover over her every waking moment, trying to force her to work behind the desk instead of with the animals. She sighed and closed the record book, tossing it into the filing cabinet and rising from behind the desk in the barn office to look out the window at the mares in the corral. She was tired of allowing everyone to dictate her decisions. She'd been hired for a job and, pregnant or not, she was going to do it.

Cougar whinnied and trotted toward the fence as Sydney approached. "Hey, mama. I certainly didn't think we'd be doing this pregnancy thing together." The horse snorted and tossed her head, shaking her copper mane. "What do you say we head out for a little ride?"

Sydney reached for a halter hanging on the fence post, and after slipping it over Cougar's head, led her into the barn. She groomed the mare and saddled her, her stomach doing a flip of excitement at the small taste of rebellion. She felt as if she'd been under someone's watchful eye since she'd arrived. If it hadn't been Scott's scrutiny, then it had been the danger presented by Kurt, and now her pregnancy had Mike and Jen watching over her as if she were made of glass.

The mare grunted as she pulled the cinch tight. "Sorry, mama. Guess I'm just frustrated." She dropped it back a bit. "Today we are going to do our own thing." She patted the horse's belly. "And you need the exercise."

She led the horse to the pasture gate, locking it behind her and hopping into the saddle. As she allowed the mare to break into a jog, she relished her freedom. It had been almost a month since Kurt had disappeared, but the rodeo standings had him listed as winning the bull-riding event at a rodeo in Oklahoma, which was far enough away from California that she felt she could relax a little. Mike had already notified the authorities, but they all knew cowboys were constantly on the move, so his warrant was pointless unless he was pulled over at some point.

Just the thought of Kurt brought back the pain of losing Valentino. He was a one-in-a-million horse. Not just because she had poured her heart and soul into him for six years after watching his birth, but also because of his raw potential to be an all-around rodeo champion. Her one consolation was the thought of seeing his offspring born over the next year.

If I'm here that long.

Scott was due to return any day, and she knew the time had come that she had to tell him about the baby. She wasn't showing yet, but she was starting to notice the changes in her body. Her breasts had grown and her jeans were getting tighter across the hips. She didn't think he'd notice, but—as Jen constantly pointed out—Scott had a right to know. This was his baby, too, and even if he didn't want to commit to her, family meant everything to him. He would want to take care of his child.

Sydney glanced around, surprised at how far she and Cougar had ridden. She had just crested the hills over-looking Scott's cabin. Memories, both good and bad, teased at the corners of her mind. She forced herself to look away from the corral toward the cabin. It was closed up tightly since Scott had been on the road for almost a month, but it still invited her, tempting her with images of Scott cooking dinner and telling her about his childhood. The memories of making love to him, of lying in his arms.

She rode toward the barn, slipping the tack from Cougar's back and turning her into one of the stalls before giving her some grain and checking to make sure the automatic water supply was on. Beside the tack room she caught sight of Valentino's saddle and bridle, and tears burned the back of her eyes.

This isn't fair. To lose Valentino and Scott?

She wanted to throw something, to release her fury at the injustice of the situation, but she knew that nothing was going to cure her grief for either. She had lost Valentino in an act of violent brutality, and she had lost Scott due to Liz's emotional brutality. She found herself walking along the path beside the house as her hand slid across her lower abdomen. She may have lost Scott, but she would always have a part of the love she felt for him. Sydney feared that telling him was going to break her heart again. She wasn't sure what she expected his reaction to be, but she knew that unless some sort of miracle happened, it wasn't going to end well for her heart.

She glanced up at the gurgling water falling from the makeshift waterfall. It showed signs of needing attention—leaves had fallen to the bottom along with some dirt—but it only served to make it fit the surroundings even more. She stared at the ripples that formed as a single leaf fell from a tree above, twirling like a dancer as it hit the surface. The memory of their playfulness haunted her, making her wish she had tried harder to reach into the depths of his soul, to find the vulnerability in him that would allow him to love her in return. What had she been lacking? How could she have been so wrong about what she thought she had read in his dark, smoldering gaze as they made love?

She had heard Scott's side of the story from several sources she trusted, and she believed them. Liz was manipulative, but even that didn't explain why he hadn't sought her out to explain himself. Or why he had yet to confess any sort of feelings for her.

But Scott was so closed off to the idea of love that, even if he wanted to love her, she knew he wouldn't risk his heart again. And if she couldn't have his whole heart, if their child couldn't have his entire heart, what hope was there? She needed to know he was as invested as she was before she could tell him about the baby. Anything less and he'd feel like she was trapping him, just as Liz tried to do. She hadn't wanted the baby to sway his feelings for her—or his lack of them. Hopelessness encircled her heart, squeezing painfully. She had to stop this.

Sydney heard footsteps behind her. Her heart skipped a beat and her body filled with heat. She probably should have been afraid, but it was as if she had conjured him by her thoughts alone. She wasn't entirely sure he wasn't just a figment of her imagination. She was afraid to speak, that it might cause him to disappear.

"I thought I might find you here."

Sydney could barely catch her breath. She hadn't seen him for a month, other than sleeping in Liz's arms. He looked tired, lines creasing the corners of his eyes and several days' beard growth along his jaw. But he had never looked more tempting to her. Her fingers itched to touch his face, her lips to kiss him. Her heart raced in her chest and she tried to breathe normally.

"Sydney, we need to talk." She wanted to answer him, but she couldn't trust her voice. Tears misted her eyes and her hand covered her stomach. "Okay," he continued. "Then I'll talk."

Scott covered the ground separating them. He met her gaze, his eyes black as the midnight sky and unreadable. "What you saw that night was a scheme Liz concocted. She was trying to drive us apart so that she could somehow get her hands on the ranch." He laughed bitterly and ran a hand through his mussed hair. "Like that was ever going to happen."

Sydney swallowed the lump in her throat and wanted to cry out to him that she didn't care about Liz, or Kurt, that she simply wanted to hear him say that he loved her. Instead she remained silent. Even the birds in the pines had quieted as if holding their breath to hear what Scott had to say next.

"I didn't make love to her. I don't love Liz. I guess I never really did."

Please, Scott. Tell me how you feel about me.

"Please say something, Sydney."

She stared down at the water, wishing her thoughts could pour out like the water on the rocks. He wasn't going to say it. Nothing had changed. His emotions were still as hidden and shut off as they ever had been.

"Look at me, princess."

Slowly, Sydney turned to face him. He cupped her face and ran his thumb against her cheek. He brushed a curl back from her temple. "I can't stand this wall that's between us. I want things to be the way they were."

He pressed a kiss to her forehead and she inhaled the scent of him. She wanted to melt into his arms, to give in to the poor imitation of love he was offering. She pressed against his chest, feeling more confident as she did.

"And how is that, Scott?" She took another step away from him, turning to look at the water again. "I follow you from rodeo to rodeo, warming your bed when you see fit."

"I have never felt like this with anyone before."

She spun on him, fire burning within her. "Tell me, Scott. What *do* you feel?"

Scott stepped back from her. "You know how I feel."

She could almost feel him retreating behind the protective barrier he'd build around his heart. "No, I don't. Your feelings are something you've kept hidden very well. I have given you everything I have: my body, my soul, and my heart. But I have to retain some dignity." Sydney brushed past him, heading toward the barn.

Scott caught up to her and reached for her arm, spinning her to face him. "I can't promise you something I don't have to give. I care about you more than I've ever cared about anyone, but I won't lie to you and profess an undying love that I don't believe in."

Sydney sighed and led Cougar out of the stall. "Just what I've always wanted to hear . . . 'I care about you.' Is that something along the lines of 'like-liking' me, Scott?" She couldn't help the sarcastic tone. How could he possibly expect her to stay?

"I believed in love when I was a kid, and in return I got a slap in the face. Love is a fantasy, something to dream about when you feel like life is throwing you a curveball. There is no such thing."

Sydney pulled on the cinch and slipped the bridle over the mare's head. "Then I guess we have nothing else to talk about." She mounted the mare, her heart shattering, the pieces coming to rest where another heart beat within her. She couldn't tell him about the baby right now, not like this. But she would tell him before she left.

"Sydney."

"Goodbye, Scott." She looked down at him and a tear

slipped down her cheek. "I love you, whether you believe in it or not."

SCOTT WATCHED AS Sydney kicked the mare into a gallop and rode away. He wanted to follow her, to make her see that he couldn't lose her, but his pride held him fast. He had given her all he could. He had searched her out, tried to explain, but she had chosen to walk out of his life. Scott looked at Noble tied to the side of the horse trailer and led him into the barn, tossing him alfalfa before grabbing his clothes from the truck.

He'd barely arrived home when he'd received a call from Mike that they couldn't find Sydney. He wasn't sure why he'd thought to look down the path; perhaps it was wishful thinking. But he hated that he was the one causing her pain. He tossed his bag onto the couch and headed for the cool beer he knew was waiting in the refrigerator, momentarily craving something stronger. He twisted off the bottle cap and tossed it into the sink, watching it slip down the drain.

"Just like everything else," he muttered, reaching into the disposal to retrieve the metal.

How was he going to work with her on a daily basis? How was he going to spend weeks on end with her, watching her working with the rest of the crew, watching rodeo contestants flirting with her? He tipped back the beer and drained the bottle. This was why he hadn't wanted Mike to hire her in the first place, he reminded himself as he reached for another. He took the beer with him, downing half of it as he turned on the shower, searching for a towel.

Tonight I am going to get rip-roaring drunk and not think about her.

Scott knew he was lying to himself but hoped the alcohol could induce amnesia, if only for one night. He polished off the second beer and stepped into the shower, the hot spray coursing over his head and shoulders. He had no idea how long he stood there, trying to let the water wash away the last few months, when he heard his cell phone ring.

He sighed and shut off the water, reaching for the towel and wrapping it around his hips. He reached the phone just as it went to voicemail. He pushed the button to redial his sister when it rang again in his hand.

"Yeah." He didn't feel like talking to anyone. The whiskey bottle in the cupboard was calling his name. Only liquor could dull the memories of Sydney's body against his better than the beer or hot water had.

"Why is Sydney packing?"

"Ask her, Jen." He pulled the phone from his ear, prepared to hang up.

"Don't you dare hang up on me, Scott," she warned.

"Look, I tried to get her to stay." He pushed the button to transfer her to the speaker on the phone while he dressed in loose jeans.

Down the hall, someone pounded on his front door.

"What the hell?" He carried the phone into the living room with him and saw his brother through the glass in the door. "I explained what happened and she left me."

Scott rolled his eyes and opened the door. "What do you want?"

"What did you say to Sydney?"

"Why don't the two of you just butt out and let me deal with this?"

"Jen?" Derek asked, jerking his chin at the phone. Scott nodded. "Jen, I've got this."

"Right." Jen's sarcasm transferred through the phone. "The same way you always do. I don't think a fist fight will help anyone right now."

"Does it matter that I don't feel like fighting with either of you?"

"I'm not here to fight at all," Derek said. "I came to talk some sense into you. Sydney loves you. Do you have any idea what you're walking away from?"

Scott narrowed his eyes at his brother. "Yes, I do. And I didn't do the walking away. She did."

"Did you tell her?" Derek noticed that Jen had grown quiet on the phone but hadn't left the conversation.

"Tell her what?"

"Don't play dumb, Scott," Jen piped in. "You have never told her that you love her, have you?"

"She knows."

Derek shoved Scott backwards, knocking him off guard, and he hit the kitchen counter. "She doesn't know, you idiot. If she did, she wouldn't be packing to leave now."

Scott glared at his brother and reached into the cabinet, pulling out a bottle of whiskey and a glass. He didn't care that the liquor was hot; he poured two fingers worth into the glass, downing it before pouring more. "You guys are ridiculous. I'm glad you and Clay have each other, Jen, but there is no such thing as love. It's hunger, lust, desire . . . whatever you want to call it and nothing more. Love is for suckers and teenagers."

"Sydney isn't Liz, Scott." Derek looked at his brother with disgust. "The sooner you realize that, the better off you'll be."

"None of this is any of your business." Scott stood toe-to-toe with his brother, daring him to make a move.

Derek shrugged. "By all means, throw away your chance with her. I'd love to pick up the pieces. I won't let my stubborn pride get in the way. I'd be thrilled to marry her."

Scott knew his brother was trying to bait him, but he wasn't about to take the bait. "She doesn't love you."

"And she wouldn't want you to raise your brother's child." Jen's words were directed at Derek but the blow knocked the wind out of Scott.

"What did you say?" Scott backed into the kitchen counter.

"What?" Derek looked at the phone as if it had grown horns.

"Scott," Jen pressed. "Go talk to her. Tell her that you love her. We all see it whenever you're with her, why can't you? I know you're afraid to feel vulnerable again, everyone is, but you can't let her go. Not like this."

"A baby?" Scott looked to Derek to confirm what Jen said, but he simply shrugged. "Are you sure?"

"No, I'm going to drop that bomb on a hunch. You

really are stupid sometimes, Scott." Jen severed the connection, leaving both brothers staring at one another.

"Mind if I have one of those?" Derek motioned to the
drink in Scott's hand. Scott held the bottle out to him.
"Well." Derek held his glass out toward Scott. "Congrats,
bro. I guess I didn't stand a chance."

"I can't talk to her tonight, not like this." Scott put the
glass on the counter. The alcohol was hitting his brain,
causing his thinking to become muddled. He made his
way to the couch, holding on to the counter for balance
before sinking into the warm leather.

"Maybe you should," Derek suggested. "You might tell
her the truth for a change."

Chapter Twenty

"MIKE, SEND ME somewhere this weekend." Sydney knew she couldn't stay on the ranch with Scott nearby. "I don't care where."

Mike was on the porch, playing with an unlit cigarette, watching the sun melt behind the hills. "I can't. I don't have anywhere for you to go." Mike shrugged his broad shoulders. "Scott is heading to Flat Rock, and that's all we have booked right now. Unless you think you're ready to talk with him."

Sydney shook her head. She needed to get away, put some distance between her and Scott without everyone in her ear. "Would you mind if I take this weekend off? Maybe go visit my family."

Mike squeezed her arm. "I think that's a great idea."

She hugged the older man. "Thanks, Mike," she whispered before hurrying into the house to pack her clothing.

She hadn't been home since she'd left and the thought

of spending some time with her family lifted her spirits. Her heart skipped nervously as she thought about telling her mother and father about their coming grandchild, but she knew deep down that they would be supportive. She grabbed her cell phone and dialed their house number, hoping to catch her mom inside.

"Hello?" Her brother's voice sounded almost as deep as their father's, and it took her a second to realize it was Chris.

"Hey! What's up, baby bro?" She tried to force the cheerfulness into her voice.

"Hey, Syd, whatcha up to? We just got in from feeding." She could hear him opening and shutting cupboards and assumed that he was searching for food, as always.

"Mom is gonna kill you if you fill up on junk before dinner."

Chris laughed. "Naw, I have two hollow legs. You know that," he teased. "You want to talk with Mom?"

"Actually, I do." She heard him yell for their mother, and a faint answer in the background.

"She said to hang on a sec. She's taking off her muddy boots."

"Okay." Sydney pressed the button to switch him to speakerphone and tossed the phone onto the bed as she began reaching for clothing, throwing them into her bag. "What's the latest news on everyone?"

"Well, Chris and his brother have pretty well clinched the number one position for team roping again."

Sydney smiled. "No surprise there."

"I know. Did Mom tell you that I finally got my pro-card? I'll be competing this weekend."

Sydney's heart dropped into her stomach and the shirt she was packing slipped onto the bed. "What? Where?"

Please, anywhere but Flat Rock.

"Flat Rock."

West Hills was the closest rodeo to her parent's ranch, but Flat Rock wasn't much farther. It made sense that they would have planned on attending. Why hadn't she thought of that? Of course they would expect her to go and support her brother, and she would want to, but she would definitely be risking an encounter with Scott. On the other hand, it might give her a chance to just watch him, to be near him, without any expectation. It wouldn't be easy, but it might be worth it.

"Hellooo? You still there, Syd?"

"What? Yeah, sorry."

"I asked if you were going to be there, since Findley Brothers is the stock contractor."

"I was actually taking the weekend off to come visit you guys, but I think Scott is working the rodeo." She tried to sound nonchalant.

"Cool. Oh, here's Mom." She heard him passing the phone. "She says she's coming home this weekend."

"You're coming home?" She heard the surprise in her mother's voice. "How did you manage to get a week-end off?" She heard something brush the phone and her mother's voice grow muffled. "Go put some fresh sheets on Sydney's bed."

"Ugh, she can make her own bed," she heard her brother complain in the background. The normal family squabbles made her smile. Going home was definitely what she needed.

SCOTT AND DEREK met Mike in the kitchen as Silvie placed breakfast on the table. The scrambled eggs, sausage, and pancakes drew groans from both men.

"Silvie, I'd love a glass of water and a couple Tylenol," Derek said sweetly.

"Hard night?" Mike asked, arching a brow at each of the brothers in turn.

Scott held up a hand. It had been a long time since Mike had scolded either of them for drinking. In reality, Scott couldn't remember a time that Mike had ever scolded him for it. He was fully regretting allowing Derek to stay, since they had polished off the bottle of whiskey. Scott couldn't remember much of the night other than visions of Sydney playing through his mind.

"Don't wave your hand at me." Mike warned. "You are *both* heading to Flat Rock after breakfast. And they want the new opening. Clay loaded up all the costumes and gear."

"Crap," Derek muttered, and Scott wanted to agree. He'd forgotten about the rodeo this weekend. He needed to get himself under control. He'd never been so distracted by a woman that it affected his ability to do his job.

"I need to talk with Sydney."

Mike shrugged. "You can't. She's not here. She left

early this morning and won't be back until Sunday evening." He leaned back in his chair and crossed his arms. "Could it have something to do with why you are in this condition this morning?"

"Where'd she go, Mike?" Scott glared at Mike as he just shrugged.

"Cut him some slack, Mike. It's not every day he finds out he's going to be a dad." Clay took the water and aspirin from Silvie and tossed them into his mouth, taking a swallow of water.

"She told you?"

Derek choked on the water and it flew from his mouth. He coughed and sputtered, trying to breath.

"You knew?" Scott asked. "And you didn't tell me? Did everyone know but me?"

"I made a promise to her."

"No," Derek managed between coughs. "Jen told him."

Mike leaned forward and adjusted his sweat-stained cowboy hat on his head. "And what do you intend to do about it now that you know?"

Scott met his gaze, even though the pounding of his head made him want to wince. "I don't know."

"Well," Mike said as he leaned back into the chair again. "I guess you'd better figure it out this weekend."

Scott glanced at Derek, who simply shrugged. His family had already offered him their advice, but he hadn't taken it. Now Sydney had left, Mike wasn't telling him where she'd gone, and he had no clue where to find the answers he needed.

SYDNEY PULLED INTO the driveway before mid-morning. As she pulled Mike's truck to a stop in front of the house, she could hear the welcoming whinnies of the horses in the front pasture. She stepped out and warm nostalgia washed over her. She watched the geldings prancing to greet her at the fence and she could almost visualize Valentino as a colt doing the same.

Sydney reached into the truck and grabbed her bag. With her arms full, she pushed the pickup door shut with her hip. "I'm fine, Mom." As she entered the front door, she was greeted by a yellow ball of fur as it slid to a stop at her feet, tripping over itself, barking happily. A little pink tongue lolled out before the puppy yipped again. Sydney headed down the hallway to drop her bag at the foot of her bed before making her way to the kitchen, the puppy following her the entire way, occasionally growling playfully and nipping at the bottom of her pant leg.

"Who's this little ball of trouble?" she asked, picking up the animal and allowing him to bathe her chin with his tongue.

"That's Cooper." Her mother rolled her eyes. "Chris's girlfriend got him for your brother for an early birthday gift."

"His birthday isn't for another two months." Sydney laughed as the puppy batted a huge paw at her cheek before laying his head on her shoulder. She scratched at his ears.

"Yeah, well, you know young love. It may be over before he even has his birthday." Her mother finished drying the last bowl and putting it away. "So what's new? How's the job going?"

"I love it." She rubbed her cheek against the puppy's fuzzy coat, avoiding her mom's stare.

"Really? Then what are you doing here when Findley Brothers has someone else working the rodeo this weekend in Flat Rock?"

The puppy yawned, giving Sydney a quick whiff of his musky breath, and she smiled. It reminded her of the main reason she had come home: to tell her parents about the baby. She put the puppy into his crate in the kitchen nook and sat down at one of the barstools across from her mother.

"I still love the job, but things have become complicated."

"You mean Valentino?" Her mother reached over and took her hand. "Baby, I'm so sorry."

A lump formed in her throat, but she was able to press on. "Not just that. You remember Scott Chandler? You met him at the roundup?"

Her mother smiled and arched a brow at her. "How could I forget him? I remember the two of you at the dance too."

Sydney nodded. "Yeah, well, things sort of progressed from there."

"But you don't sound happy about it?" Her mother leaned on the bar and folded her hands.

"I was. I mean . . . I don't know." Sydney dropped her forehead into her palms. "I thought he cared about me. He says he does, but it's just not enough, Mom."

"You're in love with him?" Her mother's voice was soft and sympathetic. Sydney nodded as a tear slipped down her cheek. "And it's not returned?" Sydney shook her head. "Aw, honey." Her mother came around the bar and surrounded her with her arms, smoothing her hair as her tears fell.

"There's more." She pulled away from her mother's embrace. "Mama, I'm going to have a baby."

Sydney saw the surprise register in her mother's eyes, but to her credit, she hid the disappointment Sydney had expected to see. "A baby?" She glanced at Sydney's stomach. "I'm going to be a grandma? When?"

"I'm only about two months along. But now you see why things are complicated? I haven't even told Scott yet."

Her mother cocked her head at her. "Sydney, you *have* to tell him," she scolded.

"I know, Mama, and I'm going to. But the last time we talked . . . it just wasn't the right time." She shrugged. "I have to go back and quit. I'll tell him then. I just can't work side by side with him."

"Because you still love him, even if he doesn't reciprocate it." Her mother finished her thought. Sydney nodded. "But what if he doesn't want to let you go?"

THE CREW ARRIVED at Flat Rock as the sun was reaching its highest peak. It was blazing hot for early June, and Scott glanced longingly at the river below as he crossed the bridge just before they reached the rodeo grounds. The image of Sydney, wet hair cascading around her in his pool, leaped into his thoughts before he could stop it. God, how he missed her. He'd never realized how often he thought of her until she had left the ranch. Mike still hadn't given him any indication of what time she would be returning. He kept glancing around, hoping that she would miraculously appear.

So far he'd spent the last twenty-four hours going through the motions, preparing for a spectacular rodeo that he really didn't care about in the least. The fact that work couldn't take his mind off of her frustrated him even more. But there was nowhere he could go that wouldn't remind him of Sydney. Just the thought of her name caused his heart to lurch. He could just picture her the last time he'd seen her beside the pool.

As beautiful as she was, her eyes had lost their fire and he was to blame. How could he have let her leave? She had laid out her heart for him and he'd thrown it back at her. She'd told him that she loved him and he'd rejected her, just as she'd feared. He didn't understand why he hadn't just told her he loved her.

Because I can't lie about something I don't even believe exists.

But would it really be a lie? He'd felt lust before and this didn't even compare. He was worried about her safety, but this wasn't just concern or even affection.

You're in love.

No sooner had the thought flashed through his mind then he realized he couldn't deny the truth of it any longer. Ever since he'd met her, Scott had known that Sydney was different. From the first night he'd held her in his arms, everything had felt so right, so perfect, so eternal. He'd known then that he never wanted to let her go. When had he lost sight of that?

Scott slowed to make the turn into the rodeo grounds, looking in his rearview mirror to see the rest of the trucks pulling in behind him. Why hadn't she told him about the baby? Didn't she realize he would have done the honorable thing—or was that exactly why she hadn't told him? Would she even believe him now if he told her that he loved her, that he always had?

The question plagued him as they unloaded the animals. "Scott, will you get your head in the game?" Derek shoved him out of the way as one of the bulls barreled through the chute into the pen.

"Thanks," he said as he wiped sweat from his forehead onto the back of his arm.

Derek gave him an odd glance before opening the next chute and stepping back. "Figured out what you want to say to her when you see her yet?"

Scott shut the gate behind the powerful animal as Clay loaded the next one from behind him. "How'd you know?"

"You look like a lovesick puppy," Derek teased. "It's written all over your face." Both men moved from the fence as the bull came through the chute, bawling furiously. "Still want to try to convince us that you don't love her?"

"I don't even know if she'd believe me if I told her." Scott looked over his shoulder at his brother. "I've really messed this up."

"I might have an idea how to fix it. Jake," Derek called. "Come take over for me. Clay, have you seen Jen?"

Clay didn't take his eyes from the fifteen-hundred-pound beast staring at him on his mount, ready to charge. "She's unloading the horses."

Scott watched as Derek ran to where Jen was leading horses to a corral. He realized that Sydney hadn't just melted the ice of his heart, but she'd also given Derek a chance to grow up and accept his responsibility to his family. She had turned his world upside down and he had to thank her for it. He just wasn't sure she was going to give him a chance.

SYDNEY LAY IN bed, the sheets cool against her heated skin. She'd tried going for a swim, but it only brought back memories, so she'd showered quickly and changed for bed. As she lay staring at the ceiling, she thought about Scott in Flat Rock and how right now he was probably sitting with the crew having a couple of beers, swapping stories and laughing before heading to bed. She slid her hand to her stomach.

Oh, Scott, if only you knew what we had done. Can you love this baby, even if you don't love its mother?

Sydney's cell phone vibrated on the dresser. She jumped at the sound and went to check the number, wondering who would possibly be calling her so late. Recognizing Jen's number, she answered it.

"Sydney?" Her voice was hoarse and raspy as she coughed.

"Jen? Are you okay? Is everyone all right?"

"Yeah, I guess. I overheard you talking to your brother the other night, so I know you're with your parents, but I really need your help."

"Anything, Jen," Sydney assured her.

"We are doing the new opening that you and Derek organized for the first time this weekend in Flat Rock, but I came down with this awful flu and there is no way I can do it."

"Jen, I don't think . . ."

"Please, Sydney? I wouldn't ask, but Mike already told them about it and they are really excited for it. Derek and Clay are playing the parts so you won't even have to worry about Scott."

"But I'd still have to see him."

"I heard you tell your brother you wanted to come see him ride. I really need your help, Sydney."

She took a deep breath. She had hoped to sneak in, watch her brother ride, and maybe catch a glimpse of Scott unobserved. But after all Mike and Jen had done for her, she couldn't let him down when he needed her help.

"Okay. I'll call you when I leave in the morning. But have Derek or Clay meet me at the gate. And I do *not* want to have to see Scott. Do you promise?"

"Thank you, Sydney. You're the best."

"You own me one," she teased. "If you feel better tomorrow, call and let me know."

Sydney knew it wouldn't stop her from going to the rodeo, but she wanted to do everything in her power to avoid Scott. She wasn't ready to face him and she certainly couldn't tell him about the baby while he was working. When sleep finally overtook her, her thoughts of Scott followed her into her slumber, haunting her dreams and stealing her will to forget him. She was again seduced by his smoldering eyes and the touch that could drive her body to frenzied passion.

Chapter Twenty-One

SYDNEY AWOKE THE next morning wondering how she could feel fearful and excited at the same time. Her parents had asked her to ride with them, but she didn't want to run the risk of having no escape plan in case she needed it.

"Besides," she reasoned with her mother, "it'll be easier to get in and out in a truck with the stock contractor's logo."

"Baby, I know you don't want to talk about Scott right now, but you're going to have to face up to a few things. Better to do it sooner than later."

"Mama, I have faced things." She gave her mother a sad smile. "Scott doesn't love me, but he never made any promises that he would. It hurts, but I can't blame him for being honest."

Her mother brushed a curl back off of her shoulder. "I'm proud of you."

"Let's get moving." Sydney's father was gruffer this morning than usual, but she could hardly blame him. She had told him about the baby last night and he'd wanted to drive to Flat Rock right then. She wasn't entirely sure how her mother had managed to convince him to stay put, but she was grateful that she had.

"Are you sure you don't want to ride with me?" Sydney asked.

Her mother winked. "I can take care of him. Don't worry, he just doesn't like to see his little girl hurting. He'll keep quiet."

"Thanks, Mama."

JEN GLANCED AT the text on her phone. "Okay, Sydney is on her way."

"I'll meet her at the gate." Derek rose and Scott had to fight the surge of jealousy. Derek smiled at Jen conspiratorially. "You know you're going to have to stay away from her for this to work. You're supposed to be sick, remember?"

Scott wished Jen and Derek hadn't lied to Sydney about Jen having the flu, but it was the only way they could think to get her take part in the opening ceremony, and he appreciated their help in getting her to the rodeo. Their plan might just work, but he would have to stay out of sight and that was going to be nearly impossible.

"Scott, leave Noble at the trailer today. We'll need him for the opening. I've got the rodeo under control and Mike will be there to make sure it's all running smoothly."

Scott put a hand on his brother's shoulder. "I trust you, Derek. Three months ago, I don't think I could have said that, but now . . ." Scott shrugged and Jen's eyes misted.

"Thanks, Scott." Derek cleared his throat. "I'll do a quick run-through with Sydney this morning, but it will be just like we practiced last night."

Scott stepped out of the trailer, knowing it was where Derek would bring Sydney to get ready and prep her for a quick run-through. He headed to where Mike inspected the roping stock, adjusting the horn wraps in preparation for the overflow of contestants.

"I'll take care of those for you, Mike." He didn't want to tell him that the offer would give him a perfect vantage point to watch Sydney practice the opening ceremony while still remaining hidden.

Mike smiled at Scott and patted his shoulder. "Scott, she's already told you that she loves you. You've got nothing to lose. Calm down, son."

"I know." But knowing she loved him didn't take away the fear that it was too late. She had given him more chances to admit his feelings for her than he could have ever deserved. He couldn't expect her to wait until he got his act together—no woman could be that patient, and he certainly didn't deserve her forgiveness for the way he'd treated her.

Mike jerked a chin toward his truck, which was pulling toward the back gate where Derek waited. "There she is."

Scott's heart stopped as he caught a glimpse of her in the driver's seat. With her hair pulled back from her face, she looked like an innocent teen girl. Her auburn curls reflected bright copper in the morning sunlight and his hungry gaze devoured her. She pulled the truck to a stop by Mike's fifth-wheel trailer. He frowned when he noticed that she avoided his eyes, parking as far away as she could.

She climbed out of the truck and gave Derek a hug as she pushed her sunglasses onto the top of her head. Even in blue jeans and a white t-shirt she was tempting. Scott fought the sharp jab of envy as Derek surrounded her shoulders with his arm. If it hadn't been for his stupidity and stubborn pride, she would be there now, with him. But, as long as everything went according to Derek's plan, by tonight it would be his arms that held Sydney.

DEREK GREETED SYDNEY warmly and she tried to keep her eyes from searching the crew for Scott. She pointed to Jake, attaching a harness to a carriage near the back gate.

"What in the world is that?"

"That is your ride, my lady."

"My what?" She laughed. "That is not exactly what we talked about. Can you even drive that thing?" She glanced at the long, open design reminiscent of medieval royalty. The deep black with gold accents would shine in the arena.

"I don't have to. Pablo is driving it." He pointed to the jet-black geldings tied nearby. "And those boys have pulled a carriage before. Come on, wait until you see the dress Jen designed."

"Okay, hang on." She locked the truck and pocketed the keys. Her eyes coasted toward the arena, where she saw Scott bent over adjusting horn wraps before they loaded a steer into the chute. As if feeling her gaze, he looked up. His black eyes were unreadable, shadowed by his cowboy hat. Her heart leaped into her throat and her breath lodged in her chest. She felt faint, leaning against the truck to catch herself. She closed her eyes and forced herself to turn away from him.

"You okay?" Derek rushed to her side.

"Yeah, I just felt a little lightheaded for a second. I probably should have eaten something."

"Come on, let's see what Jen has." He led her over to Jen's trailer, knocking before opening the door.

"Come in." Jen's voice sounded almost cheerful, and Sydney wondered if she couldn't hide on the hillside with the rest of the spectators.

One look at Jen crushed any hope for escape Sydney held. She looked horrible. Her normal olive complexion was pallid, her nose and cheeks flush, and her eyes swollen.

"How are you feeling?"

"Awful." She pointed toward the small closet beside the bed. "The dress is in there."

Sydney reached inside and caught her breath as she pulled out the heavy gown. She was almost afraid to touch the dress. She fingered the medieval costume, the sun catching the silver and gold threads, making them shimmer.

"Derek, get out so she can put it on. We'll let you know when she's ready."

"Okay." He chuckled. "I'll be back in ten minutes. We don't have a lot of time, since the rodeo starts in two hours."

As soon as Derek had left the trailer, Jen rose from the bed, wearing sweats, her hair pulled back. She coughed into her hand. "Start getting dressed and I'll be right back." She rushed to the bathroom, shutting the door behind her.

Even the closed door didn't hide the sounds of Jen vomiting in the bathroom. Sydney felt guilty that she had even thought about turning back on the drive over. She slid her jeans off and pulled the t-shirt over her head before dropping the gown over her shoulders. After wiggling into a few unnatural positions, she was able to zip the back of the dress most of the way up.

The dress bared her shoulders but fit snugly across them with braided golden trim over the silver metallic brocade. The bodice tapered to a waist that seemed impossibly small, while the sleeves draped from the elbow to the ground. The entire upper portion was made to look like a jacket, while the lower part of the dress was a loose and flowing golden brocade that matched the color of her eyes. The same gold braiding lined the sleeves and the bottom hem of the dress.

She glanced back at the hanger and saw a bag with what appeared to be a crown. She pulled it off and saw a delicate silver lace veil attached to the gold-and-silver crown. She pulled the rubber band from her ponytail and shook her hair loose, placing the crown on her head as Jen returned.

"Sydney, you look amazing." She reached for her comb and a couple of hairpins. "Let's just pull back a few of your curls and pin them. There. Look," she instructed.

Sydney looked in the mirror and gave a girlish giggle. "I can't believe you designed this. It's amazing." She lifted the skirt slightly and noticed her sock-covered feet. "Hmm, I guess boots would probably be best."

A knock sounded at the door. "Come on in, Derek," Jen called.

Derek stepped into the room and Sydney broke into laughter. He was covered in chain mail and a blue-and-silver tunic, carrying a silver helmet. He arched a brow at her. "This was your idea, you know."

"I know, it's just all so . . ." She searched for the right word.

"Romantic?" he offered.

"Ridiculous," she corrected.

"All right, you guys don't have any time to waste," Jen scolded as she crawled back into the bed. "Sydney, you'll be in the carriage, and while the announcer is reading the script, you'll just sit looking regal. Your knight will ride into the arena." She pointed at Derek, who bowed.

Jen rolled her eyes and Sydney laughed. "Can we please be serious for just a minute?"

Sydney pinched her lips between her teeth to hide her smile and Derek winked at her. "Yes, sis."

"The Black Knight—" she began.

"Clay," Derek interrupted.

"Will ride in. The announcer will hype the crowd as

the two of them fight for you. After Derek wins, he will come lift you onto his horse and you will ride out."

"Into the sunset?" Sydney asked.

"Maybe. They will start with the national anthem and a few introductions, then you guys will go in. Once you exit, Scott will come in as the announcer compares the knights of the past to modern-day cowboys. What do you think?"

"I think the crowd is going to eat it up," Sydney laughed.

"That's what the Flat Rock rodeo committee is hoping for."

SCOTT WAS READY for this day to be over. They had already had the first group of cattle ropers post their times and he was already tired of the complaints. The rodeo hadn't even started yet, but by the looks of it, it might be a long weekend.

"Hey, I want to talk with you."

Scott turned around, prepared to listen to another cowboy complain about the stock when he recognized the young man. He couldn't be more than twenty, and Scott couldn't remember how he knew him, other than seeing him in the chute that morning. It didn't matter when the younger man shoved him in the chest.

"Hey, let's just take a second and calm down. I don't want you to have to eat dust again."

"You don't remember me, do you?"

Scott held his hands in front of him in a gesture of guarded friendship. "Other than from this morning?"

"Chris Thomas. Sydney's my sister."

"Oh, hey!" Scott instantly understood the younger man's attack. "I don't think you realize what's going on."

"I don't really care what *you* think is going on. She's pregnant and you dumped her?" Chris shoved him back against the metal panels of the corral. The horses inside shied to the other side of the corral as Scott bounced off of them.

"Look, Chris." Scott tried to diffuse his indignation. He understood the need for a brother to defend his sister's honor; he would have done the same thing for Jen. "I'm going to make this right. If you let me go, you'll see what I mean in just a few minutes." Chris narrowed his eyes, obviously unsure whether to believe him or not. "Look, if you keep me any longer, I won't be able to fix this. I have to get to that trailer right now." Scott pointed to Derek's trailer.

Chris looked over as Derek rushed inside. "That knight costume has my name written all over it. But if you'd rather we stand here talking about this, by all means, let's beat each other's brains in and accomplish nothing."

"How do I know you're not just trying to save yourself now?"

Scott didn't want to insult the kids so he humored his bravado. "If I don't make this right, you know where to find me after the opening ceremony. I'll let you beat the crap out of me then, but let me at least try." Scott eyed him.

"Fine, go." Chris waved him off. "But I'll be watching and waiting back here for you," he warned.

THE STANDS WERE packed for the ten o'clock rodeo. Sydney sat in the carriage, waiting for their cue, glancing to the hillside where she saw her parents sitting with her brother. The black geldings pulled against the reins, drawing her attention back to the arena. Pablo easily held them in position until she heard the trumpets sound as the rodeo announcer reached the point in the script where he welcomed the visiting "royalty." The music played as the wagon jerked to a start, harnesses jangling as the horses broke into a slow gallop into the arena, their hooves pounding even in the soft dirt. The music softened and Sydney waved at the crowd as the carriage circled the arena and came to a halt at one end. The crowd audibly gasped as she came into full view. Sydney glanced to the other end of the arena, knowing that Derek and Clay were both waiting just beyond the view of the audience for their cues.

They were bound to prove why Findley Brothers were masters of showmanship. The announcer introduced the "Black Knight," and she stood, feigning fear, her gown gleaming as the silver and gold caught the sun. On cue, Clay rode into the arena. He wore black chain mail, a costume identical to the one Derek was wearing but with a black-and-silver tunic. As he reached the center of the arena, the horse reared, pawing at the air. The Black Knight played to the crowd as he raised a sword into the air, circling the arena to the cheers and boos from the crowd.

The announcer informed the crowd that their only hope was Sir Findley. All eyes turned toward the end of the arena where Derek suddenly charged in on Noble; he held his sword high as trumpets blared. Sydney felt her heart skip at the sight of the horse, her breath catching. He looked magnificent with a blanket matching Derek's tunic flowing around his legs while his black-and-white mane whipped backward. Derek was entirely encased in a shining suit of armor, complete with gloves and helmet. She watched as the horse ate up the arena in long strides. The crowd broke into a wild cheer.

The rodeo announcer urged the cheers into a full uproar as he encouraged the audience to choose their knight as they rode toward one another at full speed before clashing swords. The clang of metal sounded through the wireless microphones that both knights wore.

"Give up, Sir Findley. The princess will be mine." Metal crashed as they circled the horses around one another in a mock battle until the Black Knight fell from his mount.

Derek leaped from Noble while Jake appeared from a back gate of the arena to hold the horse. Clay approached Derek and they continued their battle on foot as the announcer called for the crowd to cheer for their knight of choice. The cries for "Sir Findley" and "Black Knight" echoed across the arena. Suddenly, Derek spun, his sword sliding across the front of Clay's stomach. Clay doubled over, appearing mortally wounded before falling to the ground.

Two men from the crew ran into the arena to put the Black Knight's body over the saddle of his horse and lead the animal from the arena amidst the cheers of the crowd. Derek made his way to the side of the carriage while Jake waited nearby with Noble. Sydney smiled at what would come next. Derek would ride up and say something ridiculously sappy before lifting her into the saddle and riding out of the arena with her. She reached for the wireless microphone attached to the inside of her belt and turned it on as she stood in the carriage.

"My princess," he acknowledged as he kneeled before her, holding out a hand to help her step down from the vehicle. As her booted feet landed in the dirt, he reached up and pulled off his helmet.

Sydney's head reeled as she stared at Scott. Her eyes shot to the gate where the Black Knight stood watching, and she saw Derek and a miraculously healthy-looking Jen beside him. She looked back at Scott, still kneeling before her, and her heart dropped to the toes of her boots.

"Scott?" she whispered. He smiled as his name echoed across the arena over her wireless mic. Her knees went weak at his lopsided grin and she held the side of the carriage.

"My princess," he repeated. His gaze met her own and she could see the mischievous glint in them before he bowed his head. Her heart pounded against her ribs as he called her "princess."

"My prince," she answered, amazed that she could even speak, let alone remember the lines she had practiced with Derek the day before. "My people and I are forever grateful to you for defending my honor." She waved a hand at the crowd surrounding the arena. "How could I ever repay the kindness you have done to this kingdom?"

"I can think of but one way." Scott paused for effect, tossing his helmet aside and taking her hand. "I have been snared by your beauty. I have tried to fight my feelings, but it has been for naught. They have won the battle and will not be ignored."

That wasn't part of the script. If he can ad lib, so can I.

"My prince," she said, slipping her hand from his as she tore her gaze away from him. She hoped her refusal to meet his eyes appeared as coyness to the crowd. "You are too bold and shouldn't speak of such things."

"Ah, princess, should I continue to keep my love for you hidden?" Scott stood and curved a finger under her chin, forcing her to look at him. His grin was cocky. Was he mocking her pain? She felt indignation rise up in her chest.

"I see that you don't believe me, so I will proclaim it to the people for all to hear." Scott spread his arms toward the crowd. A cheer went up as the spectators watched enthralled at the drama taking place before them. "I love you, princess."

An explosion of applause sounded. Sydney's eyes narrowed as she stepped towards Scott, standing toe-to-toe with him. "You don't believe in love, remember?" she hissed.

"Princess," he said, glancing at the crowd to remind her of their audience, "I was but a stupid fool."

Her heart galloped in her chest. What was he trying to do? Hadn't he hurt her enough? Why would Jen and Derek have called her to be a part of something that would be so painful for her? Her mind swirled with questions as she tried frantically to register any answers.

"Princess, how could you doubt the depths of my feelings for you? I have just risked life and limb to save you from the Black Knight."

I don't know what you're trying to do, Scott Chandler, but I've had enough of this.

She arched a brow, assuming the regal posture of the queen the crowd imagined her to be. "A gesture of an honorable man. Kneel and I will knight you, sir."

"The prize I prefer is far more valuable." Scott turned and walked to where Jake stood, still holding Noble. Reaching into his saddle, he retrieved a package before returning to her. Scott dropped to one knee and she heard a gasp from the crowd. "Sydney Thomas, will you marry me?"

The crowd went wild as she looked down at him. He held out the diamond ring for her to see.

"Why?" she whispered, barely able to make a sound.

"Because I need you and I love you. Without you, my life means nothing." Scott smiled up at her.

She could see nerves where she had seen cockiness only moments before. But she could see that his heart was completely exposed to her. He'd opened up for the entire world to see his vulnerability, and she couldn't help but be touched by it. She wasn't sure how things would work out in the future, but she had to take a chance on the love they had discovered.

Scott reached for her hand. "What do you say, princess? Marry me?"

She cupped his face, her answer swallowed by her laughter. "What was that?" the announcer asked.

"I said, 'Yes.'"

The audience rose from their seats, cheering as Scott pulled Sydney into his arms, his lips finding her own. Sydney forgot that they were standing in the middle of an arena during a rodeo and wound her arms around his neck, her fingers catching on the chain-mail hood he wore. With Scott's lips against hers again, she tasted his passion mingled with her tears. For the first time since finding out about the baby, she was excited about their future.

Scott slipped an arm under her knees and lifted her into Noble's saddle. He swung a leg over the saddle behind her and they rode out of the arena to the sound of thunderous applause.

"I have no idea how we are going to follow that up tomorrow," He chuckled as they rode out of the gate.

CHRIS STOOD AT the back arena gate as they passed. "Okay, Chandler, I'd say you took care of it."

Sydney looked at her brother before glancing at Scott over her shoulder. "What was that about?"

"Someone came to defend your honor earlier. I promised him I was going to make an honorable woman out of you before the day was done."

"A little sure of yourself?"

"I was stupid enough to let you walk away once. I wasn't about to let it happen twice." Scott pressed a kiss to the hollow behind her ear, causing warmth to spread through every limb. She melted into his arms as he headed toward his trailer.

She'd started the day with the certainty that she would never be with Scott again, and now her entire reality had been flipped on end. She saw her parents approaching the trailers and wondered what her father would say. Within minutes they were surrounded by family and friends offering congratulatory wishes. She laughed at Scott's nervousness when her father shook his hand while they made plans for dinner later that evening. Clay excused himself to prepare for the first event, reminding them that there was still a rodeo to run.

Scott pressed a quick kiss to Sydney's lips. She wanted him to linger but he groaned and pulled away. "I have to change and get out there."

"Go." She pushed him toward the trailer. "We'll talk more after the rodeo is over."

Scott pulled the tunic over his head as he hurried into the trailer, appearing moments later in a long-sleeved, maroon Western shirt emblazoned with Findley Brothers patches. He pulled his chaps over his slim hips, clipping the buckles on the back of his legs. Jake had already changed Noble's tack and Scott jumped into the saddle, winking at her as he rode to the arena. She lifted the skirt of her gown and headed toward Jen's trailer to retrieve her clothes.

"If it isn't the bride to be."

Sydney arched a brow and looked at Derek. "I suppose you're going to tell me you didn't have anything to do with this?"

Derek rolled his eyes. "Please, this was *all* me." He leaned back against the side of the truck, crossing his arms.

"I should be furious at you."

He shrugged. "But you're not." Derek's eyes twinkled.

"No, I'm not," she agreed.

"Why didn't you tell me about the baby?"

Sydney felt the color drain from her face. "Jen?" Derek nodded and she couldn't meet his scrutiny. "When was I supposed to tell you? Better yet, *how* was I supposed tell you? I haven't even told Scott yet."

"I would have taken care of you and the baby, even if Scott hadn't stepped up."

She was touched and saddened by his revelation. He had proclaimed his feelings for her but she hadn't realized how deep they were. She wasn't sure how to respond. "Derek, I . . ."

He held up a hand. "It's okay, Sydney. We weren't meant to be."

"I'm sorry, Derek."

"Don't be. I'll have the most beautiful sister-in-law ever." Derek pushed himself away from the truck and pressed a kiss to Sydney's forehead. "And I'm going to spoil that little cowboy like you won't believe."

WORD HAD SPREAD about the opening ceremonies, and Sydney was stopped constantly, either to be told how touching the event had been or to show off her diamond. She couldn't wait for the rodeo to be over so that she could have Scott all to herself. She knew that she had a surprise for him as well, and tonight would be the perfect night to share it. Mike had already agreed to meet with the committee at the rodeo dance so that Scott's presence wasn't required. If they could only finish the last event.

The bull riding was always a crowd favorite and it never failed to bring the crowd to the edge of their seats. She watched from the warm-up arena as she finished exercising one of the black geldings who would be pulling the carriage again the next day. Her stomach flipped when she realized that both Derek and Scott were going to be the pick-up men for the event, responsible for lifting the thrown rider to safety while the bull sought any moving target. It was a dangerous job, second only to the rodeo clowns.

She watched Scott lope across the arena and say something to his brother. It was shocking to watch the two of them together. In the last two months they had grown from bitter enemies to respected peers. Scott patted his brother on the shoulder and rode back to his post. There was a rodeo clown between them, and another one preparing to leap into a padded barrel that had been placed in a strategic location to distract the bull.

She heard the commotion from the chute and a slam as the door burst open to a flourish of heavy metal rock meant to charge the crowd. She couldn't watch with Scott and Derek both in the line of harm, so she made her way to the EMT tent where she could be useful for any injuries that were bound to occur. She heard a collective gasp from the crowd. The EMTs ran past her, carrying a backboard, and her heart dropped to her knees. She hurried back to the arena in time to see the bull turn and attempt to charge Noble.

Sydney's breath caught in her throat as Noble dodged the bull, spinning deftly before Scott tightened the rope around the bull's head and led the animal toward the exit gate. She breathed a sigh as Scott released the rope and the bull was through the gate. Sydney hurried back to the trailers to offer any assistance that might be needed behind the scenes. She heard the announcer commending the cowboy and a cheer went up from the stands. She tied the gelding to the stock trailer and ran toward the ambulance that was always present during a rodeo.

She pulled up short as she saw a familiar limp heading toward the chutes. She hurried under the grandstands where she could get a better look. It couldn't possibly be Kurt. Why would he have come here? Now?

"Sydney." She heard the hushed voice from the corral and turned to see Jen wave to her. Sydney raised a hand to let her know she heard but was busy. "Come here," Jen insisted.

Sydney shot a glance back toward the chute but had

lost the cowboy. She made her way to where Jen waited. "What? You don't . . ."

"It's Kurt. He came in this afternoon as a late sign-up for the bull riding."

"What . . ."

"I already called the police. They are on their way."

"What would possess him to show up here?"

"He's crazy," Jen shook her head. "We already know that. But he probably doesn't think he can be caught and he can just take the prize money and leave. It would be another jab at Scott that he was right under our noses. I only found out by accident."

The chute burst open and another rider was thrown within a few seconds. Several riders rode their animals to the buzzer when suddenly the crew grew quiet. The only sounds the women could hear were the bulls shifting in the chutes. Sydney thought she heard Kurt's voice yelling at one of the crew and hurried to the back gate where she could see better. She stood on the railing of the fence as the gate burst open.

Kurt had drawn one of the larger bulls, which usually accounted for a lower score since they didn't buck as hard, but Diablo Gold was known for his ability to spin before twisting. She saw the surprise register on Scott's face when he recognized Kurt on the back of the animal. Kurt's body was balanced as the bull spun in one direction before switching and cutting to the inside. Time seemed to stand still. Sydney was waiting to hear the horn blare, signaling the completion of his eight-second ride, when the bull twisted again in the opposite direction, pinning Kurt between the chain link fence and the side of the bull. As the bull turned back toward the center of the arena, Kurt's spur caught in the fence, pulling him from the animal's back.

Scott and Derek hurried in to distract the bull as the clown helped a shaken Kurt to his feet and shoved him toward the gate. Before Scott could even build his loop the bull stopped and turned back behind the pick-up men before heading straight for the retreating backs of the clown and the thrown cowboy. Derek yelled out as the bull charged the pair. The clown, a bullfighter who had worked with Findley Brothers for nearly ten years, heard Derek and jumped onto the fence, pulling himself higher than the bull's horns to the relief of the spectators.

Sydney watched in horror as the bull scraped his horn along the chain-link fence before heading straight toward Kurt. He glanced over his shoulder in time to jump onto the chute, but he wasn't about to get high enough to avoid the onslaught from the animal. The first hit in his low back was enough to knock him from the gate and send the cowboys running from the chutes, trying to reach him and pull him over.

Sydney saw the fear flit over his face as he reached for the hands of another cowboy only to slip from his grasp and hit the dirt, directly below the bull's head and the chute. The bull backed up and lowered his head as Kurt rolled into a ball, attempting to minimize the damage to his body. The crowd seemed to hold their breath collectively. The bullfighters ran to his aid as the bull charged again, this time pounding Kurt's sides with his front hooves before dropping his head and slamming Kurt between his horns and the gate again.

Scott tossed the rope expertly, slapping it across the bull's back in an attempt to redirect the animal's attention as the bullfighters jumped in front of the animal. Derek tossed a second loop over the bull's horns as they tried to drag the mass of pulsating muscle toward the gate. Sydney heard the crackle of a walkie-talkie as someone from behind the chutes called the EMTs out to the arena. She heard the ambulance roar to life and knew that it was only brought in for the most serious cases.

She dropped from the gate as she saw Scott and Derek release the bull into the corral. She caught Scott's eye as he headed back into the arena, and she could see that he was torn between worry for a fellow competitor and hatred for the man that had caused so much misery in his life and Sydney's. She opened the gate for the ambulance driver, then stepped into the arena as the entire rodeo came to a halt while they EMTs worked on the man who still lay unmoving on the ground. Cowboys exited their chutes to wait and pray for the safety of a fellow competitor as the announcer talked about the dangers of rodeo to the crowd.

The EMTs tried to block the cowboy from the view of the spectators as much as possible, but Sydney had a clear view from where she stood. She could see the blood spreading quickly on the back of Kurt's shirt. The paramedics worked furiously, cutting off his shirt in an attempt to stem the flow. He still hadn't regained consciousness as they slipped an IV into him, lifted him into the truck, and left the arena with sirens blaring.

Sydney stood by, waiting for Scott as they released the bulls from the chutes and guided them back to the corral. The announcer informed the crowd that they were going to redraw the bulls since the animals had been in the chutes too long and explained the rules that kept the animals safe and healthy. Scott rode over to her at the gate and dismounted, pulling her into his arms.

"Are you okay?"

"Scott, what was he doing here?" She buried her face into his chest and wrapped her arms around his waist.

"I don't know, but it was a joke to him. He made sure to catch my eye from the chute and give me that smirk."

"Jen called the police already, so we'll send them on to the hospital." She shook her head. "It didn't look good."

Scott kissed the top of her head. "I think he got gored."

She tipped her chin up so she could meet his gaze. "Scott, you tried to save him. Even after all that he's done." She shook her head in disbelief.

"I couldn't just let it happen."

"Scott." Jen appeared at the gate. "They are loading in the next set of bulls. And the police are here."

Sydney pushed him back toward the arena. "Go ahead. I'll talk to the police."

Chapter Twenty-Two

SYDNEY LAY CURLED against Scott's chest. She inhaled the scent of him, humming in tune to the song playing quietly on radio. Scott's fingers feathered over her ribcage before resting on her abs, her t-shirt bunching under his palm.

"When are you planning on telling me?"

She looked up at him, startled. "How did you know?"

"Jen told me." He pressed a kiss to her forehead. "Why didn't you tell me that day at the pool?"

Guilt flooded her. Sydney wanted to be angry with Jen for betraying her confidence, but if she had told him, Jen wouldn't have felt the need. "You're not angry that I didn't tell you?"

Scott tipped her chin up with the pad of his finger before running his thumb across her lips. "I wish you had told me." His eyes darkened with sadness and regret. "But I also understand that you had to find out where *we* stood before telling me about our child."

"I was going to tell you, but I didn't want you to feel trapped. And that day ..." She shrugged, her fingers splayed across his chest. "Everything fell apart, and it just wasn't the time. You weren't in a place to hear it." Sydney raised herself onto her elbow and looked down at him. "Scott, I swear, I wasn't going to keep you from your child. I was going to tell you before I quit."

Scott laughed. "You're crazy if you think Mike would have let you quit."

Sydney tried to hide her smile. "That's what he said the first time I tried."

Scott rolled over her so she lay under him. She ran her hand over his stubbled jaw. "Princess, I wouldn't have let you go either." He brushed a curl from her forehead. "It might have taken me a little longer, but I would have figured it out."

She smiled up at him. "I love you, Scott Chandler."

His kiss was tender but desperate, as if she were an apparition that was bound to disappear. She held his face, tasting his love, savoring the feel of his body weighing on her, his hand still protectively covering their child. He wound his fingers into her hair and leaned his forehead against hers, slightly breathless.

"I don't know what I would have done if I'd lost you. Thank God Derek stepped in and helped me see what was right in front of me all along."

"How did that happen? I thought the two of you could barely be in a room together?"

Scott smiled. "Let's just say that after a bottle of whiskey, Derek can get his point across. Even if it means a monster hangover the next day." Scott nuzzled the hollow of her jaw. "You've given me back my brother as well as my heart."

Sydney jumped as someone pounded on the door of the trailer. Most of the crew had headed to the rodeo barbeque and the dance. She could still hear the band in the distance, so she wondered who could be needing them now.

"Scott!" It was Jen's voice. "Sydney!"

Scott jumped from the bed and hurried to the door. "What's wrong? I thought you guys were going to the dance."

"We were. The police came to inform us that Kurt didn't make it."

Scott reached for Sydney as she approached and wound his arm around her waist. "What happened?"

"They said that there was too much damage to the liver and spleen. He never came to once they left."

Sydney buried her face in Scott's side. "It's finally over?"

THE MORNING OF the wedding dawned bright and breezy. It had been a whirlwind of activity on the ranch trying to plan a wedding in less than a month while keeping the stock moving from rodeo to rodeo. Sydney had asked Alicia and her mother to stay at the ranch and help her plan the event with Jen and Silvie. Against everyone else's wishes, Sydney insisted on the ceremony being held in the corral at Scott's cabin. Only Scott seemed to understand that she needed to close the door on the past and see the place of Valentino's death in a new light with a happy memory.

The guests had begun to arrive and were being seated in the corral, waiting for the bride to make her appearance. She knew that Chris had already arrived, and according to her father and brother, Scott was becoming more nervous with every passing moment as he was greeted by several rodeo friends.

Sydney rose from the end of the bed and stood in front of the full-length mirror. The gown of white satin and tulle surrounded her like a cloud. The modest, princess-cut neckline was covered in beads and tiny pearls and cut in at the waist, giving the bodice of the dress a heart-like appearance. The full sleeves, while slightly impractical for a summer wedding, were made of delicate lace cut out and tapered to a tight cuff at the wrist. The tulle, accented with pearls and sequins, billowed from her waist to the floor, the train trailing behind her.

"Are you ready?" Sydney looked back and saw her father enter the room. She smoothed the skirt of the dress and noticed that her hands were trembling.

"I'm scared."

Her father came and kissed the curls piled inside the veiled crown on her head. "Come here." He led her to the large picture window that overlooked the corral. "Do you see that man out there?" He pointed at Scott, standing between the preacher and Derek. "He loves you and you love him. The two of you are going to have a child soon, and you're going to adore him or her. That's all you need to remember."

She stared at Scott. He was gorgeous. He stood talking to Derek and Clay, his groomsmen, with this hair damp and curling beneath his black cowboy hat. Freshly shaven, he wore black Levis and boots paired with a tuxedo jacket, shirt, and vest. She had never seen him look more handsome. She smiled up at her father. "I love you, Daddy."

"WE BETTER GO find those ladies and get this started," Clay laughed as he gave Scott a hug and patted his shoulder.

Scott stood at the head of the aisle. He tried not to fidget, but he couldn't seem to keep his hands still. He wasn't nervous, but he was anxious to call Sydney his wife. Scott held his breath as Clay escorted Jen into the corral. His sister beamed, her smile spread from one cheek to the other. Derek, with Alicia's arm in the crook of his own, smiled down at the woman walking with him. His breath caught in his chest as he saw Bill Thomas escorting his daughter toward him, a vision in white.

She was breathtakingly beautiful as she took another step, closing the distance between them. Scott felt as if he had waited for this moment since he had nearly run her over at the rodeo with his horse. Time seemed to stand still as Sydney approached him.

Her father slipped her hand from the crook of his elbow and placed it in Scott's hand. He lifted the veil covering his daughter's face and pressed a kiss to her cheek. Scott could see the tears shimmering in the man's eyes. "Take good care of her, son."

"I promise, sir." Scott smiled as he stared down at the woman who had become the reason his heart beat.

The preacher began to speak, saying the words they had practiced the night before at the rehearsal, but Scott tuned him out. His entire being focused on the way her hair fell to her shoulders and curled around her cheeks. He could only think of the sweetness of her lips as he watched them move, repeating the vows to love, honor, and cherish him. Scott said the same words, wanting nothing more than to take her into his arms as he felt her hands shake in his own.

He slipped the ring onto her finger, forever proclaiming her as his wife, and kissed the band on her hand. "I love you," he whispered.

A tear fell from her cheek, coursing to her chin, and he reached up to wipe it away with his thumb, not even thinking about the people surrounding them.

"I now pronounce you, man and wife."

Their friends and family cheered as Scott pulled his bride into his arms and pressed his lips to hers. He curved his arm around her back and pulled her closer, branding her as his for all eternity.

Epilogue

"SYDNEY," SCOTT CALLED as he shook her shoulder gently. "Come on, sleepyhead. Wake up."

She stretched and yawned, opening her eyes, and rolled onto her back, smiling at the sight before her. Scott sat beside her on the bed, his black eyes shining. She reached up and touched his cheek.

"Your daughter is hungry," he pointed out as the bundle in his arms mewed, letting everyone know she was not pleased.

Sydney scooted into a sitting position in the bed. Reaching for her three-month-old daughter in her husband's arms, she opened her gown. Scott watched the tender moment as their child nursed. Kassie had quickly wiggled her way into her father's heart. Any remaining desire to keep his love for his girls hidden was gone. Kassie's eyes, as dark as his own but shimmering with the gold flecks that indicated the fiery temperament of her mother, had melted any remaining reservations.

"Are you going to stare all day?" Scott leaned over and tasted his wife's lips. He could see the passion flame in her eyes. He smiled, knowing that he would never grow tired of the woman he had married.

Scott glanced down at the baby nursing at Sydney's breast. "Lucky girl," he teased, winking. Sydney wiggled her index finger at him. He cocked his head and gave her a rakish grin. "Now, woman, I cannot simply service you at the snap of your fingers." He touched his lips to her own again, tasting the sweetness of her mouth as their tongues dueled. A knock at the door halted their kiss and Scott growled at the intrusion.

"Scott." Jen's voice sounded through the closed door.

Sydney laughed and pulled the blanket over her to cover her breast. "Come in, Jen," Sydney called to her sister-in-law.

"Good morning." Jen waddled in with her hand at her lower back, her very pregnant belly leading the way. "How is Kassie this morning?"

"Hungry again," Scott remarked. He wished they could have had more privacy, even gone on a honeymoon, but Sydney's pregnancy had prevented it. But once the mares foaled, he promised himself, they were going on a trip, just the two of them.

Jen leaned down and whispered into Scott's ear. "What?" Sydney asked as Scott's face broke into a broad grin.

"Hurry and get dressed." He reached to take Kassie

from her arms, his heart racing as he thought about how surprised she would be. "I'll make her a bottle."

"No, I'll feed her," Sydney argued. "Why? What is it?"

"Trust me. Just get dressed." He slipped the baby from her arms and immediately heard her mewing protests. "Oh, you can wait two seconds for a bottle." Scott reached for a nearby pacifier and slipped it into her mouth as he headed into the kitchen to prepare a bottle.

"I don't understand what the big deal is," Sydney muttered as she climbed out the bed, watching Scott leave the room.

WHEN SCOTT RETURNED, holding a bottle in his daughter's mouth, he found Sydney dressed in blue jeans and a t-shirt, reaching for a hairbrush. "Not now. Come on. We don't have time for that," he grumbled.

"What is so important that I can't even run a brush through my hair?" she asked as he herded her toward the door and out toward the back patio doors. Jen had followed them, and as they reached the barn he held Kassie out to her aunt.

Sydney opened the doors as he led her past the corral and to the barn. "Ready?"

She nodded and he slid the large door open. He led her to Cougar's stall. As Sydney walked up, he pointed toward the mare. "He's yours."

Who is mine?

Sydney looked at the mare who would be foaling any day and noticed that she seemed thinner. She looked around the stall and noticed the small, smoky gray mound near one wall. She gasped as a small head lifted and stared at her with dark, liquid eyes. The colt unwound his long legs from beneath him and tried to stand. After several attempts, he finally managed to balance himself on four spindly legs. Sydney laughed as the young colt shook on uncertain legs before making his way to her, cautiously, curiously.

"Have you imprinted him?" She looked back over her shoulder at Scott in the doorway.

"We were waiting for you to do it." He smiled down at her.

Sydney squatted on the balls of her feet, careful not to startle the foal. Slowly, he stuck his nose out to smell the stranger. Cougar nudged Sydney with her nose.

"You did good, mama." She kissed the mare's velvety muzzle as the foal nudged her in the chest.

She ran her hands over the fur of his neck and looked into his eyes. The eyes that stared back at her bravely were Valentino's.

"They say the eyes are the windows to the soul," Scott commented.

Sydney looked back at Scott as she continued to rub the foal's legs and chest, getting him accustomed to being touched by humans. She knew he must have noticed the same thing she had. "What should we name him?"

"He's yours. What do you want to name him?"

"Let's see . . . what about Smokey?" She ran her hands over his forehead and ears.

The colt whinnied and shook his head. She laughed,

amazed that he was just as opinionated as his sire had been. "Okay, picky, what do you think of Casanova?" She reached for one of his now sturdy legs and patted the bottom of a hoof. The colt nudged her neck with his muzzle and nibbled at her ear. "Casanova it is." She laughed.

Sydney stood and stepped into Scott's arms as they looked at the colt. "He looks just like Valentino did when he was born."

"Valentino is a big part of him."

Sydney leaned backward and kissed his lips tenderly. "Thank you."

"You are very welcome. I love you, Mrs. Chandler." He grinned against her lips. "The smartest thing I ever did was ask you to marry me."

"You can say that again," she teased, her voice husky with barely contained passion. He raised his brow at her. "But the smartest thing I ever did was to say yes."

She scooped a handful of grain from a bucket nearby and held it out to the mare. "You've got her eating out of the palm of your hand."

Sydney smiled and gave him a sidelong glance. "The way you eat out of mine?"

Scott reached for Sydney's free hand and brought her palm to his lips, nipping at the sensitive flesh. "Is that what you had in mind?"

Her limbs went liquid as she gazed into the black eyes that she had once thought belonged to the devil, eyes that still held the power to drown her in passion. "Not exactly." She sighed.

Scott led her back into the house, past Kassie's room where Jen was already rocking their daughter to sleep. He bent and scooped Sydney into his arms, carrying her to their room and shutting the door behind him with a worn cowboy boot. She saw where he was headed and pushed against his chest.

"Scott, we can't. Derek will be here any second and Jen is just down the hall," she protested.

"To hell with them." Scott grinned mischievously. "We're newlyweds. They'll understand." Sydney ran her fingers through the curls at the nape of his neck.

"I love you, princess. I always have."

"Always?" She asked, smiling. "I remember a time when you couldn't stand to have me around."

"I always wanted you around. I just didn't want to admit it." He pressed his lips to hers.

"I love you."

"Princess, I love you more than I can even put into words."

Sydney could see the truth shining in his eyes and wrapped her arms around his neck, content to be held by her cowboy for eternity.

About the Author

T. J. Kline was raised competing in rodeos and rodeo queen competitions from the age of fourteen and has thorough knowledge of the sport as well as the culture involved. She has written several articles about rodeo for small periodicals, as well as a more recent how-to article for *RevWriter*, and has written a nonfiction health book and two inspirational fiction titles under the name Tina Klinesmith. She is also an avid reader and book reviewer for both Tyndale and Multnomah. In her spare time, she can be found laughing hysterically with her husband, children, and their menagerie of pets in Northern California.

Visit www.AuthorTracker.com for exclusive information on your favorite HarperCollins authors.

Give in to your impulses . . .
Read on for a sneak peek at four brand-new
e-book original tales of romance
from Avon Books.
Available now wherever e-books are sold.

RESCUED BY A STRANGER
By Lizbeth Selvig

CHASING MORGAN
BOOK FOUR: THE HUNTED SERIES
By Jennifer Ryan

THROWING HEAT
A DIAMONDS AND DUGOUTS NOVEL
By Jennifer Seasons

PRIVATE RESEARCH
AN EROTIC NOVELLA
By Sabrina Darby

An Excerpt from

RESCUED BY A STRANGER

by Lizbeth Selvig

When a stranger arrives in town on a vintage
motorcycle, Jill Carpenter has no idea her life
is about to change forever. She never expected
that her own personal knight in shining armor
would be an incredibly charming and handsome
southern man—but one with a deep secret. When
Jill's dreams of becoming an Olympic equestrian
start coming true, Chase's past finally returns to
haunt him. Can they get beyond dreams to find the
love that will rescue their two hearts? Find out in
the follow-up to *The Rancher and the Rock Star*.

An Excerpt from

RESCUED BY A STRANGER

by Lisbeth Schott

"Angel?" Jill called. "C'mon, girl. Let's go get you something to eat." She'd responded to her new name all evening. Jill frowned.

Chase gave a soft, staccato, dog-calling whistle. Angel stuck her head out from a stall a third of the way down the aisle. "There she is. C'mon, girl."

Angel disappeared into the stall.

"Weird," Jill said, heading down the aisle.

At the door to a freshly bedded empty stall, they found Angel curled beside a mound of sweet, fragrant hay, staring up as if expecting them.

"Silly girl," Jill said. "You don't have to stay here. We're taking you home. Come."

Angel didn't budge. She rested her head between her paws and gazed through raised doggy brows. Chase led the way into the stall. "Everything all right, pup?" He stroked her head.

Jill reached for the dog, too, and her hand landed on Chase's. They both froze. Slowly he rotated his palm and wove his fingers through hers. The few minor fireworks she'd felt in the car earlier were nothing compared to the explosion now detonating up her arm and down her back.

"I've been trying to avoid this since I got off that dang horse." His voice cracked into a low whisper.

"Why?"

He stood and pulled her to her feet. "Because I am not a guy someone as young and good as you are should let do this."

"You've saved my life and rescued a dog. Are you trying to tell me I should be *worried* about you?"

She touched his face, bold enough in the dark to do what light had made her too shy to try.

"Maybe."

The hard, smooth fingertips of his free hand slid inexorably up her forearm and covered the hand on his cheek. Drawing it down to his side, he pulled her whole body close, and the little twister of excitement in her stomach burst into a thousand quicksilver thrills. Her eyelids slipped closed, and his next question touched them in warm puffs of breath.

"If I were to kiss you right now, would it be too soon?"

Her eyes flew open, and she searched his shadowy gaze, incredulous. "You're asking permission? Who does that?"

"Seemed like the right thing."

"Well, permission granted. Now hush."

She freed her hands, placed them on his cheeks, roughened with beard stubble, and rose on tiptoe to meet his mouth while he gripped the back of her head.

The soft kiss nearly knocked her breathless. Chase dropped more hot kisses on each corner of her mouth and down her chin, feathered her nose and her cheeks, and finally returned to her mouth. Again and again he plied her bottom lip with his teeth, stunning her with his insistent exploration. The pressure of his lips and the clean, masculine scent of his skin took away her equilibrium. She could only follow the motions of his head and revel in the heat stoking the fire in her belly.

He pulled away at last and pressed parted lips to her forehead.

An Excerpt from

CHASING MORGAN
Book Four: The Hunted Series
by Jennifer Ryan

Morgan Standish can see things other people can't. She can see the past and future. These hidden gifts have prevented her from getting close to anyone—except FBI agent Tyler Reed. Morgan is connected to him in a way even she can't explain. She's solved several cases for him in the past, but will her gifts be enough to bring down a serial killer whose ultimate goal is to kill her? Find out in Book Four of The Hunted Series.

Morgan's fingers flew across the laptop keyboard propped on her knees. She took a deep breath, cleared her mind, and looked out past her pink-painted toes resting on the railing and across her yard to the densely wooded area at the edge of her property. Her mind's eye found her guest winding his way through the trees. She still had time before Jack stepped out of the woods separating her land from his. She couldn't wait to meet him.

Images, knowings, they just came to her. She'd accepted that part of herself a long time ago. As she got older, she'd learned to use her gift to seek out answers.

She finished her buy-and-sell orders and switched from her day trading page to check her psychic website and read the questions submitted by customers. She answered several quickly, letting the others settle in her mind until the answers came to her.

One stood out. The innocuous question about getting a job held an eerie vibe.

The familiar strange pulsation came over her. The world disappeared, as though a door had slammed on reality. The images came to her like hammer blows, one right after the other, and she took the onslaught, knowing something important needed to be seen and understood.

An older woman lying in a bed, hooked up to a machine feeding her medication. Frail and ill, she had translucent skin and dark circles marring her tortured eyes. Her pain washed over Morgan like a tsunami.

The woman yelled at someone, her face contorted into something mean and hateful. An unhappy woman—one who'd spent her whole life blaming others and trying to make them as miserable as she was.

A pristine white pillow floating down, inciting panic, amplified to terror when it covered the woman's face, her frail body swallowed by the sheets.

Morgan had an overwhelming feeling of suffocation.

The woman tried desperately to suck in a breath, but couldn't. Unable to move her lethargic limbs, she lay petrified and helpless under his unyielding hands. Lights flashed on her closed eyelids.

Death came calling.

A man stood next to the bed, holding the pillow like a shield. His mouth opened on a contorted, evil, hysterical laugh that rang in her ears and made her skin crawl. She squeezed her eyes closed to blot out his malevolent image and thoughts.

Murderer!

The word rang in her head as the terrifying emotions overtook her.

Morgan threw up a wall in her mind, blocking the cascade of disturbing pictures and feelings. She took several deep breaths and concentrated on the white roses growing in profusion just below the porch railing. Their sweet fragrance filled the air. With every breath, she centered herself and found her inner calm, pushing out the anger and rage left over from the vision. Her body felt like a lead weight, lightening as her energy came back. The drowsiness faded with each new breath. She'd be fine in a few minutes.

The man on horseback emerged from the trees, coming toward her home. Her guest had arrived.

Focused on the computer screen, she slowly and meticulously typed her answer to the man who had asked about a job and inadvertently opened himself up to telling her who he really was at heart.

She replied simply:

You'll get the job, but you can't hide from what you did.
You need help. Turn yourself in to the police.

An Excerpt from

THROWING HEAT
A Diamonds and Dugouts Novel
by Jennifer Seasons

Nightclub manager Leslie Cutter has never
been one to back down from a bet. So when
Peter Kowalskin, pitcher for the Denver
Rush baseball team, bets her that she can't
keep her hands off of him, she's not about
to let the arrogant, gorgeous playboy win.
But as things heat up, this combustible pair
will have to decide just how much they're
willing to wager on one another ... and on
a future that just might last forever.

"Is there something you want?" he demanded with a raised eyebrow, amused at being able to throw her words right back at her.

"You wish," Leslie retorted and tossed him a dismissive glance. Only he caught the gleam of interest in her eyes and knew her for the liar that she was.

Peter took a step toward her, closing the gap by a good foot until only an arm's reach separated them. He leaned forward and caged her in by placing a hand on each armrest of her chair. Her eyes widened the tiniest bit, but she held her ground.

"I wish many, many things."

"Really?" she questioned and shifted slightly away from him in her chair. "Such as what?"

Peter couldn't help noticing that her breathing had gone

shallow. How about that? "I wish to win the World Series this season." It would be a hell of a way to go out.

Her gaze landed on his mouth and flicked away. "Boring."

Humor sparked inside him at that, and he chuckled. "You want exciting?"

She shrugged. "Why not? Amuse me."

That worked for him. Hell yeah. If she didn't watch herself, he was going to excite the pants right off of her.

Just excitement, arousal, and sexual pleasure. That was what he was looking for this time around. And it was going to be fun leading her up to it.

But if he wanted her there, then he had to start.

Pushing until he'd tipped her chair back and only the balls of her feet were on the desk, her painted toes curling for a grip, Peter lowered his head until his mouth was against her ear. She smelled like coconut again, and his gut went tight.

"I wish I had you bent over this desk right here with your hot bare ass in the air."

She made a small sound in her throat and replied, "Less boring."

Peter grinned. Christ, the woman was tough. "Do you remember what I did to you that night in Miami? The thing that made you come hard, twice—one on top of the other?" He sure as hell did. It had involved his tongue, his fingers, and Leslie on all fours with her face buried in a pillow, moaning his name like she was begging for deliverance.

She tried to cover it, but he heard her quick intake of breath. "It wasn't that memorable."

Bullshit.

He slid a hand from the armrest and squeezed the top of her right leg, his thumb rubbing lazily back and forth on the skin of her inner thigh. Her muscles tensed, but she didn't pull away.

"Need a reminder?"

An Excerpt from

PRIVATE RESEARCH
An Erotic Novella
by *Sabrina Darby*

The last person Mina Cavallari expects to
encounter in the depths of the National
Archives while doing research on a thesis is
Sebastian Graham, an outrageously sexy financial
whiz. Sebastian is conducting a little research of
his own into the history of what he thinks is just
another London underworld myth, the fabled
Harridan House. When he discovers that the
private sex club still exists, he convinces Mina
to join him on an odyssey into the intricacies of
desire, pleasure, and, most surprisingly of all, love.

It was the most innocuous of sentences: "A cappuccino, please." Three words—without a verb to ground them, even. Yet, at the sound, my hand stilled mid-motion, my own paper coffee cup paused halfway between table and mouth. I looked over to the counter of the cafe. It was mid-afternoon, quieter than it had been when I'd come in earlier for a quick lunch, and only three people were in line behind the tall, slim-hipped, blond-haired man whose curve of shoulder and loose-limbed stance struck a chord in me as clearly as his voice.

Of course it couldn't be. In two years, surely, I had forgotten the exact tenor of his voice, was now confusing some other deep, posh English accent with his. Yet I watched the man, waited for him to turn around, as if there were any significant chance that in a city of eight million people, during the middle of the business day, I'd run into the one English acquaintance I had. At the National Archives, no less.

At the first glimpse of his profile, I sucked in my breath sharply, nearly dropping my coffee. Then he turned fully, looking around, likely for the counter with napkins and sugar. I watched his gaze pass over me and then snap back in recognition. I was both pleased and terrified. I'd come to London to put the past behind me, not to face down my demons. I'd been doing rather well these last months, but maybe this was part of some cosmic plan. As my time in England wound down, in order to move forward with my life, I had to come face to face with Sebastian Graham again.

"Mina!" He had an impressive way of making his voice heard across a room without shouting, and as he walked toward me, I put my cup down and stood, all too aware that while he looked like a fashionable professional about town, I still looked like a grad student——no makeup, hair pulled back in a ponytail, wearing jeans, sneakers, and a sweater.

"This is a pleasant surprise. Research for your dissertation? Anne Gracechurch, right?"

I nodded, bemused that he remembered a detail from what had surely been a throwaway conversation two years earlier. But of course I really shouldn't have been. Seb was brilliant, and brilliance wasn't the sort of thing that just faded away.

Neither, apparently, was his ability to make my pulse beat a bit faster or to tie up my tongue for a few seconds before I found my stride. He wasn't traditionally handsome, at least not in an American way. Too lean, too angular, hair receding a bit at the temples, and I was fairly certain he was now just shy of thirty. But I'd found him attractive from the first moment I'd met him.

I still did.

"That's right. What are you doing here? I mean, at the Archives."

"Ah." He shifted and smiled at me, and there was something about that smile that felt wicked and secretive. "A small genealogical project. Mind if I join you?"

I shook my head and sat back down. He pulled out his chair and sat, too, folding his long legs one over the other. Why was that sexy to me?

I focused on his face. He was pale. Much paler than he'd been in New Jersey, like he now spent most of his time indoors. Which should have been a turn-off. Yet, despite everything, I sat there imagining him in the kitchen of my apartment wearing nothing but boxer shorts. Apparently my memory was as good as his.

And I still remembered the crushing humiliation and disappointment of that last time we'd talked.